Praise for *New York Times* Bestselling Author Susan Wittig Albert's China Bayles Mysteries

"[China Bayles is] such a joy . . . An instant friend."
—Carolyn Hart, *New York Times* bestselling author of the Death on Demand Mysteries

"[Albert] consistently turns out some of the best-plotted mysteries on the market." —*Houston Chronicle*

"China continues to appeal with her herbal information and savvy sleuthing." —*Booklist* (starred review)

"One of the best-written and [most] well-plotted mysteries I've read in a long time." —*Los Angeles Times*

"Albert's dialogue and characterizations put her in a class with lady sleuths V. I. Warshawski and Stephanie Plum." —*Publishers Weekly*

"Engrossing." —*The Times-Picayune*

"Mystery lovers . . . will be captivated by this unique series." —*Seattle Post-Intelligencer*

"Breezy . . . The characters are an appealing bunch." —*Chicago Tribune*

"Albert's skill in weaving everything together into a multilayered whole makes the reading smooth, interesting, and enjoyable." —*San Antonio Express-News*

"It's the interactions between the characters in the series and their growth and change that make the China Bayles Mysteries one of my favorite series." —*Gumshoe*

SUSAN WITTIG ALBERT

BLOOD ORANGE

BERKLEY PRIME CRIME
New York

BERKLEY PRIME CRIME
Published by Berkley
An imprint of Penguin Random House LLC
375 Hudson Street, New York, New York 10014

Copyright © 2016 by Susan Wittig Albert
Penguin Random House supports copyright. Copyright fuels creativity, encourages
diverse voices, promotes free speech, and creates a vibrant culture. Thank you for buying
an authorized edition of this book and for complying with copyright laws by not
reproducing, scanning, or distributing any part of it in any form without permission.
You are supporting writers and allowing Penguin Random House to continue to
publish books for every reader.

BERKLEY is a registered trademark and BERKLEY PRIME CRIME and the B colophon
are trademarks of Penguin Random House LLC.

ISBN: 9780425280010

Berkley Prime Crime hardcover edition / March 2016
Berkley mass-market edition / April 2017

Printed in the United States of America
1   3   5   7   9   10   8   6   4   2

Cover illustration by Joe Burleson
Cover design by Judith Lagerman
Cover art: *Shattered Glass* © by Carlos Caetano/Shutterstock
Book design by Tiffany Estreicher

Chapter One

Today's commercial beers are almost exclusively brewed with hops, the female flowers of the hop plant (*Humulus lupulus*). The result is a uniform, easily controlled flavor.

But before hops began to be widely used (around the ninth century), beer was flavored, bittered, and preserved with an herb mixture called *gruit*. A brewer's gruit depended on what was locally available; hence, it was distinctive and often unique. The most important herbs in gruit might be sweetgale (*Myrica gale*), mugwort (*Artemisia vulgaris*), yarrow (*Achillea millefolium*), ground ivy (*Glechoma hederacea*), horehound (*Marrubium vulgare*), and/or heather (*Calluna vulgaris*). Other herbs and spices might include chile peppers, juniper berries, black henbane, ginger, caraway seed, aniseed, nutmeg, cinnamon, vanilla, woodruff, cardamom, anise, and hops. Local beers were also flavored with seasonal fruits, such as raspberry, cherry, sweet and bitter orange, blood orange, cranberry, strawberry, peach—and even banana!

Modern artisanal beers—brewed to appeal to local tastes and traditions, using locally preferred flavorings—are a return to the distinctive, unique beers of the past and a popular alternative to commercial beers. Blood orange beer, anyone?

China Bayles
"Botanical Drinkables"
Pecan Springs Enterprise

"Excuse me." I put down my teacup. "I don't think I heard that right, Ruby. I thought you said that Ramona has bought a *brewery*."

"That's exactly what I said." Ruby sank into the chair opposite mine at her kitchen table and ran her fingers through her frizzy red hair. "My ditzy sister has just bought a controlling interest in the Comanche Creek Brewing Company, out in your direction." She made a face. "You know the phrase 'more money than sense'? It fits Ramona perfectly."

Ruby's sister Ramona has her good points, I'm sure. (Don't we all?) But I have to confess that her name doesn't appear among the top ten on my friends list. In fact, I think of her as Ruby's "evil twin," and I usually agree when somebody says snarky things about her. Not this time, though.

"Comanche Creek does craft beer," I said, "and craft beer is huge right now. People like it because it has much more flavor than mass-produced beer. And much more variety. I read the other day that there are almost four thousand small breweries in the U.S. and over a hundred right here in Texas. Ramona could be onto a good thing."

"But she doesn't *like* beer, China," Ruby protested. She poured herself a cup of tea. "She hasn't drunk enough of it to understand it."

"That's a good point," I conceded. "But most of us don't understand how the transmission works when we buy a new car. I doubt if many investors know the first thing about the nuts and bolts of the business they're investing in. They're just looking for a place to put their money to work."

"I suppose," Ruby said slowly. "But you know Ramona. She is a hands-on kind of person with very definite ideas. I can't imagine her not being totally involved in a business she's put her money into. And she's had such a hard time making up her mind. Remember when she wanted to buy into the children's bookstore next door to the shops? Then she was all gung-ho about the cupcake business. After that, it was the florist shop. And then she decided she'd buy *me* out."

"That's another good point," I agreed. The previous summer, Ramona—who had gotten a substantial divorce settlement from her philandering doctor husband—had decided that her sister needed a rest. *She* was going to buy Ruby's shop and her share of our tearoom and our catering businesses and go into partnership with *me*. That idea panicked me, until Ruby assured me that she wasn't selling out to anybody, much less to Ramona. I have learned to be cautious about Ramona's great ideas.

"You bet it's a good point," Ruby said. "This brewery is just another in a long string of impulses. Ramona has a habit of jumping into things without looking, and it gets her into trouble." She picked up her teacup and looked at me over the rim. "I have a bad feeling about this, China. My sister could be in for a hard time. And I don't know what to do about it."

I have learned to pay serious attention to Ruby's bad feelings. She is highly intuitive, especially when it comes to reading people's fears and motivations and anticipating what lies ahead for them. She tries very hard not to poke her psychic nose into the private affairs of people she cares for, but sometimes she can't help herself.

So I wasn't going to argue. Something was wrong, and Ruby sensed it. But both of us knew that there wasn't any point in trying to get Ramona to change her mind. When she decides to do something, she is going to *do* it, come hell or high water. Or both.

"How did Ramona happen to get involved with the brewery?" I asked curiously. "Seems kind of strange."

The oven timer went off. "It's a long story." Ruby put down her teacup and pushed her chair back. "I'll get our muffins out and tell you while we eat."

While Ruby goes to the oven to pull out the batch of muffins she's been baking, I'll take the opportunity to give you a little context for what's happening here. It is early morning on the second Monday in April, and Ruby Wilcox and I (we're business partners as well as best friends) are having our monthly planning session. Our shops—my herb shop, Ruby's Crystal Cave, and our tearoom—are closed on Mondays, which gives us a chance to catch up on business matters without having to tend to customers. Last month, we met at my house. This month, we're at Ruby's. Both of us have brought our laptops and a list of topics we want to talk about.

I love coming here. Ruby's Painted Lady—a gaudy old Victorian on Pecan Street—is dazzling, outside and in. The exterior is a wonderfully wild palette of smoke gray, spring green, fuchsia, and plum, and the wicker porch furniture is daffodil yellow with red tropical-print cushions. Indoors, Ruby has polished the pine floors to a shimmer and painted the walls in bright orange, yellow, and blue. The kitchen is a warm red, with a watermelon wallpaper border above a yellow-painted beadboard wainscot. A lamp with a green shade hangs over a red-painted table and four green and red chairs. Vintage tea-towel curtains hang at the window, and clay pots of red geraniums bloom gaily on the windowsill. Ruby's house will make you blink.

Ruby makes you blink as well. This morning, she had just gotten back from her extra-early yoga class and was wearing multicolored leggings vividly striped in a yellow and purple Aztec pattern, a loose purple tunic, and yellow open-toed sandals that displayed purple painted toes. Ruby has mile-long legs (she's six-feet-something in heels) and Orphan Annie–red hair, and the sight of her makes me smile. But Ruby makes everybody smile, whatever she's wearing. We're all just responding to her natural exuberance and love of life, and her ability to live fully in the present.

Ruby owns the Crystal Cave, the only New Age shop in Pecan Springs, which is adjacent to my herb shop, Thyme and Seasons. At the Cave, Ruby sells incense and rune stones and tarot cards and books; teaches classes in astrology and meditation and the tarot; and offers birth chart readings and Ouija board sessions. As partners, the two of us own and manage Thyme for Tea (our tearoom, directly behind our shops) and Party Thyme (our catering service). With our friend Cass Wilde, we jointly own the Thymely Gourmet, a meals-to-go food delivery service that Cass manages. She also manages the tearoom kitchen and helps with the catering.

And there's Thyme and Seasons Cottage, a remodeled stone stable on the alley behind the shops. Ruby and I used to use it for workshops and classes, but we recently cleaned up the loft over our shops and moved our workshops into that space. Now, I'm renting the cottage as a bed-and-breakfast.

In fact, it was rented right now. Kelly Kaufman, who works at our local hospice, has rented the cottage for the week—an unhappy family situation, she said, and mentioned that she was getting a divorce. Staying at the cottage would give her a breather while she got her act together and started looking for another place to live.

There was a time when I knew Kelly fairly well. She used to be a member of the Pecan Springs herb guild, and we had worked together often. But that had been several years ago, and we'd lost touch. Checking in on Friday, she had seemed unhappy when she mentioned the family situation. But I didn't pry. Kelly's reason for taking the cottage was none of my business. I was just glad the place was available when she needed it and I could help her out.

So there you have it: what Ruby and I do for a living. "A three-ring circus," Ruby calls it, and she's 100 percent right. Ruby, Cass, and I are ringmasters, jugglers, acrobats, tightrope walkers, fire-eaters, and lion tamers. Sometimes we're the sideshow, too—and sometimes we're the clowns. Running a small business is like that. Multiply it by several small businesses, all under one big top, and it's even more so. To make this circus work, we all have to be very good friends.

You know that old saying about opposites attracting? It's certainly true where Ruby and I are concerned. She has a wild sense of style, while I am a jeans-and-sneakers kind of gal. She is highly imaginative and often uncomfortably intuitive. I, on the other hand, am much more methodical. Where Ruby boldly goes, I am cautious. Where she's associative and leapfrogs to unexpected conclusions, I'm literal and linear, taking things step-by-step. Maybe it's my training as a lawyer, but when I finally reach a conclusion, I know how I got there and can document my sources.

My name is China Bayles. Some years ago, I cashed in my retirement account and left the large Houston criminal law firm where I was practicing. I moved to Pecan Springs, a friendly Texas Hill Country town halfway between Austin and San Antonio, where I bought an herb shop—Thyme and Seasons—in a century-old stone building surrounded by gardens. The business took several years of love, hard work, and long hours to build up, but now it's something I can be proud of. Best of all, I recalibrated myself from the fast track to the slow, learned to appreciate real friendships, discovered who I was, and began to enjoy the work I do.

A few years after I bought the shop, I married Mike Mc-Quaid, a former Houston homicide detective, currently a part-time faculty member in the Criminal Justice department at CTSU—Central Texas State University—and a more or less full-time private investigator in partnership with Blackie Blackwell. Blackie, a retired Adams County sheriff, is married to Sheila Dawson, the chief of the Pecan Springs Police. This makes for some interesting dinner table conversation when the four of us get together: a retired criminal defense attorney, two ex-cop private eyes, and a police chief. Mc-Quaid and I are the parents of two amazing kids: his son Brian, now in his second semester at the University of Texas at Austin, majoring in Environmental Science and minoring in girls; and thirteen-year-old Caitlin, my niece and our adopted daughter. Caitie plays the violin with a remarkably unchildlike virtuosity (which she certainly didn't get from my side of the family!) and runs a chicken-and-egg business on the side.

Ruby popped the muffins out of the tin and put them on a plate in the middle of the table with butter. We always have a little something to eat—usually a recipe we're trying out for the tearoom menu—and catch up on each other's personal news before we settle down to business. Our shops are so hectic that we don't have much time to chat when we're on the job, so getting together like this helps keep us connected.

"Tell me what you think about the muffins," she said. "And how about some more tea?" When I held up my cup, she filled it.

I broke the muffin and took a sniff. "Orange!" I said.

"Smells yummy." I nibbled at one of the pieces. "Tastes yummy, too. Just enough orange. And there's also—"

"Rosemary," Ruby said. She sat down, watching me to see how I liked it. "Do you think it might work as a menu item?"

"Absolutely. Different, not too sweet. How about giving your recipe to Cass and see what she does with it?"

"I'll do it," Ruby said promptly. "I think it will pair nicely with her quiche."

"I agree," I said. Cass' signature lavender quiche is a favorite in the tearoom, especially for Saturday brunch. It comes with a salad (whatever is in season), and a muffin would be a lovely addition. I spread butter on my muffin and took a bite. "So, tell me about Ramona," I prompted, my mouth half full, "and how she got interested in the brewery."

"How do you suppose?" Ruby reached for a muffin. "She got interested in the brewmaster. A guy named Rich. A hunk, to hear her tell it, five or six years younger than she is and very, very sexy. On the one hand, they are madly in love." She paused, frowning. "On the other hand, he's married— although Ramona says that's only a temporary problem. His wife is being stubborn about the divorce. Ramona is hoping she'll change her mind soon, so she and her hunk can get married."

"Sounds tricky," I said.

Ruby's laugh was brittle. "Sounds a lot like Ramona. You know what she's like when she makes up her mind to something. It's full speed ahead and damn the torpedoes. I hope this guy's wife really wants a divorce, because if that's what Ramona wants, it will happen."

"I'm afraid you're right," I said. I wouldn't say this to Ruby, but her sister is one of the most manipulative women I have ever met. Sipping my tea, I went back to the subject of the brewery. "McQuaid and I took a tour of Comanche Creek

8

and tasted some of their beers. It's an attractive place. Have you been out there?"

The Comanche Creek Brewing Company is just off Lime-kiln Road, about ten miles west of Pecan Springs and just a couple of miles from my house. It occupies a large industrial-looking metal building with a smaller limestone structure tacked to the front. The whole thing is parked on a stony hilltop, surrounded by a low forest of Ashe junipers, mesquite, prickly pear cactus, and bluebonnets, in season—all very Texas. The small stone building in front is the tasting room.

Ruby buttered her muffin. "I know where it is, but I've never been inside. I'm a wine girl myself. Beer is for guys."

"It might be a calorie thing," I said. "But when we did the tour, women made up about half the group, and they seemed to enjoy the tasting." I paused. "Tell me how your sister met her new guy. This brewmaster, I mean. Did she just happen to drop in out there for a taste or two?"

"Kate told Ramona that the brewery was looking for an investor and suggested that she consider it." Kate Rodriguez is the partner of Ruby's twenty-something daughter, Amy. Together, Kate and Amy have a beautiful little girl, Grace, now almost four, who is the apple of Ruby's eye. Kate is an accountant, and a good one. Ruby and I use her for our businesses, and McQuaid and Blackie are her clients, too.

"If Kate recommends it, the brewery must have something going for it," I said.

Ruby nodded. "Anyway, Ramona went out there to look around. The brewmaster took her for a private tour, and bam! She said it was like two magnets clicking together. A week later, she pulled out her checkbook and now she owns a chunk of the business. And you know Ramona. She rolled up her sleeves and began having ideas."

"Does this brewmaster own the place?" Buying into a

business with somebody you've fallen for is not the brightest idea in the world, in my opinion.

"Half owner, I think. According to Ramona, his wife owns the other half."

"Yeah." I tilted my head. "That's how it works in a community-property state. What's 'ours' is half mine, half yours. This guy can sell his half, but he can't sell his wife's. If they split and the wife keeps her share of the brewery, Ramona may wind up in partnership with her boyfriend's ex."

Ruby made a face. "I wish I could feel good about what my baby sister is doing, China, but I just can't."

Ramona is three years younger than Ruby, which I guess qualifies her to be the baby sister. But as kids, the two of them weren't especially close, mostly because they are . . . well, different. Sure, they have the same frizzy red hair and freckles, although Ramona is short, a little on the plump side, and highly competitive. And yes, Ramona shares what Ruby calls their "gift," which they inherited from their Gram Gifford, who inherited it from *her* mother, who brought it with her from Ireland, along with the red curls and freckles that also seem to run in that family.

The "gift" is a certain psychic talent that Ruby tries not to use unless she is forced into it. In fact, she goes out of her way to avoid situations where she might be tempted to employ it. I know for a fact that she can quite often hear what people are thinking or connect with their feelings and desires, but that she makes a deliberate effort *not* to. And that she can occasionally be surprised by a compelling glimpse into the future—or the past—but that this aspect of her gift frightens her, especially when it descends on her unexpectedly. She's afraid that she'll get pulled (she says) into something she can't get out of, like somebody who falls into deep water and can't swim. She manages to be comfortable and even lighthearted with what she calls parlor tricks, like the readings she does with her Ouija board or the *I Ching* or the tarot cards. But she always sets limits for herself to keep from getting sucked in.

Now, I am an educated and logical person (Ruby says I am overeducated and exceedingly left-brained), and when I first began to glimpse her hidden talents, I was more than a little skeptical. But I have seen her in action often enough to know that whatever is going on here, it's very real. It's also a huge drain on her physical and psychological resources, so I understand why she's so respectful of it—afraid, almost. It must be something like being suddenly charged up by an energy surge, and when the power's turned off, the energy ebbs, leaving her drained and limp. No wonder Ruby avoids it when she can.

Unfortunately, Ramona doesn't know how to set limits, and she never seems to be bothered by the kind of energy ebb that Ruby experiences. While she can occasionally tune in to what other people are feeling or thinking, she usually misunderstands it or is careless with the way she uses the information. And when she loses her temper or gets spooked, weirdness happens. Things fly around the room, fall off shelves, or explode, as if a poltergeist is at play.

Really. I am not making this up. I've witnessed it myself, especially when Ramona is excited, nervous, or trying to hide something. Ruby has attempted to work with her sister to help her use her capabilities more responsibly, but Ramona isn't very cooperative, perhaps because there's a strong subtext of competition between the two sisters, especially when it comes to their "gift." Ruby says she suspects that Ramona secretly enjoys surprising and even disturbing people, and that she often does it just to get attention. This seems to me to have become more pronounced after Ramona moved to Pecan Springs and took up temporary residence in Ruby's guest room.

11

But after a couple of months, Ruby began to feel that her sister was taking advantage (it's easy to feel that way with Ramona), and that if she *really* wanted a new start, she ought to begin by getting a place of her own. That took a little longer, because it turned out that Ramona enjoyed living with her sister. (In large part, I suspected, because Ruby managed everything and all Ramona had to do was show up for dinner and put the dishes in the dishwasher afterward.)

Meanwhile, she's been looking for something she really wants to do with her life. A "business opportunity," she says. "A place to watch my money grow." She certainly has plenty of it, thanks to that liberal divorce settlement. And now, according to Ruby, she's found a new opportunity—and a new guy into the bargain. Maybe.

"Tell me about him," I said. "Are they serious?"

"*She's* serious about *him*," Ruby replied slowly. "She says he wants to get married, as soon as he can get unhooked from his current wife."

"That's not a very promising way to get started," I said. Jumping out of one long-term relationship and into another is not a good idea, to my way of thinking. You can get into some serious trouble that way. "But of course, lots of people do," I added, wanting to soften my remark.

"Courting disaster, if you ask me." Ruby made a little face. "I don't know much about him, and of course I'm clueless about the beer business. I just wish Ramona would think a little longer before she . . ."

Her voice trailed off, and I guessed that she was thinking of that "bad feeling" she had about the situation. I eyed her curiously, wondering if she was going to tell me. But after a moment's hesitation, she decided to keep it to herself. Instead, she said, "She says he'll be with her at Sheila's birthday party next month. They've promised to bring the beer."

Sheila Dawson and Blackie Blackwell live on Hickory

Street, the next block over. As a couple, they are especially popular with their neighbors, who like the idea of having the police chief and her ex-sheriff husband living practically next door. At Christmas, Sheila had held a holiday open house for an overflow crowd. Now, Ruby had invited everybody in the neighborhood to a backyard potluck to celebrate Sheila's birthday.

"I'll meet him then, too," I said. "McQuaid says he'll be in town that week, so we'll both be here. I'm bringing salad, right?"

"Right." Ruby eyed me. "McQuaid's been doing a lot of traveling lately, hasn't he? Where is he this time?"

"Out in El Paso," I said, "doing an investigation for Charlie Lipman. McQuaid didn't give me the details, but I'm sure it's the standard thing—Charlie asked him to develop a dossier on somebody who's suing one of his clients."

"In other words, dig up all the dirt," Ruby said, pulling her mouth down. "Look for all the other guy's human failings so they can be used to discredit him."

"You got it." I grinned wryly. "That's what PIs do for a living, you know. Dig up dirt that nobody else knows anything about. That's why they call them *private* investigators."

"But at least that kind of work is safe," Ruby said, "as opposed to some of the other investigations he might be involved in. Does he tell you what he's doing?"

"Not so much, actually." I shivered, remembering the trip that McQuaid and Blackie had made to Mexico to retrieve a small boy who had been abducted by his mother and taken across the border. *That* trip had been truly dangerous. I hated to interfere with his professional work, but I had asked him to promise that he wouldn't take another case that required him to go across the border. And he had agreed.

"And I don't ask about what he's doing," I added. "I'm just glad to be out of the crime business."

13

It was true. I left the law because I was fed up to here with bad guys, who—as a criminal defense attorney—I had the responsibility of defending. Too many of them were guilty as sin, and when I got them off, I felt a) proud of myself for pulling off an acquittal in a difficult case; and b) guilty for having gotten away with murder—or theft or conspiracy or whatever. I was doing a damn good job, but the job was making me somebody I didn't want to be. Every year since I bailed out, my hands have felt a little cleaner.

So since McQuaid hung up his shingle as a private investigator, I have rarely been tempted to get involved. I listen when he feels like telling me about a case he's working on, and if I'm asked, I may even proffer a helpful suggestion or two based on my past experience with the dark side. But crooks, criminals, and investigations are *his* business. My business is Thyme and Seasons. Where I'm concerned, plants—and especially herbs—are the *good* guys.

Which reminded me of what Ruby and I were supposed to be doing. I finished my muffin, brushed the crumbs off my fingers, and reached for my list. "How about if we go over the workshop and class schedule for the next couple of months? We're mailing the newsletter later this week, and I want to make sure I haven't left something out."

Ruby opened her laptop and booted it up. "Here's my calendar," she said after a minute, turning her laptop around so I could see the monitor. "There's the class and workshop schedule"—she pointed—"and there are the special events Cass has cooked up for the tearoom. Can you think of anything I've left out?"

I scanned her calendar. Ruby was teaching her regular schedule of tarot, astrology, and meditation classes, plus a class on making and using incense. Over the next two months, I was teaching classes on making herbal liqueurs and cordials, using dye plants, and crafting herbal ointments and salves. Ruby was leading a paint-your-own-teapot workshop, and I was following that up with a workshop on growing and blending your own herbal teas. We were going to be busy.

"I think that's everything," I said, turning her laptop back around. "I'm wondering about the liqueurs class, though. It's the first time I've taught it. I hope we get enough people to make it worth the time I'm putting into the prep." Since most liqueurs have to be aged for at least a month, I had already invested quite a few hours in those I planned to offer for tasting, and there was more work yet to be done.

"I don't think enrollment will be a problem," Ruby said confidently. "Since this is the first time you've offered it, you'll have a good turnout." She frowned. "I hope you're going to include some nonalcoholic drinks as well, though. Lots of our friends are teetotalers."

"I've been thinking of that. Some of the liqueurs can also be made with vinegar instead of grain alcohol. They're called shrubs. Back in the day, before soft drinks, shrubs were a favorite family treat. I think people will enjoy learning how to make them. And I'm following up with a class on herb teas. Lots of botanical drinkables."

"Sounds good," Ruby said. "If you think the calendar is more or less okay, how about if I send you the file right now? That way, you can just copy it into the newsletter, add whatever Cass gives you, and you're good to go."

"Super." I booted up my laptop, and a few moments later I was watching Ruby's calendar file land in my inbox, as if by magic.

At that moment, Ruby's cell phone buzzed and she picked it up. She listened, then smiled happily. "Of course, Amy. Why don't you bring her over right now, instead of waiting until after lunch? After China and I are finished, I'm going to the shop to do some restocking, and Grace can come with me." She listened again, said, "See you then, sweetie," and clicked off the phone.

"Babysitting today?" I asked with a smile. I've never been a huge fan of little kids, but Grace is a charmer. And Amy is finally growing up and settling down. Grace—and Kate, too—are good for her.

Ruby put down her phone. "Yes," she said, fluffing her hair with her fingers. "I *love* Mondays. That's when I get to be Grandma."

I looked at her in her Aztec leggings, purple tunic, and mop of frizzy red hair. I shook my head. Grandmas are getting wilder all the time.

Chapter Two

Most of us view henbit (*Lamium amplexicaule*) as a nuisance garden weed and its common name, henbit, reminds us that it is a favorite of chickens. A member of the mint family, it is also called "dead nettle." But this edible herb—raw or cooked, it tastes like a peppery spinach—is packed with vitamins, iron, and antioxidants, and it's been on the dinner menu for centuries. John Gerard describes it in his famous 1597 *The Herball, or Generall Historie of Plantes*:

> The floures are baked with sugar as Roses are, which is called Sugar roses: as also the distilled water of them, which is used to make the heart merry, to make a good colour in the face, and to refresh the vitall spirits.

And Margaret Grieve, in her *A Modern Herbal* (1931) describes its medicinal properties:

> The whole plant [henbit] is of an astringent nature, and in herbal medicine is considered of use for arresting hemorrhages, as in spitting of blood and dysentery. Cotton-wool, dipped in a tincture of the fresh herb, is efficacious in

staunching bleeding and a homoeopathic tincture prepared from the flowers is used for internal bleeding.

China Bayles
"Wild Weeds That Are Good for Us"
Pecan Springs Enterprise

The shops are closed on Mondays, yes, but that doesn't mean we have the day off. It was just ten when Ruby and I wrapped up our planning session. I climbed into my white Toyota and headed for Thyme and Seasons, where I planned to meet the members of the local herb guild who volunteer to help me maintain the gardens around the shop.

It was a perfect morning for outdoor work anywhere in the Hill Country. The weather report had promised an afternoon in the upper seventies, and the morning clouds had already given way to blue skies and April sunshine. In the medians and along the curbs, oleander and Texas mountain laurels (the "grape Kool-Aid tree") were blooming, surrounded by bluebonnets, Indian paintbrush, and wine cups. In people's neat yards, fire-red tulips, gold and purple and white iris, and red and orange poppies were in full bloom, as were purple wisteria and some late bright yellow forsythia and bridal wreath spirea. Color, color, everywhere I looked.

Thyme and Seasons is situated in a century-old two-story building a couple of blocks east of the town square, on Crockett Street. Pecan Springs was established in the late 1840s by German immigrants who came to America because they had run out of land at home and understood that there was plenty of it—empty, too—on the other side of the Atlantic. The colonists arrived by ship at Galveston and drove horses and wagons overland to the hills of the Edwards Plateau. For safety, they traveled in well-armed groups, which was smart, considering that the land wasn't really empty. The local Native American residents were understandably uneasy when they saw these foreigners—most of them ill-equipped and ill-prepared for survival—moving into the neighborhood.

But the colonists' persistence and firepower made up for their lack of know-how, and over the next several decades, the Native Americans were forced to give way, as they were everywhere else in the country. Settlers built their first houses out of cypress logs. But as time went on, the German stonemasons began building more permanently, with square-cut blocks of light-colored native limestone. The old stone building that houses Thyme and Seasons and the Crystal Cave is a relic of that period, with its pine floors and beamed wooden ceilings.

When I first bought the place, it was surrounded by wide green swaths of Bermuda grass that required frequent irrigation. Over time, I've replaced almost all of the lawn with herbal theme gardens: the kitchen garden, with the usual culinary mix of parsley, sage, thyme, mint, savory, and so on; the fragrance garden, filled with roses, nicotiana, sweet peas, lavender, and rosemary; the astrologer's garden, with a traditional herb for every sign of the zodiac; the dyer's garden, with coreopsis, tansy, Turk's cap, yarrow, and a prickly pear cactus; and the apothecary garden. Stepping-stone paths border the various gardens, and there's a lovely stone fountain that provides drinking and bathing facilities for all the birds in the neighborhood.

I appreciate the volunteers who help keep the gardens neat, and as thanks for their work, they get to choose a tray of plant seedlings to take home with them, plus cuttings and snippets from the established stock plants. This morning, there were four volunteers, and they were working on the apothecary garden, raking out the winter debris of leaves and twigs and pulling out the weeds that compete with the echinacea, St. John's wort, plantain, feverfew, sage, comfrey, lavender, garlic, and chickweed. Khat, a large and elegant Siamese, was supervising their efforts from the top rail of a low wooden fence on the other side of the path.

When Khat came to me from his unfortunately deceased owner, he was called Pudding, which neither he nor I liked. I couldn't think of anything else, so I fell into the habit of calling him Cat, after Brian's favorite Kipling story, "The Cat That Walked by Himself." But Ruby objected that "Cat" wasn't sufficiently distinctive for an animal with such a sovereign air. She is a great admirer of Koko, Qwilleran's talented Siamese cat-sleuth in the *Cat Who* mysteries, and has always wanted a cat who could tell time, read backward, and has fourteen tales. In honor of Koko, Cat became Khat K'o Kung.

Like many Siamese, Khat is arrogant, conceited, and obnoxiously imperial, easy to admire from a distance but hard to love up close and personal. He lives full-time at Thyme and Seasons and holds the position of shop security guard, as one startled Pecan Springs patrolman discovered when he was looking for a rabid raccoon that had been reported in the neighborhood. He thought he saw the creature climbing the trellis beside the back porch and went to look. Khat launched himself off the porch roof and sank all eighteen of his claws—ten on his front paws and eight on his rear—into the patrolman's back. Trespassers, beware. Thyme and Seasons is patrolled by an attack cat who takes his work seriously.

Now Khat jumped down from the fence and came to inspect the garden work. Miriam Johnston, who coordinates the volunteer group, straightened up from her work. Miriam has stunning white hair, glasses, and a wide smile. A breast cancer survivor, she loves gardening and is a natural teacher who worked for years with kids in a pioneer cabin project. These days, she's passionate about straw-bale gardening. She and her husband, Dean, a naturalist by profession, are making it work in their backyard garden. In addition to volunteering to work in the Thyme and Seasons herb garden, Miriam often comes in to help out in the shops, both Ruby's and mine.

"Hey, China," she asked, "is it okay if we take some of this henbit home? There's a *lot* of it. And plantain, too."

Like many of our native "weeds," henbit is edible. Raw or cooked, it tastes like a peppery spinach and is packed with vitamins, iron, and antioxidants. At home, I include some of it in our spring salads, and Caitie feeds a *lot* of it to her chickens, who adore it. (Hence the plant's common name, "henbit.")

"Take all the henbit you can carry away," I said, bending over to stroke Khat's charcoal ears. "We need to clean it out as much as we can, or it will take over. Let's keep three or four of the largest plantains, though—I'm going to make some salve." Plantain leaves are edible, too, raw (when they're young), or steamed or boiled. And when the seed heads are young, you can use them in stir-fries and, steamed, in salads, like baby ears of corn. "Leave some space beside the plantain," I added, "and I'll make a plant marker for it."

"Oh, good," Miriam said. "Yes, I know about plantain. When I was working on the pioneer cabin project, I used it to make salves and ointments, all by itself and with sage, jewelweed, and calendula flowers. It's a shame that so many people think of it in the 'weed' category."

Doris, on her knees with a trowel, looked up. "That's my husband. If I don't stop him, he will dig every single plantain out of the lawn. Dandelions, as well."

"Mine sprays them with herbicide," Reba chimed in. "And the peppergrass, too. I tell him that they're all medicinal, but he does it anyway. He says he doesn't want our next-door neighbors to be mad at us for spreading weed seeds."

We were shaking our heads about that when my cell phone rang. Everybody looked up, startled, and I fished it out of my jeans pocket as quickly as I could. When Brian was home the previous weekend, he downloaded a police siren ringtone onto my phone as a joke. He forgot to take it off before he went back to school, and I can't seem to delete it. I've turned the darn thing down as far as I can, but it's still way too loud. So I'm stuck with a police siren—a highly realistic, totally convincing, earsplitting siren—on my phone until next weekend, when Brian will be home again.

The caller was Charlie Lipman. "Hey, Charlie," I said. "What's up?"

For most of the years I've known Charlie, he has been Pecan Springs' best and most popular attorney. He is also a longtime family friend who throws a lot of work in Mc-Quaid's direction, especially divorce work, which is Charlie's stock-in-trade. McQuaid would almost always rather be doing something else (there's nothing particularly uplifting about tailing an adulterous spouse to a lovers' hideaway), but since Charlie is a friend, he takes the cases when he can.

"Got a little problem," Charlie said. "I'm hoping you can help me."

"I'll try," I said warily. "What's up?" For too long, Charlie has been drinking too much, especially on weekends. This might not be so awkward, professionally speaking, since judges like to take the weekend off, too. But Charlie's weekends are a little longer than normal, usually beginning on Thursday night and ending around Tuesday afternoon or so. And this was only Monday, which accounts for my guardedness.

But Charlie sounded entirely sober when he said, "I understand that Kelly Kaufman is stayin' in that cottage behind your shop. She had a nine o'clock appointment with me this mornin', and she didn't show up. I've tried her cell phone but I'm not getting any answer. I figure she forgot to set her clock and maybe let her cell run out of juice. Reckon you could bang on the door a couple times and roust that gal outta bed for me?"

Charlie Lipman grew up in the upscale Highland Park area of Dallas, took an undergraduate degree from Princeton, and spent a year at Oxford before entering University of Texas Law and passing the Texas bar exam with a stratospheric score. But in Pecan Springs, it pays to talk like your average local cedar chopper, and Charlie (who occasionally imagines that he might make a run for a seat in the state legislature) is conveniently bidialectal. He writes like a law professor and talks down-home Texan. It's part of his charm.

"Sure thing," I said. "I'm in the shop garden right now. I'll go back there and knock on the door." I was curious about why Kelly had an appointment with Charlie. But he does a lot of divorce work, and she *had* mentioned a divorce.

"She probably overslept," I added. "Do you still bill people by the minute when they're late?"

It was an old joke between us. Charlie chuckled. "By the quarter hour. Encourages discipline, y'know."

"Encourages people to look for another lawyer," I said. "Will you bill Kelly for being late?"

"Ain't decided," he said cheerfully. Lawyers never answer questions about fees—they just send the invoice. "Talk to you later, China."

Thyme Cottage was built in the days when every respectable property owner had a horse and buggy. Originally a large stone stable, it had been erected at the back of the garden, parallel to the alley. Sometime before World War II, somebody turned the stable into a garage for his new 1937 Buick, with wooden doors and a parking area at one end. How do I know about the Buick? Because the proud owner of his new car took a snapshot of it in front of his new garage and framed the photo for posterity. Ruby discovered it when we were renovating the second floor of the shop building and it is hanging in the cottage hallway right now.

But it was the next transformation that really counted. The previous owner, an architect, reincarnated the stable-cum-garage as a lovely one-bedroom guesthouse with a fireplace, a built-in kitchen, and a hot tub in its own private deck. Until early this year, Ruby and Cass and I scheduled workshops there, since the main room—we call it the Gathering Room—was large enough to accommodate a modest crowd and the open-plan kitchen was ideal for cooking and crafting demonstrations.

I had been in the habit of renting the cottage as a guesthouse when it wasn't in use for our events. But when we remodeled the second floor of the main building this past winter and moved our classes there, the cottage became available full-time. I advertise on the Internet and in the Pecan Springs Bed-and-Breakfast Guide and take bookings in advance. The rental comes with linens, towels, and a breakfast that Cass makes up the afternoon before and stashes in the cottage's refrigerator, so the lucky resident can heat it up in the microwave while she's waiting for the coffeemaker to brew that first morning cup. There's also a television, a radio, and (of course) Wi-Fi. The cottage is proving to be a reliable source of extra income and only a little extra work.

A few minutes later, I was ringing the bell at the front door. Once, twice, three times—and getting no answer. Which was odd, I thought. The doorbell rings in the main hallway, loud enough to wake even the soundest sleeper.

I stood for a moment with my hands in my pockets, debating whether to go back to the shop and get the key from the hook on the wall beside the kitchen door. Or go around to the deck on the right and try the French doors that open onto the bedroom. The French doors first, I decided, although the gate to the deck was probably latched from the inside, in which case I'd have to get the key after all.

I walked around the side of the cottage to the deck, which is surrounded on three sides by a five-foot privacy fence draped in cross vine, blooming now in a gorgeous orange and yellow profusion. The hummingbirds arrive around the middle of March and head straight for that cross vine, which providentially begins to bloom just about the time they show up. There are two gates in that fence, one to the garden, the other to the alley, where the garbage cans are kept for the early-morning pickup. I gave the garden gate a tentative pull and, to my surprise, found it unlatched. I stepped up on the deck and saw that one of the French doors was slightly ajar.

Oh, good, I thought. Kelly had probably gotten up late, eaten her breakfast on the deck, and was getting ready for her meeting with Charlie. I opened the door a little wider, stuck my head through into the bedroom, and called out expectantly, "Kelly. Hey, Kelly. Your lawyer called to tell you he's waiting—and his billing clock is running!"

Nothing. Nada, zilch, *nein*. No answer.

I stood there for a moment, frowning, then called again—louder this time. But the place had an empty, unoccupied feeling, and I was suddenly, skin-prickly sure that Kelly wasn't here.

I pulled the door open and stepped into the bedroom. The bed hadn't been made. There was a filmy blue nightie on the pillow, a pair of orange scrub bottoms draped over a chair, and a pair of white Reeboks on the floor. The closet door was open, revealing several outfits hanging on hangers. So was her suitcase, on the luggage rack, its contents still neatly arranged. A black leather shoulder bag on the dresser was open, too.

In a half dozen strides, I was in the bathroom. A damp

towel lay in a heap on the floor. The showerhead was dripping warm water, the shower curtain was wet, and a wet washcloth was wadded up on the rim of the tub. The makeup light was on, and the makeup mirror was swung out over an open makeup case. A hair dryer lay beside the case, its cord dangling.

I left everything as it was and ran down the hall toward the galley kitchen. The overhead light was on, and the breakfast tray Cass had put in the fridge the night before—a pint jar of her "overnight oatmeal," an egg-and-cheese breakfast burrito, a cranberry mini-muffin, and a glass of orange juice— was sitting on the counter, still completely covered with plastic wrap. Beside it there were two red ceramic mugs of coffee, black. *Two* cups.

I stood there for a moment, frowning down at the cups. Behind me, the coffeemaker was burping, and I reached to turn it off, then half-consciously thought better of what I was doing. Without pausing to think about it, I picked up a table knife and used the rounded tip to flick the switch off.

Then I realized what I had done, and why, and stood very still.

I had used the knife to turn off the coffeemaker because some old criminal-lawyer part of my brain had blinked on for an instant to remind me that there might be some useful fingerprints on the switch. Because Kelly was gone. Because she might have gone away with somebody, either willingly or otherwise.

Otherwise? I shivered, not liking the idea that was gathering at the back of my mind. But why *else* would she leave the French doors open, the lights on, her breakfast and coffee on the counter, and—most important—her shoes on the floor and her shoulder bag on the dresser?

Oh, come on, now, China, I chided myself. Get real. There were no signs of a struggle, no upset furniture, no traces of blood. She had probably glanced at her watch, realized how late she was, and dashed out without eating her breakfast, turning out the lights, or closing and locking the French doors. She was likely wearing flats or heels, not Reeboks, to her appointment with Charlie, and she probably picked up another purse. It was a good bet that she was already seated in Charlie's client chair or on her way to his office.

And then I thought of the car. When she checked in on the previous Friday, Kelly had been driving a blue Kia two-door, several years old, and I'd shown her where to park it. I hurried to the narrow window next to the living room fireplace and peered out through the wooden shutter.

Kelly's car was still parked on the gravel apron just off the alley outside the window.

Chapter Three

Writer Amy Stewart got the idea for her book *The Drunken Botanist* in a conversation with a fellow garden writer who confessed that he didn't care for gin.

> "How can anyone with even a passing interest in botany not be fascinated by this stuff?" [Stewart] said. "Look at the ingredients. Juniper! That's a conifer. Coriander, which is, of course, the fruit of a cilantro plant. All gins have citrus peel in them. This one has lavender buds, too. Gin is nothing but an alcohol extraction of all these crazy plants from around the world—tree bark and leaves and seeds and flowers and fruit."

Stewart and her friend visited a liquor store and realized that they could assign a genus and species to almost every bottle on the shelves. She reports:

> "Bourbon? *Zea mays*, an overgrown grass. Absinthe? *Artemisia absinthium*, a much-misunderstood Mediterranean herb. Polish vodka? *Solanum tuberosum*—a nightshade . . . Beer? *Humulus lupulus*, a sticky climbing vine that happens to be a close cousin to cannabis."

Blood Orange

In every culture around the world, herbs, flowers, shrubs, and trees have been used to brew flavorful and intoxicating drinks.

China Bayles
"Botanical Drinkables"
Pecan Springs Enterprise

It probably says something about me that I didn't yank out my cell and call 911. One way or another, I've had quite a few experiences with the cops, and I know that, when they're called to take a look, they like to see real evidence of a crime—a dead body, signs of a struggle, a spent cartridge or two, a smear of blood. Anything that says, "Hey, something happened here." A call on a suspected disappearance, when the disappearee has been gone for only an hour or two—is not likely to be met with enormous enthusiasm.

Instead, I called Charlie Lipman. He might or might not be Kelly Kaufman's lawyer (an appointment with an attorney doesn't necessarily mean that you'll hire her or that she'll agree to represent you). But despite his human frailties, Charlie is a trustworthy man who carries the confidences of a great many local folk, past and present. He knows where the bodies are buried, what the dirty linen looked like before it was washed, and whose closets are full of skeletons. Anyway, he was planning to meet with Kelly, so I needed to let him know that she was a no-show. Moreover, he might have a good guess where she had gone, and with whom.

So Charlie got my first call. And then I began to pace.

* * *

LIKE all the other small towns up and down the I-35 corridor between Austin and San Antonio, Pecan Springs is growing fast, with urban development strung north and south along the freeway and residential development east and west along and between the feeder roads. The city council thinks all this growth is just dandy, of course, since an expanding tax base is pure gold in the city coffers. But a lot of locals don't agree. If it's five fifteen and you're trying to get from the courthouse square to the freeway on-ramp, you can bet on sitting in traffic for twenty minutes, even though that stretch of Sam Houston Drive is only ten blocks long.

But this was Monday morning, Charlie's office is no more than six blocks away, and he was here in under five minutes in his truck. When he goes to Dallas or Houston, he drives a silver Lexus. Around town, a man of the people, he drives a burnt-orange ten-year-old Dodge pickup with dinged fenders. (He's a loyal University of Texas alum and bleeds orange blood.) I heard his tires crunching on the gravel parking area and opened the front door before he could knock.

He didn't say *How the heck are you?* or even *Hello*, just "She turn up yet?" But I understood from the way he asked the question that he already knew the answer.

Stepping back, I shook my head. "Come in. Everything's the way I found it—haven't touched a thing." I glanced down. "Except for this doorknob. Haven't called the cops yet, either. I thought we might like to do that after you have a look around. A *quick* look," I added. The more I thought about it, the more I thought that calling the police was a smart idea. Kelly Kaufman wasn't just a friend; she was a paying guest. And as an innkeeper, I could have some liability. The idea made me nervous.

Charlie Lipman is a big guy, balding, thick through the

chest and hips, and perennially untidy, with cigar and cigarette ashes scattered liberally on his rumpled suit, coffee
stains on his tie, and a shirt left over from the day before. It's
hard to tell whether this country-lawyer look is part of his act
or the consequences of a life without a significant other. All
I can tell you is that, once upon a time, he was trim and
rather good-looking and smiled nicely, just like everybody
else. Now, his shoulders sag, the pouches under his eyes sag
onto his fleshy cheeks, and his belly sags over his belt. He
doesn't smile much anymore, and when he does, he doesn't
look like he means it. I don't know whether his profession
has soured him, or whether a string of unhappy love affairs
are the cause of his unhappiness. I worry that his drinking
and his personal problems, whatever they are, are taking the
edge off his professional abilities. Even McQuaid says Charlie's not quite as sharp as he used to be.

Maybe. But he needed only a few moments to see what I
had seen in the kitchen, the bathroom, and the bedroom. And
he saw something else—or rather, he didn't see something
he was expecting to see. In search of it, he opened the drawers in the bedroom dresser, looked under the bed and quickly
through her suitcase, then checked the shelves in the closet
and the cupboards in the bathroom and kitchen.

We were standing in the bedroom, and I saw his glance
flick across the bed and note that it had been slept in, but
only by one person. Kelly hadn't entertained an overnight
guest. He pulled out a cigarette, caught my warning look,
and put it away.

"Were you here when she moved in?" he asked.

"Yes," I said. "I checked her in on Friday afternoon, about
five o'clock. I walked her through the house, showed her the
controls for the air-conditioning, the breakfast arrangements,
the locks on the doors, the emergency phone numbers, my
home phone, that kind of thing."

SUSAN WITTIG ALBERT

I don't want my guests to be unduly alarmed, but security is always on my mind—not so much when there's a couple, but certainly when a woman is staying here alone. The cottage is on the alley, and the nearest neighbor is Mary Beth Jenkins, on the opposite side. And then there's old Mr. Cowan. I usually tell my guests that they are likely to hear his dog, a yappy little Peke named Miss Lula, who feels it her duty to alert the neighborhood to every trespassing cat, dog, and bird.

"How did she seem?" Charlie asked. "Was she nervous? Concerned? Did she say anything about why she was staying here? Or mention anything about"—he glanced at me under his eyebrows—"her dealings with me? Her job?"

"She was a little nervous, maybe," I said.

Come to think of it, more than a little, although she'd been trying not to show it. In her mid-thirties, pretty, with short-cropped blond hair and a wholesome girl-next-door face that doesn't require a lot of makeup, Kelly had reminded me that we'd once worked together on a couple of garden projects and asked if I ever needed help in the shop gardens. I'd said something like, "Sure, love to have you," which was definitely the truth. I can use all the volunteer help I can get.

"She didn't say anything about you," I added. "Or about her job. She let me know that staying here had something to do with a family situation. She said she was getting a divorce." If I'd thought about it, I probably would have attributed her nervousness to that. Now I wondered why he was asking about her job.

He nodded toward the open suitcase. "Was that all she brought? Just her bag?"

"No, she—" I stopped, suddenly remembering. "She had her computer with her. It was in one of those black wheelie cases that are designed to carry a laptop and a printer or a scanner. And she made a point of getting the Wi-Fi password

32

and the login procedure, so I thought she might be intending to use it."

"Yes. Her computer." Something was going on behind Charlie's eyes. "Which doesn't seem to be here now."

He was right. There weren't many places where she might have stashed the case, and we had already looked in all of them. I paused, wanting to cover all the bases, then suggested what seemed to me to be a reasonable alternative.

"Maybe she decided to take it with her. When she left, I mean."

Charlie gave me a reproving look that said, *Can't you do better than that?* "This is her purse, I assume." He went to the shoulder bag on the dresser, opened it, and silently held up her car keys.

We already knew she hadn't taken her car. "She could have gone away with someone," I said lamely.

In answer, Charlie reached back into the handbag. "Without this?" He pulled out a red leather wallet. "You might not carry a lot of money around with you, but I'll bet you don't go *anywhere* without your ID and your credit cards." He dropped the wallet back into the purse and fished again. "And here's this." He held up her cell phone. "You go places without your cell, do you?"

That did it. "Look. I'm not trying to intrude on attorney-client privilege, Charlie. But Kelly Kaufman is a sweet young woman, and I care what happened to her. What's more, she is *my* guest, and she seems to have disappeared from *my* premises. So if you have any idea where she is and with whom, I would appreciate hearing it. If you don't, I think we ought to let the police know what's happened." I paused. "Just in case," I added. I didn't like to think what that might mean.

Charlie thought for a moment, pushing his lips in and out, then gave me a nonanswer. "If I did have an idea, you already know I'm not gonna tell you what it is. But I have no objection to you callin' the cops. Just in case." He took out his phone. "But let me make a couple of other calls first."

He went out on the deck and closed the door behind him—checking with a member of Kelly's family, I assumed. Her husband, maybe, or somebody else who might have a line on where she was.

But he must have been unsuccessful. When he came back, he said, "No problem with me if you want to call the cops, China." Lawyers involve the police only when they can no longer avoid it—that is, only when *not* to call might result in a bit of unlawyerly unpleasantness, such as an obstruction of justice charge. If the call was to be made, I would be the one making it. He eyed me with wry amusement. "You want to go straight to the top and call your buddy Chief Dawson?"

There's no personal animosity between Charlie and Sheila that I know of, just a mutually wary professional respect. They have been known to get crosswise occasionally, how- ever, since Charlie represents his fair share of the men and women arrested by Sheila's officers. Every now and then he accuses her of kowtowing to the politicos on the city council and she charges him with being anti-cop, but it's a kind of ritualistic sparring. They haven't come to blows. Yet.

"We don't need the chief," I said. "Let's just get somebody over here who will put this situation on the record." I reached into my jeans pocket, pulled out my cell phone, and punched in 911.

Twenty minutes later, the officer—a slight but serious- looking young Latina—was following us through the house, asking all the right questions and making detailed notes. When we got to the bedroom, she opened the doors onto the deck, looked around, and said exactly what I'd been expect- ing to hear.

"There's no sign of a struggle and nothing to suggest that Ms. Kaufman didn't leave with a friend who dropped by unexpectedly." She glanced at Charlie. "Maybe she just forgot about her appointment with you." She looked at me. "And left in such a hurry that she forgot to take her purse and lock the door."

"Left without breakfast, huh?" I said skeptically.

"Wouldn't be the first time. You'd be amazed by what people do when they've got something urgent on their minds." The officer paused, then added significantly, "Given all that, do either of you want to file a missing persons report?"

Charlie wasn't looking at me, which I took to be a strong signal. "Not right now," I said. In Texas, there's no official waiting time for a missing persons report. "I would appreciate it if you'd give me the ID on your incident report, though. I'll call with an update if I have any new information to add."

The officer nodded. "Here it is," she said, and I wrote down the number she gave. "I suggest that you lock this place until Ms. Kaufman shows up again," she said. Or not, I thought, which would make it a crime scene.

After the officer left, I looked for the key and found it on the bedroom dresser, lying in plain sight right next to the shoulder bag. I put it in my pocket. If Kelly wanted to get back in, she'd have to get in touch with me. I scribbled two notes with my cell number on both. I would post them where she would see them when she came back. When, I told myself firmly. Not if.

"Nothing more to do here," Charlie said. "I need to get on my way."

Accompanying him to the front door, I said, "I assume that your phone calls went to Kelly's husband. And the hospice where she works."

Charlie considered, then decided he could tell me that

much. "To her husband, yes. He hasn't heard from her since last Thursday. But not to the hospice. She doesn't work there anymore."

"Oh, yeah?" That was news to me. "Where does she work?"

Charlie shook his head.

"Give me a break," I said impatiently. "That's not privileged."

He thought about that, frowned, and gave in. "I believe she's currently unemployed." He opened the door to leave, then thought of something else. "Hey, China, would you tell McQuaid I'm not going to need him for that El Paso job? Instead, I want him to go down to Brownsville for me. Not right away—maybe in a couple of weeks."

"But he's already *in* El Paso," I reminded him gently. "He drove out there last Thursday." If Charlie had forgotten that McQuaid was clocking billable hours on his tab, he really must be losing his grip.

Charlie chuckled, happy to put me in my place. "Well, if McQuaid's in El Paso, it's not on my nickel. In fact, he hasn't worked for me for over a month now. He knew that the El Paso investigation might not gel. So tell him Brownsville instead. Or don't tell him anything—I'll call him next week, when I know what's what."

I stared at him, feeling suddenly disoriented. "But he called me last night from El Paso, Charlie. He mentioned talking to a former cop buddy—Willard Beck—at the Border Patrol Museum there." I had assumed that his visit to the museum had something to do with the case he was working on, although now that I thought of it, I didn't know that for sure. He and Beck had worked together in homicide, back in Houston. Maybe he'd just dropped in to catch up on the news.

"And I *know* he said he was working for you," I added.

Charlie raised one eyebrow, thinking about that, then gave me a casual Don't-ask-me-I-don't-know-a-thing-about-it shrug—what guys do when they're covering for a friend. He raised a hand. "If you hear from Kelly, tell her I need to talk to her. Okay?"

"Okay," I said slowly. I shut the door and leaned against it, frowning, still trying to puzzle this out. McQuaid had called me late the night before from his room at the Holiday Inn in El Paso. Of course, he hadn't talked about the investigation he was working on—he rarely did that, and I rarely asked about it. As I had told Ruby, I'm out of the crime business and I try to keep it that way. But if he wasn't working for Charlie, what was he doing out there?

And then another thought: he hadn't called from the phone in his room, but from his cell phone. Which meant that he could have called from anywhere. What made me think he was staying at the Holiday Inn? He hadn't said so last night, had he? I went back to the conversation we'd had while he was packing. That was when he'd mentioned the Holiday Inn, the one at Sunland Park Drive and I-10, where he'd stayed on earlier trips.

And then something else snaked into my mind, a deeply unsettling memory that doesn't trouble me often but one I can't easily dismiss. Her name is Margaret. Margaret Graham, a Texas Ranger with softly waved dark hair, a rich contralto voice, and deep-set eyes the color of smoky lavender. A very attractive, very sexy woman with whom McQuaid had had a brief affair the year before we were married. If I remembered right, Margaret had been promoted to lieutenant—the highest rank ever held by a female Texas Ranger—and transferred to El Paso.

At least, that's what Sheila had told me. As a fellow female law enforcement officer, Sheila knows Margaret quite well and has kept track of her upward progress through the ranks of the Texas Rangers. Which I'm sure isn't hard to do, given that there are only two female Rangers in that bastion of Anglo male supremacy. When the first female Ranger was hired, back in the 1990s, a male Ranger was quoted in the press as saying, "Texas is going to have to change a hell of a lot before a female can ride into some dusty little town and tell the sheriff, 'Hey, I'm the resident Ranger on this case.' I don't care if she's nine feet tall and meaner than a barrel of alligators. He's not going to cooperate with her."

Things hadn't changed that much since then, and I didn't envy Margaret. Her job was even harder than mine had been, back when I was slugging it out in a profession dominated by competitive males who were ten feet tall and meaner than two barrels of alligators. But I certainly respected her for trying and for getting out there every day and going toe-to-toe with lawmen who thought they owned the right to enforce the laws of Texas.

But respect is simply that: respect. What I felt was a wedge of the old, cold fear deep down in my belly, like a large chunk of the ancient Antarctic that refused to melt. I had long ago made my peace with McQuaid over his affair with Margaret. I'd made my peace with Margaret, too. Yes, I'd been jealous of her, so jealous I felt as if I'd swallowed burning acid. But after McQuaid was shot and nearly killed, Margaret and I teamed up to finish the job he had started. And when push came to shove, in the midst of all my pain and anger, I found that I couldn't help respecting the woman for her competence and courage—and even liking her. A little.

But I liked Margaret best as long as she was part of the past, the *distant* past, and behind us. McQuaid and I were married now, and happy. At least I thought we were happy. *I* was happy, anyway. And I didn't want Margaret, or anybody else, to share our present. I shut my eyes and wrapped my arms around myself hard, hating the memory of McQuaid with her. Hating—

Stop! I commanded, and opened my eyes wide.

You quit this shit right now, you hear, China Bayles? You have no idea what's going on out there in West Texas—if anything at all. You don't know that Margaret is in El Paso, or if McQuaid is seeing her. You can just stop worrying and trust your husband. You got that, girl?

I'm no girl, but I got it. I shook myself, straightened up, and went toward the bedroom. I needed to lock up Thyme Cottage and keep it locked until Kelly returned or—

I didn't want to think about that, either.

But still, when I went through the bedroom to lock the French doors, I paused, seeing that open shoulder bag on the dresser. I frowned at it, weighing my aversion to snooping in Kelly's private life against my concern about what might be going on with her.

The concern won out. I reached into the bag, pulled out her wallet, and began to look through it. There was money— six brand-new fifties that looked as if they'd just come from the bank—as they had, for with them was a withdrawal slip for three hundred dollars. Also in her wallet: four credit cards, a driver's license with an address on Post Oak Drive, a health insurance card for a regional HMO, a card identifying her as a licensed RN, a membership card for the Fancy Dance Gym, and an ID card identifying her as an employee of the Pecan Springs Community Hospice—out-of-date, according to Charlie, since she didn't work there now.

And then another ID card identifying her as an employee, a *new* employee (since the card bore a start date from the week before), at the Madison Health Clinic on Greenbriar Drive.

I glanced at the orange scrubs on the chair. It looked like she'd gotten a new job in the same line of work—which didn't explain why Charlie had told me that she was currently unemployed. Lawyers don't know everything, however, even when they think they do.

I took out my cell and punched in the number of the Madison Health Clinic. When the receptionist answered, I asked for Kelly Kaufman.

"Hang on a minute," the receptionist said. A moment later she was back with, "Sorry, she's not here. Looks like she's not scheduled to work for the next few days."

"Oh, dear," I said. "I'm a friend. I hope she's not sick."

"No, just taking some personal time. Do you want to leave a message?"

Why not? I thought. "Sure," I said. "If she phones in, tell her that if she wants to get into the cottage, she needs to call China Bayles for the key." I gave her my cell number for a callback and clicked off.

I looked through the purse more carefully now. I found two sets of keys—one to her Kia, and on a separate key ring, what looked like house keys, probably to the house on Post Oak Drive. In addition to her cell phone, I also found a miscellany: compact, comb, lipstick, breath mints, a tampon in a purple plastic tube, an assortment of coins. I held the cell in my hand. It was turned off. I debated whether to turn it on and check for calls. But that would be an even more serious invasion of her privacy, and a violation of one of my firm personal rules.

I found a pencil and paper and noted the address on her driver's license and the addresses of both the Pecan Springs Community Hospice and the Madison Health Clinic. I folded the paper and tucked it into the back pocket of my jeans, put the purse out of sight in the bottom drawer of the dresser, and went to the patio door to lock it and draw the drapes.

Standing there, I noticed something I hadn't seen before. There are two tall gates in the five-foot-high cedar fence that surround the deck: the one on the garden side that I had used to enter the cottage, the other to the alley. Both gates have a heavy-duty sliding bolt latch on the inside, low enough so that somebody can't reach an arm over the top, slide the bolt back, and unlatch the gate. The garden gate was unlatched, as I had left it when I entered earlier. But the alley gate was unlatched, too. Which meant that Kelly could have gone out—or been taken out—that way.

I opened the gate and stepped down into the alley. The garbage can was lying on its side a couple of yards away, empty, a sure clue that the garbage truck had already made its pickup. I was setting it upright and restoring its lid when I heard a dry cough and turned to see Mr. Cowan coming through his back gate with his Peke, Miss Lula, who looks like an animated brown dust mop with a scrunched-up doggy face.

Miss Lula glared at me. The two of us are not on the best of terms just now. She and Mr. Cowan were taking a shortcut through my garden a couple of weeks ago when Miss Lula was possessed of a sudden dislike for a customer's miniature poodle, who defended herself and her mistress fiercely. It took three humans to separate those two little dogs.

Mr. Cowan—stooped, grizzled, just to the north of ninety—has staked out his position in the neighborhood watch program. He's a "window watcher." When he's not out patrolling the block in front of his house or the alley in back (with the devoted Miss Lula on a pink leather leash), he spends hours looking out the window, watching for stray kids, loose dogs, suspicious loiterers, and the like. He keeps pencil notes on these street-side happenings on yellow legal pads. I wouldn't go so far as to call him a twenty-four-hour voyeur, but since he's an insomniac, he's often on duty at night, as well. Window watching is his hobby. Nothing—absolutely nothing—escapes his notice.

Which he proved once again by saying, in his scratchy old voice, "See you had the p'lice over at your place this morning, Miz McQuaid." He fully understands that I have kept my own name, but he refuses to believe it's legitimate. Married women wear their husband's names, and that's that.

I like the old man, in spite of his stubborn irascibility. "So I did," I said cheerfully, and asked him a leading question. "How'd you know?"

He narrowed his eyes. "Squad car was parked on *my* side of the alley. Miss Lula was out in the backyard bird-watchin' and reported it."

"Ah," I said, and understood immediately what had happened. When Charlie Lipman arrived, he parked his truck on the gravel apron next to Kelly's blue Kia. Which meant that the police officer had parked in the alley, which has "sides" only in Mr. Cowan's imagination. And of course Miss Lula reported it. She reports everything. At four times the volume you might expect from a toy dog about the size of a football.

"Next time, you tell the p'lice to park on *your* side," Mr. Cowan said. He added, in a mutter, "Don't see how a slip of a girl like that'un can hope to handle a criminal twice her size. Some big hulkin' guy is gonna make mincemeat outta that little bit of a thing."

I assumed he was referring to the police officer. "I'm sure she learned a few tricks at the academy," I replied. Miss Lula had caught the scent of Khat on my jeans and was sniffing suspiciously around my calf. Remembering her attack on the innocent poodle, I took two steps sideways. "You didn't happen to notice anything else that might've gone on in the alley this morning, I suppose?"

"Reckon I did." Mr. Cowan gave me a superior smile—a good citizen, pleased to share the neighborhood bulletins. "Miz Jenkins, next door on the east, put out her garbage at seven twenty. The garbage truck showed up at seven thirty-two, with them guys whistlin' and shoutin' and bangin' them can lids like they was Gabriel announcin' the Second Coming.

At eight twenty-seven, that girl who's stayin' in your stable this week left for work. The Roper twins on the west—"

"You saw her *leave*?" I asked excitedly. We had just upped the ante. "My guest, I mean. Did somebody pick her up?"

The Peke walked purposefully off to the full length of her leash and squatted. "Atta girl, Miss Lula," Mr. Cowan called approvingly. "Good pee, little lady."

He turned back to me, his brow furrowed. "Well, I didn't 'zactly see *her*, I reckon. The guy that came to get her pulled his van right up next to the gate in your cedar fence. It had them dark-tinted windows in the back, so I couldn't see who was doin' what. But I figured she just climbed right in."

I felt my stomach muscles contract. Maybe Kelly had *climbed* right in, and maybe she hadn't. The tall cedar gate opened inward and the van had blocked Mr. Cowan's view. She might have been shoved in, or lifted in. But then again—

"Anyway," Mr. Cowan was saying, "all I saw was him, getting in and out. He was a nurse or something. Medic, maybe."

"How do you know?" I asked. "That he was a nurse, I mean."

"'Cuz he was wearing them blue short-sleeved pajamas I see on nurses over at the hospital, that's how. The pants got a string holding 'em up instead of a belt." He shook his head. "Wouldn't catch me wearin' pajamas out in public. What do they do when the string breaks?"

Short-sleeved pajamas. "Oh, scrubs," I said.

"I saw your girl getting into her car Saturday," he went on. "She was wearin' the same pajama thingies, only orange, so I figured she was a nurse, too. His were blue. Blue bottoms, blue top." He pushed his lips in and out. "Big, burly guy, he was. Muscles. Dark hair cut short."

I exhaled. We were getting somewhere. "Did you notice what kind of van he was driving?"

"Gray, is all I can tell you. Kinda metallic, maybe." Mr. Cowan raised his voice. "Miss Lula, *why* are you diggin' under Miz Jenkins' crape myrtle?" He tugged on the dog's leash. "Get over here, right now, before she sees you."

But it was too late. At the back of the house next door, the screen banged open and Mrs. Jenkins came barreling down the steps, swinging a broom. "I've told you and told you and *told* you to keep that fuzz-mop of yours out of my yard!" she yelled. "If that creature digs in my herb borders again, I am going to——"

"Sorry, Miz Jenkins," Mr. Cowan called hastily. "Miss Lula promises to be good."

"I don't want promises, Mr. Cowan," Mrs. Jenkins cried. "I want *action*." She went back inside and banged the door.

Mr. Cowan yanked on the leash. "Come on, Miss Lula. We gotta go home."

"Wait a minute," I said. "You didn't happen to jot down the van's license plate, did you? And maybe you saw the guy drive up?" I was trying to figure out how he'd gotten into the cottage. The most likely scenario: Kelly knew him, and when he knocked at the door, she simply let him in. Maybe even poured that mug of coffee for him to drink while he waited for her to get ready to go. But go *where*? Without her purse and cell phone and keys? With her computer but without locking the French doors or calling Charlie to tell him she intended to miss their nine o'clock appointment?

"No, I didn't jot down the license plate," Mr. Cowan parroted. He gave me a withering look. "Just who the blue blazes do you think I am? James Bond?" And tugging Miss Lula behind him, he marched toward his house.

I stood in the alley for a moment, considering. Unlike Mr. Cowan, who is only an unofficial window watcher, Mrs.

Jenkins, who lives in the house next to his on the east, holds an *official* neighborhood watch position. As the coordinator, she puts up signs, recruits people to the program, and gets everybody together every so often to share ideas for better neighborhood security—a good thing, since it's a mixed neighborhood of older homes occupied by seniors like Mr. Cowan and Mrs. Jenkins and families with schoolchildren. Pecan Springs is a sweet little town, but no place is crime free these days. Neighborhood watch is a good way to get people to cooperate on security issues.

I went up the walk to Mrs. Jenkins' brick patio. In spite of Miss Lula's alleged depredations, the colorful border of herbs on both sides of the path was stunning: bright orange nasturtiums, golden calendula, butter-yellow coreopsis, black-eyed Susans, and yellow-gold yarrow, interplanted with parsley, thyme, and garlic chives. On the patio was a potted pineapple sage and several large wooden tubs of miniature citrus trees, none of them more than five feet high: a satsuma mandarin orange, a Meyer lemon, and what I thought was a calamondin orange. All three were heavily loaded with green fruit— citrus doesn't ripen here in Central Texas until late fall. But the calamondin (which is valued more as an ornamental plant) was still in flower, and the fragrance of the little white blooms was heavenly. If I stood here and breathed long enough, all my worries would vanish and I would simply melt into a puddle of pure pleasure.

Mary Beth Jenkins had left her broom behind when she opened the screen door and came down her back porch steps to greet me. We've worked together on a couple of neighborhood beautification projects, so we're on a first-name basis. She is a slender, athletic woman in her sixties, with sharp features and short, boy-cut gray hair. This morning, she was wearing green twill pants and a flower-printed sweatshirt with the sleeves pushed up.

"Sorry for losing my temper," she said apologetically. "But that dog dug up my chocolate mint the day before yesterday, and I consider that a *sacrilege*, plain and simple. If she's not digging in my yard, she's doing her business under the crape myrtle or—" She stopped, chuckling. "But I'll bet you'd rather talk about my citrus collection. This isn't all, you know. On the porch, I have a blood orange and a tangerine. I grew the tangerine from seed."

"From seed!" I exclaimed. "Now, that takes patience." I looked at the miniature trees. "Do you take these indoors in the winter?"

"I wrap them in an old blanket," Mary Beth said. "And they go in the garage. The tangerine stays out on the porch, though. It's fairly cold-hardy." She paused. "You should try citrus, China. They're easier than you might think. And there are so many uses for the fruit." She turned toward the flowering plant and fingered its glossy green leaves. "For example, these little calamondin oranges are almost too bitter to eat, but they make wonderful marmalade. And that blood orange makes the loveliest granita."

"I'm tempted," I admitted. I hate to take on plants that require special cold-weather attention, but those blossoms were an almost sexual experience. And there was that gorgeous pineapple sage. "I wonder," I said, "if I could harvest some of your pineapple sage. I want to make something non-alcoholic for my class on herbal liqueurs. My pineapple sage got frosted and I've had to start over."

"Help yourself," she said, and gestured to her border. "Anything you want, just let me know. As you can see, there's plenty." She frowned. "That is, as long as that dreadful little dog leaves the plants alone."

"Great. Thanks!" I pulled my attention back to my reason for stopping. "I have a Neighborhood Watch question, Mary

Beth. I wondered whether you might have noticed a gray van in the alley this morning."

Mary Beth tilted her head. "Yes, as a matter of fact, I did. Mrs. Cutter—three doors down on the other side of the street—has been under the weather for the past couple of weeks, and I came out to gather some flowers for her. Orange and yellow blossoms are always so cheerful, and I thought they might make her feel better. I was just about to go back indoors when I looked up and saw that van stopping." She pointed. "Right there, in front of your gate."

I caught my breath. Blessings on those who pick flowers for the sick—and who look every now and then while they're doing it. "Did you get a good look at the driver? Was he alone?"

"Not a *good* look, I'd say. He was in a hurry. Got right out of the van and went on in."

"He used the back way?" But the gate couldn't be opened from the alley side. If he went in that way, Kelly must have unlocked the gate for him.

Mary Beth nodded. "As far as being alone is concerned, I guess he was. I didn't see anybody else." She regarded me curiously. "Why? Is something wrong?"

Since she'd asked, I couldn't see any reason to make a secret out of what happened. "Because my guest—Kelly Kaufman—has disappeared. When I went into the cottage, it looked like she'd left in a hurry."

Mary Beth's gray eyebrows arched up. "Kelly Kaufman? The girl who works at the hospice?"

I grew up and worked in Houston, where the only people you know are the ones who have the desk right next to yours or who buy you a drink at happy hour in the bar across the street. So I'm still surprised by the multiple connections that link people who live in small towns.

"Yes, that's her," I said, although I wouldn't exactly call her a girl. "Do you know her?"

She nodded. "When my sister was in her last days, Kelly was her hospice nurse. I honestly don't know how I would have gotten through that terrible time without her. Kelly went above and beyond. That last week, she even stayed all night, several nights in a row, bless her heart."

"That's good to know," I said. "But Kelly doesn't work at the hospice now. I understand that she's over at the Madison Clinic, on Greenbriar."

"That's too bad," Mary Beth said. "She was a wonderful hospice nurse—so compassionate with my sister, who wasn't the easiest patient in the world. But now that I know that's who you're talking about, I don't think it's at all strange that another nurse—that guy in the blue scrubs—came to pick her up. It was probably an emergency call, and Kelly dropped everything else and just went off to do what had to be done. That's the kind of person she is."

"But you didn't see her get into the vehicle," I persisted.

"I couldn't. The van was in the way. And anyway, I was looking at him." She chuckled. "Big, burly guy, dark hair pulled back in a ponytail, blue scrubs, tattoos on both arms. The kind of nurse you need to handle some of the larger patients. I did hear the other door slam, though. The passenger door, I mean. So I assume that she got in and left with him."

My ears had caught a piece of new information. "Tattoos? What kind?" And Mr. Cowan said that the driver had dark hair cut short, not a ponytail. But Mr. Cowan's eyes were thirty-some years older than Mary Beth's, and Mary Beth was nearer to the action.

"I couldn't tell you," she said apologetically. "I wasn't watching *that* closely. Just . . . tattoos. You know. Snaky blue things." She stopped. "Wait there, China. I've got something for you."

48

A moment later, she was back, carrying a pretty glass bottle tied with a raffia bow. "Orange-rosemary liqueur," she said. "Made with my mandarin oranges—which is nice, because I know they haven't been sprayed with a noxious chemical. You can use it as a marinade or in vinaigrette. You can even add it to your iced tea." She uncapped the bottle. "Sniff."

I sniffed. It had a lovely citrus scent, with an unmistakable hint of rosemary. "Luscious," I said, taking the bottle. "If you're willing to share your recipe, I could add this to the tasting table for my class on herbal liqueurs."

"I'd love to." She smiled. "And I wouldn't worry about Kelly, if I were you. That girl is smart and strong. Whatever she's doing, I'm sure she can take care of herself."

I just wished I shared her optimism. I kept thinking about that big guy with muscles and a ponytail. And snaky blue tattoos. Yes, I was worrying about Kelly Kaufman. And not just because she was a guest in my B and B. I was worried about her because I didn't think she was the sort of person to skip out on an appointment with Charlie Lipman—probably about her divorce—without letting him know.

And because I really couldn't believe that she would leave three hundred dollars and her cell phone in an open purse on the dresser and forget to lock the door.

Chapter Four

In the early 1990s, a gardener in Moorpark, California, was startled when she saw something very unusual on her favorite Valencia orange tree. The oranges on one limb of the tree were reddish and the fruit was *blood* red. A local farm adviser clued her in. Her Valencia orange had repeated a mutation that first occurred in China, where blood oranges made their first appearance centuries ago.

Traditional Chinese herbalists used oranges to treat the digestive and respiratory systems: improve digestion, relieve intestinal gas and bloating, and reduce phlegm. But the medicinal orange came into its own in the west in 1747, when a ship's doctor in the British Royal Navy discovered that oranges (and other citrus fruits) prevented scurvy in sailors on long sea voyages. Now, we know that oranges are high in vitamin C, and that citrus flavonoids are potentially antioxidant, antiviral, and anti-inflammatory.

China Bayles
"Oranges in Your Garden"
Pecan Springs Enterprise

I phoned Charlie's office, got his answering machine, and related the gist of my conversations with Mr. Cowan and Mary Beth Jenkins. At the end, I added, "I'm assuming that Kelly Kaufman is your client, so I'm leaving it to you to decide whether to pass this new information along to the police."

I paused. Of course, while we now had more information about how Kelly might have left the cottage, it was possible that she had gone under her own steam, on perfectly legitimate business—on an emergency nursing call, as Mary Beth had suggested. I didn't think so, given the purse she'd left behind and the Reeboks and the unlocked doors. Was there enough to persuade Charlie to make a call to the cops? Probably not—as I said, lawyers hate to say "client" and "cop" in the same sentence. But *I* might, if Kelly didn't show up by this afternoon.

It wasn't just Kelly that was bothering me, though. There were two heavy-duty problems circling warily in my mind like a pair of supersized sumo wrestlers, and there was nothing I could do to make them put on some clothes and go for a latte grande. But I might be able to get rid of them if I got busy, and there is always plenty to do around the shop.

Miriam and her team of volunteer gardeners had already left, and I was in no mood to work in the garden. But Caitie had after-school orchestra practice and I wasn't supposed to pick her up until five. I swept the floor, dusted the shelves with my handy-dandy feather duster, and finally sat down at my desk to update the sales tax report, a job I hate so much that I put it off until the state of Texas begins to make threatening gestures in my direction.

But stare as I might at those little green numbers doing pushups across my computer monitor, what I saw were those two sumo-size problems. I might be able to push Kelly

Kaufman off to the sidelines, but I couldn't stop thinking about McQuaid. I was obviously far more bothered than I wanted to admit by Charlie's revelation that my husband was not working for him in El Paso. In fact, it was all I could do not to take out my cell phone, call McQuaid, and let him know what I was thinking.

But what *was* I thinking? I finally made myself face that question. And I didn't like the answer I came up with.

This may sound strange, but the problem, as I had been seeing it for some time, was that my marriage to McQuaid was tranquil, settled, and stable. We cooperated to get the necessary things done around the house and in our two businesses, and we did what we needed to do to make life comfortable for each other and safe, interesting, and fun for Caitie, the one remaining child at home. We spent our days at work, and our evenings at home were quiet, almost placid. We might disagree over minor things, but there wasn't a lot of conflict or controversy, which should be a good sign, wouldn't you think? And sex is just fine, thank you very much, and well above the curve, at least in my experience.

But it seemed to me that we were living on a plateau, in a landscape where there wasn't a lot of excitement or romance or mystery or surprise. For all I knew, of course, this was the plateau that every midlife marriage settles into, when a lot of the getting-there goals and challenges have been met. This might be what marriage *is*, as married couples relax into the long haul together. Which wasn't a problem—unless you happen to be longing for excitement, romance, mystery, or surprise.

And maybe I wouldn't have thought of this as a personal problem if I hadn't begun to notice, a few months before, that McQuaid's job was taking him out of town much more regularly. And not just for a day or two, either. He wasn't teaching at the university this semester, which meant that he didn't have to stick around to meet his classes, and lately, he'd been gone for a week or ten days at a time. When he was home, he was a little distant—well, not *distant*, exactly. Just preoccupied, as if he had something on his mind.

And now *this*.

So. This what?

Well, for starters, this whatever-McQuaid-was-doing out there in El Paso that he wasn't doing for Charlie Lipman, who hadn't used him for a month or more. Although now, thinking about it, I wasn't sure that he'd actually *said* he was working for Charlie. I think maybe I just assumed that he was, since he hadn't mentioned the name of another client.

But the thing of it was . . . well, the thing of it was that Ranger Margaret Graham was in El Paso, too. Or was she? I saved the computer file—the damned tax report wasn't actually due for another week, anyway—and sat back in my chair, thinking.

I'd learned from Sheila that Margaret had been promoted and reassigned to the West Texas Ranger field office. But that had been a year or so ago. There were six field offices in Texas, plus the Austin headquarters, and the Rangers moved around quite a bit. And even within the West Texas office, the Rangers were stationed in various far-flung outposts—Midland, San Angelo, Fort Stockton, and so on. Maybe Margaret had already been assigned somewhere else. I could call Sheila and find out.

I pinched the bridge of my nose, trying out first one fictional explanation and then another. But I couldn't think of a reason to ask Sheila about Margaret's current whereabouts except the truth: I was afraid that my husband might be seeing her behind my back. But that would be admitting to jealousy, insecurity, and mistrust—and I didn't like to think I was that sort of person. I *wasn't*, was I? Of course not.

But maybe there was another way to dig up the information

I needed. Staring me in the face at this very moment was the big Google search box on my computer home page. I was a skilled and resourceful computer sleuth. And if it turned out that Margaret wasn't in El Paso after all, I wouldn't have a thing to worry about.

Fifteen seconds later, I had my answer. I typed "Texas Rangers El Paso" into the search bar, clicked on the first link that came up, and went to a page that announced, "Welcome to the web page of Company E!" in large letters across the top. Beneath that was a flattering recital of Ranger history and a display of individual Ranger photographs, with the commanding officer (Major Burns) at the top, two lieutenants below, and fourteen Rangers beneath that. They all wore white shirts, ties, and jackets, as well as silver star-within-a-wheel badges and white Stetsons. All of the fourteen Rangers were men. One of the lieutenants was a woman. That woman was Margaret.

And she was no longer just attractive, damn it. Even wearing that too-large white Stetson and the prissy girls'-school crisscross necktie, she was beautiful. I stared at her for a long moment, scarcely even aware that I was holding my breath. Then I exhaled, and with a sinking feeling in my stomach, I turned the computer off.

One of my sumo wrestlers had just gained about three hundred pounds and was squatting right in the center of the mat.

It was four o'clock by the time I got in the car and headed over to Cavette's Market to pick up something for Caitie and me for supper. Cavette's is a couple of blocks down Crockett Street, next door to the Sophie Briggs Historical Museum.

Still holding its own in a world dominated by Safeways and Randalls, Cavette's is a small, family-owned market with wooden bins and wicker baskets of fresh fruits and veggies lined up on the sidewalk and a gorgeous display of custom cakes in its bakery section. Perhaps its very uniqueness accounts for its survival, for the owners—three generations of Cavettes—know every single product they have on their shelves. What's more, they know all their customers and they call each one by name.

"Good afternoon to you, Miz Bayles."

Young Mr. Cavette—seventy and bald as an onion—straightened up from a box of fresh broccoli he was putting out on the produce counter and offered me the second half of his ritual greeting. "The good Lord takin' care of you today?"

"He sure is," I said with a feigned cheerfulness, and smiled. I was lying through my teeth. But it was the expected ritual response, and I couldn't upset Young Mr. Cavette (who is a Baptist) by telling him that I was obsessing over my husband's possible—or imagined—unfaithfulness.

Sheila once remarked that she thought the shop and all three of its owners ought to be registered as historical landmarks, and I agree. The market has been in its current location since Old Mr. Cavette's father built it in the year William McKinley was assassinated and Teddy Roosevelt moved into the White House. Old Mr. Cavette celebrated his ninetieth birthday not long ago with a block party featuring birthday cake, balloons, and party hats, to which we were all invited. Young Mr. Cavette was widowed at sixty-three and remarried at sixty-five; his bride, famous for her custom-baked and decorated cakes, is some five years his senior. The youngest Cavette, Young Mr. Cavette's son Junior, is now nearly fifty, but he still makes in-town deliveries to home-bound seniors. You can see him buzzing around Pecan Springs on his red motorbike every day but Sunday. You don't get that kind of service from Safeway.

Thinking about supper for Caitie and me, I picked up a package of tortellini—Caitie likes it—and snagged an avocado and a couple of beautiful blood oranges. We'd have salad tonight with fresh spinach out of the garden and a vinaigrette flavored with Mary Beth's rosemary-orange liqueur.

I held up one of the oranges. "I didn't know these were still in season," I said to Young Mr. Cavette.

"They ain't." He piled another head of fresh broccoli in the produce bin. "We get the Texas bloods in the winter. Them are Florida bloods, Taroccos. The brewmaster fella out at Comanche Creek brewery said he needed some. Says he's thinking of using 'em to make beer." He wrinkled his nose. "Seems sorta sacrilegious to me, but the customer is always right. So I got him a box. What you see there is what's left."

"In that case, I'll take a few more," I said, adding them to my basket. I was remembering a recipe I had seen for a blood orange liqueur. It would make an interesting addition to the liqueurs I was making for my class. I read somewhere that the Tarocco blood orange has the highest vitamin C content of any orange in the world. It certainly has the most delicious fragrance. And blood oranges are beautiful—like shimmering slices of rubies.

"I'll just have to take the rest of those oranges," said a woman behind me, taking the two that were left. "They're positively seductive, don't you think?"

"Why, hello, Janet." I turned quickly. It was Janet Parker, one of my regular customers at the herb shop. Or at least, she had been. "Golly," I said. "I haven't seen you in a while. Where have you been keeping yourself?"

"I'm a working girl now," Janet said. She's tall, angular, and attractive. She was dressed in a tailored white blouse, a slim gray skirt, and a blue jacket, and her dark hair was pulled into a neat bun. "Our youngest is going to college this year, over at A and M. I'm sure you know what that means."

"I'm afraid I do," I said ruefully. "Brian has a partial scholarship at UT, but it still costs an arm and a leg."

That's no lie. I'm sure UT is cheaper than a private university, but Brian's tuition and fees (even with the scholarship) amount to $2,500 a semester and the rest of it—off-campus room and meals in Austin, books, his car, and a little for extras—adds up to about $6,500. Brian is McQuaid's son, so he and Brian's mother, Sally (McQuaid's ditzy first wife), are picking up the tab together. But I've heard the two of them discussing the cost, and I know how it mounts up. To make things even more awkward, Sally wheedles to reduce her contribution and then cleverly manages to forget how much she owes when it's time to write the check. (Tacky, yes. But true.)

Janet nodded. "Anyway, both of the kids are out of the house now, which gave me more free time. So I went out and found myself a job." Her smile was just a little smug. "The perfect job, I have to say. And I'm making enough to pay the college bills, which is wonderful. There's even a little left over for me."

"The perfect job?" I reached over the now-empty blood orange bin and picked up a gorgeous bunch of grapes. "That certainly sounds intriguing. I might be jealous if I didn't think *I* had the perfect job." I put the grapes into a plastic bag and dropped them into my cart. "Where are you working?"

"At the Pecan Springs Community Hospice. I process the new admissions and schedule all the nurses' visits." She peered into my basket. "Avocado, oranges, grapes—looks like you're making a salad."

I nodded. "Plus spinach from the garden and some goat cheese that my neighbor makes. With an orange vinaigrette. Mary Beth Jenkins gave me some orange-rosemary liqueur, and I thought I'd use that to flavor it."

"Sounds absolutely perfect," Janet said. "I'll give that salad a try. Unfortunately, Harold won't touch goat cheese—blue cheese, either. Nothing but good old Velveeta for him."

With a sigh, she picked up a bunch of grapes. "The bad thing about working is that I'm always totally wrung out at the end of a long day. I love the people I work with at the hospice, but there's such a lot of stress. And then I have to go home and cook supper. Seems like we end up going out to eat a lot these days, which probably isn't too good for our cholesterol." She reached for an avocado. "You still have a little girl at home, don't you?"

"Yes," I said. "Caitlin. She's thirteen." Then it clicked. "Oh, you're working at the *hospice*! Gosh, that's a coincidence. I ran into Kelly Kaufman just the other day. She's working there too, I understand."

I gave myself a mental slap on the wrist for telling a lie. But I was fishing for information. And I got a bite.

"She *was*, yes," Janet said with another little sigh. She bagged the grapes and put them into her basket. "But not anymore. Which is just too bad, if you ask me. Kelly is a very good nurse, especially in a hospice situation. I really couldn't understand why Ms. Blake let her go. And neither could anybody else. The staff, I mean. We were totally in the dark."

"Well, gosh," I said sympathetically. "Whatever happened must have blown up very suddenly. I mean, Kelly seemed to really love her hospice work. And she is *so* responsible." Except for missing her appointment with her lawyer, of course, and leaving without her purse and her phone and forgetting to lock the door.

"Yes, suddenly," Janet replied, frowning. "Although Kelly has been pretty upset lately, with her divorce and all." She leaned forward and lowered her voice. "There's another woman, I'm afraid. It's apparently been going on for some time, but Kelly has only known for a couple of weeks. She told me that there's a serious disagreement over the property settlement. She and her husband have a business together."

"Yes, a business makes it hard," I said. "And so does another woman." I thought fleetingly of Margaret, then pushed the thought away.

"In a way, knowing the reason seemed to make it easier for her," Janet said. "The other woman, I mean. But that wasn't what set off her disagreement with Ms. Blake. Whatever *that* was, it must have been pretty serious, because afterward, Ms. Blake got the whole staff together—the nurses and the office people—and lectured us about breaching patient confidentiality. We're supposed to bring any concerns about patient care directly to *her*, not share them among ourselves. And etcetera. I looked around, and we were all like, *what*? What's this supposed to be about?"

"When was that?" I asked curiously. I remembered being part of a corporation and attending meetings like that, and the memory wasn't a very pleasant one.

"A couple of weeks ago," she said vaguely. She picked up a kiwi, sniffed it, and put it back. "I'm afraid Harold would turn up his nose at kiwis," she said. Instead, she chose several bananas. "The problem for me," she went on, "is that Kelly was carrying a big patient load. With her gone, I've had to shuffle quite a few schedules—not easy when you're seriously understaffed in the first place. I really wish Marla would hire a few more people. Some of our nurses have had to take on extra shifts."

"Extra shifts are hard when you have a family." I frowned and suddenly made the connection. "Oh, you're talking about Marla Blake! I know her. Is she the hospice manager?"

"Yes, and also the owner," Janet said. "Or part owner, anyway. She bought the business a couple of years ago with one of our staff doctors. The main office is here in Pecan Springs, but there are branches in Seguin and Lufkin, as well. I handle the scheduling for them, too. Altogether, we have nearly eight hundred clients. We're quite large, still growing. In fact, we're planning to open a branch in Fredericksburg, although that's been delayed. Marla has been out sick quite a bit lately." She chuckled. "And I'm sure you do know her. Over the years, she's been a member of practically every civic organization in town. The Pecan Springs Hospital Auxiliary, the ladies' club, the Friends of the Library."

"Of course," I said. My path had intersected with Marla's in the Friends of the Library. For a while, she had pretty much run the show for the Friends—which I had to admit was a good thing, since she had a knack for organizing activities and people and getting things done. Yes, she rubbed some people the wrong way—me, too, sometimes. But I had to admire her management skills, however grudgingly. Volunteer organizations need people who are driven to see that the job gets done right, even when they're stepping on other people's toes. And now that I thought about it, I remembered hearing that she had dropped out of most of her volunteer activities when she got involved with some sort of healthcare business. That must have been when she took over the hospice.

"Marla is a very hands-on manager," Janet said, in an explanatory tone. "Very attentive to detail. Which is good, because we're mostly funded by Medicare and there's so much record-keeping. But Marla has developed her own software, which makes things much easier and frees up staff time for other duties. And the fact that we're small and locally owned makes us much more responsive to the needs of the community than the big HMOs." She cocked her head to one side. "Dealing with end-of-life issues is such a difficult task, you know. We're large enough to be able to offer all the necessary services—but small enough to be sensitive to the special requirements of each individual and family. We're devoted to easing the pain that so many families have to go through at the end of a loved one's life."

"Sounds impressive," I said, although Janet's spiel struck me as canned. I wondered if she was mentally reading off the script she handed to people who were considering placing their loved ones in hospice care. But who am I to criticize? Mary Beth Jenkins had just told me what a difference hospice care had made during her sister's last days.

Janet smiled, accepting the compliment. "I've really enjoyed working there. So much so that I've been spreading the word about our work." Her smiled broadened. "In fact, Marla has just hired my sister-in-law to work in sales. Dorothy started last week."

"Sales?" I was surprised. "What does a hospice *sell*?"

Janet's eyebrows went up. "Why, our services, of course. There are a lot of options out there for end-of-life care, and people need help in choosing the very best for their loved ones. All of us on the staff help in recruiting, which is good because Marla pays nice bonuses when we bring in patients. Dorothy—that's my sister-in-law—will go out and talk to doctors, nursing homes, assisted living facilities, and individuals to let them know who we are and what we do, so they can refer patients to us. She used to sell real estate," she added earnestly, "so I'm sure she'll do very well."

I didn't quite get the connection between real estate and health-care services, but I didn't let my ignorance show. "Sounds like a match," I said politely, thinking that—with the graying of the nation's population—hospice care must be a growth industry, especially since it was funded by the government. "Maybe you'll get so busy that Marla will have to ask Kelly to come back to work."

"I sincerely doubt that," Janet said regretfully. "I didn't hear what went on between them, but I saw Kelly when she ran out of the office. She was crying. And Marla was so upset, she hasn't really been the same since. Others probably can't

61

tell that, but I can." She pushed out her lips. "Orange vinaigrette, you said?"

I nodded. "I make it with minced garlic and a spoonful of Dijon mustard."

"Oh, good," Janet said happily. "Howard just loves mustard. I'm so glad I ran into you, China. You have a great evening, now." She waggled her fingers in farewell as we said good-bye.

Chapter Five

Interestingly, some of the oldest herbal liqueurs are strongly associated with colors. Green Chartreuse, for instance, was created as a medicinal drink by Carthusian monks at their monastery in the Chartreuse Mountains of France in 1764. The secret recipe reportedly contains a blend of 130 herbs, including wormwood, lemon balm, hyssop, sweet flag, peppermint, angelica, and cardamom. The aromatic green liqueur gave its name to the color chartreuse in 1884.

Strega, a popular Italian digestif (served after meals to enhance digestion), is colored a distinctive yellow with saffron, one of the seventy-some herbs and spices, including mint and fennel, that flavor the drink.

Campari, an Italian aperitif (served before meals to enhance appetite), was originally colored red with a dye derived from crushed cochineal insects, found on prickly pear cactus. Among other herbs, Campari also contains gentian, wormwood, and quinine (extracted from the bark of the cinchona tree).

The first of the orange liqueurs, Curaçao, is named for the Caribbean island, where Valencia oranges were planted by Spanish settlers. The Valencias didn't thrive in the island's arid climate and were abandoned. The fruits of their wild descendants (called "laraha") were bitter and inedible. But it was discovered that sun-dried laraha peels had a heady orange aroma and flavor. These—with sugar, cinnamon, nutmeg, and cloves— were added to the local rum, and Curaçao was born.

China Bayles
"Botanical Drinkables"
Pecan Springs Enterprise

I picked Caitlin up on the way home from the market. She recently celebrated her thirteenth birthday, so she is officially a teenager. But she is fine-boned and small for her age, and there is often a waiflike sadness in her eyes that makes me want to throw protective arms around her and hold her close. It reminds me of the tragedies that have taken so much from this young girl: her mother's accidental drowning, her father's murder, and the death from cancer of her beloved aunt. Dark-haired and dark-eyed, she is my niece, daughter of my half brother Miles, whom I didn't meet until the last weeks of his life. My family relationship with Caitie might seem a little distant, but our heart connection has been strong from the very beginning, and I find it hard to imagine life without her. Now she is officially our daughter, and her resilience and growing self-confidence have made me very proud.

As a young woman, I was never sold on marriage, partly because my parents had a terrible marriage (witness the decades-long affair that produced my half brother Miles). I valued my single status and cherished my independence and my autonomy, first in my law career, and later, after I bought Thyme and Seasons and settled down in Pecan Springs. Even after McQuaid and I moved in together and I found myself being a mother to his son Brian, I didn't consider myself a genuinely domesticated person. I was still an *I*, first person singular, who just happened to live with a guy and his son.

But that began to change when McQuaid and I married and bought a large and rather shabby two-story farmhouse on Limekiln Road, some twelve miles west of Pecan Springs, in the Texas Hill Country. The house is white with green shutters, has a porch on three sides and a turret in the front corner, and is set back nearly a half mile from the road behind a dense stand of hackberry, cedar, and oak and a grassy meadow that, in the spring, is gloriously carpeted with bluebonnets, paintbrush, and wine cups.

It was the privacy that sold us on the place, and the extra room it offered. There are bedrooms for the kids (Caitie has claimed the round turret room), craft space for me, and office space for McQuaid. The house is separated by a low stone wall from an old, worn-out peach orchard on one side and dense woods on the other. There's a kitchen and herb garden in back, and deep in the woods, a hundred yards beyond the garden, a clear, spring-fed creek ripples over limestone ledges between banks of maidenhair ferns under a canopy of cypress trees. All of us love the place, inside and out, and it's hard to think of myself as an independent *I* here. It hasn't always been easy, but I've learned to think of myself as an interdependent *we*—first person plural. Which may be why, come to think of it, I was so bothered by the idea of McQuaid and Margaret.

When we got home, Caitie ran into the house and bestowed a quick hug on her orange tabby cat, Mr. Pumpkin (aka Mr. P), and on our new basset puppy, Winchester, then rushed up to her turret room to change out of her school clothes into the bib overalls, T-shirt, and sneakers she wears around the house. Back downstairs, she dashed out to the chicken coop that McQuaid and Brian built for her, to gather eggs and check on her chickens. Mr. P went along to make sure the chickens didn't try anything tricky. When it comes to Caitie, that cat is very possessive. A battered, bedraggled old reprobate, the tomcat was obviously at the tail end of his ninth life when he showed up on our doorstep one rainy evening, angling for supper and a dry place to sleep. What he got was Caitie, who fell in love and begged to keep him.

I had been doubtful. "You already have a lot to do taking care of your chickens. Are you sure you can handle another project?"

"Of course I can," Caitie replied staunchly, and when she added, "He's just like me—he needs a home," I had to give her a hug and agree.

She started her flock about a year and a half ago, with three Rhode Island Reds, three white leghorns, and (a little later) Rooster Boy, a fetching, red-feathered fellow who is inordinately proud of his iridescent ruff and sweep of colorful tail. Then our neighbor gave her a pair of Golden Laced Polish chickens—docile birds with glossy brown feathers mottled with gold highlights and an amazing ornamental frizzle of feathers on their heads. They look like feather dusters darting after bugs in the grass. She named them Goofy and Doofus and plans to exhibit them at the Adams County fair this summer. As Caitie banged the door behind her on her way out to the coop, I reminded myself that some teenagers are boy-crazy or clothes-crazy or (worse) both. Our teenager is chicken-crazy, and I admit to being relieved. Boys and clothes can wait.

In the kitchen, I was greeted by Winchester, who had been contemplating the change in his life situation from his basket in the corner of the kitchen. Winchester came to us just a few weeks ago from a basset rescue organization in Austin. He is heir and successor to our beloved Howard Cosell, who crossed the rainbow bridge the previous year but whose exploits live on, with love, in family legend. Every now and then, one of us thinks of Howard and says something like, "Do you remember when Howard Cosell cornered that stupid armadillo and . . ."

And then we all shake our heads and laugh and sigh a little sadly, because Howard was truly a dog of remarkable talents, and we miss him.

Like Howard, Winchester is long and low-slung, with droopy basset jowls and floppy basset ears that have a tendency to dangle in his food and water bowls. He's only about three years old, but from his mournful expression we suspect that he must have already endured an exceptionally hard life, overflowing with disappointments and disasters. He frequently gives voice (long and loud, embroidered with plaintive little yips and a yodel) to the belief that the world is going to hell in a handbasket and he does not expect the situation to improve anytime soon. Among other issues, he hasn't yet settled the question of unlimited access to McQuaid's leather recliner; who owns the entire foot of the bed; and whether bassets are allowed to eat bagels. There is also the little matter of Mr. P, an infinitely wily (but ultimately irrelevant) creature who is waiting to clean up any leftover kibble the instant Winchester retires for his nap.

However, Winchester's weeks in our household have taught him that when Mom comes home, she usually puts more kibble into his bowl. So he brightened when he saw me, scrambled out of his basset basket, and stationed himself hopefully beside his bowl: his very own, because it has his name on it, W-I-N-C-H-E-S-T-E-R, in big orange letters. When the food arrived, Winchester enjoyed that one brief, shining moment when his bowl was exactly as full as it should be, then got down to business. Like Mae West, he believes that he who hesitates is a damn fool. It's always better to eat fast, just in case another dog or two might have been inadvertently invited to dinner. And of course, there is always the cat.

I glanced at the answering machine on the counter, noticed that there were two messages, and played them as I unloaded the groceries. The first was from my mother, letting me know that her husband (Sam, whom I love dearly) had breezed through his latest stress test as if it were a stroll in the park and that Sam's doctor had announced that he's on his way to a full recovery. I breathed a quiet *hallelujah*. Sam gave us a bad scare last Thanksgiving. He had to have coronary surgery, and he and Leatha (my mother) were forced to postpone their plan to open their Uvalde County ranch as a birding retreat. We've all been worried about his health, so this was good news. Very good news.

The second call, not so much. It was from McQuaid.

"Sorry I missed you, China," he said, gruff and heavily apologetic. "I'm probably going to be out of touch for the next couple of days. This investigation is taking me into an area where there might not be cell phone coverage. There's no problem, and no danger, so don't worry if you don't hear from me for a while. I'll call when I can. Hope everything is okay with you and Caitie." There was a moment's pause, during which I heard the unmistakable clinking of glasses. McQuaid took a breath, then added, with emphasis, "Lots of love to my two best girls."

His two best girls? I hoped so, but my conversation with Charlie—and the revelation that McQuaid wasn't working for him in El Paso now and hadn't worked for him there in some time—had raised some great big red flags. I didn't like the way I was feeling. Why hadn't he called my cell phone instead of leaving a message on our answering machine? Did he want to avoid talking to me or answering my questions? For instance, where in Texas—or New Mexico, for that matter—was there no cell phone coverage? Who was clinking those glasses in the background of his call? And what about Margaret? Was he seeing her?

I frowned and played the message again, trying to find some little bit of something I could hang on to, something that would ease my ugly suspicions, or at least let me paper over them. But I couldn't, so I deleted both calls, wishing I could erase McQuaid's call from my mind as easily as I could wipe it out of the telephone's digital memory. I didn't need to be worrying about something I couldn't control. I turned away and forced myself to give some serious thought to supper. It was time to eat, and part of the salad was still out in the garden.

In our part of Texas, garden vegetables often do better in the fall than in the spring. The spring garden is cut short by our brutal summertime heat, which can strike as early as mid-May. But so far, the weather had been mild and the early veggies were thriving. We had already had several meals of Sugar Ann peas, and the Kentucky Wonder pole beans looked as if they'd be ready to harvest in another couple of weeks. The spring greens—spinach, kale, collard, and chard—were flourishing, and I gathered enough beautifully fresh spinach for our supper salads, a handful of radishes, and several green onions.

Back in the kitchen, I washed the veggies in the sink, put the water on to boil for the tortellini, and began making the lemony sauce that Caitie likes: butter, lemon zest and juice, chopped green onion tops, fresh basil, and parmesan cheese. I was stirring the green onion tops and minced basil into the melted butter when the telephone rang. I dried my hands hurriedly and reached for the phone, hoping it was McQuaid. And then remembered that I wasn't going to worry about something I couldn't control.

But it wasn't McQuaid—and I was in for a jaw-dropping surprise.

"China, this is Kelly."

"Kelly? *Kelly Kaufman?*" I turned off the burner under the butter. "Where *are* you? Are you okay? What—"

"I'm sorry," she said quickly. Her voice was light and high. "Really. I'm *very* sorry. I hated to do it the way I did, but I couldn't think of another way. I know it was clumsy. I hope you're not too angry with me."

"Angry?" I laughed shortly. "Well, I wouldn't say that, exactly. But you certainly succeeded in worrying me. You could at least have left a note, you know." I was trying not to sound accusing but not succeeding very well.

"I thought of that," she said. "But I was afraid somebody else might find it." She sounded rueful. "And if I let you in on my plan ahead of time, I figured you'd tell me not to do it."

I chuckled ironically. "Oh, you think?"

She reacted to my obvious sarcasm. "This isn't a game, China. It's important." She dropped her voice. "I probably did a stupid thing when I left the cottage, but I did it for my own safety. I'm afraid. I mean, I'm really, really scared. I was absolutely desperate to get away."

For her *safety*? This call was beginning to sound like a script for a B-movie thriller. But I could hear the fear in her voice, and I didn't want to underplay it. "I understand that, Kelly," I said more softly. "I get that you're afraid. But just so you know, Charlie Lipman and I reported your disappearance to the cops."

"I thought you might. But *please* don't tell the police you've talked to me and that I'm okay," she added, drawing out the word *please*. "Don't tell Mr. Lipman, either. I'm not sure I can trust him. It's better for me if he doesn't know where I am. I'm calling you because I think you can help me."

She couldn't trust her *lawyer*? My puzzlement deepened. "Kelly, I've known Charlie Lipman for a long time. He may be going through a rough patch lately, but he's perfectly competent to handle your divorce. He—"

"This isn't about my divorce, China. It isn't about me at all. It's about—" She lowered her voice again, as if there was somebody else in the room with her. "It's about a murder. I know that you were involved with stuff like that before, back when you were practicing law. That's why I'm hoping you'll be willing to help me."

I was alarmed. "A murder? You mean you think you've *killed* somebody?" I thought immediately of a case I'd read about, where a nurse inadvertently administered a fatal dose of the wrong medication. Her patient died. She was convicted of criminally negligent homicide.

"No, not me," Kelly said hurriedly, and rushed on. "*I* didn't kill anybody, China. But I know who did, or at least I think I do. And there's another legal thing I need to talk to you about. I've got a lot of evidence about the other cases— the unqualified people, I mean. All that documentation is on my laptop. There's bound to be some sort of evidence of the murder, too, but I don't have it." Her words were tumbling together and she stopped, breathless. "I have some ideas, but that's why I need you, China. To help me get evidence that will stand up in court. About the murder, and this other legal thing."

Unqualified people? This other legal thing?

"Whoa," I said. "You're going way too fast, Kelly. There's a whole lot of backstory to fill in. First of all, I need to know why you left the cottage the way you did. Second, why don't you trust Charlie Lipman? He's your lawyer, and you ought to—"

"Look," she broke in. "I want to answer all your questions. But the thing is really complicated, and I'd rather not go into it over the phone. Could you, like, drive over to my friend Lara's house this evening? That's where I'm staying. It's near Wimberley. We could go over the files and I could explain everything."

Explain everything? I was beginning to think I was being used for some purpose I didn't understand, and I didn't like it. I didn't like getting in Charlie Lipman's face, either. Kelly was his client. Whatever this thing was, she ought to take it to him first. If she didn't like the way he responded, she should get herself another lawyer. But not me. I've kept my membership in the bar, in case of emergencies—that is, if the shop goes broke and I absolutely, positively have to have money. Otherwise, I'm out of the business.

Yeah. Well, that's all true. But on the other hand, now that the question of murder had been raised, I was curious. I wanted to know what Kelly was talking about.

"Sorry, but I can't drive over to where you're staying," I said. "We live in the country and I don't think it's a good idea to leave my daughter alone in the house at night." I paused. "Do you have access to a vehicle? I'm out on Limekiln Road. If you want to talk, why don't you come over here?"

There was a silence. "I suppose I could do that," she said slowly. "But it would have to be after dark. I don't want to risk being seen. And I'll have to be careful." She laughed ruefully. "My driver's license is in my shoulder bag, which is on the—"

"I put it in the bottom drawer of the bedroom dresser," I said, "and I locked the cottage doors. I'll be glad to loan you my key, since you left yours behind. All your other belongings are in the bedroom, too."

She sighed. "I kinda messed up, I guess. Leaving your

place and my stuff like that. Maybe I should've done it a different way."

Well, duh, I thought. Aloud, I said, "What time do you want to come over?"

She was hesitant. "What's good for you?"

I glanced at the clock. It was six fifteen. "Give me a couple of hours, at least. Caitie and I usually sit down with her homework after supper." It's a quiet mom-and-daughter time, and I didn't want to give it up. "And then I have a little kitchen project."

"How about nine?" she asked. "It should be dark by then. And China, please, *please* don't tell Mr. Lipman—or anybody else. You won't, will you? I'll explain why when I see you."

"I won't," I said reluctantly, and hung up.

If I had known what was going to happen, I would have handled things differently. But I didn't, and there's no going back, no undoing what has been done.

In the end, it's the utter finality that's so hard to live with.

AT supper, Caitie seemed a little quieter than usual, and I was preoccupied, too—trying not to think about Kelly. It was that business about murder that intrigued me. What did she know, or suspect? What was this business about "unqualified people"? And what was she afraid of?

The questions buzzed around my head like a swarm of inquisitive flies while Caitie and I finished eating, put the dishes in the dishwasher, and completed an hour's worth of decimals, subject-verb agreement, and reading comprehension questions. Or rather, Caitie proudly demonstrated that she could do all those things, while I was an admiring audience of one.

Make that two. Winchester had draped himself across my

feet under the table and occasionally thumped his tail on the floor, signaling his approval of what was happening over his head. Of course, since Winchester is only knee high, everything taller than one of Caitie's chickens happens over his head. He must be used to that by now.

"Well, that's it, Mom," Caitie said finally, pushing her chair back. "I'm going upstairs to finish *Anne of Green Gables*. I have to write a report on it, and I still have ten or twelve pages to go."

Some mothers are called Mom from the minute their kids can say their first words. I've come by my name relatively late in the game, and I'm still thrilled whenever I hear it. I leaned over and dropped a quick kiss on Caitie's head, smelling the sweet floral fragrance of her hair and thinking that it's nice to know that girls—some girls, anyway—are still reading a book that was written over a century ago.

"Sounds good." I glanced at the time display on the microwave. I needed to get started on my kitchen project, and Kelly would be arriving before too long. "One of my friends is coming over in a little while," I added. "You may hear us talking."

She nodded. "Will it bother you if I decide to practice my violin? I'm working on something for the spring recital."

"Absolutely not," I said. When Caitie came to live with us, my mother gave her the violin I scorned when I was eleven, and she immediately fell in love with it. She's studying with Sandra Trevor, who teaches strings at CTSU and says that Caitie is exceptionally talented. When she told McQuaid and me this, Sandra added that she hoped that we would make sure that our daughter leads a normal life in spite of her talent. She grinned when she said it, but we took her seriously—which is where the cat and the chickens come in. "What are you working on?" I asked.

"Telemann," she replied. "'Twelve Fantasias.'" She stood

there for a moment, and I noticed that her shoulders were sagging.

"Is something wrong?"

"Not wrong, exactly," she said, wrinkling her forehead. "But there's this new kid—Kevin. He moved here from Chicago a couple of months ago. He's a good violinist. Really good, I mean." She met my eyes. "Dr. Trevor made him concertmaster today. I'm still in first, but I had to move over."

"Oh," I said. Concertmaster is the title given to the violinist who occupies the first chair in the violin section. It usually goes to the best and most reliable player, who is assigned to play the solo parts and help everybody tune up before they start playing. Caitie has been concertmaster since the current school year started. Up to now.

"Well, that's interesting." I took a breath. "Are you okay with it?"

"Not really," she said, and pressed her lips together. "I mean, nobody really likes playing second fiddle, do they?" She laughed a little and I joined in with a chuckle. "But I'm not really second—I mean, I'm still playing first violin, just not first chair. And Dr. Trevor says she'll rotate our positions. She wants to give Kevin a chance to get some experience, which I think is right. His fingering is better than mine, although his bowing isn't nearly as good."

"So what did you do when this happened?" I asked lightly. "I hope you didn't throw rocks at him."

"I wanted to." She smiled crookedly, showing her mouthful of braces. "But I congratulated him instead. After all, he earned it, and he'll do a good job. And I like him." She blushed. "I mean, he's okay—pretty much. For a boy. But I told him not to get too comfortable in that chair, because I intend to get it back."

"That's my girl." I got up and put my arms around her, thinking that there weren't many adults who could congratulate someone who had just taken something from them that they had worked hard for and wanted to keep. "I'm proud of you."

I was. Prouder than I could say. Grace in adversity, that's what it was, in a thirteen-year-old girl who was more mature than some women twice her age.

She hugged me back, and we stood there for a moment. Then she dropped her arms. "I need to work on the Telemann. It's awfully hard, but Dr. Trevor says she knows I can do it. I just have to practice, that's all."

"We'll love listening," I said. "It'll be background music." A little Telemann was just what we needed to accompany Kelly's tale of murder and who knew what else.

"But first I have to finish *Anne*." Caitie scooped up Mr. P, who had just come in from his evening yard patrol. She headed for the door, then paused. "Hey, when Dad calls, let me talk to him, okay? I want to tell him about Kevin."

"Okay," I said, "but don't be disappointed if he doesn't call tonight. He's somewhere out in West Texas, where there aren't any cell phone towers." At least, that's what he'd said.

She nodded. "Well, if he does, I want to talk to him."

Caitie headed upstairs, the cat draped over her arm like an orange fur stole. Winchester roused himself to inquire about the availability of cookies, but when none were offered, he stumped over his basket, draped one long ear over his eyes, and fell asleep again.

I went to the counter and set up the coffeemaker for a pot of Colombian coffee. The evening project I had in mind was making a coffee pecan liqueur for the class I'd be teaching in four weeks. This was super simple and wouldn't take more than a few minutes, but I didn't want to put it off, since all liqueurs need time to age. I would demonstrate how to make it during the class, but the one I was making tonight would be just about ready by the time it appeared on the tasting table along with the others I had already made. My favorites so far: a heady spiced rum (with cardamom, anise, and vanilla) and a peach-and-vanilla liqueur that reminded me of summer's gorgeous Texas peaches. Still on the to-do list: a strawberry shrub.

While the coffee was brewing, I got out the vodka and brandy, found the pecan, vanilla, and orange extracts in the cupboard, and measured out the sugar and salt. I poured the alcohol and extracts into a clean mason jar. When the coffee was ready, I poured a cup of it into a small saucepan, stirred in the white and brown sugars and salt, and brought it to a boil on the stove, making a simple syrup. I was setting the syrup aside to cool when I heard the crunch of car tires on gravel.

I glanced up at the clock. Kelly was a little early, but it didn't matter, since my project was just about finished. And I was just as glad. Her remark about murder had been nagging at my mind, and by this time, I was more than just curious. I wanted to know what the heck was going on. I reached into the cupboard and took out two coffee mugs. We would have coffee while we talked.

When I heard the knock, I went to the kitchen door and turned on the porch light. But I was startled. The woman who stood on the back step was dark haired rather than blond, and not the person I was expecting.

"Hey, China," she said jauntily. "Bet you're surprised to see me, huh?"

Chapter Six

The ancient beers, created independently around the
world between 10,000 and 30,000 years ago, were quite
different from what we know as beer today. There were
hundreds if not thousands of them, using some 20 different kinds of yeast, perhaps 15 different sugar sources,
and more than 200 different plant adjuncts. Many were
sacred beers, scores were highly inebriating or psycho-
tropic, and hundreds contained medicinal herbs. They
were made for sacred ceremonies, for communicating
with the ancestors, as potent nutrient foods, and for
healing. Such beers were the expression of an entirely
different way of seeing the world.

Stephen Harrod Buhner
Sacred and Herbal Healing Beers

It wasn't Kelly—it was Ruby's sister, Ramona. She was
wearing a gray jogging suit, white sneakers, and a blue
cap that read *Comanche Creek Brewing Company*. Her short
red hair was softly waved and she looked as though she'd
slimmed down quite a bit since the last time I saw her. Ruby
had said that she'd fallen in love. Maybe love had changed her.

"I know I should have called," Ramona said brightly, "but

I was out at the brewery and I suddenly got this really fabulous idea. About you. And beer. And herbs. And since you live so close, I decided to just pop over and tell you. About my idea, I mean."

Love might have changed the way she looked but it hadn't changed *her*. Ramona is notorious for her "fabulous" ideas. She has them by the dozen and acts on every single one as fast as she can, and in no particular order. It's only afterward that she discovers that most of them aren't that great after all.

"Gosh, Ramona, I'm sorry," I said, "but as it happens, I'm expecting company. In fact, when I heard the car, I thought you were my friend. So I really can't—"

"But this won't take more than a few minutes," Ramona said confidently. She stepped over the threshold. "I'll be really quick."

I sighed. Obviously, she wasn't waiting for an invitation—but that's Ramona. She always assumes that if *she* wants something it will be just fine with everybody else. Given this unfortunate character trait, I was probably right in thinking that the quicker I invited her in and heard her out, the sooner she would be on her way again.

"Well, okay," I said, following her into the kitchen. I added a cautionary, "But let's make it fast."

Hearing voices, Winchester raised his head. When he saw that company had arrived, he clambered out of his basket, trotted over to Ramona, sat upright on his haunches, and politely offered her both his front paws, held out straight.

"What a weird-looking dog," Ramona said, taking a step backward. "He's not going to jump on me, is he? I can't abide dogs that jump."

"I doubt it." I refrained from pointing out that he wasn't weird; he was a basset. And that this particular basset was hardly in a position to jump when he was making such a valiant effort to balance himself on his haunches, in hopes of impressing a new acquaintance with his I'm-a-good-dog stunt.

"His name is Winchester," I said, "and he's showing you his very best trick. He'd really appreciate it if you'd shake his paw and let him know what a fine boy he is."

You can tell a lot about a person by the way she greets a dog. Ramona wrinkled her nose distastefully. With a sigh, she bent over, took Winchester's right paw between her thumb and forefinger, and gave it a quick shake. "Good dog, Winnie. Now go lie down."

Winchester whimpered and looked up at me with a plaintive What-is-this-*Winnie*-stuff? expression. If he could have rolled his eyes, he would have.

I took pity on him. "That's a wonderful trick, Winchester," I said heartily, and gave his paw an affectionate shake. "You are a *very* fine boy. Would you like a treat?"

Not a dog to carry a grudge, he dropped down on all fours, graciously accepted my tacit apology for the bad manners of my guest, and took his treats (I gave him two, to make up for Ramona's rudeness) to his basket to get acquainted with them. But he kept an eye on Ramona, as if he didn't quite trust her, which was intuitive of him, as things turned out.

Making herself at home, Ramona spotted the two coffee mugs on the counter. She picked up the coffee carafe and filled one for herself. "Want some coffee, China?" she asked, as if this were *her* kitchen.

"Don't mind if I do," I said dryly, took the filled mug she handed me, and sat down. I turned just in time, though, to see the carafe teetering on the edge of the counter. I leapt up and rescued it.

Ramona didn't appear to notice. "Maybe Ruby told you my big news." She put her shoulder bag on the floor beside her chair and sat down with her coffee. "I am now a part owner of the Comanche Creek Brewing Company."

"I heard about that this morning." I pulled out a chair and sat down across from her. "Congratulations. But it's kind of a departure for you, isn't it? I had no idea that you were into beer."

Of course, that had never stopped her before. To my certain knowledge, the only flower Ramona can recognize is the homecoming chrysanthemum, and yet she came within an inch of buying a florist shop. Ditto the cupcake factory. Ramona has no doubt eaten her share, but she bragged that she had never baked one. Still, she was "over the moon" (she said) about cupcakes. Until she wasn't.

"I'm not into beer *per se*," Ramona said, spreading her fingers. "But I *am* into money. And once I started looking into it, I could see that beer is an absolutely amazing investment. Especially right now. Craft beer is really *hot*."

"So I understand," I said. "I've never been a huge fan of beer myself, but I've read that some of the smaller breweries around the country are doing some really interesting things. In fact, Young Mr. Cavette, at the market, told me that the brewmaster out at Comanche Creek ordered some blood oranges."

"That was my idea," Ramona said. "I am trying to encourage Rich—he's Comanche's brewmaster—to try some different things." She eyed me. "I suppose Ruby told you that he and I are engaged."

The kitchen lights flickered briefly, then flickered again. Winchester raised his head and stared at Ramona, growling low in his throat.

"Engaged? Not exactly." I was surprised. Ruby had said that the guy's current wife was being stubborn about the divorce. "She did mention that you're seeing one of the Comanche owners. But she didn't go into details."

"Well, we are." Ramona's smile had the look of smug achievement. "I am simply gaga about Rich. And being his

81

Susan Wittig Albert

business partner is a lot of fun." She wrinkled her nose. "Of course, it'll be more fun when his other . . . partner is out of the picture."

I realized that she must be talking about the man's wife, who apparently owned the other half of Comanche Creek. "Well, congratulations," I said again, not knowing what else to say. "So when is the wedding?"

"We haven't set a date yet." She didn't meet my eyes. "There are a few things that we have to—"

Outdoors, Ramona's car alarm suddenly hiccupped and began to shriek. Startled, I half jumped out of my chair. Winchester lifted his head and howled.

"That stupid alarm," she muttered, fishing for her keys in her purse. "I don't know why it does that."

She found the keys at last and went out on the back porch. The car alarm gave one last prolonged shriek, burped twice, and was silent. I frowned, thinking back to the other times I had witnessed Ramona's poltergeist tendencies, which seemed to emerge when she was excited or nervous or trying to hide something. The carafe, the flickering kitchen lights, the car alarm—was that what was happening here?

She came back into the kitchen, sat down, and dropped her keys back into her purse. "Now, where were we?" she asked, propping her elbows on the table and picking up her coffee mug.

"You were saying that you hadn't set a wedding date yet," I prompted.

"Oh, yes. Well, it's likely to be a while," she replied. "There are some things that Rich and I have to take care of."

Like getting rid of the current wife, I thought wryly. Which might not be so easy if his wife was really stubborn about the divorce. In Texas, each spouse gets half of the community property the couple has acquired during their marriage. What's more, a spouse can't sell or otherwise transfer

82

a piece of community property—in this case, the brewery—without the other spouse's permission. Rich's current wife would seem to be very much in control of the situation. Or at least, that's the way it looked to me.

Ramona was going on. "Oh, and about those oranges. Rich has been brewing beer forever, and he's very good at doing what he does. But I'm afraid he's not as adventurous as he might be when it comes to anything new. I read about another brewery that was making a blood orange beer, and I thought it sounded like a great idea. So I got Rich to order the oranges. I want him to try them out."

"Interesting," I said. Ramona at her manipulative best. I was already beginning to feel a little sorry for Rich. "Actually, I was glad to find the oranges," I added. "I got almost all of the ones that were left at Cavette's. I'm teaching a class on liqueurs, so I'm going to use them."

The strains of Telemann began to drift down the stairs. Caitie had finished her book.

Ramona cocked her head. "What's that?"

"My daughter. She's practicing her violin. I can shut the kitchen door if it bothers you."

"No, it's nice." Leaning back in her chair, she said, "I've been collecting ideas for other beers, too. There are some that I think would go over really well around here."

"Oh? Like what?" I was intrigued in spite of myself.

She began ticking them off on her fingers. "Chipotle, prickly pear, mint chocolate, coconut—really, there are a gazillion possibilities."

Chipotle beer I could imagine. Chiles have been used to flavor all kinds of drinks, including hot chocolate. And for centuries, Mexicans have been brewing a sweet, fizzy drink called *colonche* from the red fruits—the *tuna*—of the prickly pear, so prickly pear beer was no surprise. As for chocolate beer, an anthropologist at Cornell discovered recently that the people who lived in Central America some three thousand years ago had brewed beer out of the sugary pulp of the cacao pod. But I had never heard of coconut beer.

"Coconut?" I asked. "Really?"

She nodded her head firmly. "Really. I don't have the recipe, but I read that it has cayenne and cinnamon in it." She began ticking the herbs and spices off on her fingers. "As well as coriander, fenugreek, ginger, and lime. I'm anxious for Rich to try some of this stuff. Doesn't it sound *wild*?"

"Wow," I said softly. Coconut beer with ginger and lime. Now I was *really* feeling sorry for the unadventurous brewmaster. He might be glad to have Ramona's money, but it wouldn't be long before he woke up and discovered that he had a tiger by the tail—if he hadn't already. When she got an idea, Ramona was ferocious.

"Anyway," she said, "those are just some of my ideas. I think it would be totally wonderful if Rich would begin to experiment with herbal beers." She was talking so fast that her words were flying around the room like sparks. "Of course, I'm not suggesting that he replace Comanche's usual lineup of beers. All he has to do is expand it. You know, strike out into new and unexplored territory. Be an innovator in the industry."

I was going to ask how Rich himself felt about being an innovator and striking out into new and unexplored territory, but she didn't give me a chance.

"Tonight, when I was leaving the brewery, I remembered Ruby telling me that you're going to teach that class on herbal liqueurs. And then it just came to me like a lightning flash that you are the very person we need. That's why I wanted to talk to you, China. You know a huge amount about herbs. You could sit down with Rich and give him some suggestions for various plants that he could experiment with, in different combinations. You could be our consultant—and of

course we'd be glad to pay the going rate, whatever that is."
She put out her hand, beaming. "Doesn't it sound exciting,
China? Doesn't it sound like *fun*?"

Cuckoo! Cuckoo!

Startled, I turned to look at the old wooden cuckoo clock
that hangs on the wall just above the microwave shelf. A
family heirloom, it came from McQuaid's mother, who got
it from her mother. It looks like a little brown Swiss chalet
with gingerbread trim, red-painted pendulum weights, and a
painted cuckoo that's supposed to pop out through a carved
door and sing. McQuaid is fond of it, because it reminds him
of family meals at home when he was a little boy, when the
cuckoo actually sang his funny song once every hour. But
the mainspring broke the year McQuaid started high school,
the clock can't be wound, and for as long as we've had it, the
cuckoo has never popped out of his door. Until now.

Cuckoo! Cuckoo!

I stared at the clock, incredulous. Winchester lifted his head
and growled deep in his throat. Ramona frowned down at her
watch. "Your clock is slow," she said. "It's ten after nine."

"Actually, the clock doesn't work," I said helplessly. "It's
hung right there ever since we moved into the house. This is
the very first time I've heard it chime."

"Well, it seems to be working now." Ramona raised an
eyebrow. "Except it's ten minutes slow. You should probably
reset it."

The door on the clock popped open again and the little
wooden bird, painted in bright colors, flew out. He called
twice—*Cuckoo! Cuckoo!*—and flew back in again.

Winchester began to whimper. He climbed out of his basket and hurried over to my chair, his brown eyes large and
distressed, his ears flopping. He leaned against my leg, and I
could feel him trembling. When the bird came out and sang
again, he threw back his head and bayed, a deep-throated,

melodious *aaarrooo!* He sounded like the Hound of the Baskervilles baying at the moon.

I stared down at him in astonishment. I've been told that bassets bay, but in all the years I had lived with Winchester's predecessor, Howard Cosell had never once bayed. And Winchester—who can be a real baby about thunderstorms and firecrackers and other loud noises—had never bayed until now.

Cuckoo! Cuckoo!

Aaarrooo!

And then, on the shelf beneath the clock, the microwave began to chirp, first slowly, then faster and faster. The kitchen lights flickered, went off, and came back on again. Winchester flung his head back and bayed again, even louder and longer this time.

I turned to look at Ramona, who had taken out a little notebook and a small gold pencil and was jotting something down, entirely oblivious to the cacophony that filled the kitchen.

"What are you doing?" I asked, raising my voice over Winchester's distress cries.

"I'm starting a list of spices that might work in beer," she said. Her face was flushed with excitement. "How about ginger? And cloves? Nutmeg, maybe? Or what would you think of rosehips or juniper or—" She was almost bouncing on her chair. "Gosh, there are so many wonderful flavors to play with!"

"No, I mean, what are you *doing*?" I cried, over the microwave's metallic *chirp-chirp-chirp.*

"Why, nothing," she said, going back to her list. "Just making a few notes, that's all."

Cuckoo! Cuckoo! Chirp-chirp-chirp.

And then, in the living room, the television set suddenly

came on, showing the Weather Channel, where the last viewer—probably me—had left it. I could hear Jim Cantore warning about the possibility of a tornado outbreak on the following day in north Texas and Arkansas. It was the very last straw.

"Ramona." I put up my hand. In a commanding tone, I said, "Ramona, just stop. *Stop* what you're doing. Okay?"

"What?" Ramona put down her pencil and, suddenly, it was quiet. The microwave timer quit chirping, the cuckoo retreated into his clock, and Jim Cantore stopped warning in mid-sentence. Winchester dropped his head and lay across my feet, and the lights stayed on.

Ramona looked at me, her eyes innocent. Too innocent. When she spoke, her tone was arch. "Stop what, China?"

Now that it seemed to be over, I didn't suppose there was any point in confronting her about her childish little poltergeisty demonstration. Ruby maintains that Ramona isn't always aware of what she is doing. And even if she was, she would likely deny the whole thing. And then start all over again, making clear that she could turn it off and on when she wanted to.

"Stop . . . stop being so excited," I said lamely.

"I don't see why," she retorted. "Aren't you? Excited, I mean. Working as a consultant to an expert brewmaster— why, just imagine the possibilities, China! And it would certainly look good on your resumé."

I took a deep breath and held it for a moment. The cuckoo stayed shut away behind his door, Winchester lay very still, and the microwave was silent. The liquid sound of Telemann floated down the stairs.

I let my breath out again. Actually, working as a consultant to a brewmaster would be a new way to use some of what I already knew, and learn new things on top of that. I always like to take advantage of opportunities to expand my knowledge base.

But I could think of several very good reasons not to do it. To start with, I was not thrilled down to my tippy-toes by the prospect of getting involved in a project with Ramona, which strikes me as a little like setting up camp on the rim of a volcano. A good place to be if you're there to photograph molten lava and flying rocks, but otherwise downright hot and dangerous. And when I added in the possibility that Ramona's intended's current wife still hadn't yielded on the divorce or the property issue, the whole thing got rather complicated.

I didn't want to say any of that to Ramona, of course. Instead, I said, "It's an interesting idea, but I don't know very much about the possible uses of herbs in beer. I would have to do a *lot* of research. And I've already got more irons in the fire than I can manage."

"I'll bet you already know absolutely everything you need to know." Ramona leaned forward eagerly. "And if you don't, just imagine all you'll *learn*. It's right up your alley, don't you think?" She paused. "And if it works out, I'm sure you could set yourself up as a consultant to—"

"Hang on a sec. There's something I need to do."

I got up from the table and went to the counter, where the saucepan of coffee syrup had been cooling. It had a lovely coffee fragrance and was the right temperature now to add to the liquor-extract mixture. And it gave me an opportunity to slow down the onrush of Ramona's ideas.

"Have you talked to your brewmaster about this experimentation thing?" I asked over my shoulder. "If he's not sold on the idea, there isn't much point in discussing it."

Ramona drained her coffee cup. "As I said, I just thought of this tonight and wanted to talk to you first. I'll discuss it with him tomorrow." With a sigh, she put her cup down. "But just between you and me, China, Rich has a lot on his mind right now. A *whole* lot."

Upstairs, Caitie hit a sour note, stopped, started again, and then again. For a child, she is dedicated to her art, to making it perfect. I poured the syrup into the jar that held the mixture of vodka and brandy, watching the coffee-colored syrup swirl into the alcohol. This was going to be *yummy*.

"Oh, really?" I said. "I'm sorry."

"So am I." Ramona's sigh was heavy and dramatic, like a repertory actress doing regret. "Sorry and frustrated. I wasn't going to tell you, but—" She took a breath. "The thing is that he's still married. He says that he and his wife were never suited in the first place and the marriage has been over for months. She promised to sell her share—that's why I got involved in the first place. But that was a few months ago. Now, she's being stubborn about it. Apparently she invested her own money in it before they were married, money she inherited from her parents, Rich says." Ramona pulled down her mouth. "Strictly speaking, she owns more of it than he does. And now she seems to want to hang on to it." Under her breath, she added, "The *bitch*."

Ah. Now I understood. Yes, strictly speaking, this was a very messy situation. If his wife had bought the business with her own money before they were married and wasn't willing to sell some or all of her shares, Ramona might not be able to buy into that brewery. No wonder she was upset. She likes being fully in control, and when she isn't, she gets crabby. And when she gets crabby—

"Sounds kind of tricky," I said sympathetically. "Are Rich and his wife the only two partners in the business?"

Ramona winced at the word *wife*. "Yes, the only two," she said, sounding resigned. "And yes, you're right, it's tricky." She was obviously glad that I was getting the full picture. "Of course, Rich is upset about the whole thing. She's conservative about what the brewery does, she doesn't agree with his decisions, and lately, he says, all they do is fight about the business. She doesn't want to let go of it and he can't figure out how to make her do it."

I screwed the lid on tight and put the liqueur into the cupboard over the counter, where it could age. It sounded to me like the wife was holding the best hand in this little game, but I wasn't going to point that out.

"And on top of all that," Ramona went on, "Rich says she's been having lots of trouble at work and he doesn't want to make things harder for her. So he's leaving it up to her to file for divorce, rather than making the first move himself. He says we have to be patient. It may take a while, unless she has a sudden change of heart." She gave an ironic little laugh. "And as you know, patience is *not* my middle name. When I want something, I want it now."

I certainly wasn't going to argue with *that*. I hated to say it, but if I listened between the lines, what I was hearing was an old, old story. Married guy gets into a hot-and-heavy out-of-bounds relationship with an attractive woman. She falls for him, and he keeps her on the string by telling her that his marriage is all washed up and a divorce is in the offing. But somehow it never materializes. It sounded to me like this guy was giving Ramona the big runaround.

And in this case, it might not be sex he was after, although that could be a bonus. Ramona had money, which made her the perfect target for this kind of scheme. Entice her to invest a big chunk of money in the business, then marry her and get control of the rest of it—and after that, who knew what might be next? Wife Number One might be in on the scam, or she might be perfectly innocent and not know a thing about her husband's affair with the other woman. In this case the *older* other woman. Hadn't I heard that Rich was five or six years younger than Ramona?

Upstairs, Caitie came to the end of a long musical phrase, made a mistake, stopped, and went back to the beginning.

Ramona gave another sigh. "It's so *complicated*, China. I mean, I've met his wife. I like her and I certainly respect her. Everybody says she's a very kind and good person, and I think it's wonderful that Rich is trying to be respectful of her feelings. But it's a terribly uncomfortable situation for both of us." She slid me a look. "I hope you won't share any of this with Ruby. She's a very sweet sister, but she worries about me too much. And she's always giving me advice."

I nodded. I understood her discomfort, and I could sympathize. But it seemed to me that she had helped to create the situation in the first place. If you get involved with a married man, you're asking for trouble. Complaining that he had a wife didn't make a lot of sense.

She made a petulant face. "I love Rich, China. I really do, but I wish he would be a little more respectful of *my* feelings. I hate it that everything's up in the air like this. So I told him that he needed to do something to get it settled. Tell her the truth about us, or move out of the house—there's plenty of room at my place—or file for divorce himself. But do *something* to get rid of her." She gave what sounded like a little laugh. "And finally, last week, he did. They had a terrible fight, just awful, Rich said. I'm sure it was very painful for him, but it had to be done. Kelly moved out."

I turned, leaning against the counter, staring at her. Ruby once explained the theory of "six degrees of separation" to me—the notion that everybody on the planet is separated from everybody else by only six relationships. According to Ruby, there have even been a couple of intriguing experiments that seem to confirm the theory. But I can tell you from my own personal experience that everybody in a town the size of Pecan Springs is separated from everybody else by only one—or at the most two—degrees of separation. And that sometimes this is a problem. A *big* problem.

"Ramona," I said, "this guy you're engaged to. Rich. Does he have a last name?"

"Of course he has a last name, silly." Ramona gave a light, mocking laugh. "It's Kaufman. Richard Kaufman. Why?" She slanted a curious look. "Do you know him?"

No, I didn't know him. But I certainly knew his wife, and I was suddenly swept by a very understandable panic. Kelly Kaufman—Mrs. Richard Kaufman—was due to knock on my door at any moment now. I looked up at the clock and saw that it was already nine twenty, so she was actually *over*due. And here was her husband's current girlfriend, the other woman in her marriage, sitting in a chair at my kitchen table, drinking coffee out of the mug I had intended for Kelly. How in the world do I get myself into jams like this?

I took a deep breath. "Nope, hadn't even heard his name until now." Which was true, since I knew only Kelly, not her husband. I pushed myself away from the counter and made a show of glancing at the clock, then doing a double take.

"Gosh, just look at the time. It's getting late."

I scurried to the table, picked up Ramona's coffee mug and mine—which wasn't quite empty—and carried both of them to the sink. "I'm willing to consider the idea of being a consultant," I said, rinsing out the cups, "but we don't have time to get into it tonight. As I said, I'm expecting a visitor. Let's talk about it tomorrow. Okay?"

"Well, that was certainly abrupt." Ramona gave me a suspicious look. "Are you sure you don't know Rich?"

"Absolutely sure," I said truthfully. I turned to face her, hands out. "Why would I lie?"

She didn't have an answer for that. She pushed back her chair, frowning distrustfully at me. "Well, okay, then. We'll do it tomorrow. What time?"

"Oh, wait," I said. "I've got to be at the shop all day, so it can't be tomorrow. Why don't I give you a call in the next day or two and we can check our schedules?"

"Well, I suppose," she said reluctantly. She reached into her shoulder bag, pulled out a business card, and put it on the table. "I hope you *will* call me, China, and the sooner the better. I'd love to get started on this new line of beers, and you're exactly the right person to help us out."

"Sure thing," I said, hustling her to the door. I was so anxious to get her out that I would have promised her the sun, the moon, anything. "Talk to you tomorrow," I warbled. "Good night, now."

She was still frowning. "Well, good night," she said, and went slowly down the path toward her car, a white Hyundai sedan.

Faster, faster, I urged silently. *Faster!*

It seemed to take forever for Ramona to get into her car, close the door, and turn the key in the ignition, but at last she was headed back down the lane. I stood in the yard, watching her twin red taillights disappearing into the darkness. When they were gone, I thought silently, *Okay, Kelly, the coast is clear. You can show up anytime now.*

A round gold moon was rising over the trees to the east, and I heard the low, breathy *who-who-whooo* of one of our pair of resident great horned owls. A couple of months ago, they moved into a vacant squirrel's nest in the live oak tree on the other side of the stone wall. The nest is on our side of the tree, and we can watch them through binoculars. They now have a couple of little owlets just beginning to scramble out of the nest and flap their wings. They will be flying soon, and in another two years, they'll have their own territories and their own families not far away in the Hill Country. A comforting thought, that. Friends may be involved in difficult relationships, husbands may disappoint you, and somebody with better fingering may come along and snatch your chair in the orchestra. But the owls go on. And on and on.

I went back into the house and found my copy of a book called *Sacred and Herbal Healing Beers* by Stephen Harrod Buhner. I wasn't going to "consult" with Ramona and her boyfriend. But if I did, this would be the book I would use as a resource. It was full of recipes for old herbal brews that everybody has forgotten about—or that we've never heard of: cardamom seed ale, broom ale, juniper beer, molasses ale, heather mead, maple beer, and on and on. I completely lost myself in its fascinating pages, and when I glanced up at the clock, I was startled to see that it was almost eleven.

McQuaid hadn't called, but I wasn't going to allow myself to wonder where he was, or with whom.

Kelly hadn't come.

And it wasn't until the next day that I would find out why.

Chapter Seven

Of course there were many kinds of ale that were dependent upon their various ingredients . . . "Hysope-Ale," "worm-wood ale," "ale of rosemary," and "Bettony." "Heather ale" was of very ancient origin in certain parts of the country and butter ale was most plentiful in the seventeenth century.

Edward Emerson, 1908
Quoted in *Sacred and Herbal Healing Beers*
Stephen Harrod Buhner

To make a Buttered Ale, take three pintes of Beere, put five yolkes of Egges to it, Straine them together, and set it in a pewter pot to the fyre, and put to it halfe a pound of Sugar, one penniworth of Nutmegs beaten, one penniworth of Cloves beaten, and a halfepenniworth of Ginger beaten, and when it is all in, take another pewter pot and brewe them together, and set it to the fire againe, and when it is readie to boyle, take it from the fire, and put a dish of Sweet butter into it, and threwe them together out of one pot into an other.

A Good Huswifes
Handmaide for the Kitchin, 1594

It was raining the next morning, for which I was very grateful. The Hill Country—in fact, most of Texas—has been clutched in the dusty grip of drought for nearly four years, making life difficult for ranchers, farmers, and gardeners. The Highland Lakes (a chain of seven large man-made reservoirs that provide water to Austin and cities downstream on the Lower Colorado River) are all dangerously low, and the Edwards and Trinity aquifers, which supply the wells of millions of rural users, are in trouble as well. Weather forecasters had been confident of an El Niño spring: warm, moisture-laden Pacific air swirling across the Baja and northern Mexico into the American Southwest, producing soaking rains all across Texas. But every forecast has proved to be yet another disappointment, and I had gotten to the point where I didn't believe it would ever rain again. Seriously rain, I mean. The way it used to.

The light morning rain that was coming down out of the low gray clouds this morning wasn't a drought buster, either. But the ranchers would welcome even a half-inch rain that would help the late-spring and early-summer pasture grasses, and if this kept up for another hour or two, I wouldn't have to water the gardens at the shop and at home until the end of the week. It could rain all day if it wanted to, without a word of complaint from me. It was warm enough to go without a jacket, too—the forecast predicted seventies by noon.

Thyme and Seasons opens for business at ten in the morning, but I'm usually there by seven thirty or eight. I took a deep breath, pulling in the lovely scents of the place, which always feels like a safe haven from the mad, mad, mad world outside. I especially love the early-morning quiet time when I have the shop all to myself and can pretend that it's the only world there is. This morning, I tied on my green Thyme and Seasons apron over the T-shirt and jeans that are my everyday uniform, made sure there was enough change in the cash register, picked up the messages on the answering machine, and checked the shelves to see what kind of restocking I needed to do. Oh, and of course I had to feed Khat, who has a bowl in the back corner by the bookshelf. He hadn't had a bite to eat since supper the night before and was on the verge of utter starvation. A seventeen-pound Siamese shop cat requires a great many calories to keep him purring.

Thyme and Seasons occupies a small, square space, with thick limestone exterior walls; tall, narrow windows, set deep into the walls; a scarred and somewhat uneven pine floor; and cypress beams supporting the embossed tin ceiling. In the middle of the room, a long, narrow wooden rack is filled with glass jars of dried culinary and medicinal herbs, along with bottles of extracts and tinctures. Antique hutches and wooden shelves along the walls are stocked with herbal vinegars, oils, jellies, and teas. The pine cupboard in one corner displays personal care products: herbal soaps, shampoos, massage oils, and bath herbs. There are three shelves of cookbooks and gardening books and a rack of stationery and cards and gift baskets. Handcrafted wreaths and swags hang on every wall, and baskets and buckets of dried herbs—yarrow, sweet Annie, larkspur, statice, and tansy—are stacked on the floor, along with bowls of fragrant potpourri. Outside the front door, there's a five-foot-tall rack of potted herbs for sale and some larger pots of shrubby herbs: lavender, rosemary, and bay.

This morning, I wanted to finish editing the monthly e-letter and calendar that goes to customers of Ruby's shop, my shop, and our tearoom, along with ads for Party Thyme and the Thymely Gourmet. I set up my laptop on the counter, pulled up a stool, and was settling down to work when I heard a knock at the door. I ignored it, and the second, louder knock as well, since there was a definitive *Closed* sign hanging in plain sight, and under that, a sign announcing the open hours. Whoever was knocking could see that the lights were on and guess that I was in the building, but you'd think he or she would respect the signs.

At the third knock—rapid-fire and more urgent than before—I lost patience. I muttered a couple of very bad words (you don't want to know what they were), climbed down off my stool, and marched to the door, ready to take somebody's head off. But the woman standing with her fist poised for an even louder knock was Sheila Dawson, our Pecan Springs chief of police. She was wearing a bright yellow rain poncho over her usual dark blue cop uniform, her blond hair was swept back and up beneath her cop cap, and she looked very official.

But also very beautiful, because that's Sheila. If she wasn't in uniform and you didn't know that she is an experienced police officer with superior field skills, you'd probably think she should be on a movie screen or the cover of a fashion magazine. Those high cheekbones, delicate features, deep-set blue eyes, creamy complexion—if she weren't such a nice person, no other woman would tolerate having her around. The evildoers she encounters in her line of work are so taken aback at their first sight of her that they forget (almost) the skullduggery they're up to. But while her friends call her Smart Cookie, "Tough Cookie" fits her even better. You don't want to mess with Sheila when she's serious about something. This morning, she had a serious look on her face. And a white paper bag from the Nueces Street Diner in her hand.

"Hey, China," she said when I opened the door. "I need to talk to you."

"We're closed, but since it's you, Sheila, I'll let you in." I said in a mock-grudging tone. "Especially because I'll bet those are jelly doughnuts in that bag."

"Right the first time," she said as she came in. "Raspberry and lemon cream."

I rolled my eyes. "To die for," I said, shutting the door behind her. Lila Jennings at the diner makes the very best jelly doughnuts in the world. Her raspberry is so good that I refuse to worry about the calories. "How about a cup of tea to go with?"

"Sounds wonderful." She took off her cap and pulled her poncho over her head. She was wearing her duty belt, loaded down with official police gear and, yes, a gun. Seeing that, I was reminded that she's not just a friend. She's a cop, and what she does is hazardous.

But right now, she was thinking of less hazardous matters. "This thing is going to drip on the floor," she said apologetically, holding the poncho at arm's length.

"Don't worry about it." I hung it beside the door. "The floor is going to get dripped on all day. That's the nature of floors in wet weather. But it's raining, which is definitely good, so you won't hear me complain. Bring those jelly doughnuts and come on back to the kitchen. I'll brew us some tea."

Khat had appeared out of the shadows and was rubbing Sheila's pant leg, rumbling an ecstatic, throaty purr. He doesn't like men and he is neutral about most women, but he absolutely adores Sheila. When she stops in, he forgets that he is top cat, drops his dignity, and behaves like a smitten kitten. Now, still purring, he trailed her as we went through the door at the back of the shop and into the tearoom.

The tearoom is about twice the size of Thyme and Seasons. It has the same limestone walls, well-worn wide-board floors, and embossed tin ceiling. With its green-painted wainscoting, chintz chair seats and place mats, terra cotta pots of herbs on the tables, and wreaths and bundles of dried herbs on the walls, it's a friendly and attractive space, designed to appeal to the local clubs and groups that meet there for lunch. When all the tables are filled (which happens once in a blue moon), we can seat forty, and French doors open out onto a wooden deck where another dozen people can enjoy the surrounding gardens.

Behind the tearoom, the kitchen is fully equipped, professionally organized, and large enough to prepare a luncheon menu for a full house, as well as the Thymely Gourmet meals that Cass and her kitchen helper prepare for afternoon delivery. Cass would be here in another half hour to start her daily work, but for now, the kitchen was dark. I turned on the lights, filled the teakettle with water at the sink, and set it on a burner.

"So, what brings you out on a rainy morning?" I asked as I took down a china teapot, two dark green mugs, and two small matching plates. Khat temporarily abandoned Sheila and settled himself at his food bowl (he has one in each shop and one in the kitchen) to enjoy a second helping of breakfast.

Sheila opened the bag. "A one-car crash," she replied evenly. "A bad accident, made worse by a malfunctioning airbag." She put a doughnut on each plate. "I think."

"You *think* it's a bad accident?" I opened the tea canister and took out a couple of chai tea bags. "You don't know for sure?"

She licked the sugar off her fingers. "I don't know if it was an accident. Or something else."

"Well, that certainly sounds intriguing enough," I said.

She turned to face me. "I understand that you're acquainted with Kelly Kaufman." It wasn't a question.

I put the tea bags into the cups. "I am," I said slowly. "Don't tell me that *she* was in the crash!" But I could already feel a cold shiver rippling across my shoulders. I had expected Kelly to show up at my house at nine o'clock the night before, and she hadn't. I wasn't sure I wanted to hear what came next.

"Kaufman was driving west on Limekiln Road last night, sometime between eight fifty and nine, alone." Sheila pulled down a paper towel and began wiping her fingers. Her voice was calm and measured, a cop's voice. "The officer who investigated the crash estimated that she was doing at least sixty-five—fifteen miles over the posted speed. Her vehicle ran off the highway just past Comanche Creek Road. It went down a steep slope and smashed head-on into a tree. She was belted in but the airbag didn't pop. She was pinned behind the wheel."

I stared at her, feeling the cold seep into my bones. I knew that part of the highway. It was narrow and twisting, just two lanes, no passing lane—and dangerous. "Oh, my God," I whispered. "Is she . . . is she okay?"

"Multiple fractures, concussion, internal bleeding. She's critical. The doc says it doesn't look good." Sheila was watching me, her head tilted. "The owner of the vehicle, a woman named Lara Metcalf, said that Kaufman had been at her place during the day and into the evening. She was on her way to your house when the crash happened."

"What was she driving?" I asked. "Was alcohol involved?" Kelly and her friend might have had some wine with dinner. "Or distracted driving?"

"She was driving a metallic gray Chevrolet Astro van that belongs to Metcalf and her husband." Sheila was studying me. "If alcohol was involved, the investigator didn't say so. There was no cell phone in the van, and no GPS, so it doesn't seem like a distracted-driver situation. The investigator thinks it was a matter of speed. Or maybe she veered to avoid a deer crossing the road."

That was certainly possible, I thought. Limekiln Road snaked through a heavily wooded area. I'd had to slow down for deer myself, driving home after dark. And once, in the rain, a mountain lion. The sight of it had taken my breath away.

"There weren't any skid marks, though," Sheila added. "Doesn't look like she braked." She wadded the paper towel and tossed it into the trash. "Metcalf says that Kelly Kaufman told her that she wanted to talk to you—something about a murder. Do you mind answering a few questions?"

Murder. The word fell like a stone into the quiet pool of kitchen sounds—the low hum of the refrigerator, Khat's rumbling purr, the click of the clock above the doorway.

Then the kettle began to hiss. I picked it up and poured boiling water over the tea bags in our mugs. I was stalling for time, trying to decide what I could—and should—say. Kelly hadn't told me much, but she wasn't my client, so nothing she'd said to me was privileged. Neither was that business about the guest cottage, renting it, then leaving it under mysterious circumstances yesterday morning—in a metallic gray van. If Sheila wanted to question me, I was duty bound to answer. So instead of making her fish for the information, I might as well tell her the whole thing, start to finish.

"It's a longish story," I said, putting the mugs and the doughnut plates on a tray. "We might be able to expedite the process if I just tell you what I know. Let's sit down at a table in the tearoom."

Khat went with us, of course. And, of course, he jumped up on Sheila's lap the minute she sat down and began rubbing his cheek against her arm while she ate her doughnut. When she finished, she held him while he snuggled up against her. Beauty and a lapful of the beast.

I told the whole story, from Kelly's first call reserving the cottage to her arrival and unconventional departure and her phone call of the night before. What she had said about the murder was still fresh in my mind, so I gave Sheila the gist of that part of the telephone conversation and told her about Kelly's being afraid. *I'm really, really scared,* she had said, and I had heard the fear in her voice.

I also told her about Charlie's visit to the guest cottage and our discussion with the police officer who had come in response to our call, as well as my back-alley encounters with Mr. Cowan and Mary Beth Jenkins. I knew that Sheila would have access to the cop's report and that she would interview Charlie, if she thought he could—or would—provide any relevant information. But if Kelly was his client, he would be limited in what he could say. Like most lawyers, Charlie observes attorney-client privilege scrupulously.

But I didn't tell Sheila everything. I intentionally left out a couple of items. For one thing, my conversation with Janet Parker at Cavette's market, about Kelly leaving the hospice. For another, Ramona's visit and her story about her relationship with Kelly's husband. If Sheila asked me, I'd tell those parts of the story, but I couldn't see that they were relevant to the car crash.

Finished with my narrative, and my doughnut, I picked up my teacup. "So," I said, and sipped, "that's what I know. Now, tell me what happened—and why you think it might not be an accident."

Car wrecks are always bad enough, especially when friends and loved ones are injured. But they happen, and we all learn to sweep up the pieces and get on with our lives the best way we can. If this wreck wasn't an accident, though, it was something else, and we were facing a whole new set of questions. Deeply disturbing questions.

Sheila told the story, briefly and factually. There were no witnesses to the crash. It occurred after eight fifty, when a patrolman drove past the site and saw nothing, and before nine twenty, when a teenager out with his best girl spotted the wreckage and phoned 911. It happened just inside the city limits, so a couple of Pecan Springs officers were on the scene within a few minutes, and EMS immediately after that. Kelly had been carrying no identification. (Of course not: her wallet was still locked in the bedroom in my guest cottage.) The officer checked the registration on the Astro, phoned the Metcalf residence, and told Lara Metcalf that her van had been wrecked. Metcalf said she had loaned the vehicle to Kelly and identified her. She also gave the officer Kelly's husband's cell phone number so he could be notified.

The wrecked van was towed into town, the lead investigating officer wrote his report, and that would have been the end of it—except that Lara Metcalf had called Sheila's office about an hour ago and caught Sheila at her desk, doing early-morning administrative chores. That's when the word *murder* entered the conversation.

Lara and her husband, Matt, had gone to the wrecking yard where their Astro had been towed. The front end was smashed, the windows were broken, and there were long scratches and several dents on the driver's side where the vehicle had scraped against obstructions as it careened down the hill. The van was a total loss.

But there was more damage—and Matt Metcalf thought it looked odd. The vehicle's left rear taillight was broken. There was a dent low on the left rear tailgate, below the hatch, and another dent on the left side of the wraparound back bumper. Both dents were concave, and the upper dent bore visible flecks of orange paint. Metcalf insisted that this was fresh damage and that the Astro had been unmarked until last night. He pointed out that the concave dents weren't the kind that a wrecker would have made when it winched the van up the hill and towed it into town. It was his opinion that somebody had rammed the vehicle from behind, causing Kelly to lose control, veer off the road to the left, and smash into that tree. Which would also explain the fact that there were no tire marks on the pavement. Kelly hadn't braked.

Metcalf's report of the rear-end damage, Sheila said, was compelling enough for her to order the Astro towed from the wrecking yard to the police department's impound lot, where it could be given a closer look by one of their crash investigators, under magnification and in the full light of day. If there had been a rear-end collision, the evidence would be found and documented.

But that wasn't the only thing that had caught Sheila's attention. She had begun to listen with both ears when Lara Metcalf added the information that, when the crash happened, Kelly Kaufman had been on her way to talk to China Bayles—about a murder. And that she had taken her laptop with her because she wanted to show Ms. Bayles some sort of evidence.

Murder. There was that word again.

Khat had put his paws on Sheila's shoulders and was rubbing his cheek against hers, purring like a steam engine. Sheila pushed him back into her lap. "So," she said, "you've already told me that Kaufman mentioned murder when she phoned last night. Do you know anything else about it?" She added, "Like maybe who or when? Or even how?"

"Sorry, Sheila. I wish I did." I paused, feeling a flicker of disquiet. "Kelly's computer—where is it?" Anything valuable left in a demolished vehicle in a wrecking yard could easily disappear.

"It was under the front seat of the van. The officer overlooked it last night when he was clearing the accident scene— easy enough to do in the dark. But Lara Metcalf found it this morning when she and her husband went to look at the wreck. She brought it to the station."

Well, that was good news. "Have you looked at it yet?"

Sheila gave up tussling with Khat and put him on the floor. He gave her a disapproving glance, then flicked his tail twice and stalked off.

"Ignore him," I said. "He'll get over it. He's too egotistical to brood over rejection for very long."

She smiled at that, then grew serious again. "Our forensics computer tech is going over the laptop now. In the meantime, I was hoping you might know something that would save us some time."

I shook my head. "When Kelly used the word *murder* in her phone call last night, my first thought was that there had been some sort of incident connected with her nursing. Like, maybe she had inadvertently administered a fatal drug, or something like that—something that involved her personally. But she immediately said that *she* hadn't killed anybody. She said she thought she knew who did, though, and she wanted me to help her get proof."

"Anything else?"

I frowned. "Yes, something about having evidence about 'the other cases,' whatever that means. But nothing more about the murder. Which of course might just be her imagination."

"You mean you think she was making it up?"

I shook my head. "Kelly doesn't strike me as the kind of person to lie about something so potentially serious. But she could be mistaken. Hospice nurses must have to deal with death all the time. Maybe she saw something and thought it was . . . something it wasn't."

Sheila leaned forward. "The other cases? Drug trafficking, maybe? A nurse might get involved in something like that."

"No clue," I said. I thought briefly of what Ramona had said and decided it was time to come clean on that—or on part of it, anyway. "There is something else, though. I understand that Kelly and her husband were having difficulties. When she rented the cottage, she told me that she was getting a divorce and that she wanted to stay in the cottage while she found another place to live. I don't know the details, but I've heard that there's been some sort of property disagreement. The two of them—Kelly and her husband—own the Comanche Creek Brewing Company."

Sheila frowned. "Comanche Creek. I've never been there, but I've heard of it. Isn't it near where the crash occurred?"

"Not far. Less than a mile, I'd think."

Then something else occurred to me. Ramona had arrived at my house on Limekiln Road, six or seven miles west of the crash, right at eight fifty and had left at nine twenty or so. She was with me when Kelly's vehicle had gone off the road. If there was another vehicle involved in the crash, it wasn't Ramona's white Hyundai. The flecks of orange paint in the fresh dent in the rear end of the Astro hadn't come from her car.

But I'm a suspicious person by nature and by training, and the first thing I thought of was whether I might have been used to provide an alibi. After all, Ramona's visit almost exactly coincided with the time frame of the car crash. How improbably convenient was that?

The second thing I thought of was the man Kelly was about to divorce. If Rich Kaufman had somehow known that Kelly was on her way to my house—or even if he had happened to pull out of the brewery and onto the highway at the moment when she was driving past—he might have seen an opportunity to take care of his problem. Divorces have the power to turn an average spouse into a psycho, fueled by bitterness and frustration. Maybe something like that had happened here.

Sheila was following my train of thought. "I'll talk to Kaufman's husband. Do you happen to know what he drives?"

"Sorry, no." But I was guessing that if he drove an orange car or truck, the cops would be taking a close look at it. Out in the shop, I heard the telephone ring. The answering machine would pick up, but it reminded me that there was a workday world waiting for me. I stood and picked up our mugs and plates.

"Kelly's things," I said. "Her suitcase, her purse, her car—they're all still at the cottage. Would you like to take a look?"

"Definitely," Sheila said, and waited for me beside the French doors while I put the dishes in the kitchen sink. I snagged the cottage key off the nail behind the kitchen door and took the lead along the gravel path through the gray morning mist. There was enough of a drizzle to make us walk fast, and we went the shortest way, through the front door. I led Sheila past the kitchen, where yesterday's breakfast things were still on the counter, and down the hallway to the bedroom.

That was where I got another major surprise. The glass in one of the French doors had been shattered and both doors stood partway open. There was a trail of wet leaves across the carpet, a large patch of damp carpet where the rain had blown in, and a single muddy shoeprint in front of the suitcase—an odd sole pattern of wedges, ridges, and lateral slices on a very large shoe, a man's shoe, most likely. The contents of Kelly's suitcase—tidily arranged the last time I'd been here—had been tossed around, some of them on the floor. The dresser drawers were all pulled open. The shoulder bag that I'd stashed in the bottom drawer was also on the floor, the contents spilled out.

"Looks like you've had a visitor," Sheila remarked. "And not a very neat one."

I bent over to pick up Kelly's wallet, but Sheila stopped me with a hand on my arm.

"Don't touch," she warned. "We may have something here. Fingerprints, maybe. That shoeprint."

"Yeah, sure." Meanwhile, the carpet was getting wetter and wetter. But the place was a crime scene now, and I needed to cooperate. I glanced back at the shoeprint. "Distinctive," I said. "Not your everyday sneaker. Might not be too hard to find a match."

"Sure," she said ironically. "All we have to do is check every closet in town." She glanced at me. "Sorry," she said. "Just being realistic."

With a sigh, I turned and went back down the hallway to look through the living room window and see whether Kelly's Kia was still there. To my relief, it was, although one of the doors was slightly open and the dome light was on. Whoever had found her purse and the money had also found her car keys and searched her car. I wondered whether he—or she—was looking for something in particular. Kelly's computer, maybe?

Sheila had come out of the bedroom and was standing behind me, looking out the window over my shoulder. "We'll check the car for prints, too." She paused. "Any idea whether this break-in is related to the car crash last night? Assuming the crash wasn't an accident, that is."

"How the hell should I know?" I asked testily. "Given the circumstances, though, I'd say there's a good possibility. Wouldn't you?"

I was beginning to feel exasperated and angry. My guest—a very nice young woman—was in the hospital as a result of a possibly deliberate collision. My cottage had been trashed. The word *murder* was coming up with a disconcerting frequency. There was something going on here, and I was being pulled into the middle of it, whatever "it" was. That made me edgy. I have learned—the hard way—that ignorance can be dangerous—deadly, even. And while it may be a personality flaw, I don't like being kept in the dark. The feeling always makes me want to start digging for information, *any* kind of information.

I took a deep breath. I was jumpy, yes, but that was no reason to jump all over Sheila. And anyway, I had a favor to ask. I moderated my tone. "Is there any chance that I can get a look at Kelly's computer?"

"You know the protocol," Sheila said, regarding me steadily. "I can't let you go on a fishing expedition, counselor. But you can tell me what you're looking for and how it's relevant. In which case I might be able to tell you when it turns up. *If* you have a reason for needing that information." We were friends, yes. But Sheila has a habit of putting that to one side when it comes to cop business. And at this moment, she was one tough cookie. "Do you? At this moment, I mean."

"No," I muttered, and stuck my hands in my jeans pockets. I was disappointed, but I knew where Sheila was coming from. The forensic tech would have a much better chance than I would of uncovering something significant. I would have no idea where to begin looking for it or what it might look like if I found it.

"I don't want to be a prick, China." Sheila went to the front door. "If you do come up with something you think might be on that computer, let me know and I'll reconsider."

"Got it. In the meantime, I need to repair the glass in that French door before the rain ruins the carpet. Do you have a problem with that?"

"I do, actually. I'll send somebody over to check for fingerprints on that door and on the dresser drawers. We might get lucky."

"Sure," I said, resigned. "But make it snappy, will you? I hate to say it, but this business, whatever it is, is getting expensive. The broken door glass, the carpet, the cleanup." And then I thought of Kelly in a hospital bed, with tubes stuck into her and machines humming around her and nurses hovering over her, and felt a sharp thrust of guilt. My trouble was a nagging mosquito bite compared to hers.

Sheila gave me a sympathetic look. "I'll ask the techs to get it wrapped up in a couple of hours." She nodded toward the bedroom. "Please don't touch anything back there until they're finished—ditto the Kia. And if you run into anything that sheds any light on all this, you'll let me know, won't you?"

"Of course I will," I said. "And you'll return the favor?"

It wasn't hard to read the look she gave me, since I already knew the answer to the question. Regardless of what happens in your favorite cozy mysteries, the police simply do not allow a nosy Miss Marple to involve herself in a criminal investigation, except under the most unusual circumstances— that is, when they're out of leads and desperate for information. Given my experience as a lawyer, I have been allowed to intrude, but only very occasionally and only because there wasn't any other way to settle the matter at issue. In this case, I had no special knowledge or reason to get involved, and Sheila had no compelling reason to allow me to trespass on her turf. Which didn't make me any less curious, of course.

But there *was* a question that she might answer for me, and I asked it as we went back along the path to the shop. Since our husbands are partners in McQuaid, Blackwell, and Associates, she and I often discuss the investigations they're working on. She might know what McQuaid was doing in El Paso.

"McQuaid is out in West Texas," I said. "I thought he was handling an investigation for Charlie, but Charlie says he isn't, so I guess I'm mistaken. He's in El Paso. Do you know what that's about?"

The drizzle had temporarily stopped when we reached the tearoom deck and Sheila turned, hesitant. "Actually, Blackie's out there, too," she said and added, as if she were weighing her response, "No, sorry, I can't tell you what it's about." And then, hurriedly, as if to correct the impression that she knew and didn't *want* to tell me: "I mean, I don't know. That's why I can't tell you."

McQuaid and Blackie were out there together? I was surprised. The two don't team up unless they have a compelling reason. Not because they don't like working together (they do), but because it's more productive—that is, they make more money—if they're conducting separate investigations. McQuaid, Blackwell, and Associates *is* a business, after all, and the purpose is to earn a living. The last time they joined forces, they were on the trail of an American child who had been taken across the border by his noncustodial Mexican mother. McQuaid and Blackie crossed into northern Mexico together because they knew it was too risky to go alone. Juárez, where they'd been headed, was especially dangerous territory. Dozens of young women factory workers have been murdered there, and drug cartels own and operate the city. Gringos aren't welcome—particularly gringos who have been hired to take a young boy away from his mom and back to Texas. I thought about this briefly, then pushed it out of my mind. After the frightening episode with the boy, McQuaid had promised me that he wouldn't go into Mexico again for any reason.

"I wonder why McQuaid didn't tell me that Blackie was going out there with him," I said. I wasn't going to mention Margaret or say anything about my online search for Margaret's current Ranger assignment. I already knew I was a jealous wife—I just didn't want to sound like one.

"I'm sure he just forgot," Sheila said, and her glance slid away. "He probably had . . . other things on his mind."

"He just forgot?" I repeated. "That's a weird thing to forget. And yesterday, McQuaid left a message on the answering machine at the house, saying that he might be out of cell tower range for a while."

I paused. To judge from the way Sheila avoided my glance, she knew what was going on—and I didn't.

"But that doesn't make sense," I added petulantly. "Are you hearing from Blackie? Is he able to call home?"

Sheila made a show of glancing at her watch. "Hey, look at the time. Gotta get my poncho and head back to the office before they send out a search team. I'll see that the crime-scene people hit your cottage within the hour so you can get that door fixed. And if you find out anything that'll help with this car-crash investigation, you'll tell me, won't you?"

I stuck my hands in my pockets. "Right," I said, disgruntled. "Yeah, sure, I will."

Chapter Eight

Research studies indicate that orange (*Citrus sinensis*) essential oil helps to calm and reduce anxiety, lift low spirits, and increase cheerfulness. The oil may be used in a room diffuser, in massage (the oil diluted in a carrier oil and massaged into the skin), or in lotions and bath fragrances.

China Bayles
"Oranges in Your Garden"
Pecan Springs Enterprise

I loved the rain that was coming down harder outside the windows of my shop, but it definitely had a dampening effect on business. A couple of women came in at ten, just after I unlocked the front door. One of them was looking for a copy of *China Bayles' Book of Days,* which I was happy to find on the bookshelf and sign for her. Her friend was "just browsing," but by the time she left, she was carrying a copy of *Culpeper's Color Herbal,* the makings of a nice potpourri, and a bag of the Moth Attack blend that I grow and mix myself—southernwood, wormwood, rue, and santolina. Ten minutes later, a police officer came in to tell me that they were finished going over the cottage and I could get the door repaired. On her way out, she bought a small bottle of lavender bath oil.

But after that promising start, the customer traffic dwindled away. The connecting door to Ruby's shop was open, and the delightful aroma of fresh oranges and the relaxing sound of New Age music wafted through the doorway. The fragrance of oranges, Ruby tells me, has been shown to lower stress levels, so she likes to use it often in her shop, in one of those diffusers that scent room air. Her theory: shoppers with less stress tend to spend more time shopping and may find more things they can't live without.

I could see that Ruby's shop traffic wasn't any better than mine, and I wondered if we'd have any lunch customers when the tearoom opened at eleven thirty. But Tuesday is soup-and-sandwich day, which makes it easy to adjust for the size of the crowd. Cass was cooking up a pot of chicken noodle soup this morning—the aroma that came from the direction of the kitchen was an excellent clue—and several kinds of sandwich fillings. And there was a tea party scheduled for the First Baptist Church Ladies Club at three, so there would be some extra traffic then.

It was just before eleven when the bell over my shop door tinkled and the door opened with a rush of fresh, rain-cooled air. I looked up with a chipper smile from the book order I was working on and offered my standard customer-relations greeting, which varies according to the weather (wet, hot, chilly, windy, etc.). "Wet out there today, isn't it? Come in and make yourself at home."

The woman closed her floral print umbrella and looked around for a place to put it.

"Right there," I said, pointing to the pottery umbrella urn. "Don't worry about the drip. That's what it's for."

"Thank you," she said. She was in her early thirties, I'd

guess, short and athletic looking, with quizzical eyebrows, gray eyes behind round gold glasses, and brown hair frizzed by the damp. She was wearing an orange and white printed scrub top, orange scrub bottoms, and white canvas flats, and was carrying a brown leather shoulder bag. "You're Ms. Bayles?"

"China," I corrected her. "Welcome to Thyme and Seasons. Can I help you find something this morning?"

"I've found her," she said. "You." She came to the counter where I was working, and I pushed my laptop to one side. "My name is Lara Metcalf. Kelly Kaufman is a friend of mine."

"Oh, gosh!" I reached across the counter and we shook hands. "How *is* she?" I asked anxiously. "Chief Dawson told me about the accident early this morning. But maybe you have a later report?"

"Things haven't changed much since last night, I'm afraid." She pushed her fingers through her damp hair. "I've just come from the hospital. Kelly is on life support. I know nurses on her floor, and I got a peek at her chart. There's internal damage, as well as head trauma." She paused. "No point in your going over there to visit, if that's what you're thinking."

"Uh-oh," I said soberly. "Sounds pretty bad."

"It is. The doctors aren't optimistic." She took a deep breath. "But as a nurse myself, I've seen miracles, people coming back from the dead almost. I'm hoping for one now." Her voice took on an edge. "Did the chief tell you about the damage to the van's rear end? Matt and I—Matt's my husband—think somebody deliberately hit the Astro from behind."

"Yes, she did. Kudos to you for noticing that rear-end damage." I paused. "Is Matt a big guy who sometimes wears blue scrubs? Does he have snaky tattoos? And maybe a pony tail?"

"That's him." Her smile was crooked. "He did a couple of

tours with the Marines in Iraq, and one of the tattoos says 'Semper Fi.' It sort of crawls up his arm, so maybe it does look snaky. He works at the hospital." She gestured at her scrubs. "I worked at the hospice with Kelly until about six months ago. Now, I'm over at the Madison Clinic."

The Madison Clinic. I guessed that Lara might have been the reason Kelly found a job there, and it occurred to me that she might know why her friend left the hospice. But at the moment, I was more interested in Lara's husband.

"Matt," I said. "He's the guy who picked Kelly up at the cottage yesterday morning?"

"You know about that?" She seemed surprised.

I smiled wryly. "Our neighborhood watch squad is on the alert twenty-four hours a day. They like to think they're on top of all suspicious activity. Sometimes they are."

She nodded. "Whatever works. Anyway, Matt was pretty close to the end of his shift at the hospital when Kelly phoned and asked if one of us could pick her up. She was kind of in a panic, so he drove on over when he got off work."

"In a panic?" I asked sharply.

"That's right. She said she woke up about four a.m. when she heard somebody trying to get in through the French doors in the bedroom. A dog across the alley started barking and the intruder took off, but she was pretty scared." She gave me a narrow-eyed, challenging look. "Tell your neighborhood watch squad that they let that one get past them."

"Miss Lula didn't," I replied. "That was her, barking." But to myself, I thought, *That settles it. I don't care what it costs. I'm installing an alarm system in that cottage.*

Lara was going on. "The three of us—Kelly and Matt and I—have been friends since nursing school. So of course we said yes when she asked if she could hang out at our house for a few days. She had this idea of making it look like she'd been kidnapped or something. I told her it was silly, all that stupid cloak-and-dagger stuff. If somebody really wanted to find her, they could probably locate her at our place just as easily." She gave a little shrug. "But as I said, she was panicked. She was hoping to throw the intruder off her trail, at least for a while. And she likes the idea of having Matt around. He's a big guy. He certainly makes *me* feel safe."

I was thinking of the attempted break-in that had frightened Kelly and the evidence of the actual break-in that Sheila and I had seen a little while ago. Whoever had tried the first time had been serious enough to come back for a retry. Had the same person rammed her vehicle from behind?

"I get that she was frightened," I said slowly. "I just think there were better ways to handle her exit. She could have called me, for instance, to let me know what was going on."

"She realized that later." Lara's voice was sympathetic, and there were smile crinkles around her gray eyes. "But we all do stupid things when we're scared. And she was plenty scared. I told her she shouldn't blame herself."

I liked this woman for her sensible compassion and for sticking up for her friend. "Actually, she was right to be afraid," I said, and told her about the break-in. The neighborhood watch team had dropped the ball on that play, I thought.

"Oh, dear," Lara said softly. "I'm glad Kelly wasn't there when *that* happened."

The shop door opened and a rotund, moon-faced woman wearing a transparent plastic raincoat came in, her bouncy gray curls hidden under a plastic rain bonnet. "Hey, China," she said. "Don't you just love the rain?"

"Absolutely, Janelle," I said heartily, past Lara's shoulder. "If you can't find what you're looking for, just ask."

"I just came for some more goldenseal root," Janelle said cheerfully, heading for the rack of bulk herbs. "Evinrude has weepy eyes, and I make a strong tea of the goldenseal and use it as an eyewash. It really helps. And Evinrude doesn't mind it at all." She frowned. "He used to growl at me when I used the chemical stuff."

I chuckled. "I'd growl at you, too," I said. "Evinrude's got the right idea." I glanced at Lara, whose eyebrows had gone up under the frizz of her hair. "Evinrude is Janelle's dog," I explained. "He's a Great Dane."

"I was wondering," Lara said, and laughed.

"Don't let him hear you say *dog*," Janelle cautioned. "He thinks he's one of us. He just happens to have four legs instead of two." A moment later, she had made her purchase and was out the door. I returned to my conversation with Lara.

"I heard from a friend that Kelly left her job at the hospice rather unhappily," I said. "Maybe you know what that was all about."

Lara hesitated, as though she was deciding whether she should share what she knew. "I know a little," she said slowly. "She and the owner—Marla Blake—disagreed about patient care."

"You mean whether the patients got as much attention as they needed?" I asked.

"Well, not so much that, I think. It was more about whether they were all qualified."

Ah. There was that term again, the same one I hadn't understood the night before, when Kelly had mentioned having documentation of "unqualified people" on her laptop.

"And there were some record-keeping issues," Lara went on. "When I worked with Kelly at the hospice, I remember that she was kind of a nut about records." She read the question on my face and added, "I mean, she thought that all the hospice nurses should keep detailed notes, not just check off their visits." She sighed. "Sorry. That's about as much as I can tell you."

Which didn't mean that it was as much as she *knew*.

119

Lara regarded me thoughtfully. "Kelly spoke very highly of you, China. In fact, she was hoping you might be able to help her . . ." She paused, and her unfinished sentence hung in the air between us like an invitation.

"Help her obtain evidence of a murder," I said. "Evidence that would stand up in court. At least, that's what she told me when she phoned last night. Unfortunately, that's as far as we got. But Chief Dawson said that you mentioned it to her." I gave her a questioning look. "What do you know about it?"

Lara shook her head. "Next to nothing. I only know what I overheard her telling you on the phone. I asked her about it before she left for your house, but she said she didn't want to tell me, because that might make me an excessive something or other."

"Accessory after the fact?" I hazarded.

She brightened. "Yes, that's it exactly. She said she'd seen it on a courtroom TV show and she didn't want to risk getting me into trouble."

Ah, so. "I don't think that would have applied in this case," I said gently, "but Kelly's concern for you is certainly admirable." I hesitated. "Do you know if the police are making any progress on their investigation into the car crash?" I wasn't counting on Sheila to keep me posted.

"I haven't heard a thing. But Matt is convinced that it was Kelly's husband, Rich, who hit her. He and Kelly have been having a lot of trouble about their divorce lately. Arguments, shouting matches, even push-and-shove stuff. In fact, Matt thinks it might've been Rich prowling around your cottage the other night. Me, I don't agree."

"What does Rich drive?"

"A Ford F-150."

"Color?"

Lara hesitated slightly. "It's orange. He went to UT, you know." She added hastily, "But Rich and I grew up together,

China. I've known him ever since we were kids. He might have threatened Kelly, but he wouldn't try to *kill* her."

"Maybe just scare her a little?" I asked. "Like, maybe he just drove up close and tapped her with his front bumper?"

"Not even that," Lara said flatly. "I'm *sure* it wasn't Rich. If you ask me, it was the same person who committed the murder Kelly wanted to tell you about. The killer knows she's onto him and was trying to shut her up for good." Her eyes filled with tears and she turned her head aside. In a lower voice, she added, "If that's who did it, he might get what he wanted. Kelly may never be able to tell anybody what she knew."

Sadly, I thought that could be true. But Lara was overlooking something and I needed to point it out.

"This county is full of University of Texas alums," I said, "and lots of them drive orange vehicles." It's true. Orange may be an unusual vehicle color choice in most states, but not in Texas. Here, to demonstrate their loyalty, some people get their cars custom-painted orange and install a fancy orange-and-chrome-plated longhorn emblem on the front of the hood. "Any one of them could have been headed west on Limekiln Road last night," I added. "Kelly might have been hit from behind by a driver who was texting, and when he saw what he'd done, he panicked and fled the scene."

"I suppose it could have happened that way," Lara conceded.

"So for the car crash, we have three possibilities." I ticked them off on my fingers. "It might have been the husband, the killer, or a distracted driver. That is, assuming that your van really *was* hit from behind." Lots of possibilities, very little evidence.

Lara propped her elbows on the counter and leaned forward on them. "Kelly was coming to you to ask if you would help her get evidence on a murder. There was another legal thing, too, but I don't know what it is. So I guess—" She pushed her lips in and out. "I guess that's why *I'm* coming to you, China. To ask you to help me find out what Kelly knew."

"Why?" I asked. "Why do you want to know?" It's a question people ought to ask themselves before they start looking for answers to questions they don't understand. Sometimes, it turns out that they really *don't* want to know, after all.

She was silent for a moment. "Well, for one thing, she's my dearest friend. She was digging into something that seemed terribly important to her. I don't know what her reasons were, but I want to help. I think I owe her that, as a friend." She paused, narrowing her eyes. "And for another, I think finding out about this murder she was talking about will lead us to the person who hit her last night."

"Fair enough," I said. "Did she give you any clues? How much do you think *she* knows about this alleged murder?"

"Well, it's not just 'alleged.'" Lara was defensive. "I mean, it really happened. At least that's what Kelly believed. From the little she said, I think she knew *who* got killed, and how, and why. Definitely why." She paused. "I mean, she didn't *tell* me these things, but she knew. It made her very apprehensive."

I'll bet it did. I reached for something a little more tangible. "On the phone, Kelly told me that she knew who the killer was—or that she thought she did. Did she say anything more than that to you? Did she give you any clue to the identity of the victim?"

"No, not in so many words. But I got the idea that this whole thing is connected to the hospice, somehow or other." Lara pulled her mouth down. "I'm sorry, China. I'm telling you what I know. I wish it could be more."

So did I. But if the murder was related to her hospice work, the victim would be the place to start. The *alleged* victim, I reminded myself, of an alleged murder. This whole thing could be a figment of Kelly's overactive imagination. If only we had a little more information—

"Do you know if Kelly told her lawyer anything about this so-called murder?" I asked.

Lara frowned at *so-called*, but she didn't try to argue. "Charlie Lipman, you mean? I doubt it. She told me she didn't trust him. That's why she wanted to see you."

"Really?" Charlie had his problems, but that didn't make him incompetent or untrustworthy. All lawyers bend the rules a little when they have to. But I'd never known Charlie to do something seriously unethical. "Do you know what her problem with him was? He was handling her divorce, wasn't he?"

"Yes, and she thought maybe he could help her with this other legal thing. But that was before she found out that he—" She stopped. "No, she didn't tell him anything about what she suspected."

I frowned. "Found out what? Come on, Lara. I can't help unless I know what's going on."

She hesitated. "Well, okay. She told me she found out that Mr. Lipman had a serious conflict of interest."

"What kind of conflict?"

"I don't know. He told her he could still represent her on the divorce, but she had to get another lawyer to represent her on this other business. She made a couple of calls from our house yesterday. She said she was calling lawyers he recommended. But she wasn't satisfied."

"Do you know who she called?"

"No," she answered slowly. "But I think I could get the numbers for you, if you need them. They're probably in my phone."

"That might help," I said, "depending on the firms she called." I picked up a business card and jotted down my cell phone number on the back and handed it to her, making a mental note to ask Charlie what the conflict was. That wasn't privileged. And under the circumstances, I might be able to persuade him to tell me. "What I really need, though," I added, "is access to her laptop. She said there were things on the computer that she wanted me to see. Documentation of some sort."

"The police have it now," Lara said. "I found it in the wreck, under the front seat."

"That's what Chief Dawson told me. Their forensics guy is supposed to be going over it today." I paused. "It was a good thing you thought to hunt for it, Lara. It may not tell the police anything, but if it had disappeared, there wouldn't be anything at all to go on."

"That might not be true," Lara said. She flipped open the top of her brown shoulder bag and took out a white envelope, folded over several times. "There's this." She put the envelope on the counter in front of me. "I found it in the glove compartment of the van this morning. The dashboard was so smashed that Matt had to take a crowbar to the glove compartment to get it open. He was looking for the registration and the insurance stuff. This was in there, too. I probably should have given it to the police, but I thought I'd take it home and look at it on my computer first. Now I think you should have it."

I opened the envelope and shook something out on the counter. It was a black gizmo the size of my thumb and weighing about as much as a saltine cracker.

I picked it up. It was a flash drive. A teensy-tiny technological miracle capable of storing every bit of data from my computer and probably from every computer on our block as well. It could give me the access I needed to Kelly's computer—*if* she had been in the habit of using it to back up her files.

"Hey, thanks," I said. "This could help." Maybe. Of course,

there might be nothing on it, or nothing of any significance. "I'll look at it as soon as I can." If it turned out to be something the cops should have, I'd give it to Sheila.

"You're welcome," Lara said. "Give me a call when you've figured it out." She glanced at her watch, then stepped back. "Sorry, China, but I gotta go. Matt's waiting for me. I'll look for those telephone numbers when I get home this afternoon."

She was halfway out the door when I called to her. "Hey, Lara, your umbrella. Don't forget it."

"I'd forget my head if it wasn't fastened on," she muttered. She snatched up the umbrella and was gone.

Chapter Nine

There's another, more indirect way to incorporate "oranges" into your garden. Before synthetic dyes, many different herbs and plants were used to produce the color orange in a variety of shades. Here are some of the most common botanical dyes:

Bloodroot (*Sanguinaria canadensis*) root: reddish orange

Butternut (*Juglans cinerea*) bark and seed husks: light yellow-orange

Carrot (*Daucus carota*) root: dark yellow-orange

Coreopsis (*Coreopsis tinctoria*) blossoms: bright orange

Eucalyptus (*Eucalyptus*) leaves and bark: rusty orange

Osage orange (*Maclura pomifera*) twigs, bark, and roots: yellow-orange

Lilac (*Syringa vulgaris*) twigs: yellow-orange

Onion (*Allium cepa*) skin: mustard orange

Pomegranate (*Punica granatum*) skin: light brownish orange

Saffron (*Crocus sativus*) flowers: burnt orange

Turmeric (*Curcuma longa*) powder: dark burnt orange

The color orange radiates warmth and vitality and has been said to energize psychic power. It is also used to warn of impending danger, as in the U.S. color-coded

threat advisory scale, where orange signals a "high"
threat level.

China Bayles
"Oranges in Your Garden"
Pecan Springs Enterprise

Lara had no sooner left the shop than the rain stopped,
the sun came out, and so did the customers. The tearoom was nearly filled for lunch, and people browsed through
both shops (and spent some money, which is always nice)
until almost one thirty. Things slowed down after that, and
Ruby and I went into the tearoom to clear the last of the tables while Cass and her helper headed for the kitchen to get
things ready for the First Baptist Ladies tea party.

Ruby was wearing a cheerful orange today—a vintage
orange cotton pique dress with three-inch orange cork wedges
that boosted her way above her normal six-foot-something.
She was also wearing a light, orange citrus scent, the per-
fume I had made her for Christmas. When she wears it, she
says, she can feel that her power is enhanced. I don't know
what that means exactly, but it certainly smells delicious.

While Ruby straightened the chairs and floral-printed ta-
blecloths, I swept the floor, listening for the bells that would
let us know that a customer had walked into one of our shops.
While we were working, I took the opportunity to fill her in
on what had happened to Kelly Kaufman and the break-in
at the cottage. But I didn't say anything about her sister's
unexpected—and uninvited—visit the night before, or about
her poltergeisty shenanigans. Ruby has enough on her mind

without trying to ride herd on Ramona's romantic and business affairs, especially when the two are scrambled together. Anyway, I had promised Ramona not to say anything about our conversation.

"That car crash sounds just *awful*," Ruby said soberly when I finished telling her about it. "I hope your friend recovers."

"I do, too," I said. "But I don't mind telling you that I'm worried. I wish I knew what happened out there on that road last night. And who broke into the cottage and why. Those two things might very well be related, which means that I'm sort of in the middle of it."

She frowned, hesitantly tucking a red curl under her yellow-and-blue headband, and then stood very still, her glance going a little inward, her head cocked as if she were listening to something—music, a distant voice—that I couldn't hear. She turned her head, her eyes widening, then put one hand to her throat and the other hand on a chair back, steadying herself.

I turned, concerned. "Are you okay, Ruby?"

She sat down abruptly on the chair. I propped my broom against the wall and went to her. "Are you okay?" I repeated urgently. "What's the matter, dear? Would you like me to get you some water?"

I'm not sure she even heard me. "Ruby?" I repeated, and put my hand to her cheek. It felt chilly. "Ruby, what's wrong? Are you sick?"

She was looking up at me, but her eyes were unfocused and vague, and when she spoke, her voice was a thin thread, uninflected and mechanical, like a voice in a dream.

"Don't go in there, China." She pulled in a half-strangled breath, let it out. "Please, no. Don't. It's not safe." The last word was said on a long, sighing breath, as if she was about to faint. She had grown very pale, and the freckles stood out on her nose.

"What? Go in where?" I leaned over her, my hand on her shoulder, feeling frightened for her, not sure what to do. "Ruby, should I—" Should I make her put her head down? Lie down on the floor? Get a doctor, maybe?

I raised my head to call out for help to Cass, who was banging a pot in the kitchen just a few yards away, but Ruby opened her eyes, stopping me.

"Something's awfully wrong, China." She put out a hand, and when I took it, her fingers were like frozen sticks. "It's dangerous," she said. "Don't go in." She pushed out a ragged breath, her voice rising. "Don't go through that door!" she cried, clinging to my hand.

By now, I was thoroughly frightened. My palms were clammy; my heart was pounding. But this was silly, I told myself. Here we were, on an ordinary day, in our usual place. There was no door, and no danger. I was standing right here beside her, not going anywhere. And then Ruby let go of my hand and put both hands to her face, covering her eyes.

"Are you all right?" I asked anxiously. "Do you want to lie down?"

"I . . . My goodness." She shook her head, then dropped her hands and took a deep breath. "I think I said something, China. Something important. Did I? What was it?"

"You said 'Don't go through that door.' You said it was dangerous."

She straightened her shoulders. "Well, don't, then," she said, in her usual Ruby voice. "If that's what I said, don't do it." She gave me a long, intense look. "Do you understand?"

And then, of course, I did. I hadn't seen Ruby use her gift very much lately. But I've watched her in action more than once, and I know she's in touch with something in the universe that the rest of us ordinary mortals simply don't understand—and that many of us don't want to believe in. I can't pretend to know how she makes it work, and to tell the truth, I'd just as soon remain ignorant. But whatever it is, it's real. And *important*, nothing like the silly, cartoonish kind of thing that Ramona does with cuckoo clocks and microwave ovens and TVs.

"I understand," I said. I added, a little reproachfully, "But there are a lot of doors in this world. It would help if I knew which one you were talking about."

"I'm afraid I can't tell you," Ruby confessed. "But please think twice before you open a strange door, will you?" She stood. "I picked up a bite to eat before the lunch crowd came in," she added. "If you want, I'll keep an eye on your shop while you sit down and have a sandwich."

"That would be wonderful," I said gratefully. Ruby and I learned long ago the multiple advantages of our adjoining shops. One of us can spell the other when we need a private moment or have to run out for a quick errand. And we're never lonely, which is an even more important benefit. I just can't imagine Thyme and Seasons without the Crystal Cave—and Ruby—on the other side of the wall. It's like two halves of a whole, somehow.

Struck by this last thought and remembering how abruptly Kelly's life had been altered by that crash, I put my arms around Ruby and hugged her, hard.

She hugged me back, then pulled away, puzzled. "What's that for?" she asked, one ginger eyebrow arched. "Did I do something especially nice?"

"You're the only friend I have who warns me about going through doors," I said with a grin. "That makes you special, doesn't it?"

She leaned over (way over: I'm only five-feet-four) and kissed me on the cheek. "If you want to talk later, China, I'm available. And maybe by that time, I'll know what door we're talking about and why you shouldn't go through it." She gave me a gentle push. "Now go and get a sandwich, sweetie. You'll feel better."

I had to laugh at that. I went to the kitchen and grabbed a chicken salad sandwich, a couple of cookies, and a glass of iced tea. Supplied with lunch, I took my laptop to a corner table in the empty tearoom. I sat down and polished off my sandwich while I was waiting for my laptop to boot up. Then I plugged Kelly's flash drive into the USB port. The drive appeared as the "E" drive under "My Computer." I clicked on it, mentally crossing my fingers that it wouldn't be password protected.

It wasn't. I was in.

Now, if you know me, you know that, normally, I'm not a snoop. I devoutly believe in safeguarding my own and other people's privacy, and under most conditions, I would never go cruising through another person's data files. That's as bad as reading somebody else's mail or pawing through the drawer where she keeps her undies.

But Kelly had seemed convinced that she had information about a serious crime, maybe even a murder, and she'd said that the documentation was on her laptop. What's more, she had been on her way to my house to discuss it with me. So I felt justified in scanning her flash drive, with the hope of seeing what she had intended to show me. Whether I would recognize it when I saw it was another question altogether.

There were four folders on the drive, along with the usual aggregation of setup and application files. The first folder was named "Pecan Springs," the second, "Seguin," the third, "Lufkin," the fourth, "Notes." I reached for a cookie and munched it as I frowned at the folders, the first three named for Central Texas towns. I remembered hearing them mentioned recently and in the same sentence. Now, where was it? Who had I been talking to when—

I was clutching at that memory when I was interrupted by the siren ringtone on my cell phone. I considered letting the call go to voice mail, but the ring was annoying. And I remembered McQuaid, who might be back in cell-tower range and calling to tell me that he'd wrapped things up in El Paso and would be home for supper tonight. I stood up and fumbled my phone out of my jeans pocket. But it wasn't McQuaid. It was Lara.

"I have those numbers Kelly called from our house yesterday, China—the lawyers Charlie Lipman recommended. There are three of them—two to Austin, one to our local area code. Want them?"

"Sure," I said, thinking how great it was that our telephones kept records for us. I took a pencil out from behind my ear and a paper napkin from the holder in the middle of the table and jotted the numbers down as she read them off. When she finished, I said, "What about the durations of the calls?"

"Each of the first two was about ten minutes. The third, the local number, was a little over four." She paused. "Are you going to follow these up?"

"I am. I don't know where they'll lead—maybe nowhere." Maybe Kelly was so fed up with Charlie that she was looking for another divorce lawyer. If so, that wouldn't tell us much. "But thanks for getting them for me." I paused. "Any word on Kelly's condition this afternoon?"

"I just talked to the charge nurse, a friend of mine." Lara took a deep breath and let it out in a long sigh. "They've been testing Kelly every hour to see if there's any neurological response. There isn't."

"Oh, no," I whispered. "Oh, Lara, I'm so, so sorry."

"Thank you. She's still on life support, but that's mainly to keep her going until her family gets here." Lara's voice was steady, the voice of an experienced nurse who has dealt with death before. But underneath the matter-of-factness I could hear a profound sadness for her friend. "Her mom is flying in from Seattle. I'm leaving in a couple of minutes to go to the airport and pick her up. I'll probably be with her at the hospital the rest of the day if you need to talk to me." She hesitated. "Have you heard anything from the police?"

"Not a word." I swallowed hard, still trying to get around the idea that Kelly wasn't going to make it. "Have you?"

"Actually I have, roundaboutly, from one of Matt's buddies who works at the brewery. Rich was at the hospital all morning, but he drove over to the brewery to do something he had to do. The cops showed up about that time and questioned him until he got irritated and told them he wouldn't answer any more questions without his lawyer."

"Uh-oh," I said. "He used the magic word. *Lawyer* always jacks up the cops' curiosity barometer a couple hundred percent. They'll figure he has something to hide. And he's already in the crosshairs, of course. When there's trouble, the spouse is always the number one person of interest."

"I suppose you're right," she said. "Anyway, after they talked to him, they went outside and took a look at his truck."

"Ah," I said. "Did they impound it?"

"If they did, I didn't hear about it," Lara said. "Why?"

"If they'd found any damage that might have been due to last night's crash, they would have towed it to their impound yard. They wouldn't have left it where he could take it to a body shop and get it repaired."

"So I was right," Lara said. "I *knew* Rich didn't do it."

"Not necessarily," I cautioned. "It just means that they didn't find any damage *yet*. They may send another investigator for a second opinion. But at least they're looking, which ought to give you some satisfaction. It means that the chief took you and Matt seriously when you reported the rear-end damage to your van. Without that, they would have written off Kelly's crash as a one-vehicle accident. Driver lost control on a bad stretch of road and smashed into a tree. End of story."

"Yes, there's that," Lara agreed. She hesitated. "You'll let me know if you want me to do any legwork, won't you?"

I blinked. "Leg work?"

"Well, as I said, I really want to help you," Lara replied. "Like, after you've called those phone numbers and you want to dig a little deeper. Or when you get into the files on that flash drive and you think I might be able to answer your questions. I want to pick up where Kelly left off—get to the bottom of this thing she was doing, whatever it is." Her voice was earnest now, as if she'd taken this on as a crusade. I could hear the tears she was holding back. "I'm your girl, China. Don't forget."

I was touched by Lara's sincerity. I thought once again of Kelly, on life support. "Thank you," I said. "I'll remember." I looked up as Ruby opened the door and several women came into the tearoom chatting and laughing. I started shutting down my computer. "But right now, I'm going to say hello to some First Baptist ladies who are early for their tea party."

Lara chuckled drily. "My," she said with mock admiration. "You lead such an *exciting* life, China Bayles, all full of thrills and chills. Have fun with the ladies. I'll check you later. I'm eager to know what you find out from those phone calls." Then her voice changed. "I'm really serious about wanting to help. Somebody tried to kill Kelly—I *know* it. I want to find out who it was."

IT had started to rain again and the customer traffic dropped off after the ladies were finished with their tea. Karin Johnson, our neighborhood handyperson, was at work on the

French doors in the cottage bedroom, and I took fifteen minutes to go back there and check on her progress. I would come in early the next morning and clean everything up, including the fingerprint powder residue on many of the surfaces. Kelly had rented the cottage for a week, so I could leave her things there for at least that long.

While I was talking to Karin, my daughter called my cell phone. I answered hurriedly, shutting off the siren ringtone as quickly as I could. Caitie's friend Sharon, also a violinist, had asked her to stay for supper and the evening. Could she? They wanted to practice together.

"It's a school night," I reminded her. Caitie is almost too self-contained, so I try to encourage her to spend time with other girls. But that usually happens on weekends. "What about your homework?"

"I've already got it pretty much done," Caitie said. "Sharon's mom says she'll bring me home about nine. Sharon's having trouble with one of our concert pieces, and Dr. Trevor suggested that we work together on it."

"Sounds okay to me, sweetie," I said. "Have fun."

We exchanged noisy mom-daughter kisses and I clicked off with a smile, thinking how much Caitie has enriched my life and wishing that her father—Miles, my half brother— could know that his little girl is already making a lovely mark on the world. He would be pleased. And so, perhaps, would be the father Miles and I shared and whom neither of us had ever fully known.

IT was nearly four o'clock before I could get back to the telephone numbers Lara had given me. But I didn't dial them on the phone. Instead, I brought up the browser on my laptop and typed the first of the three into the search bar. It turned out to be the telephone number for the law office of Stevens,

Worth, and Bullock in Austin, and the search engine's listing included a link to the firm's website. That told me what I needed to know. They were False Claims Act lawyers.

I sat very still, staring wide-eyed at the web page on my laptop. Although False Claims wasn't in my special skill set as a lawyer, I had a general knowledge of it, and I didn't have to read more than a few sentences to get a glimpse of Kelly's backstory. But one gust of wind doesn't make a hurricane, I reminded myself quickly. I had another couple of numbers to check out.

I typed the second number into the browser, clicked on the web link, and a moment later, I was looking at the website of Prince and Rosato, Attorneys at Law, specializing in False Claims and *qui tam* litigation.

And with a nearly audible click, the universe seemed to settle into an orderly, familiar arrangement of fact, law, and proceedings. I still knew next to nothing about what Kelly suspected or who was involved or what was at stake. But at least I knew what league we were playing in—or I thought I did. Unless I was mistaken, the name of this game was Let's Blow the Whistle, and the rules were all very clearly spelled out in the federal government's playbook, under the False Claims Act. Kelly must have wanted help with a whistle-blowing case.

I had to reach pretty far back in my law school memory banks for this one. Congress enacted the first False Claims Act during the Civil War, in order to catch suppliers and manufacturers who were cheating the federal government. The law included a qui tam provision that allowed people who had knowledge of the fraud but weren't connected to the government to file a lawsuit on behalf of the government. What's more, it gave them the right to collect a certain portion of the fines and penalties. Qui tam comes from a medieval Latin phrase that means "he who sues for the king and himself"—the "king," in this case being Uncle Sam. As I said, it was old law school exam material, especially that medieval qui tam bit.

But qui tam is also very current, very simple, and very much in the news these days. The law—which has been updated in the years since the Civil War—rewards people for doing the right thing: notifying the Department of Justice of any fraud that involves federal funds and providing the evidence (or at least the initial evidence) that leads to a conviction. In Texas and elsewhere, state legislatures have climbed on the antifraud bandwagon.

Any fraud involving government funds? That covers a lot of territory, doesn't it? Just think of the gazillions of taxpayer dollars Uncle Sam shells out annually on health care, schools and colleges, highways and bridges, farm subsidies, and defense contracts. Add space exploration, research and development funding, and homeland security, and you get a glimpse of just how much money we're talking about and how widely it is dispersed.

And anywhere and everywhere that kind of money is spent, some of it is going to be slipped into people's pockets, instead of going where it's supposed to go. Contracts are illegally bid, kickbacks are paid, defective products are sold, regulations are ignored, the government is overcharged—and that's just the beginning of the ways greedy people divert money into their offshore bank accounts, where they seldom pay income tax on their ill-gotten gains. Which means that the IRS can be involved as well.

The False Claims Act encourages whistle-blowers to tell the truth about fraud they see on the job and institutes legal proceedings designed to return those dollars, plus a hefty fine, to the federal kitty. The FCA also safeguards the whistle-blower from retaliation by an employer and rewards him or her for having the courage to do something most people don't like to do: *snitch*. And the reward is definitely enticing. Under the law, for every dollar Uncle Sam collects from fraudsters, the whistle-blower may earn from fifteen to as high as thirty cents, depending on the case.

The total amounts of these payoffs can be staggering. I read recently that the guy who blew the whistle on the Union Bank of Switzerland's U.S. tax fraud pocketed $104 million. A group of six Pfizer employees were awarded $102 million for exposing the illegal promotion of the arthritis drug Bextra. And $96 million was paid to a woman who identified faults in manufacturing at the pharmaceutical company GlaxoSmith-Kline. Not all rewards are this large, of course. The average case settles for $2 million or less, for which the average whistle-blower earns about $320,000 and the average lawyer 40 percent.

And that's as it should be, for the process is a complicated one and there are plenty of ways to go astray. For one thing, a whistle-blower's False Claims case has to be fully and completely documented according to federal rules, and is initially filed "under seal." That is, everything about the case is strictly hush-hush and nobody but the court and the Department of Justice sees the evidence the whistle-blower has assembled. Once the case is filed, the Department of Justice opens its own investigation. If the case is solid and there's potentially enough fraud to make it worth the attorney's time, the DOJ will step in and litigate on behalf of the government *and* the whistle-blower.

Meanwhile, everything is still under seal, and the defendant (the alleged fraudster), is completely in the dark. He doesn't know that a whistle-blower has filed a lawsuit until the DOJ decides to deal itself in. Or out, in which case the whistle-blower has to decide whether to go forward on his own or drop the whole thing. You can see why I said that this is a matter for the attorneys who know how to litigate stuff like this. It's not a job for the unlearned or the fainthearted.

But there's another wrinkle. If a qui tam case ends in a large penalty for the wrongdoer, the first to file is the one who gets the goodies. Say, for example, that two or three employees have observed the same corporate fraud. The "first to file" rule means that the one who gets to the courthouse first gets 100 percent of the credit for reporting the fraud, even if someone comes along later with a briefcase full of more and better evidence.

And that's it in a nutshell. Of course, I could be way off base on this one. Kelly might have been onto something else entirely. But people don't go shopping for a False Claims attorney just for the fun of it. If Charlie Lipman had suggested that Kelly call those attorneys, it was because he thought she needed somebody like Stevens, Worth, and Bullock to represent her. Ergo, she must have told him that she had some sort of knowledge of a fraud and wanted to become a whistle-blower. But I still had no idea what she might know or whether a False Claims attorney would consider her case substantial enough to make it worth pursuing.

But whatever it was, it could have potentially put her in danger. Whistle-blowers do not lead charmed lives. I shivered as I remembered what had happened to Karen Silkwood, an employee of Kerr-McGee Corporation, a company that manufactured plutonium pellets for nuclear reactor fuel rods at an Oklahoma site. Silkwood, twenty-eight, was a whistle-blower who went to the Atomic Energy Commission with her concerns about workers' exposure to radioactive material at KMC's Oklahoma factory. And as I remembered the story (retold in the movie *Silkwood*, with Meryl Streep), she was taking certain documents to a *New York Times* reporter when her car was hit from behind and forced off the road. She was pronounced dead on arrival at a local hospital. The documents—she had told friends that they were proof that Kerr-McGee was covering up faults in the handling of highly radioactive materials—were missing from her wrecked car. They were never found.

I sat up straight, my heart pounding. But I shouldn't let the similarity between the car crashes—Karen Silkwood's and Kelly Kaufman's—lead me to misconstrue the situation. Kelly could have been onto something else entirely or onto nothing at all. I am not a conspiracy theorist by nature, but I have been known occasionally to leap to a conclusion on pretty flimsy evidence or connect a few dots that, on closer inspection, didn't exist. If I was doing that in Kelly Kaufman's case, it wouldn't be the first time.

Anyway, I still had the third of Lara's three phone numbers—the local number—to check out. I glanced at what I'd jotted down on the napkin and frowned, thinking that it looked familiar. Pretty darned familiar, in fact. I punched it into my cell phone, and as I did, the ID in my cell phone came up. Kelly hadn't called a local attorney. She had called Jessica Nelson at the *Pecan Springs Enterprise*. I thought I knew why—and that it was a seriously bad idea.

Jessica Nelson is a dedicated young reporter who became famous a couple of years ago. She was on what seemed like a routine story assignment when she was kidnapped by a guy who was desperate to cover up a botched drug-related arson-murder. But Jessica managed to get away in a rather dramatic fashion. The day after her release, she was interviewed on CNN, NBC, and CBS, and the week after that, on ABC's *Good Morning America*. She told how she had waited in fear in the dark, bound and gagged and wondering if she was going to be killed. And how she had slipped her bonds and taken down her captor entirely by herself, armed only with a seven iron from his golf bag. The media loved that part of the tale, and by the end of the first interview, Anderson Cooper had dubbed Jessica the Seven-Iron Slugger. Three hours later, she had been contacted by a New York literary agent. Her book was published not long afterward and did very well as true crime.

Jessica and I have remained friends and I see her often these days, at the newspaper and around town. She hangs around the police station, where she's good friends with Sheila and knows most of the detectives. She's always on the lookout for a good story—especially another true crime.

Jessica picked up on the first ring. "Jessie Nelson," she said crisply. "What can I do you for?"

"Huh," I said. "Can't you come up with something a little less corny than that?"

"Hark gets what he pays for," Jessica retorted. "Pure corn." She had recognized my voice, or more likely, my caller ID on her phone. "What's up, China? Are you calling to say that you won't be meeting the deadline for your page—again?"

Hark Hibler is the editor of the *Enterprise*, and Jessica's boss. My boss, too, at least on Thursdays, when my garden column is published. I write it in return for free advertising for the shop, which has turned out to be a pretty good deal. Hark is also Ruby's boyfriend, at least at the moment.

"Nope. I'm calling to ask you something," I said. "Got a spare minute?"

"Just. I'm finishing a story and it's due in the boss' computer in half an hour."

"Plenty of time," I said. "Did a gal named Kelly Kaufman phone you yesterday?"

There was a moment's silence. Then a guarded, "Well, maybe. Who's asking? You or somebody else? If it's you, why?"

"Me," I said. "Me and me only. Did she?"

Jessica's "Yeah" was also guarded. "And why exactly are you wanting to know?"

I countered with, "Did she tell you why exactly she was calling?"

Jessica sighed, and I pictured her rolling her eyes. "Well, yes and no. That is, she told me that she was calling with a heads-up about a story and hinted that it involved some local people and might make a pretty big local splash. Maybe a few national ripples as well. I didn't take it too seriously. I hear that a lot from people who are looking to get their five minutes of fame. But then—" She stopped.

Damn. I took a deep breath. "So? What happened? Did she tell you why she was calling? What was it about?"

A pause. I could hear the sound of a pencil tapping on the desk. Jessica operates on pulses of nervous energy. "So, what happened was that she didn't want to talk to me on the phone. Too hush-hush or something, or maybe she was afraid that Homeland Security or the FBI has my phone tapped. We made a date to get together for lunch today at Beans'." More tapping. "The thing is, she didn't show."

"I see," I said. Of course she didn't. She was in the hospital.

"In case you're curious," she added, "since I was there, I went ahead and ate. I had Bob's cabrito fajitas, which are truly spectacular. If you don't have anything better to do tonight, go over there for supper."

"So she didn't tell you what she was calling about?"

"Nope. And like I said, she didn't show. But what I'm saying, China, is that you absolutely *have* to have some of Bob's cabrito fajitas." Bob Godwin owns Beans' Bar and Grill and is famous for his cabrito. "You'd love them. He says he uses orange zest, garlic, and a couple of different chiles in his rub, then he slow roasts it and serves the cabrito thin-sliced, with warm flour tortillas and salsa. I'm telling you, it's out of this world."

So Kelly hadn't told her story to Jessica, which was a good thing. "I'm on my own for dinner tonight," I said. "I think I'll do Beans'." I didn't even pause for breath. I was eager to get off the line before she could start asking questions. "Thanks a bunch, Jessie. You have a great afternoon now. Talk to you later."

But I didn't click off quite fast enough.

"Hey, whoa," she said quickly. "Where're you going, China? Hang on a sec. You know about that car crash last night?"

"Which crash?" I asked, playing for time.

"Out your way, on Limekiln Road. A one-car crash. Kelly Kaufman was involved. You haven't heard?"

"Oh, that one." I don't mind messing with the truth, and I'll even fabricate a story when necessary. But I hate to lie in answer to a direct question. It's too much like perjury. I sighed. "Yes, I heard."

"Well, I hadn't. Not until I got back from lunch and found out why she didn't show." Jessica took a breath. "There's no official word from the hospital, but I called a buddy of mine over there and learned that Kaufman is critical, on life support. Then I talked to Sheila, and found out that they're looking for a vehicle that might have rear-ended her. Maybe you can tell me something about that?"

I heard the *clickety-click* of Jessica's computer keyboard and guessed that she was opening a file. It wouldn't do any good to tell her to stop. She has a nose for news that just won't quit. She was smelling a story.

"All I know is that Kelly is in the hospital," I said evasively. Now I really wanted to end the conversation. "Sorry, Jessie, but something has just come up here that I need to—"

"Sheila told me that there are fresh dents in the rear end of the Astro Kaufman was driving," Jessica said insistently. "And flecks of orange paints in the dents. You wouldn't happen to have heard about that, would you? That wouldn't be why you're calling, would it, mmm?"

Clickety-click.

"I'm afraid I don't know any more than you do," I hedged, which might or might not have been true, since I didn't actually know how much Jessica knew, or guessed, or was inclined to speculate.

"Jimmy went out to the PSPD's impound yard to get some photographs of the van and sent me a couple from his cell phone. I just saw them. The Astro looks like it was pretty well totaled." Jimmy is the newspaper's staff photographer, a college kid who is working his way to a journalism degree at CTSU. "Sheila told me that Kaufman was heading west on Limekiln Road when it happened, and that they're operating on the theory that the van was struck from behind." She paused. "So naturally I'm wondering about that, since you've called to ask me about her. You live out west on Limekiln, don't you?" She didn't wait for me to answer. Jessica knows very well where I live because she's been there, quite a few times. "Was Kelly Kaufman on her way to see you when she went off the road?"

"No comment," I said firmly.

Clickety-click.

"Did her reason for coming to see you have anything to do with her reason for calling me?"

"How the heck should I know?" I asked testily. "I have absolutely no clue why she called you." Which was not exactly true, since I knew whom Kelly had called before she called Jessica, which gave me a couple of pretty good clues. "And no, you may not quote me."

That didn't stop her. "Let's try again. Do you *think* the car

crash might have had anything to do with her reason for calling me yesterday afternoon? Or for seeing you last night? For
all I know, you two might be working together on this story
she wanted to talk to me about. You have been known to
solve a mystery or two around this town, you know."

"No, we aren't working together," I said flatly. "Jessica, I
wish you wouldn't—"

"But she *was* on her way to your house?"

"I answered that already, Jessica. *No comment*."

"Well, okay. But you've got to admit that it looks suspicious. Kaufman hinted to me that she had a big story I might
be interested in writing about. And now you turn up, asking
questions about her. It's not a huge stretch to connect the
dots." Her tone became confidential. "Come on, China. If
there's something going on behind the scenes here, you and
I would both be better off if we put our heads together and
shared what we know. We've done it before. There's no reason not to do it this time. Right?"

Wrong. There was a very good reason not to. But I couldn't
tell Jessica what it was or why it had been a very bad idea for
Kelly to approach a reporter with her story.

Here's the thing. When a whistle-blower files a False
Claims lawsuit under qui tam rules, the case is immediately
sealed. No matter what the substance is or who's involved,
nobody, but *nobody*, is supposed to know a thing about it—
except, of course, for the whistle-blower herself and her lawyers, the court, and the legal eagles at the Department of
Justice.

Yes, there have been and continue to be other situations
where a whistle-blower may want to air his findings on the
Internet or head for a hungry reporter and spill all the beans
in order to get the story out. That was what Karen Silkwood
had to do, since, at the time she was trying to protect the
safety of her coworkers, whistle-blowers at nuclear plants

weren't protected. That's what CIA whistle-blower Edward Snowden did, because the Whistleblower Protection Act doesn't apply to him or to any employees of the CIA, the FBI, and the Government Accountability Office.

But it applied to Kelly and to her case—if she had one, that is.

And although I confess to having only a general knowledge of the qui tam rules, I knew that if Jessica Nelson, zealous young journalist, smelled a story, she would feel duty bound to dig as deeply as she could into it. And when she'd found out as much as she could about it, she would write a story that Hark Hibler would plaster all over the front page of the *Enterprise*. Which meant that if Kelly actually had a viable False Claims case, it would go down the drain as soon as the newspaper hit the streets. The fraudster would learn about the case against him, the Department of Justice would refuse to participate, and Kelly could become ineligible to receive whatever reward she might have had coming.

Assuming that she was alive to claim it, of course. That might be a rather slender assumption to hang on to, but I was going to cling to it until . . . well, until it was no longer assumable. Or something like that.

"Jessica," I said carefully, "I'm your friend. You know that, don't you? I wouldn't steer you wrong. If there was a story here that you could use, I wouldn't stand in your way. Please believe me when I say that Kelly was not fully informed when she telephoned you, and that if I had been her lawyer, I would have advised her not to—"

"Ah-*ha*!" Jessica chortled. "There *is* a story here, and there is some sort of lawyerly reason why I'm not supposed to have it. That's it, right? And don't try to tell me that you're her lawyer, because I know you don't take clients. So there's no issue of client privilege."

I sighed. "If you won't listen to reason, there is no point in talking to you."

"I am listening, China," Jessica said, now very sober. "And what I'm hearing is that there is a story here." She repeated the word with emphasis. "A *story*. And Kelly wanted to let me in on it. But you don't want her to, for reasons you're not willing or able to give me. So since you won't help, I'll just have to track down this story on my own. Is that what you want?"

No, it was *not* what I wanted, most definitely. I hesitated, thinking that maybe I'd call Hark and tell him to call off his newshound. But the minute that thought crossed my mind, I pushed it away. Hark Hibler is compelled by the same journalistic impulses that drive Jessica. Ask him to rein her in, and he'd only spur her on.

But there might be another way to go about this. No whistle-blower suit had yet been filed, so there was no case—yet—and no seal. Maybe I could enlist Jessica's cooperation on a part of the story and get her promise of silence with the assurance of a much bigger story later, when it was ready for public consumption. Also, now that I thought about it, Jessica probably had fairly easy access to information I might need, depending on how deeply *I* dug into Kelly's story. Maybe I could use her.

"Caitie's having supper with a friend and McQuaid's out of town, so I'm heading to Beans' tonight to treat myself to Bob's fajitas," I said. "How about meeting me there."

"Changed your tune, have you?" She chortled. "Why? You going to let me in on the story?"

"I may be able to tell you one or two things you might like to know," I said judiciously.

She didn't hesitate. "What time?"

"Six thirty suit you? I'm afraid I can't stay out late." I'd left Winchester in his outdoor dog run, so he was fine. But he would certainly be ready for his dinner. And Caitie would be home at nine.

She laughed at that. "Curfew, huh? Sure, six thirty is fine. I'll see you there."

Shaking my head, I clicked off the call. On the one hand, there was Lara, eager to help me track down the person who (she thought) landed Kelly in the hospital on life support. On the other hand, there was Jessica, going for Kelly's story, full steam ahead.

I sat for a moment, trying to sort through the maze of speculative detail and determine what might happen if Lara and Jessica got deep enough into the story to find out what it was all about. Maybe Kelly didn't have a whistle-blower's claim, and maybe she wouldn't live to pursue it. But if she did, either or both of these young women could jeopardize it by making the story public. Or—and this was another possibility, given the qui tam first-to-file rule—either of them could get in line ahead of Kelly for the reward if they managed to uncover the evidence that she had been putting together.

And there was someone else involved in this matter. The cops were operating on the theory that the van had been struck from behind. Yes, it might have been an accident—a random hit-and-run on a winding road on a dark night. But I couldn't stop there. If it had been deliberate, who stood to benefit? The husband, probably. I was sure that Sheila and her crew were putting him through the wringer. But there was another candidate: the person who was committing the fraud that Kelly had been about to blow the whistle on.

But maybe this was a bridge too far. I glanced over my shoulder at the shop clock. It was nearly five o'clock. If I was going to catch Charlie Lipman in the office today, now was the time. I went back to my phone, and a moment later, his secretary was telling me that he was out but would be back around five thirty and she'd pencil me in for a quickie. But it would have to be short, she said frostily. He was leaving for Austin at six.

I raised my eyebrows, but Charlie's current secretary (they don't seem to stay long) is a prim, straitlaced lady of fifty-something who is married to the principal of Pecan Springs High School. Her name is Rosie Caulfield. It was probably fair to assume that by "quickie," Rosie meant something like a short consultation.

"Five thirty is fine," I said.

"But do be punctual," she warned. "I lock up when I leave, which is promptly at five thirty. And he *must* leave by six."

"I'll do my best," I promised, feeling like a third-grader who has been told to report to the principal's office for after-school detention.

It was a squeeze. But I managed to check out the shop and the tearoom cash registers (cash in one stack, checks and credit card slips in another) and make up the daily bank deposit, tidy up the shop, feed Khat, and say good night to Ruby. Then I zipped my laptop into its leather case, grabbed the deposit bag, locked the door, and headed for the bank, feeling reasonably satisfied. For a rainy Tuesday, it hadn't been a bad day, sales-wise.

Otherwise . . . With a shiver, I thought of Kelly, for whom it had been a very bad day.

Chapter Ten

Long before the Spanish arrived in Mexico in 1521, the Aztecs had produced a fermented beverage from the heart of the blue agave (*Agave tequilana*). When the Spanish conquistadors ran out of the brandy they had brought with them, they began to drink tequila—and liked it even better. Tequila is traditionally produced in and around the Mexican state of Jalisco, where agave, a succulent, thrives in the area's volcanic soil and dry, high-altitude climate. The plant, which has fleshy, spiky leaves, is harvested at maturity (eight to twelve years). The large heart (*piña*) of the plant is peeled, roasted, and crushed, and its sap is fermented and distilled twice to produce tequila.

China Bayles
"Botanical Drinkables"
Pecan Springs Enterprise

Charlie's office is in an older section of Pecan Springs, where the houses have been turned into professional office space and the lawns have been replaced by an attractive xeriscape of Southwestern native shrubs, grasses, yuccas, agaves, and wildflowers that tolerate heat and don't need much water—a big issue in Central Texas, where we are learning to live with drought and climate change. His office is in a small gray house with blue shutters, set well back from the street under a couple of large live oak trees, with a cobbled parking area off to one side. By the time I arrived, Charlie's old truck was the only one in the small lot. I pulled up next to it and went inside.

Soberly dressed in a black polyester suit and a tailored white blouse, Rosie was sitting at her desk with her purse on her lap, ready to leave for the night. She stood, pointed me in the direction of Charlie's back-room office, and announced that she was locking up.

She was stern. "He has only thirty minutes. I hope he won't be late for his Austin appointment."

"I understand," I said meekly. "We'll make it a quickie."

Charlie was sitting at his desk, staring at his computer monitor, a cigarette dangling from one corner of his mouth and an empty shot glass at his elbow.

Most lawyers I know are neatniks, not eager for clients to see stacks of files and mounds of loose paper. Or they hire neatnik secretaries who are instructed to step in and tidy up the desk the minute the boss leaves for court or lunch or handball. Not so for Charlie. His secretaries are forbidden to touch his desk under pain of excommunication, and the top surface is always buried beneath mounds of papers, briefs, folders, books, and the relics of various takeout meals and snacks. A bottle of his favorite tequila lives in his bottom drawer.

"Ah, China." He stubbed out his cigarette in an overflowing ashtray. "Punctual as always."

"I was warned," I said.

"No doubt," he replied drily. "Bar's open." He opened the

drawer, took out a bottle of Siete Leguas and tipped it into his shot glass, then pulled out another glass for me. "Join me in a drink?"

"No, thanks." I'm partial to a good tequila sunrise but it's easy for me to say no to straight tequila. I moved a stack of briefs from one of the client chairs to the other. "Have you heard about Kelly Kaufman?"

His face darkened. "Yes. On life support, I understand. Fine young woman. Terrible, terrible accident."

Terrible, yes. Accident, probably not. But I didn't want to go into that with him. I sat down on the empty chair. "There are a couple of things—"

"Hey," he said. He put the bottle and glass back in the drawer. "I've figured out what McQuaid's doing out there in El Paso. Who he might be working for, that is."

"Oh, yeah?" He had my full attention. "Who?"

"Last year, I had a client down in Jim Wells County—Zumwalt Oil Drilling—who was losing a lot of equipment. Oil field theft. It's a booming business these days, really crazy. Hundreds of thousands of dollars' worth of trucks, equipment, tools, materials, stolen from drilling sites and storage yards. The stuff ends up all over the map—Houston, Dallas, Oklahoma City, down in South America, up in North Dakota." Charlie tipped back his head and tossed back his tequila.

I wasn't quite seeing the point. "So?" I prompted.

"Anywhere there's oil action—and there's a helluva lot of fracking going on these days—there's theft. Big stuff, little stuff, stuff you wouldn't think of." Charlie waved a hand. "Solar panels and batteries are the current hot items. The bad guys cruise the back roads looking for solar panels on isolated well sites, then swoop in and rip off the panels, the batteries, and all the copper wire they can grab. These wells are isolated, maybe two, three wells to a site, and they're easy pickings. The equipment loss can amount to nine or ten thousand a well—and there's the downtime, too. No batteries, no power, no pumping. The pump sits there idle until somebody comes along and spots the theft." He chuckled drily. "Some of the operators have installed surveillance cameras, but these crooks know what they're doing. They steal the cameras, too."

I was getting impatient. I only had a half hour to find out what Charlie knew about Kelly, and the clock was running. "Sounds like a pretty efficient operation. But what's this got to do with McQuaid?"

"Hold your horses, China. I'm coming to that." He opened the bottom drawer, considered a moment, and shut it again. "Like I said, a lot of the stuff is ending up in Mexico. Turns out that some of the thieves here in Texas are working for the drug cartels. Instead of selling the stolen stuff—big rigs, equipment, pipes—the cartels take it back home and put it to work. They're using it to tap into Pemex oil pipelines. They've gotten smart about it, too. They used to kidnap Pemex employees and force them to handle the technical stuff. Now, they just co-opt the Pemex workers and pay for the inside information and expertise they need."

"Pemex. That's the state-owned Mexican oil company, isn't it?"

"Yep." He pulled a package of Marlboros out of his shirt pocket, lit one, and leaned back. "We ain't talkin' loose change here, China. Pemex says it's losing some five billion dollars a year in illegal taps. The cartels have morphed into oil field pirates. And they're pretty damned good at it."

I frowned. "You're not saying that McQuaid—" I paused. Blackie was out there, too, according to Sheila. "You're not telling me that McQuaid and Blackie are doing an oil field theft investigation for Zumwalt Drilling?"

"Oh, hell, no." Charlie dismissed my question with a wave

of his hand. "Zumwalt is small-fry. A couple of months ago, I got a call from an outfit calling itself the Oil Field Theft Task Force. It's a coalition of local and federal law enforcement, along with a handful of private investigators working for the drillers and oil operators who want their own men on the job. The Mexican Federales are involved too—they're trying to crack down on the cartels on their side of the border." He picked up his glass. "Anyway, somebody at the task force was looking for a reference for McQuaid, Blackwell, and Associates, checking them out for their investigation. I was glad to give your boy two big thumbs up. So I reckon that's why he's out there."

I was beginning to put this jigsaw puzzle together, and the picture that emerged had nothing to do with the beautiful Margaret Graham or the possibility of McQuaid's continuing friendship with her. It was more frightening than that. Much more.

"So he decided not to tell me who he was working for or where," I said painfully, "because he's working for the task force and he figured he might have to go down into Mexico to track down some of that missing equipment. He was breaking his promise, and he didn't want me to know." I swallowed hard. Going into Mexico meant trespassing on the cartels' territory. And in this case, he might be intending to interrupt their piracy. People who did stuff like that didn't always come back.

Charlie's eyebrows went up and he cocked his head. "Breaking his promise?"

I straightened my shoulders. That part of it was between McQuaid and me, and I wasn't going to cry on Charlie's shoulder.

"No big deal," I said past the hurt in my throat and the cold fear in my belly. McQuaid tells me I'm phobic about Mexico and the cartels, and he's right. I *am* phobic. But he had promised. Shouldn't I trust him? If I didn't, what did that say about me?

"Really, no big deal," I repeated as casually as I could. "That's not what I'm here for, anyway."

"That's what Rosie told me." Charlie winked at me, and I saw a little of his old self. "She said you wanted a quickie."

"Rosie told me that a quickie was all you had time for," I countered, and we both chuckled. I glanced at the clock and saw, with some chagrin, that it was quarter to six. If Charlie had been trying to stall me—to keep me from asking him about Kelly Kaufman—he had certainly pushed the right buttons.

"So?" Charlie asked, eyeing me. "What's on your mind, if it's not your old man?"

"Can't you guess?" I replied. "Kelly Kaufman."

"Forget it, China." Charlie leaned forward to tap his cigarette into the ashtray. "You know I can't talk about her. Whatever happens over there at the hospital, she's a client. Privileged."

He was right in one regard. Attorney-client privilege persists even after the client's death. But that wasn't the issue I wanted to pursue.

"Not so fast," I said. "You were acting for her in the matter of her divorce, right?"

He considered that, pushed his mouth in and out, and finally nodded. "That's right."

"And you turned her down on the other matter she asked you about. You told her you had a conflict, and you gave her the names of two lawyers in Austin. Stevens, Worth, and Bullock was one of them. Prince and Rosato was the other." I watched him, waiting.

"Ah, yes," he said. He narrowed his eyes. "Did Kelly tell you that?"

"No."

"Then how did you—"

"She made the calls from a friend's house. The friend found the numbers in her telephone and gave them to me." I paused. "Kelly told you she thought she had a whistle-blower claim, didn't she?"

Charlie frowned. "Well, now, China, you know I can't—"

"Oh, yes, you can, Charlie," I said flatly. "This isn't tid-dlywinks. We've got a situation here. The police think some-body forced that young woman off the road last night. Could have been somebody who was afraid that she had informa-tion that could be used in a government fraud case. What I want to know from you is why you referred her to another firm. What's your conflict?"

Charlie reflected for a moment, then tried out an answer. "Maybe I don't feel confident in taking on a whistle-blower case. False Claims is a pretty specialized field. Plenty of ways to get crosswise of the feds and lose the whole shebang." He blew out a stream of gray smoke. "Maybe I didn't think her case had sufficient merit to make it worth my time. Or maybe—"

"Uh-uh." I shook my head. "Those dogs won't hunt, Char-lie. Kelly told her friend that you said you had a conflict of interest." I grinned mirthlessly. "I've known you for a long time, and I've never known you to let a potential client slip out of your net. If you had been able to take Kelly's case, you would have. Then you would have brought a False Claims firm into the case and shared a part of the reward. You couldn't take the case because you have a conflict. Who's the client that's creating the conflict?"

There was a long silence, then a long sigh, and I could see the regret written across his face. "I can't tell you that, China. And I think you know why."

"Could be several reasons," I said. "The one that comes to

mind first is that you represent the client who is the potential target of Kelly's suit, if there is one." I paused, and a thought I didn't like elbowed unpleasantly into my mind. "She told you enough about it to cause you to send her to another law firm. I hope you didn't pass that information along to your client—the one who's creating the conflict of interest." I took a breath. "You didn't, did you?"

Charlie's expression darkened. "If you're suggesting that my client is responsible for Kelly Kaufman's accident—" He stopped.

"You said it, Charlie. I didn't." I watched him. Was he thinking of what Kelly had told him before he stopped her with his conflict-of-interest statement? Was he remembering that, after she left, he had picked up the phone and made a call to his client? Was he wondering whether his client had acted on the information he had passed along, and as a result, Kelly lay, gravely injured, on life support in the hospital? But if those thoughts were going through his mind, they weren't written on his face.

He was silent for a moment. Then he tried again. "China, you and I both know that privilege covers—"

I broke in briskly. "You and I both know that privilege does *not* cover the mere fact of an attorney-client relationship, Charlie. You are free to tell me who your client is, anytime you feel like it. So don't try to hide behind the privilege shield. What's more, privilege does *not* cover information you may have about the furtherance of a crime or fraud. If you suspect that your client had anything to do with Kelly's accident—"

He didn't let me get the rest of that sentence out and on the record.

"I would like to help you, but I can't." All business now, Charlie pushed back his chair and stood up. "This is as far as we go in this matter." He glanced down at his watch. "I have to head for Austin. I have a bar association committee meeting tonight."

I wanted to say that I hoped it wasn't the ethics committee, but I thought better of it. "That's okay, Charlie. I'm meeting a friend at Beans'." I paused. "Let's stay in touch on this, shall we?"

"Sure thing," he said, and walked with me to the front door. He unlocked it to let me out. "No hard feelings, I hope. Still friends?"

"Of course," I said cordially. "Professional disagreement, that's all."

At least, that's what it was until I noticed Charlie's truck, sitting next to my Toyota in the small parking area at the side of the house. It was an old Dodge crew cab pickup with badly dinged fenders, a deep crimp in the tailgate, and a rash of rust spots, like a bad case of the measles.

The truck was familiar, of course. And it was orange. Burnt orange.

I stood for a moment, calculating. Then, since I'm the kind of person who likes to get all the information possible about a given subject, I glanced over my shoulder to make sure Charlie wasn't coming out of the back door or watching out of the window, then ducked around in front of his truck to give it a close look. He has never been what you'd call a cautious driver, and the dents and scrapes on his truck, front and back, are silent witnesses to his close calls, some of them obviously recent. I bent over, squinting. Had any of them been made as recently as last night?

It was possible, yes—the crease in the front fender looked highly suspicious. But I couldn't form an opinion with a quick, casual glance in the afternoon light. That would require a search warrant and a forensic examination of the paint flecks on the Astro van and the paint on the Dodge.

I straightened up and hurriedly climbed into my car. *Come on, China,* I reprimanded myself guiltily. This is complicated enough without inventing a boogieman. It was hard to imagine that Charlie could have rear-ended Kelly—and even harder to come up with a reason why.

But as I got into my Toyota, it certainly gave me something to think about. I shivered. As if I didn't already have plenty on my mind, with Charlie's suggestion that McQuaid and Blackie were working for the Oil Field Theft Task Force and might be down in cartel country at this very moment. I put the key into the ignition and started the car, reminding myself that McQuaid and Blackie were both big guys who had plenty of experience taking care of themselves in tough corners. But I am a worrywart, and the possibility of danger always looms large in my mind. It's the downside of being married to somebody who is married to his job as a private investigator. If I wanted to live with him, I had to learn to live with what he did for a living. Nobody had ever said that life would be easy.

I put the Toyota in gear and pulled onto the street. What I needed was a glass of wine in a familiar place with familiar people. And I needed it *now.* I was glad that it was just a few blocks away.

BACK when Pecan Springs was a true small town, Beans' Bar and Grill was at the center of its social life, and everybody met friends there for lunch or dinner at least once a week. Now that Pecan Springs is just another bead on the string of thriving communities along the I-35 Corridor (Buda, Kyle, San Marcos, New Braunfels), things have changed. You can sit down to an excellent Japanese, Chinese, Thai, Greek, or Cuban meal, all within a fifteen-minute drive. If you want to travel a little farther north, there is a glittering galaxy of upscale places to eat in Austin, where at least one glitzy new restaurant is born every week. Southbound, there's another galaxy of good eating in San Antonio.

But that doesn't mean that Beans' Bar and Grill is running short on customers these days. If anything, its appeal may be even stronger, since people who are crazy about down-home Texas usually aren't nuts about Thai or Greek and they'd just as soon not dodge the big rigs that dominate the heavy truck traffic on I-35. Beans' is located in a two-story stone building between Purley's Tire Company and the Missouri Pacific Railroad tracks, across the street from the Old Fire House Dance Hall. Built sometime in the 1930s, it has a well-worn wooden floor, a white-painted pressed-tin ceiling, an antique bar along the right side of the main room, and a couple dozen mismatched tables and chairs painted red, green, yellow, blue—whatever color happened to be cheap at Banger's Hardware when the chair or table was acquired. Old wooden wagon wheels hang from the ceiling, studded with lights shaped like red and green jalapeño peppers. A carved wooden Indian stands in the corner with a politically correct sign around his neck, requesting that people refer to him as a Native American. On the walls: posters of Texas politicos—Lyndon Johnson on a horse, rounding up steers on his ranch; white-haired former Governor Ann Richards in white cowgirl garb on a white Harley; George W. Bush in dirty jeans with a chain saw in one hand and a Lone Star longneck in the other. The posters are full of holes. They're used as targets for dart games.

Bob Godwin has run Beans' for five or six years. His food is good and, yes, often great. But not everybody goes there to eat. Some go to sit at the bar and cheer for the Texas Longhorns on TV, play pool (eight-ball, nine-ball, or one-pocket), or throw darts. Others go there to drink with friends and

catch up on the gossip or listen to gen-u-ine cowboy music—
the Sons of the Pioneers or Tex Ritter or Gene Autry—on the
wheezy old Wurlitzer jukebox.

But when you get right down to it, it's the down-home food
that brings most people, as it brought me that night. There's
always barbecue on the menu—beef, chicken, and pork
grilled out back in old metal half-drums over mesquite fires.
Chicken-fried steak smothered in Bob Godwin's special
cream gravy. Big bowls of Bob's secret-ingredient chili (be
warned: it's *spicy*), served with hot-water cornbread flattened
into five-inch pancakes and fried. One of Bob's neighbors
raises goats, so there's usually cabrito in various forms—
kabobs, or drunken goat stew, or (as it was this week) fajitas.
Plus, there are the sides: mac and cheese, mashed potatoes,
deep-fried pickled jalapeños, frijoles, black-eyed peas, col-
lards, coleslaw. Desserts, if you're still able—pecan pie,
peach cobbler, fried ice cream.

And when you're ready to settle your tab, you can whistle
for Bud (short for Budweiser), Bob's golden retriever. Bud
trots over to the table wearing a sporty blue bandana and a
leather saddlebag with pockets marked *Cash*, *Credit Cards*,
and *Tip*, as well as a little sign that says, *Don't feed me
French fries, but steak is great.* Bud is very professional: he
always brings back the change.

I parked my Toyota in the gravel lot beside the railroad
tracks and headed for Beans'. I was turning the corner of the
building when I was barged into, hard, by a bulky, heavyset
man wearing a red sweatshirt over jeans. He had a narrow
mustache and metal-rimmed glasses and a scar from the
corner of his right eye to his jaw, relic of a motorcycle
accident.

"Oh, hell, China, sorry," he said, putting out a hand to
steady me. "You okay? Shoulda looked where I was going."

"Oh, hi, Jack," I said breathlessly, righting myself. "I'm okay. But you pack a wallop."

It was Jack Bremer, the owner of the strip center where McQuaid, Blackwell, and Associates has its office, on the south side of town. The strip is a little seedy, but McQuaid likes it. A PI's office ought to look a little seedy, he says.

"Yeah," Jack said, grinning. "Your guy wouldn't be too happy with me if he thought I'd knocked his pretty wife down and walked over her." Jack talks fast and it's hard to get a word in edgewise. "He back from Mexico yet? Chihuahua was what he told me, I think."

"Chihuahua?" I asked. "He said he was going to *Chihuahua*?" That's the Mexican state just south of the border, across from El Paso.

Jack tilted his head. "I think I'm remembering right. I told him to watch himself and pack plenty of firepower. And stay away from the señoritas."

I was having trouble with my breathing, and it wasn't because I had nearly been knocked over. "Did he . . . did he tell you what he was doing down there?"

"Working for one of the big oil companies, with some kind of federal SWAT team, was what he said," Jack replied. "We don't hear much about it up here, but Pemex—the Mexican oil company—has *mucho* trouble with the cartels." He patted my arm reassuringly. "You don't have to worry, China. McQuaid may be a danger junkie, but he knows how to handle himself."

A danger junkie, I thought. Oh, right. I steadied my breathing. "I never worry," I lied.

"Good girl," Jack said. "You have a great evening, now." He strode away.

I stood for a moment, holding myself against the fear that was sweeping me. McQuaid was going into one of the most hazardous of the northern Mexican states, on a mission so dangerous that I didn't even want to think about it. With the fear came a quick rush of anger—he had broken his promise—and a hot rash of guilty shame: I hadn't trusted him. I had thought he might be seeing Margaret. So many feelings, all swirling together.

I closed my eyes, took a deep breath, and waited for the whirlpool to subside. I couldn't let myself think of this, of any of it. If I did, I'd be pulled under, and there were things I had to do. I straightened my shoulders, turned the corner of the building, and went into Beans'.

Chapter Eleven

Cilantro doesn't always get the respect it deserves. Some people love it and can't get enough of it. Some people hate it—and don't mind telling the world how they feel. Julia Child, the famous author of *Mastering the Art of French Cooking*, once said that cilantro was one herb she positively didn't like. If it was served to her, she told an interviewer, "I would pick it out if I saw it and throw it on the floor."

Many people agree passionately with Julia Child. The problem, it seems, is created by cilantro's odor, which to some smells like soap, with a strong top note of bugs. Chemists tell us that these odors are created by fat molecules called aldehydes, which are also present in soaps and, yes, bugs. If you don't like cilantro, you may be responding to memory associations with unpleasant odors. Or, some scientists say, the aversion may be genetic. That is, your dislike of cilantro may be encoded in your DNA.

China Bayles
"The Great Cilantro Debate"
Pecan Springs Enterprise

Blood Orange

It was still light outdoors, but inside it was dim and smoky. (The city council has been debating a "Smoke-Free Pecan Springs" ordinance, but they haven't been able to pass it yet.) When I went in, the Riders in the Sky were doing the great old Gene Autry song "Back in the Saddle Again" on the Wurlitzer, and Pittsburgh was playing Cincinnati on the TV on the wall in the corner. Bob Godwin was behind the bar, wearing a black T-shirt that warned *EASILY PISSED HEAVILY ARMED* and a white canvas apron tied over his black jeans. A burly Army vet, Bob has gingery hair and furry red brows that meet like two antagonistic wooly caterpillars over his thick red nose. He wears a tattooed broken heart on one thick forearm and a coiled snake on the other. He and Bud live in a single-wide north of town.

"Hey, China," he called over the Wurlitzer and the ESPN game. "Good to see you."

At the bar, a couple of guys' heads turned. The bald head belonged to Jake Robinson from the feed store where we buy Caitie's chicken pellets, the pony-tailed head to Lyle Vargas, from Purley's Tires next door. Lyle recently sold Ruby and me two new rear tires for Big Red Mama, our shop van, while Ruby flirted with him outrageously. Both guys raised their hands in greeting, and Lyle patted the empty stool next to him with a welcoming grin.

This is odd to say, since I'm a married girl and don't hang out with the guys, but Beans' is a kind of refuge for me. I needed that just now, and its down-home comfort settled across my shoulders like a much-loved ratty old sweater that smelled of tobacco smoke and beer and hot frying grease. I shook my head and smiled my thanks to Lyle, lifted my laptop case to signify that I would be occupied, and pointed to a table in the back corner.

"Wine," I mouthed to Bob, who couldn't hear me over the TV crowd's bases-loaded roar. I held up one finger. "Red."

Bob nodded and winked. "Comin' up," he mouthed.

Jessica wasn't due for a while, and I thought I'd use the time to peek into Kelly's files. So I headed for my favorite table at the rear of the large room, sat down with my back to the wall, and took out my laptop. I was booting it up as Bob arrived with my wine, a red plastic bowl of warm tortilla chips, and a dish of superhot salsa.

He set the food down. "Meetin' somebody, or are you all by your lonesome tonight?" Bud was with him, and the dog put his golden muzzle on my jeans-clad thigh and grinned up at me. Bud and I are old friends.

"A friend will be along in a little while. We'll be having supper." I reached down and scratched Bud between his ears. "How ya doin', old buddy?" Bud wagged his tail fervently.

"He's great," Bob said, smiling down at the dog. "He caught an armadillo the other evening. Couldn't quite figure out what to do with him, though. Didn't have a can opener, so he couldn't eat him—finally decided he'd better let him go." He laughed loudly, then leaned closer. I caught a strong whiff of beer and garlic. "Understand that McQuaid is headed across the border tonight, into Juárez. You've got one brave hubby there, girl."

"Juárez?" I stared at him, taken aback, and my heart jumped into my throat. "*Tonight?* Where'd you hear that?"

Juárez is on the other side of the Rio Grande, opposite El Paso, in the state of Chihuahua. The two cities are so close that you can sit on a bench in Ascarate Park in El Paso and watch a woman hanging her family's washing on a bare Juárez hillside. Juárez had been at the heart of the so-called narco war of a few years ago, when more than eleven thousand people were murdered in and around the city in the

Blood Orange

space of thirty-six months. Its reputation as a crime center has almost completely strangled American tourist traffic.

He straightened. "Blackie and McQuaid were talking at the bar the other evening. What I heard was that they were going out to El Paso together on a job for the Oil Field Theft Task Force. They expected to cross over into Juárez and see what they could find out about what's going on down there." He frowned at my look of surprise. "Why? Is it supposed to be a secret? Are they"—he bent over again and dropped his voice to a whisper—"undercover?" He straightened up with a gleeful look. "I'll bet that's it, ain't it? They're undercover! Prob'ly connecting with some of them cartel guys. Making some sort of deal."

"It's possible," I said slowly, not wanting him to know that everybody in town seemed to know about McQuaid's job—everybody but me. "But I don't think so. Undercover, I mean."

Bob's question gave me something more to worry about, though. Surely McQuaid and Blackie weren't going to try to infiltrate one of the cartels. That would ratchet up the danger a couple hundred percent. I shivered.

Bob grinned, showing one broken tooth. "I told those boys I'd be glad to go with them sometime, when they pick up a job that could maybe give 'em some trouble." He flexed a bicep, showing me his bulging muscle. "I could back 'em up. I'm a black belt—damned good marksman, too." He tilted his head, a faraway look in his eyes, as if he were imagining himself riding shotgun alongside McQuaid and Blackie, through a dark canyon with a potential sniper behind every boulder.

"I like runnin' Beans', y'know?" he went on in a reflective tone. "Great folks, decent living, got my dog and my trailer, even got me a girlfriend. But every so often, a man yearns to get out there and mix it up with the bad guys, like we did

167

back in the old days, in the army. Y'know how it is?" He refocused his eyes and dropped a hammy hand on my shoulder. "Well, maybe you don't, since you're a girl. Things are prob'ly diff'rent with you. But McQuaid understands. That's why he liked bein' a cop. And now that he ain't, he misses the danger, same way I do. You tell him for me, China—I'm his boy in a tight spot. He needs me, all he has to do is say the word."

"Thank you," I said, reaching for my wine. "I will."

You tell him for me, China—I'm his boy. Bob's words stayed with me after he walked away. A new idea was coming to me: that McQuaid had left me in the dark out of kindness, wanting to spare me from being worried or afraid. A misplaced kindness, yes. But maybe he would have told me about his work for the task force if I'd been a little more open to the kind of jobs he took, or been a little more of a cheerleader. Yes, I'm a worrywart. And yes, I *hate* the idea that he might be putting himself in danger. But I'll always be his girl in a tight spot. Always. I need to tell him that.

But right now, there was something else I needed to do, and I wanted to get into it before Jessica arrived. I inserted Kelly's thumb drive, brought up her four files ("Pecan Springs," "Seguin," "Lufkin," and "Notes"), and opened the first one.

The Pecan Springs file was captioned "Pecan Springs Community Hospice Patient Records." It was a fairly straightforward listing of patients' names and addresses; dates of admission; dates of termination (with categories for death, discharge, and transfer); names of certifying physicians; and various codes for physical condition and treatment. There were also names and contact information for family members. At a glance, it looked as if the listing spanned at least two years, maybe more, and included both current and discharged patients. I scrolled through the file from beginning to end. Several dozen or so of the names were highlighted in yellow, a couple of dozen were highlighted in pink, and a lesser number in blue.

The files for Seguin and Lufkin, the other two towns that the hospice served, had identical formats, with fewer patient listings—understandably, since the towns are much smaller. Each file had maybe a couple of dozen entries highlighted in yellow, a smaller number in pink. Scanning the entries in all three files, I could see that these records had been updated the previous Friday, which was a surprise, since I distinctly remembered Janet Parker telling me that Kelly had left the hospice a few weeks before.

Which made me wonder just when and under what circumstances Kelly had created these files. I went back to the main page, clicked on the "File" tab, and looked at "Properties." I was even more surprised to see that the file I was looking at had been copied at 11:42 p.m. on Saturday. Saturday *night*? Wasn't that a little unusual?

No, it was more than unusual—it was downright strange. Why in the world would Kelly be copying hospice patient records at nearly midnight on a Saturday night? But the instant I asked that question, I knew the answer. She did it at night because she didn't want anybody to know she was doing it.

But why would she want to do it at all? What was she getting at here? I opened the "Notes" file, hoping to find an answer. But there were only three text entries, numbered, and several hyperlinks to articles on the Internet. The text entries looked like a simple description of the highlighting in the files:

1. Pink: overstays
2. Yellow: potentially unqualified patients (check certifying doctors and signatures)
3. Blue: unnecessary general inpatient care?

Okay, that was helpful, sort of—except that I didn't understand the significance of *overstays* in the first item. Why did the length of the stay matter? In the second item, the word *unqualified*, which Kelly had mentioned on the telephone, still had me stumped. And the third item was a total mystery.

I picked up a tortilla chip but passed on Bob's salsa (it's hot enough to melt tonsils). Maybe the links would help. Bob gives his regular customers passwords so we can use his Wi-Fi. I logged in, clicked on the first link, and brought up an article entitled "Medicare Pays Billions to Cheating Hospice Firms." So while the Sons of the Pioneers sang "Cool Water" and "Empty Saddles," I got a quick lesson in the services that hospices offer—and ways that hospices are cheating Medicare.

According to the writer, hospice care provides medical services, emotional support, and spiritual resources for people who are in the last six months of a terminal illness, and their families. They offer care in the patient's or caregiver's home or in a hospice center, nursing home, or hospital. For these services, the hospice receives a standard "reimbursement." This was $172 a day when the article was written, and up to four times more if patients qualified for a stay in a treatment facility. They get this money whether the patient is visited daily, once a week, or even less often.

It turns out, though, that some hospices cheat by admitting "unqualified patients"—people who are not only *not* knocking on death's door but are healthy enough to walk several miles a day or go out to dinner or attend a grandson's wedding. (The writer offered several eyebrow-raising examples, such as the "terminally ill" patient who was photographed shopping for a hunting rifle. The guy had been "qualified" by a doctor who received a kickback for his referral.)

Hospices also cheat by claiming the Medicare reimbursement for patients who live longer than six months. In one case, for instance, a hospice billed Medicare nearly five thousand dollars a month for weekly one-hour visits to a "terminal" patient—for over two years. Other hospices fraudulently billed Medicare for bogus "general inpatient care" at a hospital or other facility, to the tune of nearly seven hundred dollars a day. And still other hospices were facing criminal prosecution for submitting documents with stolen Social Security numbers, forged doctors' signatures, and fake patient histories. Obviously, Medicare fraud was a booming business. And it paid off big-time.

Ah. So that's what this was all about—or some of it, at least. By the time I finished reading, I thought I understood what Kelly had uncovered, and I had a fairly clear idea what kind of whistle she had been planning to blow, and on whom.

And then I thought of something else. I brought up my browser, searched for the Pecan Springs Community Hospice, and found its website—a very attractive one, with a montage of photographs of appealing patients and helpful nurses in pleasant settings, all wearing pleasant smiles. But I was looking for something more, something very specific. I clicked on the "About Us" tab and brought up the names of an advisory board, a dozen of them, as well as the hospice's owner and manager, Marla Blake, and the physician "team," three local doctors: Cynthia Harris, Christopher Burgess, and Gene Gulling.

As it happened, a year or so ago, I had met Christopher Burgess, a charming young man, tall, dark, with an angular face, a dimple in his chin, and a wicked grin. He had one arm in a sling—a hang-gliding accident, he said. We had met at the refreshment table at a Friends of the Library fund-raiser, and when he'd found out who I was and what I did for a living, he'd asked me several questions about medicinal herbs. We'd gotten into a conversation about opium poppies—an interesting topic for a casual chat.

And I knew someone else on that page. Charles Lipman was a member of the advisory board.

I sat back, reflecting. *This* was his conflict of interest, or a piece of it. There might be more, of course. The hospice was a for-profit organization. Was he a behind-the-scenes investor, too? Did his law firm represent the hospice? But even if he was just an advisory board member and nothing else, that was probably enough right there to require him to refuse to take Kelly's whistle-blower case. And once again, reluctantly, I thought of Charlie's old Dodge pickup, his burnt-orange pickup. I hated to say it, but Charlie had been known to drink and drive. Had he—

"Hey, China. Sorry to be a little late. I got caught by the telephone just as I was leaving."

I looked up to see Jessica Nelson, a frosty margarita in her hand. "Hey, Jessica," I said, and closed the files, then closed my laptop. "Thanks for meeting me."

"Well, I'm intrigued," Jessica said, pulling out a chair and sitting down. In her mid-twenties, she is a petite young woman with boy-cut blond hair and freckles, an easygoing manner, and a soft Southern voice that's at odds with the watchful, intent expression in her brown eyes. She was wearing jeans, a University of Texas sweatshirt, and white sneakers. She pushed up her sweatshirt sleeves and folded her forearms on the table.

"I want to know how you think we might work together on this thing, China. But before we get to that, I've just been on the phone with a friend who works in the ER, over at the hospital. The officials are mum, as usual, but my friend says that Kelly Kaufman is still on life support."

Bless energetic reporters with friends in the ER. I leaned forward. "How is she?"

Jessica shook her head, her expression sober. "It's looking grim, I'm afraid. There's been no measurable brain activity since an hour or two after she was brought in. When her mother gets here from out of town and there's a little time to say good-bye, she will likely be taken off life support. Barring a miracle, of course."

"It's so sad," I said, remembering the lively young woman who had rented my cottage, ready to begin a new life on her own.

"Yes." Jessica sighed. "Life is fragile." Another shake of her head. "That's a cliché, but it's true. And when something like this happens, all we can think of are clichés. There's just never any new or striking way to say how sorry we are."

Bob Godwin appeared at the table, order book in hand. "What'll you ladies have tonight?"

I didn't need a menu. "Cabrito fajitas for me," I said. "And a go-box." I wouldn't be able to eat the whole plateful, but I could take the rest of it home.

"Tortilla soup," Jessica said. "But cut the cilantro," she added sternly. "If there's cilantro in it, it goes back to the kitchen."

"Yes, ma'am," Bob said, looking offended. He made a couple of notes on his order pad and left.

"Woman after my own heart," I said. I am *not* a fan of cilantro, and Bob's cooks seem to think that tortilla soup isn't perfect without a hefty dressing of chopped cilantro on top. "Somebody told me the other day that I should try a cilantro margarita," I added. "I thought it sounded unspeakably bad."

"Amen to *that*," Jessica said emphatically. She picked up her margarita glass, licked salt off the rim, and glanced at the closed laptop on the table. "You've been doing some research. On the Kaufman case?"

I waggled my hand in a maybe-yes, maybe-no gesture.

Jessica tilted her head, frowning. "Well, I have one more thing to tell you about Kaufman. But then you're not hearing another word from me until I hear something from you. Something I don't already know." She narrowed her eyes. "Deal?"

"Deal," I said promptly, since I already had that something in mind. "What's your one more thing?"

"I checked with one of my informants at the police department. The cops are now saying that the van Kelly was driving was definitely struck from behind. The paint flecks on the van itself aren't quite large enough for analysis, but Sheila sent a tech out to the scene of the crash. He prowled around and picked up several larger chips of paint, which means that they may be able to identify the make, model, and year of the vehicle that hit her. He even found a couple of shards of glass, maybe from a broken headlight. They may have come from an earlier wreck, though."

"Interesting," I said, "but circumstantial." The prosecutor was going to need much more than that to make a case that a good defense attorney couldn't knock down. That is, assuming that the cops were able to locate the vehicle and its driver, which was certainly no slam dunk.

"Yeah. Circumstantial. Nevertheless . . ." She took another sip of her margarita and pulled the basket of chips toward her. "Your turn."

I paused for dramatic effect, holding her gaze. "When Kelly telephoned me last night," I said at last, "she said she wanted to talk to me about a murder."

I thought that would get her attention. Jessica's eyes opened wide. She stopped in mid-motion, her hand poised over the basket of chips. "She *did*? Omigod! What else did she say? What—"

"Whoa." I held up my hand. "That's all she said. We didn't

get to have that conversation, remember? She was on her way to my house when the accident happened."

"It was no accident," Jessica said grimly. She picked up a chip and dipped it into the salsa. "Kelly had a story to tell and somebody didn't want her to tell it."

"Granted," I said, "although it was a pretty clumsy effort, wouldn't you say? Maybe even opportunistic. If you're serious about shutting somebody up, there are more definitive ways to make sure it happens." I helped myself to a chip. "But that's not the point, at least at the moment. The point is that I *don't* know what 'murder' she was talking about—or even if there was one. That's where you come in."

"I do?" Jessica's eyes were watering from the superhot salsa. She took a big gulp of her margarita. "That's good to hear. What do I do?"

"You're a kick-ass researcher." It wasn't an idle compliment. Jessica possesses the bulldog tenacity that is the hallmark of all dedicated researchers—and of truly good investigative reporters. She never stops digging until she gets answers. I added, "And you have easy access to information from the *Enterprise* morgue."

That was a big thing. Given what I was after, I would have to do lots of online searches, and they'd be hit-and-miss. Jessica could get into the back issues of the newspaper through the in-house *Enterprise* computer files.

She nodded eagerly. "Both true. What do you need?"

Carefully, I went through what I wanted her to do and how I thought she might go about it, stressing the need to keep everything as confidential as possible. By the time I was finished, a large serving of fajitas, flour tortillas, fixings, and a dish of fragrant black beans was in front of me. I picked up a warm flour tortilla, laid it flat on my clean plate, then added a streak of guacamole down the center, with a strip of sour cream alongside, just two-thirds the length of the tortilla.

Jessica was dipping her spoon into a bowl of tortilla soup—with *no* cilantro—and still thinking about her assignment. "I'll be glad to see what I can do." She gave me a straight, hard look. "As long as you guarantee that I'll get an exclusive."

I had been thinking about this. I needed to protect Kelly's rights as a whistle-blower and make sure that her evidence was preserved for presentation to the court, where it would be sealed—if the case got that far, that is. But a murder—assuming there was one—was a criminal matter, and a different thing entirely. That was where Jessica could help. And that was where she could earn the right to the story.

"Yes," I said, "you can have an exclusive on this part of the case. If you're able to dig up the murder that Kelly was talking about—assuming there *was* one, of course—you'll get the story." I looked up at her. "You don't have to figure out whodunit," I added. "All I need is the victim's name and circumstances."

To my fajita, I added a couple of thin slices of cabrito and a generous spoonful of salsa borracha, then the onions and the cheese, just enough of each, and finally a strip of green pepper. Then I folded the bottom up and sides over, constructing a tidy, ready-to-eat package, guaranteed not to drip.

Jessica is sharp. Frowning, she went back to her soup. "*This part* of the case?" she asked thoughtfully. "You mean, there's another part?"

"Yes, but that's not part of the deal. And no, I can't tell you why. At least, not yet. I will when I can. I promise." I bit into my fajita, closed my eyes, and chewed. It was wonderful. After a moment, I opened my eyes. "For Pete's sake, Jess. Isn't murder enough to move you?"

She had to chuckle at that. "Okay. You're on. I'll get back to you with a progress report as soon as I've done enough research to know where we are. And I'll wait—impatiently—to learn the other part of the story. How's that?"

"That works," I said. Holding my fajita in my left hand (rule number one when you're eating a fajita: never put it down, or it will come apart and you'll have to reconstruct), I began on my beans, which were also terrific. Both of us fell silent as we worked on our food.

Silent, that is, until my phone went off, and every head in the room swiveled toward me. Reddening with embarrassment, I grabbed for it. If it was McQuaid—

But it was only a nuisance call, and I clicked off immediately with a mutter.

"What's with the ringtone?" Jessica asked curiously. "It is *fierce.*"

"Brian put it on for a joke," I said. "I can't figure out how to delete it. I'm hoping he can do it when he gets home this weekend."

"That's easy," she said, reaching for it. "I'll show you." But after a moment, she frowned and handed it back. "I can't get it off, either. Hope it's not some sort of malware."

We went back to our food until, finally, I pushed my plate away. "I think I'll never eat again," I said. Then I picked up the go-box. "But just in case I'm hungry tomorrow . . ."

We didn't linger after we finished our meal. Bud arrived promptly with the check. We put our credit cards into his leather saddlebag and completed the transaction when he trotted back to the table. For a tail-wagging tip, I gave him the bit of cabrito I had saved on my plate and an extra pat on the head. I waved good-bye to Bob as we left and went out into the April evening. The sun would be setting in another ten minutes, but the sky was still light and the air was scented with spring. Across the street, a band at the Old Fire House was just getting warmed up for the night. The place is a hangout for the kids from CTSU, and they have live music almost every night.

Jessica's blue Volt was parked next to my Toyota in the lot. "Headed home?" she asked as we reached our cars.

I looked down at my watch. It was just seven thirty. Winchester was good for another hour, and Caitie wouldn't be home until nine. "Yes, but maybe not right away," I replied. "You?"

She grinned as she got into her car. "I've got a research project to get started on. I'm going back to the *Enterprise*. Don't go to bed early. If I find something interesting, I'll call you."

In my car, I pulled up Lara Metcalf's number on my cell and phoned her. I caught her just as she was leaving Kelly's mother in her daughter's hospital room. They were saying a final good-bye before Kelly was taken into surgery for organ donation.

"Oh, it's just so awful, China," Lara said, in tears. "The brain stem tests confirmed that there's been no brain activity at all for over eighteen hours. It's heartbreaking."

"Lara, I'm so, so sorry." I took a deep breath. "How's her mom?"

"Trying to be brave, but not carrying it off very well. And Rich, too. He seems terribly broken up. And, of course, it's worse because, as her husband, he's the one who has to give the final order." She sighed. "You know, if this hadn't happened, I believe they might have gotten back together again. In spite of everything, Kelly still loved Rich. She wasn't the one who wanted the divorce, and I believe, down deep in my heart, that Rich didn't, either. If it hadn't been for the other woman—" She stopped, and I heard her blow her nose. "Well, the less said about that, the better. It's all water under the bridge. There's nothing to be done about it now."

I thought of Ramona, the other woman, and remembered

once again that I was her alibi for the time of Kelly's car wreck. But I wasn't going to say a word about that to Lara. I sat back in the seat, thinking quickly.

Lara's sad news, clad in the utter finality of death, changed things substantially. The records I had on my computer were Kelly's, the documentation for a whistle-blower case that had the potential for a substantial reward if she had prevailed. But it might also be important evidence in a criminal case. That's where this thing seemed headed now.

I said, "Listen, Lara. I wonder if we could put our heads together for ten or fifteen minutes. There's something I want to show you. I'm headed home, but I could stop at the hospital if you're going to be there. It's on my way."

"I'll be here until Kelly's mother is ready to leave," she said. Then, more hopefully: "What do you want to show me? Have you learned something?"

"You'll understand when you see it," I said. At least, I hoped she would. "Where can we meet?"

"Kelly is in Intensive Care, in the first-floor wing. I told her mother I'd wait for her in the lounge at the south end of the main corridor. Do you know where that is?"

"I do," I said. "I'll see you there in about ten minutes." I clicked off the call and sat there, thinking of Kelly, remembering the last time I had seen her, bright and full of life. And now—

I turned the key in the ignition. And now that lovely young woman was dead, and the thought that her death might profit a killer was like sharp, hot acid at the back of my throat.

Chapter Twelve

The familiar marigold (*Tagetes* sp.) has a rich history. The original wild marigolds of Mexico (*T. erecta*, often called African marigolds) grow three to four feet high, with large orange flowers streaked with red. For the Aztecs, who practiced ritual human sacrifice, the orange marigold was *flor de muerto*, the flower of death. The streaks of red in the blossoms symbolized blood, while the brilliant orange color represented the House of the Sun, where sacrificial victims spent the afterlife.

In today's Mexico, the marigold is a central symbol in the *Dia de los Muertos* (Day of the Dead). In the rituals of this ancient celebration, the scent of the flower and its bright orange color are thought to guide the spirits of the dead to the family's altar, where they can rejoin the living.

China Bayles
"The *Dia de los Muertos*"
Pecan Springs Enterprise

The Adams County Hospital is in the process of adding a new wing. The project has been under construction for the past six months or so, and a big section of the main parking lot is closed off. I managed to find a space within walking distance, shouldered my laptop case and my purse, and set off.

The two-story hospital is built of red brick and set back from the street behind a sweeping lawn and a row of beautiful old live oaks. Located just a half block from the Pecan River, the old building has a mannerly, gracious look about it, the way hospitals used to look in decades past. For a while, there was talk of constructing a shiny new hospital on I-35, complete with every gizmo known to modern medicine. But as medical facilities in Austin and San Antonio expanded, competing with them began to seem less like a good idea, and wiser heads prevailed. The hospital board compromised by adding a second wing on the west side of the main building to match the utilitarian one-story wing that angles off to the east. There will be enough beds to suit the community's needs without going broke in the process.

I stopped at the nurses' station at the entrance to the wing. Helen Berger, a friend and fellow member of the herb guild, was on duty, in maroon scrubs with her hair pinned up. She looked up from her work and saw me.

"Hello, China. Haven't seen you here for quite a while."

"Since Caitie had her tonsils out last summer," I replied, with a little smile. "Thanks for being so sweet to her." Caitie had been kept overnight, and with Helen's help, we'd made a little party for her with balloons, party hats, and ice cream.

"Caitie's a lovely little girl. And so talented—her violin, I mean. My daughter tells me that my grandson, Kevin, has quite a crush on her."

A boy has a crush on my Caitie? I wanted to whimper,

"Oh, no, I'm not ready for this!" But I managed to gulp back the words, and say, "Kevin is your grandson?" in something like well-behaved surprise. "Congratulations to him, by the way," I added. "Caitie tells me that he's been promoted to concertmaster."

"Yes, for now, at least. He's afraid Caitie will snatch it back." Helen chuckled. "Actually, I was glad to hear that. Kevin is inclined to be lazy. A little competition from Caitie might push him to try harder—test himself. Kids need that sometimes." She glanced at the clock. "Visiting hours are just ending. Did you want to see one of our patients?"

"I'm meeting a friend of Kelly Kaufman's in the lounge. Lara Metcalf." I gave her a crooked smile, and added lightly, "Do I need a hall pass?"

Helen lifted an eyebrow, and said, "Of course not." Then she added soberly, "Such a terrible, terrible thing, Kelly's accident. She was a wonderful nurse, you know. Everyone who's had any experience with the hospice speaks very highly of her. We're all in a state of shock."

I heard the past tense and regretted my flip question about the hall pass. "Kelly's . . . gone, then?" I asked hesitantly.

Helen nodded, pressing her lips together. "She was removed from life support just a few moments ago. I'm afraid there was never any question, China. Her injuries were just too severe."

"Thank you," I said, and turned away. There was nothing more I could say.

The overhead fluorescents cast an unfriendly glare on the polished floor of the long, gray-painted hallway. Since visiting hours were over, it was deserted, and most of the doors were closed. And then, halfway down the hall, one of them opened and a woman came out, turned, and began walking toward me. I didn't recognize her until we were almost face-to-face. It was Marla Blake, whom I hadn't seen since we worked together on a couple of projects for the Friends of the Library.

"China Bayles, isn't it?" she said, stopping. She was dressed in a chic gray jogging suit, with a nifty little University of Texas emblem on the zipper top and the word *Longhorns* striped vertically on her right leg, expensive-looking orange-and-white running shoes, and a fanny pack. She was wearing her dark hair differently—a sleek, short bob with bangs that looked almost like a wig—and she'd lost quite a lot of weight since I last saw her. Her eyes were dark and shadowed and her cheekbones were even more clearly defined in her angular face, and there was a gaunt look about her. I wondered if she had been ill. But she still held her mouth with the firm determination I remembered from our time together, and she wore the same impatient expression, as though she were on her way somewhere, on some sort of important mission, and disliked being interrupted before she got there. She had always been wound tight with a nervous energy. Tonight, she seemed wound even tighter.

"Yes, it's China," I said. "Hello, Marla."

"Goodness, how long has it been since we've seen each other?" she asked, wrinkling her forehead as if she were checking an internal calendar. "A year? Two?"

"Three," I replied, "since Friends of the Library." I added the first thing that came to my mind. "You stopped in to see Kelly Kaufman?"

An almost imperceptible shadow crossed her face, and she nodded shortly. "I walk along the river in the evenings, so I dropped in for a moment to speak to her mother and her husband. You're a friend?" She didn't wait for my answer. "Such a sad, sad thing. Kelly worked for me at the hospice, as I'm sure you know. She was an excellent nurse. We all just loved her."

"That's what I've heard," I replied, remembering that

Janet Parker had told me that the staff was dismayed when Kelly left—or was let go. Which was it? "But she had left the hospice, hadn't she? I heard that she was working at the Madison Clinic."

Marla's mouth tightened, and she slid me a glance that let me know that I was speaking out of turn. "Well, everyone needs to grow and move forward," she said briskly. "She saw an opportunity and took it, and I wished her well." She gave a heavy sigh. "And now this terrible accident, ending such a promising life . . ." Her voice trailed away and she shook her head. "We'll all miss her."

"Yes," I said. "We will." And then there was nothing more to say. Awkwardly, I pointed to the lounge at the end of the hall, where I could see Lara waiting. "Excuse me, but I'm meeting someone. Lara Metcalf," I added, and then, a half breath later, "She used to work at the hospice too, I understand."

An unreadable expression flickered across Marla's face. "Oh, yes. Lara." Her tone was just short of dismissive, but she managed a brittle smile. "Give her my best. So nice to have seen you, China."

"Yes, nice," I replied. I went forward down the long corridor to the lounge, wondering what Lara had done to get crosswise of Marla. I was also thinking of the files on the laptop I carried over my shoulder and wondering how and where Marla might fit into the picture that was beginning to emerge.

The lounge was filled with furniture as utilitarian as the wing itself. A row of windows looked out across a curving bed of rosemary and salvia, interplanted with various species of marigolds. In the gathering dusk, their bright orange and yellow blossoms were like coins of fallen sunshine. A cheerful assemblage of children's crayon drawings was taped to one plaster wall over a lighted aquarium filled with colorful fish swimming lazily through an underwater jungle of green plants. A coffeemaker and cups sat on a shelf, a soft-drink machine hummed busily in one corner, and a large-screen TV set, muted, displayed a CNN news feature.

Lara was slumped on one of the plastic couches facing the television set, a tissue clutched in one hand. She was dressed in jeans, a blue-and-white striped top, and a blue knitted cardigan. Her eyes were red and swollen.

"Hello, China." She sounded weary. "I saw you talking to Marla Blake just now. Did she tell you that Kelly was taken off life support a little bit ago?"

"Helen Berger told me," I said. "I'm very sorry." I began to swing my laptop case off my shoulder, then stopped. "This has been awfully rough on you, Lara. Maybe you don't feel like talking right now, or you'd rather go back to Kelly's room. We can put this off until tomorrow if you like."

She sighed. "Thank you, but no. Rich and her mother are still with her, and that's as it should be. And I need to wait until Kelly's mom is ready to go. I'm taking her to her motel. So let's do it now. What's on your mind?"

I sat down beside Lara, unzipped the case, and took out my laptop. "You know that thumb drive you gave me this afternoon?" I booted up the computer. "I'd like you to see what's on it and tell me what you think."

She fished in her purse, found another tissue, and blew her nose. "Sure, if I can. I'm curious, anyway."

Kelly's folders came up on the laptop monitor, and I turned it so that Lara could see. "These computer files were created last Saturday night," I said. "They appear to be patient records for the Pecan Springs Community Hospice, for all three locations: Pecan Springs, Lufkin, and Seguin."

"Really?" Lara said. "Gosh. I wonder how Kelly got these. And why."

"Good question," I said, and opened the Pecan Springs file.

"I recognize the format," Lara said thoughtfully. "It's the system that Marla Blake set up after she took over the hospice. It wasn't operating very efficiently at the time, and the old records were on an obsolete machine in a format that couldn't be upgraded easily. All of us knew something had to be done. We were glad when Marla got the new system up and running."

"And that was when?"

"She bought the hospice about three years ago, I think." She paused, frowning. "Yes. Three years. We used the old system for a year or so, until she set up her records." She tilted her head, frowning. "Hey, wait a minute, China. Did you say that these files were created last *Saturday night*? That can't be right. Are you sure?"

I clicked on the "File" tab, then "Info," and brought up "Properties." I pointed to the entry marked "Created." "See? Saturday, 11:42 p.m."

"Gosh," Lara said in a wondering tone. "That is *weird*."

"Yes. Not exactly office hours. So, first off, I'm wondering how Kelly managed to get these records. Could she have logged into the hospice records from a remote location outside the office?" As I asked that question, I realized that Kelly had rented my cottage on Friday, so her "remote location" would have been *my* B and B.

But Lara was shaking her head. "I don't think so, China. Marla made a big thing about setting up her record system on an office computer that wasn't tied to the Internet. She was really freaky about security—somebody hacking into the system and stealing patient identities. So if Kelly actually created these files on Saturday night, she would have to have *been* there. In the office, I mean. Working on the office computer." She shook her head. "Which doesn't exactly make sense. I mean, the office has an alarm. She had to let

186

herself in, disarm it, and work in the dark." She shivered. "It's *creepy*."

"Do you know if she had a key to the office?"

"Well, sure," Lara said. "When she was working there, she had a key. All the nurses had keys. There's a supply room stocked with anything the patients might need—saline solution, catheter irrigation kits, test strips for the blood tests for people on blood thinners, that sort of thing. Patients don't get charged for supplies or equipment, since the hospice reimbursement from Medicare and insurance is supposed to include that cost. Big things like electric beds and commodes and oxygen equipment and wheelchairs—we had a contract with a supplier in Dallas for stuff like that."

"What about drugs?"

She looked uncomfortable. "Oh, yes, drugs. Well, most of the time, the docs prescribed what was necessary, and the pharmacy delivered it to the patient. Whatever we had at the office was kept in a locked drawer in the supply room. Mostly what we had was lorazepam, for anxiety. And maybe morphine, for pain."

"Morphine? But that's a controlled substance."

"Well, yes." She shifted, frowning. "We weren't supposed to have drugs. We would let the doc know when a patient ran out of something. The doc wrote the prescription and faxed it to the pharmacy for the family to pick up. But sometimes the family didn't tell us they were running out, so to make sure we could help our patients in an emergency, we kept a small stash in a locked drawer in the supply room at the office." She chuckled. "Kelly and I used to joke that what we really needed was medical marijuana, which is so much better than prescription drugs and painkillers. Last I heard, it was legal in twenty-three states." She made a face. "But not in Texas, of course."

"There's actually quite a bit of underground support for it," I said. "A bill to legalize medical cannabis was introduced a couple of years ago. But it's stuck in legislative committee—it'll probably be there for a long time."

She nodded. "Well, even Texas will approve it eventually. When it does, you should go into the business."

I winced at the thought of all the red tape the state legislature would wrap around the use of medical pot. Much better left to people who deal only in marijuana, I thought.

"But back to the keys," I said. "Did you turn yours in when you quit working at the hospice?"

"Yes, I did. Marla Blake was pretty strict about that." She slid me a half-guilty glance. "But most of the nurses made copies, in case we lost the ones Marla gave us. I kept mine. I'll bet Kelly did, too."

That made sense. One more question. "Are the on-call staff on the premises at night?"

"No." She shook her head. "The office opens at eight and closes at five. After hours and on weekends, the phone is picked up by an answering service. If one of the patients or a family member phones in with an urgent need for help or some sort of special care, the service pages the on-call triage nurse. She makes whatever arrangements are necessary."

I nodded. "Okay. So let's assume for the moment that Kelly kept a key, and that she let herself into the hospice office late Saturday night, when no one was there. She sat down at the office computer and copied the patient records onto a thumb drive." I pointed to the screen, which still displayed the properties. "According to the 'Last Modified' date and time, she worked on the file on Sunday, at 10:11 a.m. That must have been when she color coded some of the entries."

"Color coded?" Lara scrolled down the page. "Oh, yes, I see. Pink, blue, yellow. I wonder what it means."

"There's a key in the "Notes" file. She used pink to mark the records of patients who were in hospice care for longer than six months. She used yellow for 'potentially unqualified patients,' and blue for patients who got general inpatient care when she didn't think it was necessary."

"I see," Lara said slowly, still scrolling through the file, frowning in concentration. "You know, I've glanced at these records in the office, when one of the girls had the system up and I happened to walk past the desk. But I've never actually *looked* at them. As nurses, we didn't have access to them. It wasn't part of our job."

"You must have kept some sort of record of your visits, though. Didn't you?"

"Oh, sure. Paper-pencil reports on each visit." She put her finger on one of the columns. "We used codes like these, for patient condition and treatment. We had to turn in our reports at the end of the week. They're filed in folders labeled with the patients' names. Eventually, somebody on the clerical staff got around to transcribing our paper-pencil records into the computer. I suggested that the nurses should have iPads, so we could update the records automatically. But Marla said there wasn't enough money for that."

"It would be pretty expensive," I said.

"But it would pay for itself in time savings," Lara pointed out. "And probably cut down on transcription errors." She was hunched over, studying the file on the laptop. "This is really interesting, China. Kelly has put quite a lot of work into this color code. The overstays—the patients she's marked with pink—are pretty easy to spot, if you know what you're after. You can look at the admissions date, and if it's longer than six months ago and there's still no discharge, it's an overstay. But these others—especially the unqualified—I'm not sure how she came up with them. Maybe she knew them from visits or something."

Now we were getting somewhere. Lara knew the magic words.

"Discharge," I said. "Can you spell that out?"

"It goes like this." She pushed her lips in and out. "According to Medicare rules, patients are expected to die within six months of the date of admission. If they're still alive at the end of that time, they're supposed to be discharged by the hospice."

I looked back at the monitor. "Do you see any cases you recognize?"

"Sure. You can tell from this file which nurses were assigned to the case." She pointed to an entry. "See? *LaM?* That's me." She smiled. "I remember this guy. Ronald MacDonald, like the McDonald clown, only spelled differently. But there was nothing funny about him. He was a pain in the neck. He was so verbally abusive that Angie, our social worker, recommended that he be discharged for cause. Even the chaplain weighed in on that one."

"Chaplain?" I asked. "Sorry—this is all new to me. The hospice has a chaplain? And a social worker?"

"Yes. Angie Strickland was our social worker when I was there. Doug Vincent, a very nice man with seminary training, was the chaplain. Doug and Angie both tried to counsel Mac-Donald, until the old guy kicked both of them out. Even Doug—who always tries to see things from the patient's point of view—agreed that he should be discharged for cause. That's Medicare's term. It means that the patient was so uncooperative that we couldn't deliver our services."

"What happened? Was he discharged?"

"Uh-uh." Lara shook her head firmly. "Marla said no. She hates to lose patients, even those who misbehave. Or to put it more precisely, she hates to lose the reimbursement." She looked back at the file and traced the data line across the screen with her finger. "But I see she lost him anyway. He died—

finally—after a long overstay. I'll bet he's one patient who won't be missed."

I fastened on a detail. "Marla hates to lose patients?"

Lara raised an eyebrow. "Well, sure. At one hundred and seventy-two dollars a day, it pays to keep them enrolled for as long as possible."

"Ah," I said. "And I suppose it costs less to keep a patient than to add a new one, considering the set-up costs, book-keeping, and all that."

"Exactly," Lara said. "But a hospice has to keep new patients coming in to replace the ones who are discharged—through death or whatever. Hospice care is a service, but it's also a business. A profitable business, or Marla wouldn't be doing it."

"How profitable?" I asked.

She tapped a finger against the monitor. "Well, you can do the math. A hundred and seventy-two dollars times a hundred patients is over seventeen thousand dollars—a *day*. I heard Marla once say that the profit margin is around twelve percent, which means that the hospice is clearing over two thousand bucks a day for every hundred patients on the books."

"Wow," I said softly. "Two thousand dollars a *day*?"

"On just a hundred patients. So . . ." She let it dangle.

"So if there are two hundred active patients, the profit must amount to something like four thousand a day." I whistled softly. "That's one hundred twenty thousand dollars a month. *Profit*."

"Right." Lara said. "And if any of them have to go to a hospital for what's called 'general inpatient care'—say, if somebody falls and breaks a bone—the reimbursement shoots way up. It's nearly seven hundred dollars a day. Of course, the hospice has to pay the hospital out of that, but—"

"But the billing could be faked?" In fact, that had been

191

mentioned in the article I'd read. The patient stayed home, but the billing was changed to inpatient care.

She frowned. "Yes, but the hospital would have to be in on it. Which would make it more complicated. But doable, I guess, if somebody worked at it." She kept on scrolling through the file, making a little humming sound under her breath. "I'd have to study this for a while before I could tell you what Kelly must have been thinking when she copied these records. That might take some research. Fieldwork, I mean. Actually going out and checking on some of the cases she's marked 'unqualified.'"

There was that word again. "Unqualified," I said. "Who actually says whether a patient is qualified?"

"A personal physician has to report the diagnosis and say that the patient is facing death in six months. The hospice doc has to sign off on it. Then the patient is 'qualified,' according to Medicare." She looked back at the computer monitor. "I can probably tell you more after I've had a chance to take a close look at this. I kept my own personal notes while I was working for the hospice. I can check those."

"That would be great," I said. "How about if I email a copy of Kelly's files to your computer right now? Not just the Pecan Springs file, but the other two files, for the branches in Lufkin and Seguin, as well. When you get home tonight, or maybe tomorrow, you could go over them and let me know what you think."

"I can do that." Lara looked at me, her forehead puckered. "But I think I've already got a pretty good idea what Kelly was trying to do here. She—" She stopped, biting her lip.

"She *what*, Lara?"

She was silent for a moment, then said slowly, "Look, China. Hospices work under fairly strict Medicare rules. Owners and managers know what they are and what can happen if the rules are violated. Kelly had a reason for pulling these files and marking the records she thought were violations. She must have been thinking about . . ." She let her voice trail off.

I finished the sentence for her. "She was thinking about filing a whistle-blower lawsuit against the hospice, Lara. Two of the phone numbers you gave me this afternoon were Austin attorneys who specialize in that area of the law. Charlie Lipman couldn't take Kelly's case because he's on the hospice board, which was a conflict of interest. He may even be the hospice's lawyer."

"A lawsuit against the hospice." Lara's mouth tightened. "Yes, that's what I was coming to. That means a suit against Marla Blake, doesn't it?"

"Right. But others could be involved as well. Other owners, for example. Or staff who were directly responsible for the violations—and profited from them."

"Marla isn't the only owner," Lara said slowly. "One of . . . one of the doctors owns half of the business."

"Really? I saw that there are three doctors on the hospice medical staff. Which one is part owner?"

Lara was chewing her lower lip. "Marla's son."

I frowned. So this was a mother-son operation. That was unusual, and interesting. "I read the doctors' names on the website," I said, "but I don't remember one named Blake."

"His name is Burgess. Christopher Burgess. He's Marla's son by her first marriage."

"I've met him," I said, remembering our conversation at the Friends fund-raiser. "He's very good-looking. And charming, easy to talk to. I had no idea he was Marla Blake's son."

"Most people at the hospice don't know, either." Lara's voice had changed, taken on an edge. "Chris doesn't hang around the office much. But then, neither of the other two docs do. They come in every couple of weeks to review the new cases, but most of the time they communicate via email and fax."

Chris? It sounded as if Lara was on friendly terms with him. "How do *you* happen to know?" I asked. "That Dr. Burgess is Marla's son, I mean."

Her glance slid away, and she didn't answer immediately.

"This might be important," I said. The fact that she had brought the relationship up suggested that it was somehow significant. There was a backstory here, and I wanted to know it. "How is it that you happen to know that Burgess is Marla's son?"

She was slow to answer. After a moment, she replied half-reluctantly, "Because I was . . . involved with him. Before Matt and I got together, I mean."

"Involved," I said. "Romantically?"

She put up a hand and rubbed her cheek. Another silence, as if she was deciding how much to tell me. Then, slowly, she said, "In the beginning, I liked Chris a lot. He was sweet and fun, and I thought we might . . . well, I thought we might even get married." Her voice took on a defensive edge. "It would have been nice, you know? Marrying a doc with an established practice and plenty of income. It might sound crass to you, but I even thought that if I married Chris, I could quit work. I was a carhop in high school, I had a half dozen jobs in college, and I waited tables to put myself through nursing school. It sometimes seems as if I've been working my whole life." She gave me a questioning look, as if she was waiting for my objection or censure.

But I was more interested in why she *hadn't* married him than why she had wanted to. "But then?" I asked sympathetically, nudging her to tell more of the story. "Sounds like it didn't work out the way you thought. Was there a reason?"

"Yeah. There was." She sighed. "I found out that he was

in trouble with the Texas Medical Board. Which wouldn't have been enough, all by itself, to make me pull away. But when I put it together with some other things . . . Well, I just got cold feet. It wasn't for me. And then Matt came back into my life, and I knew that he was the one."

I'd had a few encounters with the medical board in my earlier incarnation as an attorney and had found that dealing with them was a challenge. They have a habit of circling the wagons, holding secret meetings, and making backdoor deals. The public can see the disciplinary action only after an investigation is final, and getting to that stage can take well over a year—if it happens at all. The investigations into complaints against doctors (and there are thousands every year) are carried out by other doctors, and doctors make up most of the board. Some cynical members of the Texas press have pointed out that when foxes guard the chicken coop, things don't usually end well. A doctor who is being investigated for harming a patient is free to continue to practice, and to harm others. And when the board actually *does* get around to disciplining a doctor, it's often just a slap on the wrist. He gets probation or a temporary suspension when his medical license should have been revoked.

I didn't want to sound as if I were cross-examining her, so I softened my tone. "So how did you happen to find out about Burgess' trouble with the medical board?"

With a certain reluctance, she replied, "Well, he said something that made me wonder. I don't remember exactly what it was, just a funny kind of comment. But later, I couldn't quite put it out of my mind. You know how those things are? So I went online and searched the medical board's disciplinary actions back three or four years. I found it."

"Found what? Was his license suspended?"

"Are you kidding?" Lara laughed shortly. "The board almost never does that. Instead, they put him on probation for a couple of years. He wasn't supposed to practice without another doctor's supervision, or prescribe narcotics or pain-killers. I guess it's okay for him to work in hospice, though. That's mostly where he works now. He's a palliative care doctor."

"Palliative care?"

"That's what it's called in hospice. The emphasis isn't on curing a patient, but on making a terminal patient comfortable through the end of life. There's a focus on symptom and pain management, and on alleviating stress for the patient and the family. Chris—Dr. Burgess—sometimes makes patient visits." She smiled a little. "That's how we happened to get together, you know. We both worked on the MacDonald case."

"Why was he suspended?" I asked. "Were the reasons posted?"

"Yes. There had been three—or maybe four, I can't remember—medical malpractice suits filed against him. But the thing they got him for—this was a couple of years before I knew him—was that he'd been writing prescriptions for painkillers for the woman he was living with, who had once been his patient. She was killed in a one-car crash, and when they did an autopsy, they found an elevated level of oxycodone in her blood. It was traced back to the prescriptions he'd been writing."

"Did you tell him what you knew about him?"

"No. Chris isn't . . . He's not the kind of person you can talk to about things like that. He is *very* self-confident, you know? He just kind of brushes criticism away. But I began to . . . well, wonder. So I went online and searched through the medical board's disciplinary records, and I found something from a later hearing that bothered me."

"For example?" I prompted.

This time, she was even slower to answer. But finally, she

took a deep breath, and said, "There were several allegations of sexual misconduct with patients. The hospital where he was working in Dallas apparently didn't report them to the police. Hospitals don't like negative publicity, you know. Co-workers cover up to keep from getting their department into trouble. And management will always believe a doctor over anybody else. But somebody at the hospital must have thought the allegations should be on his record, and they were sent to the medical board. That's where I found them."

"I see," I said. "And then what?"

"Well, I began to think about our relationship. He was . . . he was a rather aggressive lover, I guess you'd say. Rough, sometimes."

"That's what you meant when you said there were 'other things' that bothered you?"

She pressed her lips together as if she wasn't sure she should be telling me this. But after a moment, she nodded. "I didn't like it, you know, but I kind of accepted it, because I thought maybe the relationship was going someplace and I could get him to change. He could be very sweet when he wanted to be. But after a while it didn't seem okay. There seemed to be a lot of narcotics around his place. And when I put all that together with his probation and the allegations, I got uncomfortable. So I told him I couldn't see him anymore."

"How did he react?"

Her mouth twisted. "Let's just say it wasn't very pleasant. I was even a little afraid. He's the kind of guy who expects things to go the way *he* thinks they should go, and when they don't, he loses it. But after a few minutes, he would seem to get a grip, and everything was okay again." She paused, thinking. "Afterward, I realized I had seen him act that way before. I was glad when it was over."

"Did you ever talk to Kelly about any of this?"

Lara shook her head. "No. I didn't want anybody to know how foolish I'd been. And of course I didn't talk to Marla. I figured she already knew about the probation, and I certainly wasn't going to tell her about the rest of it—the personal stuff, I mean, about Chris and me. But I think he must have told her. Told her something, anyway. She began acting . . . well, a little hostile toward me. It made me uncomfortable."

I remembered the expression that had flickered across Marla's face when I mentioned Lara's name. "Is that why you left the hospice?"

"Yes. I didn't want to get teamed up with Chris on case assignments, and I didn't know what he might have told his mother. I quit and got a job over at the Madison Clinic right away, and for better pay, so I came out all right. I just wish that Kelly—" Her voice had a tremor in it, and she had to clear her throat before she could go on. "I don't know why I've told you this, China. It doesn't have anything to do with . . ." She gestured toward the files on the computer.

"You never know," I said softly. "It just might."

If she heard me, she didn't respond. She was squinting at the monitor screen again. Half under her breath, she said, "Kelly took a really big risk, sneaking into the office at midnight to copy these files. Do you think this might have something to do with that murder she was talking about?" She looked up at me, her eyes dark. "Or with her car wreck?"

"I think it could," I said. "But we won't know until we've looked at this stuff a little more closely." I hesitated. "She didn't tell you what she knew about the murder, and she didn't tell me. Do you think she might have told her husband?"

Lara thought about that for a moment. "I don't think so," she said. "She and Rich were barely talking about their marriage and the business they owned together—the brewery, I mean. I doubt very much that she would have said anything to him about her suspicions."

"Sounds logical," I said. I slanted her a look. "Do you happen to know if the cops have cleared him as a suspect in the car crash?"

She nodded. "Apparently. Turns out that he was at the brewery last night, with three other guys, one of them an off-duty police officer. They were together until the police called to tell him about Kelly's wreck." She took a deep breath. "Okay, China. Please go ahead and send Kelly's files to me. I'll go over them tonight after I get home."

I got her email address, attached the files, and hit the *Send* button. I glanced up at the clock and blinked when I saw how late it was.

"Hey. My daughter will be getting home soon, and our dog has probably written me off." I began zipping my laptop back into its case. "Call me when you've come to some conclusion about the files."

We stood, a little awkwardly, and Lara leaned forward and put her arms around me. "Thanks," she said, her voice muffled against my shoulder. "Thank you very much, China."

"For what?" I asked, returning her hug.

"For giving me something to think about besides what's happening in Kelly's hospital room. I was going crazy, sitting here, just waiting. Waiting for my best friend to die." After a moment, she stepped back, her voice intense. "Now I've got something to do, and it's not just busywork. It's something that Kelly started, for a reason. It was important to her, which makes it important to *me*. And I'm going to finish what she started." She reached out and gave my hand a hard squeeze. "Thank you, China." The tears were running down her cheeks, but she was smiling. "So, yes. I'll call you as soon as I've got something figured out."

"Good," I said, and returned the squeeze. I wasn't as confident as she was, and I was concerned. "But please don't mention Kelly's files to anybody, Lara. Not to her mother or her husband—not to anybody. If she was endangered by what she knew, you could be, too."

Lara's eyes got large. "You're right," she said soberly. "I won't say a word."

I drove home through the deepening dark, mulling over what Lara had told me. There were a lot of odd little bits of complicated information to process, but I was beginning to see a shape emerging out of the scattered confusion. I was grateful for Lara's help. Now, if Jessica could come up with one or two of the things I'd asked her to search for, we might be able to make some forward progress.

The puzzle was almost intriguing enough to blot out my worry about McQuaid, which was sharper now after talking to the guys at Beans'.

Almost enough. But not quite.

Chapter Thirteen

Not all botanical drinkables are alcoholic, of course. Drinks brewed from various herbs are drunk for their stimulant or relaxant properties, for medicinal purposes, or simply for their taste.

Stimulant drinks are brewed from coffee and tea plants as well as from herbs such as rosemary, guarana, ginseng, and yerba maté. If you're looking for a calming, relaxing bedtime tea, you have several good choices. My favorite: a blend of dried chamomile, hibiscus, and passionflower blossoms, with dried blackberry and peppermint leaves and orange peel for a citrusy flavor. Other options: lavender, lemon balm, skullcap.

China Bayles
"Botanical Drinkables"
Pecan Springs Enterprise

Winchester began barking with delight when he saw my headlights coming down the drive, and when I let him out of his dog run, he danced ahead of me on the path to the house. Yes, bassets can actually dance, although they're always a little embarrassed when they find themselves doing it and stop the minute they know someone's watching. Bassets are mindful of their dignity.

In the kitchen, I dished out Winchester's dog food and added a couple of chunks of cabrito and half a flour tortilla from the take-out box I'd brought home from Beans', as an apology for being late. When he was finished, Winchester looked up at me with mournful brown eyes, silently pleading for the rest of that tortilla so he wouldn't starve during the long, lonesome night ahead, when the refrigerator door was closed and all the snacks were put away on shelves he was too short to reach. Bassets are champion moochers.

"Oh, all right," I said, and dropped it on his plate. He scarfed it down and wagged a fervent thank-you with his stout, white-tipped tail, just as car tires crunched on the gravel drive. A moment later, Caitie ran into the kitchen, dropped her books and violin, grabbed a basket, and ran out again to pick up eggs and make sure that her girls were safely tucked into their skunk- and fox-proof coop for the night. Mr. P came down the stairs to inquire about the whereabouts of his dinner and was waiting beside the door when Caitie came back into the kitchen, carrying eight brown-shelled eggs in her basket.

"I'll take all of these, sweetie," I said. "I want to make some deviled eggs when your dad gets home."

"When will that be?" she asked. "Soon, I hope."

I took a deep breath. "I do, too," I said, keeping my voice level. I penciled a note on the pad we keep on the kitchen counter. Eight eggs times twenty cents an egg: $1.60. A little pricey compared to store-bought, but Caitie's eggs are in a different class altogether.

"How much do I have now?" she asked, getting a can of cat food out of the cupboard and a can opener out of the drawer. To Mr. P's loud meow, she said, "I'm hurrying as fast as I can. Just be a little patient."

I added $1.60 to $11.40. "Thirteen dollars even," I said.

Blood Orange

"Good," she said. "The girls need more laying pellets, and that's more than enough. Can we pick up a sack tomorrow?"

"Sure thing," I said. That's our deal with Caitie. We pay her for the eggs we eat, out of which she pays for her chicken feed. She sells extra eggs to the neighbors and keeps whatever she earns. During the summer, when there are extra *extra* eggs, she peddles them to the customers at the herb shop. Caitie has the soul of a musician and the mind of an entrepreneur. I have the feeling that whatever she does for a living when she's grown up, she'll always have plenty of pocket change.

I filled the teakettle at the sink. "Did you and Sharon have a nice evening?" I asked, putting the kettle on the stove.

"Boys." Caitie puffed out her breath as if she was short on patience. "Sharon lives across the street from Kevin. He heard us working on our concert piece and came over with his violin." She spooned Mr. P's supper into his dish. Winchester trotted over to watch and graciously offered to dispose of anything left in the can. "Not for puppies," she said, and Winchester gave a heavy sigh.

"Ah," I said. "Kevin." I wondered if she knew he had a crush on her. And then, belatedly, I wondered if she had gone home with Sharon tonight *because* she knew that Kevin lived across the street. After all, she is thirteen. "How did that work out?" I asked.

Caitie put Mr. P's dish on the floor. "Well, three violins is better than two when it comes to practice," she said judiciously. "And Kevin's not so bad when he's not showing off for Dr. Trevor or for the other boys. When he's by himself, he's kind of nice. Well, he was tonight, anyway." She bent over and gave Winchester a little push. "Winnie, this is *not* your supper. Go lie down in your basket."

Winchester was not in the mood to follow orders. He gave her a reproachful look, flopped down flat on the floor (the "flat basset" position, his I-am-not-moving-one-inch posture, with rear legs splayed and tail on the floor), and put his nose between his paws. The cat, wise to the ways of silly dogs, ignored him and gobbled his dinner.

"Does Kevin do that? Show off for Dr. Trevor, I mean." I got the tea out of the cupboard—my favorite home-crafted bedtime blend of chamomile, hibiscus, and passionflower blossoms, with blackberry and peppermint leaves and dried orange peel. I felt I needed it after my eventful evening. And then I thought of Kelly and I was ashamed of myself. *I* needed comforting when Kelly's mom was coping with the loss of her daughter? Death is the greatest finality, and losing a son or a daughter must be the hardest death to face.

"Kevin is the biggest show-off in the whole wide world," Caitie declared dramatically. "I told him he could get an Oscar for Best Show-off." She went to the fridge and poured herself a glass of milk. "I'm going upstairs to call Sharon."

"But you just left Sharon," I pointed out, spooning the loose tea into an infuser and dropping it into the two-cup china pot my mother had given me. "And it's almost bedtime."

Caitie put her head on one side. "Oh, Mom, please? It won't take long, I promise. I forgot to tell her something."

I thought of Kelly and Kelly's mom, and turned and gave my daughter a hard hug. "Okay. You can call Sharon, but use your cell, please. I'm expecting your dad to call. Don't forget to watch your minutes. And bedtime."

I ruffled her hair, gave her one more hug, and let her go. *Hoping* that McQuaid would call was more like it, actually. Hoping that he hadn't gone south across the border. Hoping that if he had, he had already come back north, all in one piece. Hoping that as soon as he could get a cell phone signal, he'd call. Hoping—

The phone rang, and I grabbed for it, feeling my heart jump into my throat and hang there, pulsing.

"Tell him I said kiss-kiss and come home *soon* 'cause we miss him." Caitie scooped up Mr. P, draped him over her shoulder, and went upstairs. Winchester, realizing that being a flat basset wasn't going to get him anywhere, lumbered to his feet. With a glance over his shoulder that said, "Someday I'll be gone and you'll miss me," he trudged to his basket and climbed in.

It wasn't McQuaid; it was Jessica.

"Oh, it's you," I said.

"Must've caught you at a bad time," Jessica said wryly. "Want me to hang up and call back next month?"

"Sorry," I said. "I was hoping— Never mind." I took a deep breath and forced a smile into my voice. "What's up?"

"What's up is that I've just emailed you some things I think you should take a look at. Do you have your laptop handy?"

"It's right here. Hang on a sec and I'll bring it up."

I put the phone on speaker, unzipped the computer case, and took out my laptop. I flicked the power switch, and a moment later I was watching Jessica's email, loaded with three attachments, drop into my in-box.

"What's in the attachments?" I asked.

"Some examples of what you might be looking for. Three stories, one from a couple of weeks ago—the date is March 30—and the other two from last year, August and November. Three deaths, two in Pecan Springs, one in Lufkin. All three unattended."

"No kidding?" I said. "You found these already? Wow. That was fast."

"Well, as you said, I'm a kick-ass researcher," Jessica said smugly. "And I do have access to the in-house *Enterprise* computer files. I did a quick-and-dirty search, just to see what might turn up. There were a couple of others—a homeless guy found dead under the I-35 bridge, a twenty-one-year-old woman who OD'd in her car—but they didn't seem to fit. If what I've sent isn't quite what you're after, you can help me narrow it down. And of course, I can go back farther into the files. Tomorrow. This is it for the night."

The kettle was steaming, and I poured hot water into the teapot and put on the china lid. "Are you still at the newspaper office?"

"I'm just turning off the lights and heading home. It's been a long day, and I'm ready to get naked and dive into a hot bath. So let's plan to talk tomorrow. Okay?"

"Sure thing," I said. "And Jessica, thanks. I'm in your debt."

"You think?" Jessica asked, with a touch of sarcasm. "I don't hang around the office computer after dinner just for fun, you know. You'd better remember this when it's time for the story you promised me."

"Yeah," I said. "Jessica, I've just come from the hospital. They took Kelly off life support tonight. She's dead."

"Ah, *hell*," she said very softly, and clicked off.

I got my favorite teacup out of the cupboard and sat down at the kitchen table. When Jessica and I were eating together at Beans', I had asked her to do some research for me. Kelly had used the word *murder*, which potentially covered a lot of time-and-place territory. But based on the computer files she had copied and color coded, I was guessing that she was looking into some irregular situations at the hospice, and that she suspected that it was a patient who had been murdered.

And that nobody knew that the death was actually a murder.

Which all by itself was odd, of course. Murder is not a minor crime. In most circumstances, when it happens, you can't miss it. Somebody finds a dead person, recognizes that the victim came to a violent end, and calls the cops. The homicide unit opens an investigation, identifies a person or persons of interest who have motive, means, and opportunity, and pursues them with bulldog determination until the killer has been captured, tried, and convicted. Or until the crime has been relegated to the cold case files.

Obviously, that wasn't the kind of murder Kelly had in mind. She knew—or thought she knew—of a murder that had not been recognized as a murder, which ruled out gunshot, strangling, stabbing, asphyxiation, and all the other violent means that couldn't be missed when the body was found. This murder had no witnesses, the autopsy turned up nothing that made the county medical examiner suspect foul play, and the justice of the peace had to have ruled it accidental or a death from natural causes.

The *Enterprise*, like all small-town newspapers, reports all deaths in its coverage area. So, as a quick first pass, I had asked Jessica to search the *Enterprise* files for newspaper reports of local-area unattended deaths—deaths that occurred when the person was alone—that met these criteria. I would match those names against the names of patients in the files Kelly had copied. If Jessica couldn't find any matches, I would look into the circumstances of the death of every hospice patient. Even if I could get Lara to help me, that was a much bigger job, and not one that I was eager to dig into.

Thinking about this, it occurred to me that there might be other, related records on Kelly's computer—a diary, maybe, or notes about the investigation she was undertaking. Once I had a better idea of what I was looking for, I could ask Sheila for permission to do a computer search. But not yet. Right now I'd just be guessing.

Anyway, if I brought the police into this, Sheila would ask me to explain all the whys and wherefores, and then she would undoubtedly take the investigation away from me. The police would have to be involved sooner or later, of course.

But right now there was no evidence of a murder, no body, and no witnesses—nothing that would justify the assignment of costly police time and effort.

I sat down at the table, poured a cup of tea, and stirred in a spoonful of honey. Then I opened the attachments Jessica had sent and quickly scanned each one, noting the circumstances. In Lufkin, a sixty-seven-year-old woman, recently released from the hospital after a serious stroke, was found by her sister, dead in a chair in her bedroom. In Pecan Springs, a seventy-three-year-old man was discovered dead at the foot of a ladder in his backyard by the guy who came to trim the shrubs. The victim had apparently fallen when he tried to replace a screen on a second-story window and died of a broken neck. I brought up Kelly's files and did a search on both names. Neither had been patients of the Pecan Springs Community Hospice. Both were out of the running as the potential murder victim—real or fictitious—that Kelly might have had in mind.

But the third one, also in Pecan Springs, was a different story, and much more gruesome. According to an *Enterprise* article published in September, the police had been called to a house at 137 Wheeler Avenue in response to a neighbor's report of a deceased resident. When they arrived, the officers discovered a severely decomposed body, identified as that of Ronald R. MacDonald, age seventy-six. The air-conditioning in the house had been turned off, and all the windows were closed. The weather had been extremely hot, and due to the advanced stage of decomposition, the Pecan Springs Fire Department Hazmat Unit was called and the residence was treated as a hazardous-materials scene. It appeared that MacDonald, who had recently been discharged as a patient of the Pecan Springs Community Hospice, had been dead for approximately ten days. There were no signs of foul play. The autopsy revealed that he had died of morphine poisoning.

Justice of the Peace Maude Porterfield ruled that the death was due to a morphine overdose, adding that it could not then be determined whether it was an accident or a suicide.

Ronald MacDonald. I frowned. Where had I—

And then I remembered. MacDonald was the hospice patient whom Lara had mentioned as a candidate for "discharge for cause." Searching Kelly's file, I found the entry easily. Ronald R. MacDonald, 137 Wheeler Avenue, deceased, August 15 (approximately). Kelly had coded the entry yellow, for "unqualified." When I studied it, I saw that she could also have coded it pink, for overstay. MacDonald had been in hospice care for just short of a year.

I picked up my cup and sipped the fragrant tea. The Texas Code of Criminal Procedure requires that unattended deaths, like all three of those Jessica had sent me, be subjected to both an autopsy and an inquest. Tom Harkins, an MD at the hospital in Pecan Springs, does the county's autopsies. Tom is smart, conscientious, and operates strictly by the book. And Maude Porterfield, whom I know quite well and whose judgment I respect, would not have ruled as she did if there had been even the slightest evidence of foul play.

So there wasn't much to go on here—when you got right down to it, nothing at all. On the surface, it looked like the tragic death of an elderly man who had gotten confused about the dosage of his painkiller, or had committed suicide when the pain of his disease became unbearable. But Kelly had used the word *murder*, and morphine has served as a handy murder weapon many times in the past. MacDonald's death met the criteria I had established, and I wasn't going to give it a quick pass.

I took out my cell and phoned Lara. I caught her on her way back home to Wimberley after she had dropped Kelly's mom at her motel. She sounded sad and weepy when she answered my call, but she perked up when I told her what I had asked Jessica to look for and what she had found. She understood the situation immediately, in part because she is a very smart woman and in part because Ronald MacDonald had been such an uncooperative patient and she remembered him well. When she learned that he was dead from an overdose of morphine, she was quick to grasp the implication.

"You're thinking *this* might be the murder Kelly had in mind?" she asked.

"It's a place to start," I said. "I have a couple of questions. Should I call you back when you get home? Or are you at a place where you can answer them?"

"Just pulling into my driveway," she said. "Shoot."

"Okay. When you were MacDonald's nurse, did you ever have any contact with his family or neighbors?"

"Nope. His wife was dead, he had no children, and as far as friends were concerned—well, he seemed to be pretty much alone in the world. The woman across the alley looked in on him every now and then, though. I'm sure I have her name in my notes. It might be worth the trouble to drop in and talk to her."

"He was an overstay," I said. "He was in hospice for eleven months before he died. And Kelly has marked him as 'unqualified'—not sick enough for hospice. Do you happen to remember right off what his illness was?"

There was a pause. "Stomach cancer is what I remember," she said slowly. "Not a surprise, given the man's diet. He wouldn't stop smoking, either. But there were some questions about the . . ."

Her voice trailed off. After a moment, she said, "Look. Kelly's death has been pretty hard for me, and I'd rather get into all this when I'm fresher. Tomorrow is my day off at the clinic. I'm scheduled to have lunch with Rich and Kelly's mom to talk about funeral arrangements. But maybe you and I could get together in the morning? We could try to connect with the woman across the alley and see if she knows anything about MacDonald's death. Also, I'd like to pick up the things Kelly left in your cottage. No point in leaving them for you to store."

"Of course," I said sympathetically. "I'll get Caitie off to school in the morning, then give you a call and we can make our plans."

"Thanks," she said, letting her breath out in a long whoosh. "You know, China, I have the very strong feeling that Kelly is riding along with us on this. It may be just wishful thinking, but I still believe that we will find out who rear-ended her—and that it was deliberate."

I wanted to say, *And then what?* but I held my tongue. Lara didn't know any more than I did, and neither of us knew enough to answer a "then what?" question. Anyway, she had enough on her plate right now. So I wished her a good night's sleep and hung up.

I sat for a moment, sipping my tea and thinking about a game plan for tomorrow, now that Lara and I were planning to get together. I glanced at the clock. It wasn't ten yet, and Ruby was a night owl. I picked up my cell and called her.

"Have you come up with any more magic words about doors and why I shouldn't go through them?" I asked.

Ruby sighed. "I hope you're not going to hold that against me."

"Not at all," I said. "I'm just seeking guidance. I'm looking for a door to go through, but I'd hate to open it and have a gun go off in my face. Or the ceiling fall down on my head. Or something."

We both chuckled. Then she said, very soberly, "I'm so sorry to hear that Kelly died this evening, China. I know that she was your friend, and you'll miss her."

"You've heard about that already?" And then I understood. "Oh," I said, remembering that this was a complicated affair, and that there were lots of different threads woven through it. "Ramona must have told you."

"Right." Another sigh. "She was here this evening, crying on my shoulder about the way things have turned out."

"Crying?" I was taken aback. "Excuse me for saying so, Ruby, but I would think your sister would be happy. Well, maybe not celebrating with champagne and party hats, but at least quietly satisfied. She got what she wanted, didn't she? Just last night, she was telling me how eager she was for her brewmaster boyfriend to divorce his wife so they could be married and spend the rest of their natural lives together, brewing blood orange beer and adding herbs to every beer recipe they can think of. And now his wife is out of the way, without even the bother of a divorce and the distribution of property. Everything that belonged to Kelly probably now belongs to her husband."

"My, aren't we snarky tonight," Ruby said.

"Well, yes," I replied drily. "And likely to get snarkier. Excuse me, but Kelly is dead and I hate the thought of your ditzy sister—your evil twin—gloating."

"She's not gloating." Ruby was very serious. "She's miserable. He told her to go away and leave him alone. Forever."

"Kelly's husband?" I asked in surprise. "Kelly's widower, I mean. He told Ramona to *go away*?"

"Yes, that one. And yes, that's what he said."

"Wait a minute, Ruby. I don't understand. Just last night, Ramona was thrilled by the idea that Rich was going to divorce Kelly and marry her and she would own a big piece of the brewery and—"

"She may end up with the brewery," Ruby said. "She's already invested quite a bit of money in it. But Rich feels terribly guilty about their affair, and now that his wife is dead, he's heartbroken. He says he's going to sell out and move away. He blames himself. He says that if he and Ramona hadn't been involved, Kelly would have been home last night, safe and sound, instead of driving on Limekiln Road."

"There might be some truth to that," I said. "But Kelly has been dead only a few hours. I'm sure Rich will feel differently before long. Ramona just needs to give him some time, and some space. If she could just be patient and stand back for a couple of months while he sorts things out—"

The minute the words were out of my mouth, I saw the problem. Ruby's sister has never been able to practice patience for one single instant, let alone a few weeks or a couple of months. What she wants, she wants *now*, and if she can't get it now, she doesn't want it. If she had been insensitive to Rich's grief and had shown that side of herself to him today, she could easily have revealed an aspect of herself that turned him away once and for all. He might even begin to blame *her* for what had happened, as well as himself.

Ruby was reading my mind. "Yes," she said sadly. "You and I both know that Ramona doesn't have a patient bone in her body. Of course she hasn't said this, but I've had the idea all along that the romance was more her idea than his. Listening to her tonight, I have the feeling that Rich really is through with her. And I don't blame him, one single bit. I hate to say it, but you're right, China."

"Right about what, exactly?"

"She really is my evil twin. And I don't know what to do about her. When she was here tonight, she flew into one of her little tizzy fits. Stuff started rocketing around the room and—" She stopped. "Sorry," she muttered. "I know that sounds idiotic, but it's true."

"It doesn't sound idiotic at all." I glanced up at the cuckoo clock, which hung sedate and silent on the wall. "When she was here last night, she got . . . excited. The cuckoo clock came back to life, the microwave went berserk, the TV switched it-self on, and Winchester joined in with his very best howl. It was a cacophony." I blew out a breath. "And I have the idea that this was just a little exercise. I hate to think of what might've happened if she had shifted into high gear."

"Sorry," Ruby said apologetically. "I'm at my wits' end. If you have any suggestions for ways we can handle her . . ." Her voice trailed off.

I sighed. If Ruby couldn't deal with her sister, nobody could. "Well, it's nothing we can solve tonight. Listen, there's something important I need to do tomorrow morning. If I open up, can you keep an eye on the shop for me for a couple of hours?"

"Oh, no problem," Ruby said. "Miriam is coming in the morning to help me put up some new shelves. Between the two of us, I'm sure we can manage. In fact, you don't even need to open up. We can handle that for you."

"Well, if you're sure," I said. "I really appreciate it, Ruby."

"It's the least I can do," she said. She paused, and in a smallish voice added, "But I'd feel a lot better, China, if I knew you were being careful about that door."

"I'd feel a lot better," I countered, "if I knew which door to be careful about. Please let me know if something comes to you."

"Oh, I will," she said earnestly. "I will. I promise."

I went upstairs, kissed Caitie good night, then took a long bath. After that I climbed into bed and read for an hour, still hoping that McQuaid would call. But I couldn't stop glanc-ing at the clock, and I finally gave up. I punched up my pil-low and turned out the light, my cell phone on the bedside table and Winchester, snoring gently, sprawled across the foot of the bed. Every so often his stumpy little legs jerked as he chased rabbits and armadillos in his sleep. He gave a gleeful little *yip* every time he caught one.

But I lay awake for a very long time, thinking about McQuaid and Blackie and wondering where they were and what they were doing. They weren't trying to infiltrate one of the Mexican drug cartels, were they? Oh, please, no. No! Sometime just before dawn, I woke up with a gasp, drenched in a cold sweat. I had dreamed that I opened a door and found McQuaid lying facedown on the floor in front of me. I awakened before I discovered whether he was alive or dead.

After that, it was impossible to get back to sleep. About four o'clock, I got up, turned on my laptop, and began doing some research on Medicare fraud.

Chapter Fourteen

The opium poppy (*Papaver somniferum*) blooms in a variety of beautiful colors, from pale lavender to an intense, vibrant orange. It's a lovely garden flower and remarkably easy to grow, but you're not going to see it in most American gardens. The plant's dried latex sap is known as opium, and opium's main psychoactive substance is morphine, named for Morpheus, the Greek god of dreams. Because it operates directly on the central nervous system, morphine is a powerful—and powerfully addictive—painkiller.

Morphine was first extracted from opium in a pure form in 1804, and rapidly came into pharmaceutical use as a painkiller. Many soldiers became addicted to morphine during the Crimean War and American Civil War, where it was widely used in battlefield hospitals. Laudanum, a tincture of opium, was used in many patent medicines and as a sleep aid, increasing the addiction problem. In 1874, a chemist attempted to create a less addictive form of morphine and synthesized heroin. But it was two to four times more potent than morphine, and addictions skyrocketed.

China Bayles
"The Opium Poppy: The Sleep Herb"
Pecan Springs Enterprise

"That's the house," Lara said, pointing to a neat yellow bungalow. I pulled over and parked half a block away from it, leaving the motor running. The morning was warm and bright with April sunshine, and bluebonnets and yellow-orange paintbrush were blooming in the grass along the curb. We had stopped at the diner and picked up coffee in cardboard to-go cups and also a couple of Lila Jennings' jelly doughnuts, strawberry for Lara and raspberry for me. That made two mornings in a row. I was beginning to feel downright decadent.

Ronald MacDonald's neighbor hadn't been listed as a contact in Kelly's file, but Lara had found her name, Mary Jo Mueller, in the personal nurse's log she had kept during her years at the hospice. "You can never keep too many records," Lara remarked, and I agreed.

It hadn't been hard to locate Mrs. Mueller's house. As Lara had recalled, it was on the other side of the alley behind 137 Wheeler Avenue, where MacDonald had lived—and died. It was in an older neighborhood of rental houses and small one- and two-story apartment complexes. We drove past the Mac-Donald address first. I wasn't surprised to see that the house had been razed, and a new one was going up in its place. Years ago, on a case back in Houston, I had gotten too close to a decomposed human body. The smell of it clung like a stubborn ghost to everything, no matter how thoroughly the site and its furnishings were disinfected, and clung to my skin and hair—for real, or perhaps just in my imagination— through a week of showers. The owner of the house in which MacDonald had died no doubt found it cheaper to tear the rental down than to clean it up.

I finished the last bite of my jelly doughnut, reached for my coffee, and studied the Mueller house. It was set back behind a small green square of lawn, bisected by a neat brick sidewalk and centered with a single large pecan tree. The morning sunlight brightened the tree's new green leaves and dappled the lawn.

"Before we talk to this woman," I said, "maybe you could bring me up to speed on MacDonald. You've said he was hard to get along with. Tell me more."

Lara licked the sugar off her fingers and picked up the spiral notebook she had brought. She looked professional today, in brown slacks, a red jacket, and a white blouse. Both of us did, in fact: I was wearing khaki slacks, a navy top and blazer, and black loafers, a big change from my usual jeans and T-shirt.

"MacDonald was admitted to hospice care with stomach cancer, on the referral of a doctor in San Antonio. Chris—Dr. Burgess—signed the admissions paperwork. Dr. Burgess and I made the first visit together, and then I made weekly visits for the next five weeks."

I saw the red stain on her cheek and wondered whether she was embarrassed by her former relationship with Burgess or whether she still might harbor some feeling for him. "Weekly visits," I said. "Is that standard for hospice?"

"It depends on the case. Yes, most patients are visited weekly by a nurse. The social worker, the chaplain, or a household helper sometimes makes additional visits. The focus is supposed to be on pain management, you know, for people who are dying. So the nurses do what they can to make the patients comfortable, see that they have what they need, and so on." She took a breath. "My first few visits with him were pretty routine, and then he began to be . . . well, abusive. Verbally abusive."

I asked the question I'd been wondering about since my predawn foray into Medicare fraud. "How ill was he, as far as you could tell?"

She reached for her coffee, parked in the cup holder. "You know, that bothered me. He was supposed to be terminal. But during the time I was assigned to him, his physical condition didn't change. Of course, stomach cancer isn't something you can actually *see*, and I've known other patients who have seemed to plateau for a time. But he didn't experience any weight loss, which I thought was strange."

"Do you know what happened in his case after you stopped making visits?"

"That's where it starts getting a little squirrely." She sipped her coffee and put it down. "Last night, I checked the file you emailed me—Kelly's computer file—and found that she had been assigned to him, too, for about six weeks. Then another nurse took over, someone whose name I didn't recognize, and several others after that. Over the eleven months of his stay in hospice, he had five or six different nurses." She finished her coffee and put the cup on the floor. "The visits weren't regular, either. There were weeks when nobody visited. Or if they did, the record is incomplete."

"Six or seven different nurses." I thought about that for a moment. "Is that the usual practice? I would think it would be a lot better for the patient if he or she had just one nurse during the stay."

"It wasn't usual, China. Most of the time, we were assigned to a patient and stayed with that patient until the end. Of course, nurses sometimes go on vacation. And if there's a late-night or weekend emergency, the on-call nurse handles the situation."

Lara leaned toward me, her gray eyes intent behind gold-rimmed glasses, her brown hair frizzing around her face. "But China, listen to this: I got up early this morning and went through Kelly's files again, looking at her 'unqualified' patients, the ones marked yellow. All of them were admitted by the same two San Antonio doctors and certified by Chris Burgess. All of them were visited by the same four or five nurses. They were nurses whose names I didn't recognize, even though it looks like we worked there at the same time." She shook her head. "It's not like the hospice was a huge business, you know. We all attended the same staff meetings at least once a month—at least, we were *supposed* to."

A mockingbird landed on the hood of the Toyota, regarded us with one bright, beady eye, then flew away. "Those four or five nurses," I said. "Is it possible that they didn't really *see* the patients? That they signed off on visits that were never made?"

She nodded slowly. "Yes. We were paid by the visit, and only occasionally supervised. So maybe they just didn't visit."

I might have been surprised if I hadn't already begun to see the pattern. "How about this?" I asked. "Could those nurses have been paid *not* to visit? And could the patients themselves—or some of them, anyway—be fictitious? So the hospice was billing Medicare one hundred seventy-two dollars a day for 'patients' who received no services at all. Is that possible?"

She chewed on her lower lip for a moment, then said, very quietly, "It's possible, China. I mean, I know that the hospice delivered real services to real patients, because I worked with many of them while I was there, and so did the other nurses. But it's also possible that some of these people in Kelly's files were never patients at all. And here's another thing. The patients Kelly coded as 'unnecessary general inpatient care' were all moved to a small medical facility down in Seguin, when it would have made a lot more sense to put them in the Pecan Springs hospital." She looked up at me. "I'm wondering whether there was some kind of kickback arrangement on those patients."

"Ah, yes," I said. "I see." And what I was seeing was the jagged outline of a very large fraud that had been playing out for a very long time, to the lucrative tune of hundreds of thousands of dollars.

Lara turned to look out the window, watching a young mother pushing a baby carriage down the sidewalk. After a moment, she said, "But whatever the case, they're not patients now."

"They're not?" I drained my coffee.

"Uh-uh. When I went through the files this morning, I saw that all of those patients—the ones Kelly coded as unqualified or unnecessary general inpatients—have been discharged."

"Discharged?" I frowned. "You mean, they died?"

"No. That's the interesting thing. They *didn't* die—except for MacDonald, of course, who was definitely dead. They were simply marked 'discharged,' every single one of them. There's no indication in the file whether or where they were transferred. They were just . . . discharged."

"Easy enough to do," I said, "if they're fictitious." Or the hijacked identities of real people with real social security numbers, fictitiously reported as "patients."

She nodded. "But wait until you hear this." She paused, making sure I was listening. "All of the discharges took place on the same day last week. On Saturday."

"On Saturday," I repeated. "When the office wasn't open." And Kelly had surreptitiously copied the files a few hours later, on Saturday night.

"Yes. If I had to guess, I'd say that somebody in the office found out that Kelly was suspicious and made a clumsy effort to get these names off the books." She took a breath. "They probably figured on coming back later and purging all of them—and maybe they already have. But the thing is that the records have already been submitted to Medicare for payment. The reimbursements have been paid. So taking them off the books isn't going to do the trick."

"In fact," I said, "taking them off the books is a crime, too. It's a cover-up." At a minimum, it can translate to obstruction of justice, with additional charges for falsification of records and making false statements. I had come across a half dozen examples of that in my early-morning online research. And in the case of Medicare fraud, the penalties for attempted cover-ups are plenty stiff. In one case I'd read about, the manager of an Arkansas hospice got five years in prison and a twenty-five-thousand-dollar fine for *each* charge, and each falsified record counted as a single charge. In a scheme like that, there could also be charges of conspiracy and money laundering.

But right now, we were dealing with murder, not Medicare fraud—unless, as I now strongly suspected, the two were closely linked.

"Getting back to MacDonald," I said. "According to the newspaper story, the man died last August, of a morphine overdose. At the inquest, it seems to have been assumed that morphine was being prescribed for pain and that he managed to hoard enough of the narcotic to serve as a lethal dose, either accidentally or deliberately." I paused and said, slowly, out loud, what I knew we were both thinking. "It's also possible that somebody brought the morphine and administered it."

"Yes," Lara replied slowly. "China, I'm willing to bet that MacDonald is the murder victim Kelly was thinking about." Puzzled, she wrinkled her forehead. "The old man was certainly abusive, maybe even crazy. But I can't come up with a good reason for killing him. Can you?"

"Perhaps," I said, and then offered the explanation that had been banging around at the back of my mind since early that morning. "Perhaps he was killed to keep him from telling what he knew about the Medicare fraud."

Lara's mouth dropped open. "What he knew—"

I tapped a finger on the steering wheel. "Try this as a scenario, Lara. Let's say that MacDonald didn't have stomach cancer, or any other illness. As a hypothesis, let's say that he was fraudulently recruited to become a hospice patient and then began to cause trouble for his recruiter. Say that he threatened to tell what he knew unless he was paid to keep his mouth shut. That he was asking for more and more money—until he became too unreliable, too much of a threat. At which point somebody took him out. And somewhere along the way, instead of risking other similar threats, it was decided that it would be safer to create fictitious patients, rather than recruit potential troublemakers."

"Wow," she said, letting out a long breath. "Just . . . wow."

"It's possible?"

"It's possible," she said slowly, "all of it. I have to admit that I never saw any evidence of illness—of a terminal illness, I mean. MacDonald was so hard to deal with that it was impossible to tell what was really going on with him. Most of the time, he wouldn't even let me check his vital signs." She hesitated. "Of course, that could have been an act—part of the scam."

I nodded. "Yes, part of the act. But we are very far out on a *very* thin limb, Lara. We have a theory of a crime, but we don't have a shred of evidence. We're identifying a murder victim that the authorities have already written off as a suicide or an accidental OD. We're conjecturing that there was a large-scale fraud and that MacDonald was involved in it. We're guessing that—"

"Yes, we're guessing," she said impatiently. "But we're not making it up, China. It's all part of a bigger picture, and the records Kelly copied prove it. She knew that somebody

223

at the hospice was defrauding Medicare and she knew how it was being done. More than that, I'll bet she knew who was doing it. That's why she was killed."

"I suppose you have a candidate," I said quietly.

"Yes." She took a deep, ragged breath. "It had to have been Chris. Dr. Christopher Burgess. He signed off on every single one of the patients that Kelly coded as unqualified. They were in hospice because he gave his approval."

"And murder?" I studied her. "Do you think Dr. Burgess would have killed somebody who threatened to reveal what he was doing?"

She tried to say something, cleared her throat, and tried again. "Yes," she said, very low. "Yes, I think . . ." She blinked fast, trying not to cry. "I think he'd do that. There was a kind of . . . ruthlessness about him. I saw it once or twice when we were together, and it scared me. It was one of the reasons I decided to break up with him."

"I'd like to hear more," I said gently, and put my hand on her arm. "But we don't have to go into that now. Let's back up. You've met MacDonald's neighbor—what can you tell me about the woman?"

Making a visible effort to pull herself together, Lara squeezed my hand. "I saw her for the first time on my second visit to MacDonald's house. She had stopped in to bring him some groceries. We left at the same time, so we had a chance to talk. She's a woman in her late sixties, I'd say. As I remember, she's retired from the library—children's librarian, I think she said. Some people might think she's a bit of a busybody, I suppose, and she seems a little nosy. But she probably does a lot of good, checking on older people in the neighborhood and keeping an eye out for kids. She seemed quite reasonable and nice, unlike MacDonald, who kept telling her to go away and never come back." A smile ghosted across her face. "*Cantankerous* doesn't begin to describe the man, China. He was a first-class jerk."

"Did you see her often?"

"Two or three times. We didn't talk much, but I had the feeling that she was . . . well, puzzled about MacDonald. She seemed curious about him."

I nodded. "Well, let's go see if she's at home, shall we?"

With its yellow walls, white shutters, and blue front door, the Mueller house was the prettiest on the street. The front steps featured pots of purple and red petunias and there was a blue-painted swing at one end of the shaded porch.

Lara had to knock several times before the door opened on a chain and an older lady peered out at us over plastic-rimmed bifocals. Her long white hair was braided and neatly coiled around her head and there was a hearing aid in one ear. Slightly stooped, she wore pink felt house slippers and a cotton housecoat that zipped up the front. The housecoat was printed with huge pink and chartreuse cabbage roses bright enough to make me blink.

"Hello, Mrs. Mueller," Lara said, smiling. "It's been quite a while, but I wonder if you remember me. I'm one of Mr. MacDonald's hospice nurses. We met when you brought him groceries one afternoon."

"Oh, yes, of course I remember." The woman spoke rapidly and in the high, shrill voice of the hard of hearing. "That poor man. He was *such* an old rascal, wasn't he?"

"Well, that's certainly one way to describe him," Lara replied with a chuckle. She gestured at me. "This is my friend China Bayles. If you're not busy just now, we'd like to chat with you for a few minutes."

"China Bayles? Why, of course! From Friends of the Library! You gave a talk in our herb garden just after it was opened. Do you remember?"

"Of course," I said. I remembered helping to plant the garden and giving the talk. I even vaguely remembered her, although I hadn't known her name. "It's good to see you again."

The chain came off the door and she stepped back. "Well, isn't this nice?" she said cheerfully. "I was just ironing tea towels, so you'll give me a little break. Come on in, girls. It's a warm morning, even if it is just April. How would you feel about a glass of lemonade?"

"Lemonade would be lovely," I said. "Thank you for your hospitality."

The kitchen was a pleasant, sunshiny room with wide, multipaned windows that gave a view of a small vegetable garden. It was planted in neat rows, the ferny tops of carrots marching in careful alignment between beets and rainbow chard. Several fuchsias in full pink and purple bloom hung from the eaves of a frame garage. Beyond the garden, I could see a low privet hedge along the alley and, on the other side of the alley, the empty lot where the MacDonald house had once stood. An ironing board was set up in front of the window, where Mrs. Mueller could watch the birds visiting the feeder on the small brick patio just outside. On one end of the board, a stack of neatly ironed tea towels sat next to an electric iron, and a slightly damp tea towel with a crocheted edge was spread on the working end, waiting its turn.

"You girls sit down right there at the table." Mrs. Mueller went to the board and turned off the iron. "Make yourselves at home."

"Thank you," Lara said as we took chairs. The table was covered with a cheery white cloth printed with little red and blue and green birds. "This is very kind of you."

"I'm always glad to have company," the old woman said. "I used to love to go to work—I was a librarian, you know—because I love seeing people. I miss that." She went to the refrigerator and took out a frosty pitcher of lemonade. "So you've come to talk about Mr. MacDonald? Well, as I told that other nurse last week, I would certainly like to see something done about the poor man's case, if it isn't too late. It just doesn't sit right with me, knowing—"

"Excuse me," I said. "The other nurse?"

"Yes. Kelly Kaufman." As Lara and I traded glances, Mrs. Mueller took three glasses out of the cupboard and began to fill them. "The girl who was in that car wreck night before last. I read about it in the *Enterprise* yesterday." She put a hand over her heart and patted herself several times. "Such a shock that was! I had to read it three times before I could get my mind around it. Would you happen to know how she is?"

"I'm sorry to tell you," Lara said soberly, "that Kelly died last night."

"Oh, dear!" Mrs. Mueller's eyes widened behind her glasses. "Oh, mercy me! What a horrible thing!" She put the pitcher down with a thump. "I am so sorry to hear it. Kelly was a lovely girl. She seemed to understand the problem and want to see what could be done to fix it." Sighing heavily, she put two filled glasses in front of us. "But it's really too late, I'm afraid. Once the bureaucracy decides a thing, it's done. St. Peter himself couldn't change it."

I made a quick stab. "You're talking about the ruling in Mr. MacDonald's death?"

"Yes, that's right. I blame myself, you know. If I'd been here, it wouldn't have happened. Not the awful way it did, anyway. I am just so sorry about that. Which is what I told Kelly." She opened an old-fashioned tin breadbox printed with yellow daffodils. "You wouldn't say no to a peanut butter cookie, would you? I make them for the little boy across the street. Gerald, his name is. He comes over every day after school for a glass of milk and a cookie, and sometimes I read

227

him a story. He's a latchkey child, you know. We have several in this neighborhood."

"We'd love a cookie," I said warmly, although the memory of Lila Jennings' sugary jelly doughnut was still with me. "And peanut butter is my favorite, hands down." I paused. "When did you talk to Kelly, Mrs. Mueller?"

"Last week," she said, putting the cookies on a plate in the middle of the table. She sat down in a chair opposite me. "It was Thursday, I think. Yes, Thursday. I'd just got back from driving old Mrs. Grumper to the beauty parlor for her regular Thursday shampoo and set. Kelly came over on her lunch hour and we had tuna salad sandwiches." She brightened and started to get up again. "Is it too early for a bite of lunch? I have bread and plenty of—"

"Oh, thank you, no, Mrs. Mueller," Lara said hastily. She picked up a cookie. "This is really perfect. Just this, and the lemonade."

"So Kelly came to discuss Mr. MacDonald's death," I said, prodding Mrs. Mueller back to the subject. "I'm sure you told her your concerns about it."

"I certainly did." Mrs. Mueller helped herself to a cookie. "And if I hadn't been out of town when the poor man died, I would have told the police about it—then, I mean. But it all happened while I was staying in Chicago, taking care of my sister. She was dying of cancer, and of course I wanted to stay with her until the end." She shook her head. "Well, what with one thing and another, I was gone from the middle of August to the end of September. By the time I got back, everything was all over and done with and settled. At least, that's what the police told me when I tried to talk to them about it." She sniffed. "They told me to go back home and mind my own business. They were nice about it, but I could tell there wasn't any use in trying to get them to listen. They just kept saying that the JP had ruled and the case was closed and that was it."

"So you were out of town when Mr. MacDonald died," I said thoughtfully. "And you didn't get back until—"

"Until after Maude Porterfield had held the inquest." She shook her head. "My older sister went to school with Maude, you know, and she used to come over to our house every Saturday. Maude is as smart as a whip but she has always been *very* opinionated. Once she's made up her mind, nothing's going to budge her. Which is what I told Kelly." She sighed heavily. "Oh, I am *so* sorry to hear about that lovely girl's death! Such a tragedy. Does anybody know how the wreck happened?"

"I think it's still under investigation," Lara said.

"Well, I hope the police do a better job than they did with poor Mr. MacDonald," Mrs. Mueller said tartly.

I cleared my throat, wanting to get the conversation back on track. "What made you want to go to the police about Mr. MacDonald? What did you want them to do?"

"Well, I just never did understand why the man was in hospice," Mrs. Mueller said. "Especially when things dragged on and on. Mrs. Patterson, two blocks down on the other side of the street, was in hospice for three months at the end of her life, the dear old thing. But she was really, truly sick, not like Mr. MacDonald. He was just playing sick. And he didn't even do that very well." She gave a sarcastic harrumph. "Stomach cancer, of all things. That's what my sister died of, you know. *She* wasn't playing sick, believe you me."

"How did you know he was playing sick?" Lara asked. She reached for another cookie. "Would you mind if I—"

"Oh, my dear child, no!" the old woman exclaimed. "I just love to see people eat my cookies. Well, about playing sick." She nodded toward the window. "I like to iron. It's my hobby,

229

you might say, so I'm there at the window a lot, ironing and watching the birds and enjoying my garden. I could see that man, out in his backyard almost every day, pushing his lawn mower, one of those old reel things. And painting the back porch, and lifting weights. And he had one of those bicycles, you know, that doesn't go anywhere. It just sits and you pedal it. It was on his back porch and he pedaled it every day for an hour, with a book propped up in front of him. My sister had a *real* case of stomach cancer, and I could tell the difference. That man was no sicker than I was. In fact, he wasn't even taking painkillers. He'd thrown them all out."

"He did?" I asked encouragingly. "How do you know?"

"Because one day last summer Mrs. Van Kirsten's German shepherd got out of the yard and got into all the garbage cans along the alley. I went out to pick mine up, and Mr. MacDonald was out there picking his up and cursing the dog. I saw what he was throwing away and it was all his medicine. Bottles and boxes of pills and things like that."

"Maybe he was just tired of taking them," Lara objected. "He was such a difficult patient. He might have been doing it just to be contrary."

"No, he said he was cleaning house," Mrs. Mueller said. "And he was getting rid of stuff because he was going to move, and anyway, he'd never needed any of it to begin with, which was why there was so much. Then the next week, when he was out mowing the backyard, I took him a nice big slice of cake. He'd had a little too much to drink, I think, and it made him want to brag. He told me right straight out that he was pulling the wool over everybody's eyes. About being sick, I mean. He said, 'I'm as fit as you or anybody else on this block, Mrs. M.' That's what he called me. Mrs. M."

"Oh, really?" I asked, thinking what a marvelous witness this woman would make, if you could keep her focused on the questions. "When was that? When you took him the cake, I mean."

"I can tell you exactly," she said, "since it was the day after my birthday, which is August tenth. Mrs. Gregory from across the street made me the most beautiful coconut cake with a gorgeous strawberry rose right in the middle. I took him a piece and some of the strawberries, because I knew he'd love it. He did love to eat, and he could eat *anything*, which is another reason I know he wasn't dying of stomach cancer."

"You were telling us," I prompted, "that he said he was pulling the wool over everybody's eyes, and that he was fit. Did he say anything else?"

"Well, he certainly did. As I said, he'd been drinking a little too much. He was feeling pretty good about himself that day. He said that all he had to do was play sick, and in return, he got free rent and his groceries delivered and a big-screen TV and money for gambling online. He especially liked Texas Hold'em, although he wasn't much of a big winner. But he said he was getting tired of being so confined and he wasn't going to play sick forever." Mrs. Mueller leaned forward and took another cookie. "He said the doctor was going to give him a lot more money and then he was going to get out of town. He was flying to Guadalajara—in fact, he had already bought his plane ticket. He was all excited about it. He had a friend who was living there, so he could move in with her until he found a place of his own. He thought it would be easy to relocate. He even demonstrated his Spanish to me."

"The doctor was going to give him more money?" Lara's voice was strained. "Did he say which doctor? Or how much?"

Mrs. Mueller pressed her lips together. "No, and I didn't ask. I may be nosy, but not as nosy as some folks think. But

I was surprised when he said that, which is why I remember it." She tilted her head to one side, her eyes bright and bird-like. "Never heard of a doctor *giving* money, you know. Usually, it goes the other direction."

Lara looked at me, and I saw that she had reached the same conclusion I had. Chris Burgess had been paying Mac-Donald to play sick. "You told Kelly Kaufman about this?" Lara asked.

Mrs. Mueller nodded. "And she was every bit as interested as you are."

I was calculating. If Mrs. Mueller's conversation with MacDonald had taken place on the day after her birthday, that would make it August 11. And just a few days later, Mac-Donald was dead. "Do you know," I asked, "whether he had any painkillers in the house? Morphine, that is?"

"Oh, I don't think so," she said definitively. "Like I told you, he was out there in the alley just the week before, throwing away all kinds of stuff like that. I suppose Ms. Blake could have left him some, when she came—although I don't know why in the world she would, since he was just playing sick." She paused. "Of course, I suppose he fooled her, too. He was proud of fooling everybody."

I pulled in my breath. "Ms. Blake? Marla Blake? When did *she* visit him?"

"Why, yes, Marla Blake." Mrs. Mueller smiled at me. "I'm sure you know her, China, from Friends of the Library. She owns the hospice now. I saw the two of them sitting out on Mr. MacDonald's back porch the morning I went to Chicago to help take care of Martha. I remember, because I was rushing around, finishing up my packing, and just happened to glance out of my upstairs bedroom window. And there they were, chatting away a mile a minute. She'd brought takeout, too. They were having an early lunch."

"And what day did you leave for Chicago?" I asked.

"August fifteenth," Mrs. Mueller said promptly. "A couple of days before, Howie—he's my brother-in-law—called from Chicago and said my sister wanted me to come and stay with her. So I called Mrs. Bosworth at the travel agency and she got me a ticket, and Mrs. Van Kirsten took me to the airport and Howie picked me up that night at O'Hare." She paused for breath. "It's amazing how you can get up in the morning in Texas and go to bed in Chicago. All in one day."

August 15. That put Marla Blake on the scene on or just before the presumed date of MacDonald's death. It wasn't definitive, but Mrs. Mueller's eyewitness testimony was likely the best the prosecuting attorney was going to get. She had taken us from possible accident or suicide to murder in the space of a few minutes, and had given us a potential murder suspect, as well. Of course, there were holes, but—

"You were gone how long?" I asked.

"Over a month and a half." She sighed. "I don't begrudge dear Martha the time I spent with her. After she passed, we had the funeral, and then I stayed on for a week to help Howie pack up her things for the Goodwill. That's always so sad, you know, and it's not easy to do." Another sigh. "But it was a long time to be away. I missed putting out my fall vegetable garden. And I didn't find out about Mr. MacDonald until the day I got back and looked across the alley and they were tearing down his house."

"My goodness," Lara said. "That must have been a shock."

"Oh, it was," Mrs. Mueller said earnestly. "You could have knocked me over with a feather when I saw it. I immediately thought, well, he's gone to Guadalajara, the way he said he would, but why in the world are they tearing down his house? So I went next door and asked Mrs. Van Kirsten what about it, and she told me that Mr. MacDonald had died just about the time I left, apparently, but they didn't find the poor man's body for quite a long time. Which was why the house had to be torn down, since the smell had got to the point where it just couldn't be cleaned up. Mrs. Van Kirsten said I should be glad I wasn't here, because it had been plenty hot and the air conditioner was shut off over there. Things got so ripe the day before they found him that the neighbors couldn't use their barbecues out in their backyards."

"Oh, dear," Lara said, wide-eyed. "How awful for everybody."

"Yes, it was, just terrible, apparently. Mrs. Van Kirsten is the one who called the police about the odor. She told me all about how the police came, and then there was the autopsy, and after that the inquest. Oh, and she gave me the mail she'd picked up at Mr. MacDonald's house. That was before she knew he was dead, you see. The man collected catalogs and they were all piled up on his porch, and she thought so much mail might invite burglars, although how a burglar could stand going into that place, I don't know. So she put everything in a shopping bag and gave it all to me. There was a letter from his friend in Guadalajara wanting to know why he hadn't arrived when he said he would. I answered that and told the lady that Mr. MacDonald was dead and wouldn't be coming to stay with her."

"Ah," I said, and let out a long breath. "I wonder—would you mind letting me see the letter from Guadalajara? Or better yet, would you loan it to me?"

"Of course," she said. "I'll get it for you before you go."

"Thank you." I paused. "You said earlier that you went to the police. Why did you do that?"

She pushed her bifocals up on her nose. "Well, I'm sure it was none of my business. But you know, I just couldn't see where that old man got so much morphine after he'd cleaned out all his painkillers, which to me meant that he didn't do it accidentally, especially since he said right out that he wasn't sick and didn't *need* any painkillers. And he'd made all these plans for Guadalajara and was really excited about going, which made me think that he wouldn't have wanted to kill himself. And that left—" She stopped.

"That left what?" I asked quietly.

She twisted uncomfortably in her chair. "Well, murder, I suppose. But that's pretty silly, isn't it? I mean, he could be unpleasant and even nasty, if he didn't want you around, which is why I suppose the nurses stopped coming. But I couldn't think of a reason in the world why anybody would want to kill him. So I did try to talk to the policeman about it, but when he asked me that question you just asked—'Well, then, if it wasn't an accident or suicide, what *was* it?'—I couldn't come up with an answer. So I tried to forget about it, until Kelly came over to lunch last week to talk to me about it." She scrunched up her face. "And now she's dead, too. Seems like a kind of curse, doesn't it?"

I chuckled mildly. "Well, if that's what it is, all I can say is that the three of us had better be careful."

Lara smiled at that, but Mrs. Mueller didn't. "Mind what I say," she said soberly. She gave me a direct look. "Didn't I hear that you used to be a lawyer, China? Maybe the police would listen if *you* went and talked to them."

"I'm not so sure about that," I said, remembering that Sheila did not always welcome my suggestions. "But I'm definitely going to give it a try."

"That's the spirit," she said, and pushed the plate toward me. "Have another cookie. It'll give you strength. I'll go look for that letter."

Chapter Fifteen

Lara didn't say much as I drove her back to her car. I didn't prod her. I guessed that she was thinking of the sadness that lay ahead of her that day: helping Kelly's mother and husband plan a funeral for a daughter and wife who'd died too young and by someone's dark intention. It wouldn't be easy.

I was silent, too. Mrs. Mueller had provided a great deal of detail, some of it relevant, some not. I needed time to sort through everything and pull out the information I intended to share with Sheila. The letter from MacDonald's friend in Guadalajara, Sarita Gomez, for instance, which Mrs. Mueller had given me. Ms. Gomez had been disturbed when her old friend—they had once been sweethearts, so it seemed from the letter—didn't arrive at the time he'd planned, and hadn't answered his phone, either. The letter was strong evidence that MacDonald wasn't a candidate for suicide, and I was confident that he'd been murdered. I thought of Mrs. Mueller's report of seeing Marla Blake at MacDonald's house on the day she left for Chicago. She might have identified his murderer as well, and Kelly had given us the motive behind the killing. There were still a few holes to fill: identifying the driver and the vehicle that had rammed Kelly, for one. That was something the police could do better than I, given their forensic capabilities. But I thought I had enough to convince Sheila to reopen the MacDonald investigation.

Before I could see Sheila, however, there was something I had to do. After I dropped off Lara, I stopped at the shop and was glad to see that Ruby—wildly resplendent in a rainbow caftan over red jeggings—had everything under control.

"I'd like to take another hour or maybe two," I said to Ruby, and told her why. "Would that be okay?"

"No problem as far as I'm concerned," Ruby said, straightening up from a box of dream catchers she was unpacking for display. "Miriam is here to help, and Cass has a helper in the tearoom. You can take the rest of the day if you need to." She held up a peacock-feather creation decorated with bits of blue and green stained glass and glittery ribbon streamers. "Isn't this gorgeous?" She pinned it to the display. "Good dreams guaranteed."

"I need one of those," I said. "Last night, I dreamed I found McQuaid facedown on the floor. In the dream, I never found out if he was alive or dead."

Ruby turned to regard me, frowning,. "You still haven't heard from McQuaid?"

I shook my head. "Not since the message he left on Monday evening."

"Oh, hon," she said sympathetically, and enveloped me in her rainbow arms. "I would tell you not to worry, but I know it wouldn't do any good. Just try to keep from worrying too much." She paused, holding me out at arm's length. "And watch out for doors. Please."

"That's still the best you can do?"

"Well, I don't know if this means anything," she answered slowly, "but when I was brushing my teeth this morning, this weird picture popped into my head. A kind of shimmery image of a door, just sort of hanging there in space. I think it was light brown, or a kind of rusty orange, maybe. Does that help?"

"Not much," I said with a frown. "But I'll be on the lookout."

"Please do," she said. "And if I get a clearer picture, I'll let you know."

THE Pecan Springs Police Department used to be located in the basement of the old brick building that also housed the town's Tourist and Information Center, the Parks and Utilities Department, and a sizable colony of Mexican free-tailed bats that lived in the attic and swarmed out at sunset on mosquito patrol. When Sheila inherited the department from the former longtime police chief, Bubba Harris, the day-shift dispatcher, receptionist, and clerk to the justice of the peace was a woman named Dorrie Hull, whose uniform consisted of jeans, a fringed Western shirt, and hoop earrings as big as saucers. Dorrie sat behind a wooden counter, greeting the people who came to pay parking and speeding fines (cash only, no checks), occasionally speaking into the dispatcher's mike, and painting her nails. She came from Lubbock. On her desk was a silver-framed, autographed photo of her rock-and-roll hero, Buddy Holly, who had also come from Lubbock, and a saguaro-shaped ashtray, always full. Dorrie was a chain-smoker. If you had to wait to see the chief, it was best to do it outdoors. The basement had no windows.

But times have changed. The police department now shares a modern office building with City Hall and the municipal court on West San Marcos Street, a block from the courthouse square. The bats moved to the I-35 bridge over the Pecan River, and Dorrie packed up her Buddy Holly photo and her nail polish and went back to Lubbock. If you want to pay your parking fine, there's an office for that, with a neat young lady behind a computer. Or you can pay with a credit card, by telephone or online. Some people say they miss Dorrie, but the work probably gets done faster. And the air is easier to breathe.

The chief's office is at the very end of the hall, behind another, smaller office that belongs to her assistant, Connie Page, a recently divorced, attractive forty-something. I expected to find Sheila at her desk, digging out from under her usual mountain of paperwork, or on the phone with the accounting office, trying to squeeze enough money out of the budget to buy body cams for her officers. The chief's job, she says, is mostly paperwork, personnel, and community relations. She'd love to get out in the field and actually fight crime, but that doesn't happen very often.

Sheila wasn't in her office, however. She was closeted with the city attorney for the rest of the morning, Connie said, and after that she was scheduled for a luncheon meeting with the mayor.

"Rats," I said. "What's her next free half hour?"

"A whole half hour?" Connie picked up a large blue plastic cup and spooned something out of it. "You're sure you can't manage with fifteen minutes? Time's tight today."

As Sheila's gatekeeper, Connie is a good friend to have, and we have occasionally worked together to get something done under the radar. Now, I frowned. "Come on, Con. I need thirty minutes at least. This is business." I paused, peering into her cup. "What's that you're eating?"

"My lunch." She opened a drawer, pulled out a plastic spoon, and dipped it into the cup. "Try it." She held up the spoon.

I tasted. "Mmm. Delicious. What is it?"

"Orange-banana slush. I keep it frozen in the dayroom

239

fridge." She sighed. "Of course, I'd rather have a cheeseburger, but this is much healthier. Plus, orange juice reduces stress. And believe me, this is a high-stress job. Nonstop stress, from the time I clock in to the time I clock out." She took off her tortoiseshell-rimmed glasses and knuckled her eyes. "You said you wanted to see her on business, didn't you?"

"Yes. Police business."

She put her glasses back on and frowned at the day's calendar on her computer screen. "Well, I suppose I can move Internal Affairs to late afternoon and give you Quintana's half hour. He'll be pissed, but what else is new? Quintana makes a career out of letting people know he's stressed." She clicked a few keys. "How about one thirty to two, when the chief gets back from lunch?"

I was glad that Ruby had said that I could take the rest of the day if I had to. "Great," I said. "I'm just happy to get on her calendar. She's a busy lady."

"You don't know the half of it," Connie said grimly. "Morning, noon, and night, that woman never stops. She doesn't miss a beat and she never forgets anything. I don't know how she does it. Me, I have to have a quiet evening with my feet up or I'm absolutely no good the next day. Plays havoc with my social life. Guys don't like to date girls who need to put their feet up in the evening." She picked up her cup and spoon. "If something happens to her lunch and she gets back to the office early, do you want her to phone you?"

"Definitely," I said. "I'll stay loose and keep my fingers crossed."

She made a face. "More likely, she'll call and say she has to do such and such with so-and-so and tell me to call you and cancel. I'm apologizing right now for that," she added, "in case I'm so stressed out that I forget to apologize when it happens."

I rolled my eyes. "Don't let her cancel, Con, please. Tell

her I need to talk to her about the Kaufman case. And the MacDonald case as well. The two are related."

Connie scowled at me over her glasses. "MacDonald? MacDonald?" She waved her spoon. "Who's that? I don't remember—"

"As in Ronald. The old man who died of morphine poisoning last August and wasn't found until he was grossly stinky."

"Oh, that one." Connie wrinkled her nose. "Phew. I remember him. But that case has been closed for months. Maude Porterfield ruled—"

"I know what Maude Porterfield ruled. Maude is a sweet old thing and we all love her dearly, but she isn't infallible. If she had known then what I know now, she would have ruled differently, I promise you." I tapped her desk with a finger for emphasis. "The chief needs to reopen that case, Con. Today, if not sooner. I'll tell her why, in detail, when I see her."

"Well, that's mildly interesting," Connie said, tilting her head. "You're telling me that this MacDonald thing is connected to the *Kaufman* case?"

"Yes, that's what I'm saying." I leaned forward, feeling urgent. "Listen, Con, if the chief says she wants to cancel, tell her that Kelly Kaufman was killed because she knew about MacDonald's murder and she had a very good idea who did it and how and why—and that *I* know what Kelly knew." I was lying. I didn't know who. Not for sure.

Connie peered at me over her glasses. "Really?"

"Really. New information on both cases, guaranteed. In fact, I'm ready to tell the chief the whole, complete backstory, beginning to end." This was an exaggeration, but not by much.

"My goodness," Connie said admiringly. "You *have* been a busy girl. But I'll be the first to say that new information on the Kaufman case will be welcome. The chief has been in a very bad mood about it." She paused. "Although she's also been worried, because she hasn't heard from that husband of hers. I understand that your guy is with him and that they've both vamoosed. Mexico, was what the chief was saying. Juárez, maybe."

"Something like that," I said. I kept my voice level, although I was troubled to hear about Sheila's concern. She certainly hadn't let me see that when we'd talked. But maybe she was trying to keep me from fretting. Now, hearing that she was worried, the level of my apprehension shot up several hundred points.

"You mustn't worry, China," Connie advised, seeing my expression. "Those guys are smart and experienced. They know what they're doing. Whatever comes along, I'm sure they can handle it easily."

"That's what everybody says," I replied. Literally everybody. Charlie, Bob, the boys at Beans', Ruby, Sheila, now Connie.

She raised both eyebrows. "You don't believe it?"

"Of course I believe it. But sometimes . . ." I wanted to say that, as a practical matter, sometimes bad things can get so huge and hairy that even the smartest and most experienced guys are overwhelmed. But I have a habit of looking under rocks for problems, and that's probably what I was doing here. I certainly didn't want to seem disloyal or appear to lack faith in my husband's ability to take care of himself. After all, he had dealt with plenty of huge, hairy bad things when he was with Houston Homicide, and he'd come through in one piece.

So I managed to find a smile and pasted it on my face. "Yes, of course I believe it," I said confidently. "They're big guys. I'm sure they'll be okay." I paused, getting away from the subject. "Say, do you happen to have a Pecan Springs phone directory handy?"

"Sure thing." She reached into a drawer and pulled it out.

I found the names I was looking for, but the residence numbers and addresses were unlisted, which wasn't surprising, since the people could easily be reached through their business. I handed the directory back to Connie. I was about to ask her to look up the numbers—after all, this was police business. But her phone rang. She put down her cup and reached for it.

I put down the directory and turned to go. "Thanks, Con," I said. "I'll see you at one thirty. On the dot."

"Unless we call and cancel," Connie reminded me, picking up the receiver.

I rolled my eyes. "No, not that. No, please!"

BACK in the car, I sat for a moment, thinking. It wasn't eleven thirty yet, which meant that I had at least two hours to kill. I could go back to the shop, but it sounded like Ruby had all the help she needed. So I might as well put the time to good use. For that, I needed those addresses. I fished out my phone and called Jessica at the *Enterprise*.

She picked up on the first ring. "Hey, China," she said briskly. "What's up?" Without waiting for an answer, she added, "Sorry I haven't gotten back to you on that research project. An eighteen-wheeler jackknifed on I-35 and a truck carrying dozens of crates of live chickens ran into it. The state police closed all six lanes, and it took a couple of hours to round up the chickens. Kinda fun to watch. But between that and the city council meeting, I've been slammed all morning."

"No problem, Jessie, really. I owe you for the clips of those items you sent me last night. One of them, the piece on Ronald MacDonald, gave me just what I was looking for. I checked it out this morning. You can put a hold on the research project until we see how this lead pans out."

"Awesome. And yes, you owe me. I hope you're not forgetting our deal. When do I get my story?"

"I'm meeting with Sheila this afternoon. There may be a couple of developments later today." I spoke with more confidence than I felt. "As soon as she gives the word, I'll call you with details. In the meantime, I need two resident addresses. They're unlisted in the directory. Do you think you can get them for me?"

"I'll see," Jessica said. "Names?"

I told her and heard keys clicking. "Looks like they're in the same neighborhood," Jessica said, and rattled off two street addresses. "That's a high-end community out there, China. These folks must be doing pretty well for themselves."

"They work in a high-profit-margin business," I said drily, remembering that the profit on the hospice could run as high as $120,000 a month. From the *honest* side of the business. There was no telling how much they were raking in from the dark side.

Jessica paused. "Wait a minute. This first name you gave me, Marla Blake. She's the owner of the Pecan Springs Community Hospice, isn't she? And the dead guy in the story I emailed you, the one who hung around so long that they had to get the hazmat unit in for the cleanup—wasn't he a hospice patient?" I heard the rattle of keys. "And this other address you're asking for. He's a hospice doctor, isn't he?"

"Jessica," I said grimly, "you are just too damn good."

"You bet," she said. "And Kelly Kaufman was a hospice nurse, wasn't she? So if she really did sniff out a murder, maybe the victim she had in mind was this guy MacDonald, who was a hospice patient. And you're sniffing out the hospice owner and a hospice doc, so you must think—"

"Back off, Jessie," I cautioned. I had enough to manage

without Jessica dealing herself into the game. "Just back off. You'll get your story later. I promise."

She didn't back off. "So you must think you're on the trail of whoever killed MacDonald and rammed Kaufman's vehicle. And you're thinking that it's got to be Blake or Burgess or both." I could hear the excitement in her voice. "Am I right? No, don't answer that. I *know* I'm right!"

"Amazing, Sherlock," I said with exaggerated sarcasm. "You get the prize for limitless leaps of logic, as one of my law professors used to say."

Jessica ignored me. "I'm going with you," she said. "You're onto the story, China. I want to be there to see what develops."

"No," I said quickly and urgently. Too urgently.

"Why?" She caught my tone and her voice changed. "You're afraid it's too dangerous? You're going after Kelly Kaufman's killer and you don't want to share the risk. That's it, isn't it?"

"No, of course not." I backpedaled swiftly. "It's not necessary, that's all." I managed a chuckle. "Jessie, you have an overactive imagination. I'm just going sightseeing. I'm sure you've got better things to do than tag along with me."

Overactive imagination . . . tag along. Those were the wrong things to say. I had insulted her, and I knew it the second the words were out of my mouth.

But to my surprise, she didn't seem to be offended. There was a brief silence. Then, "Well, you can't blame a girl for trying," she said lightly. "Oops, there goes my other line blinking. Maybe they're chasing pigs this time. Gotta go."

I breathed a sigh of relief. "Talk to you later. And thanks again."

"You're welcome," Jessica said. "And don't forget my story."

* * *

ACCORDING to the addresses Jessica gave me, Marla Blake and her son, Christopher Burgess, lived about six blocks apart off Sierra Hills Drive on the far west side of Pecan Springs. Some fifteen years ago, the upscale development was carved out of beautiful, untouched ranch country—cedar-clad hills, limestone ledges, clear creeks, wooded slopes, open meadows—and to the developer's credit, the character of the landscape was largely unchanged. There were no aboveground utilities, the lots were wide and deep, and the main street curled at a leisurely pace around and up and over Turkey Ridge, the houses becoming larger and more expensive as the road wound upward.

I found Christopher Burgess' house first, at the far end of a cul-de-sac at the highest point of the ridge. There was a mailbox at the curb, and I checked the street number to be sure I had the right place. The house, barely visible, jutted out of a high, steep hill that lifted up and away from the street, and the curving driveway was screened from view by several strategically placed plantings of dense junipers. I drove past the place slowly, looking up at the hill, but the house offered almost no public presence. All I could see was the slope of a roof, a wide expanse of glass windows facing east, and a cantilevered wooden deck facing west, no doubt providing inspirational views of the sun rising and setting across the Hill Country.

I turned and drove back the way I had come, parking around a curve some thirty yards away from the house. I wasn't exactly sure what I was looking for or why I had driven up here, except that I had some free time and wanted to put it to use. When I phoned Jessica for the addresses, I had the vague idea of taking a quick look at both residences so I could provide Sheila with a little more background on the main characters when I told her the story. I imagine that most doctors are wealthy, even one who has incurred the displeasure of the Texas Medical Board. But the Burgess house, in a neighborhood where the properties are worth somewhere north of five or six million dollars, gave concrete expression to the somewhat abstract notion of Medicare fraud.

I lowered the car window and sat for a moment, enjoying the juniper-scented fresh spring breeze. The late-morning sun washed the trees with a cheerful brightness, a mocking-bird performed his borrowed songs on a live oak limb, and a yellow skimmer, its butterfly wings the color of ripe lemons, perched on the hood of my car. A gray cat with a bright blue collar strolled out of a nearby drive, taking his sweet time to cross the street in front of me. At the base of a mailbox, a clump of native flowers—mealy blue sage, Mexican gold poppy, and lavender prairie penstemon—brightened the curb. It was a lovely morning to simply take a deep breath, relax, and enjoy the moment. To just *be* in the moment, as Ruby is always advising me.

But as I have frequently admitted to Ruby, I would much rather *do* than *be*, and I often find myself doing something just because I'm curious. In fact, as McQuaid will tell you, curiosity is one of my character flaws. It has occasionally gotten me into trouble, when I've failed to look where I was going or forgotten that a little healthy fear can be a useful thing.

But there was nothing to fear here. The morning was pretty, the neighborhood was safe and quiet, and I wasn't going to do anything to invite trouble. All I wanted was a closer look so I could give Sheila a better idea of at least one of the people at the center of this case. Nothing wrong with that, was there? Like the Burgess house, the other houses were set so far back from the street or were so carefully screened with trees that they couldn't be seen. And since it was late morning, in the middle of the week, most of the occupants would be away from home.

I mulled this over for a moment, feeling the curiosity nudging me, pushing me. If I got out and walked around, it wasn't likely that I would be seen, much less stopped and questioned. But it might be a good idea to have a cover story, just in case. I reached over the back of the seat and snagged the green Thyme and Seasons clipboard that held extra sheets from one of my walk-and-talk sessions with an herb class in the garden. Then I fished under the passenger seat and found a navy blue cap emblazoned with the words *Pedernales Electric Cooperative*. It had been forgotten at our house by a friend of McQuaid's and had made its way to my car one rainy morning. I stuck it on my head and pulled down the bill. My khaki slacks and navy blazer didn't look much like a uniform, but I figured I could pass for a PEC employee checking out transformers.

I dropped a pen and my cell phone into my blazer pocket, stuck the clipboard under my arm, and locked my purse in the car, then walked up the street jauntily, as if I had every reason in the world for being there. At the Burgess mailbox, I paused and (in case somebody was watching from one of those concealed houses) pretended to make a note on the clipboard. A wide wooden stair with rustic cedar railings ascended the steep hill in the direction of the house high above, but I ignored it. Instead, I turned and walked up the sloping asphalt driveway, which curved to the right around a limestone outcrop bright with Texas lantana and scarlet hedgehog cactus, and then back to the left, where it widened out onto an asphalt apron in front of the garage.

I was maybe fifty yards from the street now, and well above it, on the slope of the hill. Ahead and above me, built against the hillside, was the house, the walls of limestone and glass with a wide wraparound wooden deck featuring clusters of expensive-looking deck furniture. A flight of shallow-set limestone steps angled up the hill to my right—another entrance to the house, I thought. And directly in front of me was a two-car garage built under the house. Off to my right, on a narrow slot of pavement, a twenty-foot sailboat sat on a trailer, neatly covered with a lashed-down blue tarp. On my left, a silver-gray Porsche 911 was parked in front of the garage door. The door was open, giving me a clear view of everything inside.

Like most garages, this one said a lot about its owner. A snazzy blue-and-white powerboat on a trailer took up most of the left bay of the garage. Around it, hung from the walls and ceiling and stacked on the floor, was enough gear to stock a small sporting-goods shop. A pair of rugged-looking mountain bikes, snow skis, water skis, life preservers, fishing rods and nets, coiled climbing ropes and bungee cords, tennis racquets, a couple of expensive-looking compound bows, the furled yellow sail of what looked like a hang glider—Chris Burgess was obviously an outdoor guy.

And that wasn't all. In the right bay of the garage was a late-model Hummer.

An *orange* Hummer.

Chapter Sixteen

Was I surprised? I was and I wasn't.

I was already confident that both Marla Blake and her doctor son, Chris Burgess, were deeply implicated in the long-running Medicare fraud at the hospice. The scheme required a doctor's input and the owner/manager's collaboration in the creation of fake or doctored patient records, so it had to be a team project. After listening to Mrs. Mueller's story that morning, it seemed clear that Ronald MacDonald had been party to the fraud and that he had been blackmailing Chris Burgess, threatening to reveal what was going on. When he made a demand that was difficult or impossible to meet, it seemed better to take him out. Marla Blake had handled that chore, if Mrs. Mueller's testimony could be believed.

Then either mother or son or both had discovered that Kelly was putting together a whistle-blower case and that she had gotten into the office and copied the patient files. Had Charlie Lipman—deliberately or inadvertently—clued them in on what she had done and let them know that she was staying in my cottage? I didn't think he would answer that question for me, but Sheila would no doubt put it to him, and he'd be hard-pressed not to answer her.

In any event, either Blake or Burgess—Burgess, I thought—had tracked Kelly to the cottage. He tried to break in while she was asleep in the wee hours of Monday but got frightened off by little, loud Miss Lula, the neighborhood watchdog. Judging from the man-size shoe print on the bedroom carpet, he was also the one who had broken in and ransacked the place, looking for Kelly's computer and her copy of those incriminating files. He had plenty of motivation, for the restitution, fines, and prison penalties for Medicare fraud are stiff. He wouldn't be in prison for life, but he'd be there until he was an old, old man. And while he might have plenty of money now, between the Medicare restitution, the penalties, and the cost of his defense, he wouldn't have a cent left when he got out.

So no, I wasn't surprised to see, parked right in front of me, the vehicle—the *orange* vehicle—that might have knocked Kelly off the road. If this was it, we were back to accident or intention. Burgess might have been trailing her, barreled up behind her, miscalculated, and struck her without intending to. That's what the defense would argue. The prosecutor, on the other hand, would argue that he had hit her on purpose, aiming to scare her off the case or shut her up permanently. And the malfunctioning airbag did the job for him.

But I *was* surprised—bowled over, almost—by the breathtaking size and sheer arrogance of the vehicle. I stood for a moment, staring at it, feeling my heart knocking against my rib cage. *Damn, that sucker is big.* Big and intimidating. Seen from the rear, the Hummer was a massive block of automotive conspicuous consumption, nearly seven feet wide by seven feet high, unapologetically tanklike, a gas guzzler and proud of it. Off-road-worthy, capable of taking the

251

Sierras in a single bound, but (I had read) sheer hell to maneuver on city streets and in heavy traffic. Still, it was the wet dream of every cool, hot-blooded American hero wealthy enough to indulge himself with this symbol of wretched excess and macho enough to think he could actually drive it.

As I stood there studying the thing, however, I knew it wasn't the Hummer's rear end I had to see. It was the *front*. If this was the vehicle that had struck the Astro, the damage, if there was any, would be to the front end, the right front. And surely there would be some damage, given the orange paint on the left rear of the Astro and the flecks the crime tech had found at the scene.

If I could confirm that, it would be all the evidence Sheila needed to tie Burgess to Kelly's death. But I needed to confirm it now, as in *right* now, this minute. With the cops on the lookout for a damaged orange vehicle, it wasn't likely that Burgess would be dumb enough to try to get the Hummer repaired. But it would be an easy matter for him to drive it down the street, wait until a witness—a jogger, a delivery truck—appeared on the scene, then pretend to lose control, run up over the curb, and ram it into a tree, destroying whatever damage there was and creating more. It was a wonder he hadn't thought to do that already. So yes, I needed to check it out right now.

But from where I was standing, it looked as if the Hummer's front bumper was snugged up tight against the back wall of the garage. The only way I could see the front end was to scoot in there and get a quick look. It was a tight fit back there, and since the garage lights were off, that corner was pretty dark—clearly, a job for somebody who was four foot ten, weighed less than a hundred pounds, and had eyes like a cat. I wished briefly for a flashlight, then decided that there was probably just enough light to see what I was looking for. If I made it snappy, I could be in and out in less than a minute.

Or maybe not. I took a step to my right and peered down the Hummer's length. The dark tinted side and rear windows made it look even more deliberately intimidating, and the damn thing was so wide that it took up more than its share of floor. There wasn't much more than eighteen inches of clearance between its right flank and the unfinished garage wall. I eyed the space and made a calculation. I'm not exactly skinny, but I'm reasonably limber and athletic, one of the benefits of spending hours every week in the garden, spading, raking, and pushing wheelbarrows. If I sucked it up, turned sideways, and sidled in, I might be able to make my way to the front of the vehicle before I had to breathe again. I looked again. Yes, I could probably do it. But *should* I?

And there I was, squarely impaled on the horns of a dilemma. My heart was racing fast, I was primed to spring into action, but I was frozen in place. My adventurous self, the part of me that loves taking chances and thrives on risk, wanted to get in there, get out, and have the job done with so she could prance off to Sheila with the results. *Easy peasy,* I could hear her saying. *Piece of cake. No problemo. Go for it, girl, right now, before Burgess shows up and asks you what you think you're doing on his property.*

On the other hand, my cautious, lawyerly self was hanging back, shouting, *You've gotta be kidding! Haven't you ever heard of* trespass, *for Pete's sake? You want to get disbarred, you freakin' idiot? Get the hell out of here this minute, before Burgess shows up and calls the cops!*

But if Burgess had damaged the right-front end when he used the Hummer to ram Kelly, he wasn't going to call the cops. No, of course not. He was going to come after me with whatever weapon he had handy. A tire tool, a crowbar, a *gun*.

Yeah, a gun. And the hell of it was, he would be legally justified in injuring or killing me, and at the thought, apprehension twisted in my gut. My plan for this little midday venture, vague as it was, had not included trespass. Strictly speaking, of course, I was trespassing on Burgess' property just by walking up his drive. But I hadn't seen a No Trespassing sign, and anyway, people—delivery guys, meter readers, tax appraisers—walk up driveways all the time. That could be more or less overlooked, whereas entering Burgess' garage and poking around among his prized sporting possessions was an entirely different matter. My lawyerly self understood what the media calls the *castle doctrine* all too clearly and was calling it to my attention, just in case I'd forgotten it. Also cleverly called the Make My Day law, it permits a homeowner to use deadly force to defend his property and gives him a free pass if he kills the intruder, even when the intruder is unarmed. If Burgess wanted to shoot me, he'd get away with murder. Happens frequently in Texas, and when it does, the gun lobby stands up and cheers.

However.

Kelly was already dead, and if this guy had killed her, I didn't want him to get away with *her* murder. Ignoring my apprehension and dropping a gag order on my lawyerly self, I darted a quick glance around. There was nobody in sight. I glanced up. Nobody on the deck, either. I stepped quickly to the left and put my hand on the hood of the Porsche. Stone cold. I told myself that Burgess likely had another vehicle— most doctors have at least three, don't they? He and his car were out somewhere tooling around Pecan Springs, doing the kinds of things that doctors do on weekday mornings. All I needed was a minute to get in, a minute to look, and a minute to get out—three minutes at the most. And then I could tell Sheila that this orange monster was the vehicle that had struck Kelly's Astro. Or wasn't, as the case may be.

With this calculation, I could feel my risk-taker self flexing her muscles, breathing deep, taking charge. I put my clipboard and cap on the driveway and stepped into the garage, sucked in my stomach, turned sideways, and began sidling between the Hummer and the wall of the garage.

It was a tighter fit than I had thought, and there wasn't much wiggle room. I felt something sharp—a protruding nail, probably—grab at the back of my jacket and hold on tight. In an attempt to get loose, I rotated my shoulders, pushing my chest against the Hummer, until I heard the cloth rip and yank free. But I was too out of breath to curse the tear in my favorite jacket. By the time I reached the front end of the orange beast, I had broken out in a cold sweat and was sucking in big gulps of air.

Unfortunately, I had been right in my first assessment of the difficulty. The front bumper was smack up against the back wall of the garage, and the corner was so tight that there was no room to bend over and get a good look. What's more, the Hummer was such a hulking monster that it blocked any light that might be coming in through the open garage door.

But even in the dimness, I could see that the right orange bumper extension undeniably hung loose. I could wiggle it with my fingers. When I bent over and reached around with my right hand and ran my fingers lightly across the end of the upper part of the bumper, I felt a noticeable crease. And then my fingers caught the sharp edge of a broken fog light, and I was sure. Jessie had said that in addition to paint flecks, Sheila's crime tech had picked up shards of glass and reported the possibility that a headlight had been broken in the collision. If the glass turned out to be a chemical match for the broken fog light, that would put the Hummer at the scene of the crash. A defense attorney might try to dance around that one when the case came to trial, but jurors like forensic testimony. The prosecutor would no doubt call this a humdinger.

I straightened up, mentally applauding my clever little joke. There was more than enough evidence here to justify a search warrant—and Sheila should tell her guys to look for running shoes while they were at it. The prosecutor would be delighted to get a match to the muddy print on the carpet in my cottage bedroom. Added to the paint flecks and the glass shards, that would pretty much clinch a charge of vehicular manslaughter, which would be upgraded to vehicular homicide if the prosecutor decided he could tie in Kelly's evidence of hospice fraud. It probably wouldn't be the first time that Medicare fraud proved to be a motive for murder.

But now that I had seen what I came to see, it was time to get the hell out. It was too tight a squeeze to turn around, so I reversed direction and began to sidle toward the rear of the vehicle, hoping I wouldn't get snagged on that nail again. But I had managed only three or four crabwise steps when I heard a loud *click*. I felt a spurt of fear and froze, turning my head, trying to track the direction of the sound. A second later, there was a raucous electronic buzz, and with a clang and a rattle, the garage door began to descend.

The door was coming down! My heart was thudding in my chest and my breath was ragged. My first thought was to make a quick break for it and try to dive down under the descending door. But I was jammed tight between the Hummer and the wall, and there was no possibility of a quick break. That door was coming down *fast*. In an awful, blood-freezing instant, I realized I was imprisoned here, in a killer's garage, pinned like a bug behind the killer's road hog.

And that wasn't all of it. That door had not decided to come down all of a sudden and all on its own. Somebody had flicked a wall switch or was operating the remote gizmo that raised and lowered it. Which meant that somebody—most likely Burgess—knew that I was here. He had seen me through a window maybe, or I had triggered some sort of silent alarm in the house when I entered the garage. He was figuring that I was there to hot-wire his Hummer and make off with it.

This conclusion was immediately ratified by the sound of a dog barking. A dog with a deep, gruff, snarly growl, the kind of sound that belongs to a *big* dog—a Doberman or a German shepherd or a pit bull. Well, of course it would be a big dog. Burgess wouldn't want to go tooling around town in his giant burnt-orange Hummer with a Peke or a mini-poodle riding shotgun. That wouldn't be cool.

But while Burgess might know I was in his garage, he didn't know *where* in his garage I was, exactly. The lights hadn't come on yet, and with the door coming down, the only light came from the row of windows near the top of the door. The garage was plunged into thick, oily-smelling twilight. I had two choices. I could stay where I was, sandwiched and helpless, an easy target the minute Burgess turned the lights on and he and his dog started looking around for me. Or, in the few seconds of darkness left, I could—

I took three crabwise steps back to my right again, back to the Hummer's massive front end. I had no plan, not even half a thought. I was acting purely on an instinct to move, to get out of a jam. I jacked up my right leg, wedged the toe of my loafer into the corner of the bumper, and heaved myself up on the Hummer's orange hood, which flexed and popped a little under my weight. Flattening myself on my belly, I squirmed across the hood and dropped to the concrete floor on the other side of the vehicle, awkwardly and hard.

Damn! As I came down, my right foot hit something on the floor. It was loose and round—a tennis ball, maybe—and my foot skidded out from under me, giving my ankle a quick, sharp twist. The pain shot up my leg to my knee, and I leaned against the vehicle to take the weight of it and bit my lip to keep from crying out.

But there wasn't time to think about my ankle or let myself feel it, even. The dog was still barking, louder now, and at any moment a door might open and the animal might come rushing out. Bending over, crouching low, I hobbled the few steps to the driver's-side door, reached up, and pulled the handle, praying that it was unlocked. It came open. I planted a foot on the running board, grabbed the steering wheel, and used it to haul myself up and into the driver's seat, thankful that the interior dome light hadn't come on. I didn't want the noise of a door slam, but I pulled it shut until I felt it latch, then groped for the door lock, found it, and pushed it down. There was a satisfying *clunk* as all the doors locked. I was still imprisoned in Burgess' garage, but at least I was locked in his Hummer, where he might not think to look for me. And if he did, he might not see me, because the windows were darkly tinted. What's more, he probably wouldn't shoot me through the window. He'd be too concerned about damaging his damn vehicle. Of course, he might have his key fob in his hand, poised to push a button and unlock all the doors. But he might *not*, in which case I'd be safe while he went to get his keys—for a few minutes, anyway.

I don't know what I was expecting the inside of a Hummer to look like, but it wasn't this. It didn't feel a whole lot roomier than your everyday SUV. The dash was a rather ordinary display of dials and buttons and a GPS screen—obviously, the hulk's appeal was in its exterior size rather than its interior appointments.

But I didn't linger to look. The front two bucket seats had a wide console between them, and I scrambled through, thinking that I'd feel a whole lot safer, and be a whole lot harder to find, on the floor in the rear. I landed on my hands and knees.

I was in luck. Burgess must have been using his Hummer to haul his hang glider or surfboards or maybe just his big dog, because he had stripped out all the rear seats to create a large cargo space. The floor was covered with a wall-to-wall rubber mat and littered with cardboard boxes, plastic crates, tools, and coils of rope. I spotted a lug wrench and picked it up, thinking that, if worse came to worst, I'd have a weapon.

And then, along one side, I saw a heavy dark green canvas tarp, not neatly folded but bunched up. Dragging the lug wrench, I crawled under the tarp, pulling it over me on the theory that if he couldn't see me, he couldn't shoot me. The tarp must have been used on some sort of recent marine expedition, because it was damp and it smelled like fish. Very *much* like fish—and something else. Fresh marijuana, and a lot of it. I had hit the evidence jackpot today. From the smell of it, I was sharing my hidey-hole with a substantial quantity of high-potency weed.

Scrambling into the Hummer, I'd been too juiced with adrenaline to notice my damaged ankle, but the minute I lay still, it began to throb so painfully that it brought tears to my eyes. I was shaking, too, both from the pain and from a half-nauseous what's-next excitement. And from anger—at myself. I'd gotten into this dangerous fix because I wanted to know whether the Hummer bore evidence of a hit-and-run. But I hadn't stopped to think, as I should have, that my presence as an intruder might compromise the evidence and make it inadmissible. Instead of scoping out the vehicle myself, all I'd had to do was trot back down to the street and telephone Sheila to report that I had seen an orange Hummer, owned by a man who had a compelling motive to put Kelly Kaufman out of business. She would have recognized the urgency, politely excused herself from her lunch with the mayor, and gotten a search warrant. She would be on her way right now.

And then, as I lay there, mentally kicking myself for being such an idiot, I heard Ruby's words in my mind. "It's dangerous," she had said. "Don't go in. Don't go through that door!"

Door. Garage door. I gritted my teeth. Damn it, Ruby had been right! There *had* been a door, and I had ignored her warning and the admonishments of my lawyerly self and had gone right through it. The door had closed behind me, and now I couldn't get out. I would be in deep, serious trouble if I was found.

And then, close by, I heard a door slam. The dog barked twice and then growled, loudly, and—through an opening in the tarp—I saw the garage overhead lights come on. I shrank back farther under the tarp. The dog's barking was louder now, and imperative, a *Eureka!* bark. He was just outside the Hummer, and I guessed he'd caught my scent. Mine or Winchester's. I'd found one of my loafers in Winchester's bed that morning. He doesn't chew, but he'd given it a good licking, inside and out.

A moment later, someone—it had to be Burgess—tried the driver's-side door. He found it locked and muttered a short, sharp "Damn it." Then he raised his voice, and said savagely, "I know you're in there. I have a gun, and it's loaded. If you don't want to get hurt, you'd better unlock the door and get out, right now." He paused, and his voice took on a jagged edge. "And if you don't come voluntarily, I'll get my keys and haul your ass out. Which is it going to be?"

I was silent, trying not to move. But I had noticed that he hadn't said, *You just hang tight while I call 911*, which is what any normal person would say to a locked-in intruder. Of course he wouldn't call the cops. He was thinking of the Hummer's front-end damage, not to mention the fresh stash of pot hidden in the rear. He wouldn't risk inviting the police anywhere within sniffing range of this vehicle. And he wouldn't turn me over to them, either, since I'd be sure to rat on that marijuana.

Which left an alternative I didn't like to think about, and my grip tightened on the lug wrench. I doubted that he was used to shooting people, so he might be a little slow. And he wouldn't expect me to come out swinging. Maybe I could take out his kneecap before he tightened his trigger finger.

He waited. Then, when his threat didn't produce any immediate results, he took a different tack. "Hey," he said, softening his voice. "Hey, there. We don't have to make a big freakin' deal out of this, you know. It's just a little misunderstanding." His tone was more gentle, inviting, enticing. "All you have to do is open the door and come out so we can talk. Okay?"

If I didn't know about Kelly—and about MacDonald and the Medicare fraud and the stiff penalties and decades of prison Burgess faced if he was convicted—I might have been persuaded. But I *did* know, and I also knew that the minute I stepped out of the Hummer, this man would shoot me dead and claim his right to defend himself and his property under Texas' castle doctrine. He'd get away with it, too.

There was a moment of silence. And then he chuckled. "Oh, I get it," he said, sounding even more friendly now. "You're scared of the gun. Well, sure—that's understandable. Okay, tell you what. I'll put it down on the floor."

Another silence. *Yeah, I bet,* I thought with a sarcastic chuckle. *Sure, he's put it down.*

His voice warmed, and there was a hint of a reassuring chuckle in it. "There. Gun's gone. Out of reach. So you don't need to be afraid. Just open the door and—"

And then my cell phone shrieked.

The police siren was earsplitting. The Hummer's tin-can cavern seemed to amplify the sound, which rose and fell in pulsing waves of absolutely authentic mimicry. Panicked, I groped in my jacket pocket trying to shut it off. And as I pulled it out and saw that it was Ruby calling, I realized that the damn thing might be my best weapon. Letting it shriek, I pulled back the tarp cautiously and peeked through the tinted window.

Burgess lied. He had *not* put the gun down. He was standing beside the Hummer, his weapon raised in one hand, trying to figure out where the siren was coming from. *Inside? Just outside, on the driveway? Down on the street?* But it must have seemed to him that it was coming from everywhere. Caught between fight and flight, he was paralyzed. Consternation, confusion, and uncertainty were written all over his face.

And in the next moment, somebody—more than one somebody—was pounding on the garage door, pounding and shouting. Amid the voices, one stood out.

"Police!" Sheila was yelling. "Drop that weapon and open the door! Right now. That's an order!"

Chapter Seventeen

In a thriller, of course, the suspect would have turned and made a run for it, through the house and out a back door into the dense stand of cedars that clothed Turkey Ridge. There, gun in hand and extra cartridges in his pocket, he would have made a last-ditch stand, killing a couple of cops and maybe even an innocent neighbor or two before he was shot by a hero sniper who had climbed the ridge behind him and taken him out with one improbable long-distance bullet. The killing would have avenged the victims, saved the state the expense of a trial and a lengthy incarceration, and created a razzle-dazzle, shoot-'em-up ending.

But that isn't what happened. It took a moment for Burgess to sort through his options, realize how limited they were, and decide that he would do better to bluff, at least until he could get lawyered up. He opened the garage door, surrendered his weapon, and began to discuss the matter with Sheila in a reasonably civil way. Seeing that he was behaving, I unlocked the Hummer and climbed out.

But Burgess participated in the discussion only until he understood that he was a prime suspect in the Kaufman hit-

and-run and that Chief Dawson had brought a search warrant and was impounding his Hummer. At that point, he shut up and refused to talk without his lawyer present, which was smart, looking at it from the lawyer's point of view. An officer escorted him to the squad car that would take him down to the police station, where he would be held for questioning and then booking. But before that happened, I caught him looking at me a time or two. I thought he had probably remembered who I was and was wondering why *I* was the one who had locked herself in his Hummer.

When Burgess was on his way, Sheila inspected the damaged front end of the Hummer, opened the rear and hauled out a large plastic garbage bag stuffed full of marijuana, and dispatched two officers into the house to search for the running shoes that might have made the print in my cottage bedroom. Then she called for a tow truck to haul the Hummer to the impound yard.

As for me, I was keeping a low profile. I propped myself against the Porsche to take the weight off my damaged ankle while I tried to figure out how Sheila, in the company of ace reporter Jessica Nelson, had managed to get to Burgess' house just in time to keep him from shooting the intruder in his garage. That would be me.

It was Jessica who filled me in. I had told her to back off and I thought she'd complied. But, like any red-blooded, ambitious reporter, she had a different idea. She figured that I knew where the story was, and she was damn well going to be there, too.

But the more she thought about it, the more she thought it might be a good idea to check it out with Sheila, rather than freelance. After all, her standing as a crime reporter depended on just how close to a crime she could get, which depended, most of the time, on the chief's goodwill. Cross

Sheila, and Sheila would cross Jessie off her list of trusted reporters. Access is the name of the game.

So she stopped at the PSPD just about the time Sheila walked in. There had been a crisis in the mayor's office, the mayor had canceled lunch, and Sheila was headed back to her desk to tackle her stack of paperwork. Jessica filled Sheila in on what she knew about the MacDonald case, the connection to the hospice, and my request for the addresses of Marla Blake and Christopher Burgess. It took Smart Cookie all of two minutes to run a vehicle check and discover that while Blake drove a red Lexus, Burgess (in addition to his silver Porsche) owned an orange Hummer.

Telling me this, Jessica laughed. "An orange Hummer. You should have seen her eyes light up, China. From that minute on, she was locked and loaded. The next stop was the JP's office down the hall, where she got a search warrant."

As a reward for her tip, Jessica got to ride along in Sheila's squad car. When the two of them got to Burgess' street, they spotted my Toyota parked a block below his house, so they knew I was there. On the driveway, they found my cap and my Thyme and Seasons clipboard. ("Sort of like following a trail of bread crumbs," Jessica said with a chuckle.) They peered through the windows in the garage door—which was a sort of rusty orange color—and saw Burgess with his gun and his dog, standing beside the Hummer.

And that was the moment Ruby called my cell and set off my police siren. Jessica recognized it and told Sheila that my phone and I were somewhere in that garage. Which was when Sheila began pounding on the garage door and shouting and Burgess came unraveled.

I shook my head in exasperation. "You don't back off, do you, Jess?"

"You bet your boobs I don't." She narrowed her eyes.

265

"And you'd just better be glad of it. You might be dead by now. And your killer would invoke the Make My Day law and get off scot-free." She pulled out her cell and dialed the *Enterprise*. "Go away. I need to call in my story."

I was glad of Jessica's intervention, yes. I was truly glad for that phone call, too, which had come at exactly the right moment. When I finally called Ruby back, I apologized for letting her call go to voice mail.

"I was sort of tied up," I said, watching as a large, tilt-bed tow truck backed up to the garage. The driver got out, climbed into the Hummer, and got out again. "I hope your call wasn't too urgent."

"I was feeling pretty urgent at the moment I called," Ruby replied, "but not so much now." She laughed a little. "Now, it seems sort of silly. Hope I didn't interrupt anything crucial."

"Actually, you interrupted something extremely crucial." The memory flickered through my mind like a bad movie. "And your timing couldn't have been better." The tow truck driver began pulling out a heavy cable, which he hooked to the Hummer's rear end. "What were you calling about? Did something happen at the shop?"

"No, everything's fine here. We've had good traffic all day, and no problems. Miriam has been a big help. She loves to answer people's questions." She paused. "Actually, I was calling to tell you that I suddenly realized what kind of door you're supposed to watch out for. I was ringing up a customer when I sort of *saw* it, all of a sudden. It just popped into my head—no idea why."

"Oh, really?" I said. "Just popped into your head, huh? So what kind of door was it?"

The tow truck winch motor whined and the Hummer began to roll backward out of the garage, and up onto the tilted truck bed. Out in the open, in good light, the damage to the front end was clearly visible. It would show up well when the prosecutor displayed the photographs to the jury and pointed out where the Hummer had made contact with the Astro and sent it careening off the road. He would also bring in that broken fog light and hand it around the jury box. Juries like show-and-tell.

"You're going to think I'm nuts," Ruby said apologetically. "But it was a garage door. Not the kind with hinges and a doorknob, that you push. It was the kind that goes up and comes down when you turn on a switch or punch a button. It was sort of rusty orange. In my mind, I suddenly saw it coming down, and I was afraid you might be in trouble. So I called."

"You are not nuts," I said softly, thinking that sometimes Ruby's relationship to the universe is impossible to understand. "It definitely *was* a garage door, a sort of rusty orange. And after it came down, I was in some pretty serious trouble."

The Hummer lurched to a stop on the tow truck's bed, and the driver began to secure it in place. Perched up there, the monster machine looked almost ignominious, a leviathan rendered helpless, piggybacking to the impound yard.

"What kind of trouble?" Ruby's voice went up a notch. "Are you okay, China? What—"

"I'm okay," I said ruefully, "although after that door came down, there were a few moments when I passionately wanted to be somewhere else. But your phone call saved the situation, and everything turned out just fine." Fine for me, of course. But not for Burgess. His troubles were just beginning. They wouldn't be over for a long, long time.

"Hey, China! Come and take a look." I glanced up. From the open garage doorway, Sheila was motioning to me.

"Gotta go now," I said to Ruby. "I'll tell you the whole story when I see you." I paused. "And thanks again. You can't possibly know how grateful I am for your call."

"That's sweet," Ruby said. "It's always nice to be appreciated."

Sheila was holding two plastic evidence bags. Sealed in each was a single running shoe. She held up the bags so that I could see the shoe soles, which displayed an odd pattern of wedges, ridges, and lateral slices. "These were found in Burgess' closet," she said. "Think one of them might be a match for that shoe print in your cottage?"

"Sure looks like it to me." I grinned. "And you didn't even have to check every closet in town. Did you find anything else of interest?"

She laughed. "You mean, in addition to that thirty-gallon trash bag full of marijuana? Well, yes. Right now, the guys are upstairs photographing and bagging a significant cache of narcotics—oxycodone, fentanyl, hydromorphone, and some exotics. They appear to have been purchased by prescription from pharmacies in San Antonio and Austin under various patient names—hospice patients, probably, and Medicare beneficiaries, which could double the charge count. I don't think this was just a matter of overprescribing. From the looks of it, he was running a retail narcotics business. There's enough stuff in this house to qualify him as your basic neighborhood drug lord."

"Wow," I said quietly. "Just wow."

"You bet. Thanks to you, maybe we'll actually be able to put this one out of business."

"You're welcome," I said modestly.

She shook her head. "Uh-uh. Don't start feeling good just yet, China." She gave me one of her chilly official glances. "Under the circumstances, I doubt that Burgess will be inclined to press charges against you." Her voice sharpened. "But before we forget about your little escapade, would you mind telling me what in the name of all that's holy prompted you to lock yourself inside that man's Hummer, inside his garage?" She leaned forward until her nose was almost touching mine. "How was it that you got out of law school without understanding the consequences of trespass and the damned *castle doctrine*?"

I stepped back. "I'm afraid I don't have a very good answer," I replied meekly. "It was just one of those things you find yourself doing—and then wish you hadn't." I straightened my shoulders. "But you could at least give me credit for digging up the MacDonald connection and figuring out what Kelly Kaufman's hospice patient files meant, and what Marla Blake and Chris Burgess have been up to at the hospice for the past couple of years. If it hadn't been for all that, you'd still be scratching your head over a few flecks of orange paint on the rear end of the Astro. If Burgess had had time to think about it, he would have banged up the Hummer so he could get it repaired legitimately. And that would have destroyed the evidence."

"I suppose you've got a point there." Sheila put a hand on my arm. "But promise me you'll stay out of other people's garages from now on. I'd hate to have to be the one to break the news to McQuaid that some irate homeowner took you for an intruder and shot you. Dead."

"If you put it that way," I said, "I promise. I agree. It was not smart."

"Good." She dropped her hand. "We'll need you down at the station this afternoon to make a statement. I'm not sure I get the MacDonald backstory, and this hospice fraud has some kinks in it that I don't understand. Jessica gave me the general outline, but she doesn't have a handle on the details. I need you to straighten all that out for me. And I'll want to go over your statement with you before I sit down with the prosecutor to discuss the charges. This is obviously a complicated case."

"Can the statement wait until after five?" I asked. "Ruby's

SUSAN WITTIG ALBERT

been holding down the fort all day, and it would be good if I went back to the shop to give her a hand."

Sheila shook her head. "Sorry. I need it right away, please. I don't think Blake is a flight risk, but I want to pick her up before she learns that her son has been detained. I hope that hasn't happened already." She looked at her watch, then up at me. "Oh, and McQuaid said for you and Caitie to go ahead and eat without him. He'll be home tonight, but it's likely to be pretty late."

I stared at her. "Well, gosh, that's great," I managed. "You . . . you heard from him?"

"Indirectly. Blackie phoned me when I was on my way up here. They're flying in this evening on a Texas Ranger plane. Both of them." She grinned. "They got what they went for, but don't tell McQuaid I said that. He'll want to tell you himself."

"Terrific," I said. I was almost too giddy with happiness and relief to ask why, if Blackie could call Sheila, McQuaid hadn't called me.

"And one other thing," Sheila said. She held out her hand. "Give me your phone."

I took it out and handed it to her. "What do you want my phone for?"

She manipulated it deftly for a moment or two, then handed it back. "Here," she said. "You are no longer impersonating a police car."

IT was after eleven. Caitie had gone to bed and McQuaid and I were sitting in the front porch swing, his arm around me, my head on his shoulder. Above us, the stars were brilliant sparks against the deep blackness of the sky, and the moon was a silver coin tossed among them. The air around us was sweet with the fragrance of the honeysuckle growing up the trellis at the end of the porch. From the nearby woods, our pair of resident owls traded quiet, meditative calls; far to the west, a chorus of boisterous coyote yips and yelps flickered across the distance. Winchester, sleeping at our feet, heard them in his dream, half woke, gave an answering snuffle, and went back to sleep again.

McQuaid put his cheek against my hair. "God, how I've missed you," he said. "Out there, every time I slow down enough to think, I think of you. And Caitie and this place and Brian, but mostly you. I love coming home."

I picked up his hand and kissed it, put it down again. "Was it a difficult job? What you were doing out there, I mean."

Caitie had still been up when he arrived, and he had told her one or two funny stories about his trip before we sent her off to bed. We had tacitly agreed to save the rest of it until we were alone. I had related my narrative quickly and without a great deal of drama and entirely omitting my misadventure in Burgess' garage, which I didn't think it was necessary for him to know. It was his turn now.

"It wasn't bad," McQuaid replied lightly. "Anyway, you don't want to hear all the gory details." His arm tightened. "I'm home. Isn't that enough? There are plenty of other things to talk about, aren't there?"

You tell him for me, China, I'm his boy. Bob Godwin's words came back to me again, and I remembered the pledge I had made. I hated the idea that McQuaid might be putting himself in danger, but I would always be his girl in a tight spot. Always and always. I needed to tell him that.

"Yes, it's enough that you're here," I said. "And I appreciate that you didn't tell me where you were going or what you were doing because you didn't want me to be afraid. But I've learned that I worry more when I don't know what's going on. When I close out anything that might affect us. Might change our future together."

I thought of my jealousy, of Margaret, of the silly things I'd conjured up. I turned my head and looked up at him, at the strong face, the firm mouth, the hard jaw. "I am with you and for you, McQuaid, wherever you are and whatever you're doing. I want you to know that."

"Really?" He kissed the tip of my nose. "After Blackie and I brought that young boy back from Mexico, you told me you didn't want me to—"

"I was wrong," I said. "There are things you have to do— that you *want* to do—that I might rather you wouldn't. But I trust you to make smart choices, whether you're here or in Mexico or wherever." I lightened my voice. "Even if you are a danger junkie."

And then I shivered, thinking of my own recent not-so-smart choice, going into Burgess' garage. Trouble can happen anywhere. MacDonald died of morphine poisoning at home. Kelly was struck on Limekiln Road. Burgess could have shot me in his garage. All of this right here in Pecan Springs.

"Well, I don't always make smart choices," McQuaid said thoughtfully. "But I'm cautious. And I do my homework. Blackie and I and Felipe knew where we were going and what we needed to do when we got there."

"Felipe?"

"Felipe Cisneros. Blackie and I were working for a task force—federal and state and local law enforcement, plus guys hired by drillers and oil companies—that's trying to curb the theft of oil field equipment in West Texas. South of the border, the Mexican police are involved, too, trying to reduce oil thefts. Mostly, the thieves are the cartels, picking up equipment—

drilling pipe, drill rigs, trucks, dozers, pumps—they can use to tap into the Mexican oil pipelines. They steal the oil, then truck it back north across the border and sell it here. Felipe has been undercover for the task force six or seven months, on both sides of the border. Blackie and I worked with him."

"Worked with him how?" I asked.

McQuaid grinned. "We were a pair of gringo wildcatters, aiming to track down our stolen equipment and buy it back. Felipe had a good lead on the two men we needed to see and was acting as a go-between. We connected with his guys in a seedy bar in Juárez, then went with them to a villa in the hills outside of town, where they were holding a big cache of stolen equipment bound for one of the cartels. We were about to fork over a bundle of pesos when the Federales showed up—surprise, surprise—and took everybody into custody. The guys at the villa went to jail, but the police turned the three of us—Felipe, Blackie, me—loose. Then they planted their own men with the equipment. When the cartel people showed up, they arrested them, too. Once that was done, we started bringing the equipment back over the border, several million dollars' worth. It should all be in El Paso by now, heading back to wherever it belongs. And as part of the hit, three oil brokers in Houston were simultaneously charged with receiving stolen Mexican fuel. Once the oil's in the system, you know, there's no stopping it. It can go to any refinery of any legitimate company."

"So the job was a success." I squeezed his hand, hoping I sounded like a cheerleader. "Congratulations!"

"Yeah. Thanks. Well, unfortunately—" He stopped.

"Go on," I prompted, and before he could ask, added, "Yes, I'm sure. I want to hear it, McQuaid. All of it."

He was silent a moment. "Unfortunately, when Blackie and I got back to headquarters, we heard that Felipe had turned that trick once too often. He was machine gunned in Juárez this afternoon. Killed instantly."

I shuddered. *It could have been you,* I thought, and the words came to my lips, but I didn't say them. Yes, it could have been McQuaid. But it could have been me, this afternoon in Burgess' garage. Life is short, and we never know what's waiting around the corner, right here in town or on a Mexican hillside. The best thing we can do—the *only* thing we can do—is to love one another now, while we have one another, while we're together.

"I'm sorry about Felipe," I said evenly. "But I'm glad you and Blackie got the job done and made it out okay."

He nodded regretfully. "It's a loss. Felipe was tough and smart, the kind of guy you want at your back in a tough place. He took too many chances, but he understood the risks. And for him, the greater the risk, the better he liked it." He paused. "Blackie is like that, too, although you wouldn't think it to look at him. Offer him a dangerous job and he'll jump on it, just for the fun of the damn thing." There was a certain grimness in his voice. "That's not me, China. I do what I have to do, but I don't love the risk."

"No?" I asked. "Then why did you take the job?"

"Because I got a percentage on the equipment we brought back across the border." He chuckled wryly. "Enough, in fact, to fund the rest of Brian's undergraduate years. So if Sally finks out on her commitment again, I can handle it."

I pulled away and looked at him. "Is that why you took on that dangerous job? For the *money*?"

He frowned. "Well, sure. I hope you don't think I do stuff like that just for kicks." He put a hand on my shoulder and looked at me, straight and hard. "I am *not* a danger junkie, China. You know that, don't you?" He shook my shoulder a little. "Don't you?"

"I know that you don't *think* you're a danger junkie." I

might have laughed when I said that, but his face was serious. Too serious.

"Huh," he grunted. "Look who's talking. The girl who went looking for trouble in a killer's garage and ended up locking herself into his Hummer while the freakin' guy stood outside, threatening her with a gun and his vicious dog. He could have killed her, too, and claimed a castle defense. In fact, he might very well have done just that if the cavalry hadn't ridden up in the nick of time." He regarded me through narrowed eyes. "Now, who's calling who a danger junkie?"

I made a face. "Who told you all that?"

"The chief of police told her husband, and he told me. Did she lie? Did he?"

"Not exactly, no." I sighed. "But there were extenuating circumstances. Several of them."

His mouth was a thin line. "There always are when you paint yourself into a tough corner, China. So don't get on my case about being a—"

I kissed him. "I'm not getting on your case, McQuaid. I love you, whoever you are."

He kissed me, long and deep. "Love me, huh?" he murmured. He lifted me to my feet and held me against him. "Care to prove that?" he asked after a moment.

"I can't think of anything I'd rather do," I said breathlessly.

Winchester clambered to his feet. He knew the signals. If we were going upstairs, he was, too. Bassets do *not* like to sleep alone on the porch.

A few weeks later, Sheila's birthday party—an old-fashioned block party—was a boisterous success. The temperature was in the low eighties, and the sky was a vivid, moving panoply of sun and clouds. Ruby's backyard, with its border of flowers

275

and rosebushes, looked gorgeous. The whole neighborhood turned out to help celebrate, along with Blackie's friends from the Adams County sheriff's office, Sheila's friends from the PSPD, and some of the guys from Beans'. Blackie and Hark Hibler had brought Ruby's TV set out to the deck and were watching a baseball game, while several people had brought guitars and fiddles, and impromptu singing groups gathered here and there around the yard. The kids were playing volleyball, and Caitie and a couple of the neighborhood girls were hunched over a large jigsaw puzzle.

The food was splendid. Bob Godwin set up a big barbecue barrel and served smoked ribs and sausages to the crowd. The potluck—salads, sides, sandwiches, breads, and a birthday cake studded with thirty-nine candles—was terrific. There was lemonade for the kids and iced tea and wine for the grown-ups. And Ramona brought several kegs of Comanche Creek beer she wanted everybody to sample and vote on. Blood orange beer and prickly pear beer came out about even in the informal rankings, but the hands-down favorite—predictably—was chipotle beer.

Ramona did not bring Rich Kaufman. They were no longer a thing, Ruby told me in a whisper. Rich, still brokenhearted over the loss of his wife, was leaving the brewery as soon as Ramona could find another brewmaster. And Ramona's passion for beer had turned into just another of her passing fancies. She was already looking for an investor to buy her share of the brewery.

"If she could settle down to just one thing and put all her energy into it, she'd be a huge success," Ruby said wistfully.

"If she could settle down to one thing, she wouldn't be Ramona," I said tartly, and Ruby had to agree.

Charlie Lipman was at the party, too. I was stretched out in a chaise longue with a glass of wine, enjoying the afternoon sunshine, when he pulled up a chair beside me. He lowered himself into it holding a glass of lemonade. He was actually sober, too, even though it was the weekend.

We were silent for several moments as a nearby group finished a raucous version of "Mammas Don't Let Your Babies Grow Up to Be Cowboys," fueled by Ramona's chipotle beer. When it was over and the group had headed back to the kegs, Charlie pulled his chair around so that we were facing each other.

"I guess maybe I owe you an apology," he said.

"I don't need an apology," I said. "But it would be kind of interesting to hear the details."

He screwed up his mouth. "Yeah. Well, I guess I owe you that, too." He took out a cigarette and lit it. "I've severed my connections with the Pecan Springs Community Hospice."

"Good plan," I replied, and waited for more. After a moment, I got it.

"Unfortunately, I was the one who told Christopher Burgess and Marla Blake that Kelly Kaufman had made unauthorized copies of the hospice records." He blew out a stream of smoke. "When Kelly told me about the Medicare fraud, I believed she was making it up—that she was a disgruntled ex-employee acting out of spite because she'd been fired. I had no idea that the hospice was anything but a hundred percent aboveboard. I thought I was doing my job, safeguarding an important organization against a frivolous, if not fraudulent, claim."

"Ah," I said. "And you also told them that Kelly was staying in my cottage?" That would explain the attempted break-in on Sunday night—fended off by Miss Lula—and the break-in after the car crash.

"Yep, that was me." He pulled out a handkerchief and mopped his forehead. "I made a big mistake. But I did it in good faith, China, acting on the information I had at the time." He took a sip of his lemonade, made a face, and set the glass down on the grass beside his chair. "I can't bring Kelly back, but I've told the police about my part in this crazy affair. That information was the key to Burgess' motive."

"For ramming Kelly's car?"

"Yes. Because they hadn't been able to come up with a motive, the best they could do was involuntary manslaughter. But when the prosecutor learned that I'd told Burgess that Kelly was onto the Medicare fraud, he upgraded the charge to murder. I understand that another upgrade might be in the works. Capital murder."

"They can probably make that stick," I said thoughtfully. "Murder committed in order to conceal another crime. And on top of that, there are felony charges of possession and trafficking for the narcotics found in the house. Who'd Burgess get to defend?"

"Sam Carson, from San Antonio. He's good."

"I know Sam from law school," I said. "He's good but not that good. If the prosecutor does a halfway decent job, Burgess is looking at a hefty prison sentence." I paused. "He hasn't been apprehended yet?"

That was the big news. Burgess had been arraigned on multiple counts and posted a half-million-dollar bail. But just a few days before the grand jury heard his case, he had up and left town, which of course didn't deter the grand jury. An all-points bulletin was issued for his arrest, but the last I heard, he was still on the lam.

"Oh, they'll get him," Charlie said confidently. "Just a matter of time." Another group of musicians fired up—"San Antonio Rose"—and Charlie leaned closer to me, raising his voice. "When I talked to the police, they said that you were the one who doped out the hospice fraud, based on the records that Kelly copied—illegally, I should point out—from the hospice computer. True?"

I ignored the remark about the illegality of Kelly's copying. It was true, but as a practical matter, it wasn't likely to be a contested issue at trial.

"True," I replied, "but I didn't dope it out on my own. I had the help of Lara Metcalf. She's the one who retrieved Kelly's laptop from the wreck and gave me the thumb drive that held the records. She'd worked as a nurse at the hospice and understood the way things operated. She knew Chris Burgess, too." I hesitated, then decided not to tell him that Lara and Burgess had once been romantically involved. He didn't need to know that.

He sat for a moment, smoking and listening to the music. Then he asked, "Are you aiming to file a whistle-blower claim? You can, you know. From what Sheila told me, it sounds like you probably have enough documentation." He gave me an amused glance. "At least, enough to interest some shyster lawyer."

"Who, me?" I raised my eyebrows. "I don't intend to file, but Lara Metcalf is seriously considering it. She's contacted one of those 'shyster' lawyers you recommended to Kelly. If she wins a whistle-blower award, she plans to use the money to create a nursing scholarship in Kelly's name."

"A worthy aim," he said drily. "But I've heard that kind of thing before. We'll see if she actually ponies up when the money comes in."

I ignored that, too. "There's a lot to be negotiated," I said, "since the hospice fraud is a motivation behind the other criminal acts, and false claims suits are supposed to be sealed." I paused. "I take it that you're not going to represent the hospice in a false claims suit."

"Correct. I've already told both Burgess and Blake that they should plan to plead, whomever they hire to defend them. Simpler and cheaper, all the way around."

"True enough," I said. "I hope they take your advice."

He pushed himself out of his chair. "Well, thanks for listening, China. I'm glad I got that off my chest. It's been bothering me." He glanced around. "Haven't seen McQuaid. Is he here?"

I pointed toward the deck, where five or six people were intent on the game. "He's watching the Rangers whup up on the Twins. Six-two, last I heard. You need to talk to him?"

"Yeah. I want him to schedule that Brownsville trip. I've got a client in big trouble down there. He needs a good investigator." He shot me a curious look. "Everything go okay in El Paso?"

I thought of Felipe, and danger, and misadventures here and there. "More or less," I said. "Ask him. I'm sure he'll tell you."

Charlie nodded, stuck his hands in his pockets, and walked away. I watched him go, thinking how glad I was not to be burdened with clients' legal troubles. I didn't envy Charlie the load he was carrying.

The afternoon wore on. The ribs and sausages disappeared, the kegs emptied out, and people began going home. It was Sunday, after all, and *Downton Abbey* was on. McQuaid, Blackie, and Hark were still out on the deck, now watching Los Angeles play Baltimore. Caitie was out there, too, still working on the puzzle with her new friends. Ruby, Sheila, and I had finished cleaning up the party things and were sitting around Ruby's kitchen table enjoying a glass of my homemade ginger ale and a slice of Sheila's cake.

"Charlie and I were talking about the Kaufman case," I said to Sheila. "What's the latest news on Burgess? Any reported sightings?"

Sheila picked up her fork and attacked her birthday cake. "I guess you haven't heard. He was picked up just a few hours ago attempting to cross the border. He's already on his way back to Pecan Springs."

"Oh, yeah? That's great!" I said enthusiastically.

"It's a good thing he didn't make it," Ruby said, sipping her ginger ale. "If he got into Mexico, he might have been hard to find."

"And hard to extradite, too," I said. "A capital murder charge would complicate things. Mexico doesn't have the death penalty. If Burgess had been apprehended there, the prosecutor might have had to agree not to go for the death penalty in order to get him extradited."

"Well, we've got him now." Sheila's voice was gritty. "And this time, there won't be any bail. He'll be cooling his heels in jail until the trial—where he'll be convicted and hauled off to prison. Burgess has seen the last of his freedom for a good long time."

Ruby frowned. "I don't think I ever heard how you know it was his Hummer that hit Kelly's van." She picked up the pitcher of ginger ale and refreshed our glasses.

"Forensics," Sheila said. "That orange Hummer paint is distinctive. And there was the fog light glass, too. Putting Burgess himself in the Hummer was a little harder. But when we searched the vehicle, we found a receipt for fuel from a Wag-A-Bag on the west side of town, time-stamped twelve minutes before the crash. The security camera at the pump shows that he was the one filling up and driving off."

"Good work, Smart Cookie," I said approvingly. "Charlie told me that Sam Carson is defending. Sounds like Sam will have his hands full."

Sheila nodded. "I saw you and Charlie talking. He tell you about his part in this? He's the one who handed us Burgess' motive. Without him, we didn't have a way to tie Burgess directly to Kelly. We had the shoeprint in your cottage, but we didn't have a *reason*. Charlie gave us what we needed."

"He told me," I said, turning my chilly glass in my hand.

"I'm wondering about Marla Blake. Mrs. Mueller was able to implicate her in the MacDonald death, but I haven't heard an update."

Sheila sighed. "The prosecutor says we don't have enough evidence to reopen the case. I assigned a detective to it, but he came up empty-handed."

"I don't understand," Ruby said, frowning. "China told me that Mrs. Mueller actually *saw* Marla Blake with Mr. Mac-Donald, right around the time he died. That's eyewitness testimony, isn't it? Isn't that enough?"

"All she saw was the two of them sitting together on the porch. That's just not enough to make a case, especially since we don't know when MacDonald actually died." Sheila finished her cake and pushed her plate away. "There will be plenty of other criminal charges against Blake, though, once the Medicare fraud investigation gets under way." She sat back in her chair. "But she's back in the hospital. And from what I hear, the prognosis isn't good."

"Hospital?" I asked, surprised. "Prognosis?"

"You don't know?" Ruby pulled down her mouth. "She has cancer."

"Oh, no!" I exclaimed.

"Ovarian cancer, stage four," Sheila said. "It's spread to her lungs and her liver. It's been diagnosed as terminal."

"But I just saw her," I protested, and then stopped. When I saw her last—at the hospital the night Kelly died—I'd noticed that she seemed to have lost quite a lot of weight, and that her sleek dark hair looked like a wig. "I guess she was keeping it a secret," I said.

Sheila nodded. "That's right. She's been going to Houston for treatment, I was told. But the cancer is aggressive and there's no keeping it a secret now. She's trying to get permission to use an experimental drug."

"Terminal," Ruby said quietly. "That's rather ironic, isn't it? I mean, she was involved in creating false hospice cases—terminal cases. She might even have killed old Mr. MacDonald. And now she's diagnosed as terminal herself. There's justice for you."

"Justice doesn't always happen in the courtroom," I said. "But it usually happens, even in an imperfect world."

"Burgess will get justice, too," Sheila said grimly. "*In* the courtroom. He will—I promise you."

Caitie stood outside the screen door. "Hey, Mom. Dad says game's over and he's ready to go home."

"Tell him I'll be just a minute," I said, and Caitie turned to yell, "She says she'll be along when she's good and ready."

"Brat," I said affectionately, and Caitie giggled.

"Happy birthday, Sheila." I paused, studying her, thinking that she somehow looked . . . different. Prettier, if that was possible. Softer, maybe. Happier. "Whatever Blackie gave you for a present, you must have liked it. You're glowing."

"I don't think I heard what it was," Ruby said. "Something special?"

"We haven't told anybody yet." Sheila's voice softened and she seemed almost shy. "And yes, I guess it's pretty special." She took a deep breath. "We're having a baby."

"A baby!" Ruby squealed, clapping her hands. "Sheila, that's awesome! That's totally wonderful!"

I stood, went behind Sheila's chair, and folded my arms around her, my hands on her belly. "Preggie," I said softly, my cheek against her hair. "I am so *happy* for you, Sheila. When are you due? Is it a boy or a girl? Are you feeling okay? What does Blackie say?" She had been pregnant once before, but it had been an ectopic pregnancy and she'd lost the baby. She and Blackie had been devastated, and all of us had felt their grief.

283

"Around the first of November," Sheila said, smiling. She folded her hands over mine. "A boy. Blackie is over the moon. And I'm feeling okay; some days more, some days less."

"Morning sickness?" Ruby asked sympathetically.

Sheila nodded, making a face. "Last time, China prescribed ginger. I've stocked up on that again." She brightened. "But this time, at least, the police department has a policy in place that covers pregnant officers. An *excellent* policy, I might add. Modified assignments, maternity uniforms, some paid leave. Even paid breaks for pumping breast milk. And breastfeeding officers can wear lighter ballistic vests, if they choose."

"You mean boob breaks?" Ruby's eyes widened. "*Paid* boob breaks?"

"Shocking," I said. "What's the cop shop saying about all this?"

"We'll see," Sheila said, smiling ruefully. "I get to be the first to try it out."

I grinned. "You done good, kid. Bright idea, to get that policy in place before you got pregnant again."

"Oh, you bet," she said smugly. "You guys don't call me Smart Cookie for nothing."

"I'll drink to that," Ruby said, lifting her glass of ginger ale, and we all laughed.

To the Reader

Here give me leave to tell you, that there are a great
number of brave Herbs and Vegitations that will do the
business of brewing as well as hops . . . Peny Royal and
Balm are noble Herbs and of excellent use in Beer or
Ale. They naturally raise and cheer the drooping Spirits
and also they add great strength and fragrancy. The
same is to be understood of Mint, Tansie, Wormwood,
Broom, Cardis, Centuary, Eye-bright, Betony, Sage,
Dandelion, and good Hay, also many others, according
to their Natures and Qualities.

Thomas Tryon
The Art of Brewing Beer, Ale, and
Other Sorts of Liquors, 1691

One of the things I've learned over the years I've been engaged in writing this long-running series is that there is
never an end to learning about plants. Just when I think I've
got a good handle on the various ways humans have used
plants, I discover an entire new range of practices. Now, having done the research for China Bayles' class on liqueurs, I
fully understand the feeling of frustration that led Amy
Stewart (in *The Drunken Botanist*) to throw up her hands
and declare:

To the Reader

It would be impossible to describe every plant that has ever flavored an alcoholic beverage. I am certain that at this very moment, a craft distiller in Brooklyn is plucking a weed from a crack in the sidewalk and wondering if it would make a good flavoring for a new line of bitters. Marc Wucher, an Alsatian eau-de-vie maker, once told a reporter, "We distill everything except our mothers-in-law," and if you've ever been to Alsace, you know he wasn't exaggerating.

Exactly. There is a wide, wild world of plant-based booze out there to be explored, and if this is your first taste of this intoxicating subject, I hope it won't be your last. In the Resources section of this novel, I've provided a list of books that will take you further into this delicious subject. And of course, if you're a teetotaler, there are plenty of tasty, refreshing nonalcoholic options. Cheers!

But drinkables aren't the only intoxicants in *Blood Orange*. In fact, the word *intoxicant* is derived from the medieval Latin word *intoxicāre*, to poison. For too many, that is exactly the danger posed by the opium poppy (*Papaver somniferum*). While its narcotic properties have been invaluable in the medical treatment of pain, its poisonous, addictive properties have haunted humans since its very first use over six thousand years ago. While there may be more dangerous plants on this planet, the opium poppy is certainly among the most notorious.

However, when they are used unwisely, even mild-mannered plants can have regrettable physical and neurological effects, especially when they are thoughtlessly combined with over-the-counter and prescription drugs. China Bayles and I hope you will seek informed advice before you use any herbs therapeutically. Do your own careful homework and

To the Reader

use all medicine with attention. China and I would not like to lose any of our readers—especially you.

As usual, thanks go to the researchers who have compiled the various books, monographs, and online articles I have consulted in my research on plants (and for this book, on hospices and Medicare fraud), and to the many readers who have supported this series throughout its long life. Also to Miriam Johnston of Peoria, Illinois, the winner of a "cameo character" raffle for the benefit of the Story Circle Network, for volunteering to help in China's and Ruby's shops and gardens. Miriam introduced me to the idea of straw-bale gardening, which China and I intend to try out in the next gardening season. To my daughter, Robin Wittig, for guiding me through the labyrinth of hospice operation and suggesting plot possibilities I hadn't thought of. And to Natalee Rosenstein, Michelle Vega, Robin Barletta, and the rest of the Berkley Prime Crime team: you've been the best support group an author could hope to have, for more years than any author has a right to expect. Thank you, thank you.

And again and always, to Bill, for everything.

Susan Wittig Albert
Bertram, Texas

Resources

I know some who are constantly drunk on books as other men are drunk on whiskey.

H. L. Mencken

Bobrow, Warren. *Apothecary Cocktails: Restorative Drinks from Yesterday and Today*. Fair Winds Press, 2013.

Buhner, Stephen Harrod. *Sacred and Herbal Healing Beers: The Secrets of Ancient Fermentation*. Brewers Publications, 1998.

Farrell, John Patrick. *Making Cordials and Liqueurs at Home*. Harper & Row, 1974.

Fisher, Joe, and Dennis Fisher. *The Homebrewer's Garden: How to Easily Grow, Prepare, and Use Your Own Hops, Brewing Herbs, Malts*. Storey, 1998.

Higgins, Patrick, Maura Kate Kilgore, and Paul Hertlein. *The Homebrewers' Recipe Guide*. Touchstone, 1996.

Proulx, Annie, and Lew Nichols. *Cider: Making, Using & Enjoying Sweet & Hard Cider*. Storey, 2003.

Rathbun, A. J. *Luscious Liqueurs: 50 Recipes for Sublime and Spirited Infusions to Sip and Savor*. Harvard Common Press, 2008.

Schloss, Andrew. *Homemade Liqueurs and Infused Spirits*. Storey, 2013.

Stewart, Amy. *The Drunken Botanist: The Plants That Create the World's Best Drinks*. Algonquin Books, 2013.

Resources

Vargas, Pattie, and Rich Gulling. *Cordials from Your Kitchen: Easy, Elegant Liqueurs You Can Make & Give*. Storey, 1997.

Vargas, Pattie, and Rich Gulling. *Making Wild Wines & Meads: 125 Unusual Recipes Using Herbs, Fruits, Flowers & More*. Storey, 1999.

Recipes

Another favourite brew was that of armsful of Meadow-sweet, Yarrow, Dandelion, and Nettles, and the mash when sweetened with old honey and well worked with barm [yeast], and then bottled in big stoneware bottles, made a drink strong enough to turn even an old toper's head.

Margaret Grieve
A Modern Herbal, 1931

Ruby's Orange-Rosemary Muffins

½ cup butter or margarine
2 cups unbleached all-purpose flour
1 teaspoon baking powder
½ teaspoon salt
¼ teaspoon baking soda
1 cup sugar
2 large eggs
1 cup yogurt
½ cup orange juice, fresh
zest of one orange
1 tablespoon fresh rosemary, finely chopped

Wash the orange thoroughly, let it dry, and zest it. Preheat oven to 400 degrees F. Line muffin tin and set aside. Melt butter and set in refrigerator to cool. In a large bowl, mix flour, baking powder, salt, and baking soda. In a separate bowl, mix cooled butter, sugar, and eggs. Add yogurt, orange juice, zest, and rosemary. Mix well. Add to flour mixture and stir until just combined. (Don't overmix.) Fill muffin cups about two-thirds full. Bake for 12–15 minutes (for mini muffins) or 20 minutes (for large muffins). Cool in pan for 3–4 minutes before removing to cool on a rack.

Mary Beth's Blood Orange Granita

4 cups blood orange juice
½ cup lemon juice
¼ cup simple sugar syrup (2 parts sugar to
    1 part water, heated to boiling)
¼ teaspoon ground cardamom

Combine all ingredients in a mixing bowl. Adjust sugar to taste. Pour liquid into large, shallow stainless steel pan and place in freezer. When frozen, scrape with fork until fluffy and serve.

Mary Beth's Orange-Rosemary Liqueur

3 oranges
1 cup sugar
2 cups water
¾ cup coarsely chopped rosemary leaves
1 cup vodka or Everclear
½ cup brandy or rum

Wash the oranges thoroughly, let them dry, and zest them. Combine the water and sugar in a medium saucepan and bring to a boil, stirring to dissolve sugar. Add the rosemary and simmer for 5–6 minutes, stirring occasionally. Strain through a fine sieve; discard the rosemary. Pour into a clean quart jar. Add orange zest and cool. Add vodka or Everclear and brandy or rum. Cover tightly and store in a cool, dark place for one month. Strain, discard the zest, and rebottle. Cover tightly and age for another month.

Blood Orange, Avocado, Grape, and Spinach Salad

4 large handfuls of spinach
2 blood oranges, segmented
1 avocado, diced
18–20 red grapes
Green onion, sliced diagonally
2 ounces (about ⅓ cup) goat cheese (or blue cheese), crumbled

ORANGE VINAIGRETTE
3 tablespoons orange juice
2 tablespoons white wine or Champagne vinegar
1 teaspoon finely minced garlic
2 teaspoons Dijon mustard
2 teaspoons honey
⅓ cup olive oil
Finely ground black pepper

To make the salad: In a large serving bowl, combine the spinach, oranges, avocado, grapes, onion, and cheese.

To make the vinaigrette: Whisk together the orange juice, vinegar, garlic, mustard, and honey. Gradually whisk in oil until well blended. Add pepper to taste. (If you have some of Mary Beth's Orange-Rosemary Liqueur, substitute that for the orange juice and increase the vinegar to 2 tablespoons.)

Drizzle dressing over the salad and toss. Serve immediately. Yield: 4 side salads or 2 dinner salads.

Spicy Henbit

4 cups henbit leaves, chopped
    (avoid tough, stringy stems)
Water to cover greens
3 tablespoons butter
1 teaspoon sweet curry powder
¼ teaspoon ground cinnamon
⅛ teaspoon ground cloves
2 tablespoons flour
¾ cup sour cream

Place henbit in a pan and cover with water, bring to a boil, and simmer for 10 minutes. In a separate pan melt three tablespoons butter. Stir in curry powder, cinnamon, and cloves. Stir and cook for 1 minute, then stir in flour. Whisk in a half cup of hot water from the simmering henbit and stir until smooth. Remove from heat and stir in sour cream. Drain the henbit and mix with the sour cream mixture. Return to heat and cook on low for 5 minutes. Serve hot.

Recipes

Cass' Overnight No-Cook Orange-Mint Oatmeal

1 cup plain or vanilla yogurt
⅓ cup uncooked old-fashioned or
   quick-cooking oats
¼ cup orange segments
1 teaspoon chopped mint
1 sprig of mint for garnish

Mix yogurt and oats. Stir in orange segments and chopped mint and top with a sprig of mint. Cover and refrigerate overnight. If you prefer, for oranges substitute ¼ cup of sliced bananas, blueberries, raspberries, pineapple tidbits, diced kiwifruit, sliced grapes. Serve with a crunchy topping, such as chopped nuts.

Caitie's Favorite Pasta: Tortellini with Lemon Basil Butter Sauce

1 package fresh or dried tortellini (14–16 ounces)
½ cup butter or margarine
1 green onion, chopped
1 teaspoon lemon zest
2 tablespoons fresh lemon juice
2 tablespoons chopped fresh basil
Grated Parmesan cheese
Extra basil for garnish, optional

Cook tortellini according to package instructions. Drain and pour into a serving bowl.

To make the sauce, melt the butter or margarine in a

small saucepan over medium heat. Add the green onion and cook until tender, about two minutes. Stir in the lemon zest, lemon juice, and basil. Cook for an additional 2 minutes.

Pour sauce over the tortellini and stir gently to combine. Garnish with Parmesan cheese and (if desired) extra basil. Serve immediately.

Coffee-Pecan Liqueur

 1 cup vodka
 1 cup brandy
 1½ teaspoons pecan extract
 1 teaspoon vanilla extract
 1 teaspoon orange zest
 1 cup strong coffee
 ⅓ cup white sugar
 ⅔ cup light brown sugar
 ¼ teaspoon salt

In a quart jar, combine vodka, brandy, extracts, and orange zest and set aside.

To make syrup: In a saucepan, over medium heat, bring coffee, sugars, and salt to a boil, stirring constantly. Reduce the heat and boil gently, stirring until the sugars have dissolved (3–5 minutes). Remove from heat and cool for 15 minutes or so.

Pour syrup into jar of alcohol mixture, stir well, and cover tightly. Store in a cool, dark place for at least one month.

Blood Orange Liqueur

4 blood oranges
1 lemon
Fresh ginger, about 2″ long, peeled and sliced
2 cups vodka
1 cup water
1 cup sugar

Wash and dry the oranges and lemon. Peel the skin, leaving as much of the pith on the fruit as possible. Put peels in a quart jar. Remove the pith from two of the oranges, reserving the other two oranges and the lemon for another use. Cut the de-pithed oranges into pieces, place in a quart jar, and smash the orange with the back of a spoon against the sides of the jar. Add ginger and stir. Pour the vodka into the jar.

To make simple syrup, combine water and sugar in a saucepan over medium-high heat. Bring to a boil and stir until the sugar has dissolved. Cool.

Pour the syrup into the fruit-alcohol mixture and cover tightly. Store in cool, dark place for at least one month, shaking occasionally.

Strain the liqueur through a double layer of cheesecloth into a pitcher. Strain a second time through a new double layer of cheesecloth into bottles. Cap and store or use immediately.

Recipes

Strawberry Shrub

1 cup sliced strawberries
1 cup sugar
1 cup red wine vinegar
½ cup mint leaves, bruised

Combine all ingredients in a medium bowl. Mash the berries to release their juice, and stir until the sugar has nearly dissolved. Refrigerate overnight. Place the fruit mixture in a nonreactive saucepan and heat gently over medium-low heat, just to dissolve remaining sugar. Strain through a mesh strainer; strain again through a coffee filter. Refrigerate. Use to flavor sparkling water or top ice cream. Makes about 2 cups.

In place of strawberries, you can use any seasonal fruit: raspberries, blackberries, blueberries, peaches, mango, pineapple. Experiment with fresh "sweet" herbs, too: lemon balm, pineapple sage, scented geraniums, tarragon, basil, rosemary (but do crush rosemary leaves). And try adding spices: cloves, nutmeg, cinnamon.

China's Homemade Ginger Ale

1½ cups chopped peeled ginger (about 8 ounces fresh ginger)
2 cups water
¾ cup sugar
Pinch salt
About 1 quart club soda
Fresh mint for garnish

To make the ginger syrup: In a small saucepan, cover chopped ginger with water and simmer for 45 minutes, partially covered. Remove from heat, cover, and let steep for 30 minutes. Strain through a sieve into a bowl, pressing ginger to remove all liquid. Discard ginger. Return liquid to saucepan. Add sugar and a pinch of salt and heat over medium heat, stirring, until sugar has dissolved. Chill.

To make a drink: Stir ginger syrup into club soda: start with ¼ cup syrup to ¾ cup club soda, adjust to taste. Serve over ice with a sprig of fresh mint. Makes 4–5 cups.

Connie's Stress-Buster Orange Banana Slush Lunch

1 6-ounce can frozen orange juice concentrate
1 peeled and frozen banana, sliced
¾ cup (6 ounces) vanilla yogurt
1 cup water (or your choice of juice)
½ teaspoon vanilla extract

In a blender, combine the orange juice concentrate, banana, yogurt, water or juice, and vanilla; cover and process until smooth. Sweeten to taste. Makes two servings; enjoy one now, and freeze the other for the next day's lunch.

The China Bayles Mysteries
by Susan Wittig Albert

Herbalist China Bayles will do anything for
a friend in trouble—even if it means
getting mixed up in murder...

Find more books by Susan Wittig Albert
by visiting prh.com/nextread

"All the elements of a good cozy...fun and engaging
characters, a solid mystery, and unique lore that pulls
you into the mystery."—Fresh Fiction on *Blood Orange*

susanalbert.com
🐦 SusanWAlbert

Penguin
Random
House